Sun, sea & sh

A Paninaro Imprint

www.paninaropublishing.co.uk
info@paninaropublishing.co.uk

www.paninaropublishing.co.uk

Contact - info@paninaropublishing.co.uk

A catalogue record for this book is available from the British Library.

ISBN - 13: 978 - 1916088573

Socials;

Twitter @johnnyroc73

Instagram @johnnyproctor90

For, Auntie Anna

If the planets align in the correct order, and you're lucky enough. You get an auntie in your life, like me. You know the type? The one that puts herself last, always. Someone who doesn't even know the meaning of the word selfish. A woman who won't be able to settle unless she knows that you have food in your belly.

I know that you wont ever read this dedication but I just wanted to say that you were there for me in a way that I will never, ever forget and that you are and will always be appreciated.

Rest in peace.

Love, JP x

Prologue - A recap of the players of Muirhouse Violet.

(Taken from Muirhouse (2020) and updated for 2022)

1. **Sepp** - Our cat between the sticks who only got the gig as keeper on account of him being a lanky bastard. While not exactly the type that you would ever put your house on saving a shot from an opponent, he *was* capable. Named Sepp due to the fact that not only was he our goalkeeper but he freakishly looked the double of the old German goalie, Sepp Maier. Should've been fucking nicknamed 'push up' due to the amount of times in a match you'd hear him screaming 'PUSH UP, VIOLET.'

2. **Bungalow**** - The kind of cunt that you'd send for some tartan paint and he'd ask you how much of it you were looking for. Name awarded specifically because of that … Fuck all up top. Claim to fame is that when he was a kid he appeared on 'Jim'll Fix It' where he got to re-enact the scene from Empire Strikes Back with Dave Prowse and Bungalow as Luke Skywalker. Apparently Prowse didn't even have his fucking Darth Vader suit on which, in my own honest opinion, would've kind of defeated the whole purpose. As a player? You'd shove him in the dependable category. Daft as a brush off and on the pitch but knew when to fucking row Z it and when to take a touch. What else are you looking for from a centre half?   **
Due to recent indiscretions Bungalow will be unavailable for selection for Muirhouse Violet until further notice. His place currently taken by **Baz Delaney**. A player who, until recently, had been waiting in the wings on his chance

coming around and on performances so far had impressed to the point that the speculation is that Bungalow may not walk straight back into the side, once he walks out the front door of Saughton. Delaney, an ex member of the Hibs Capital City Service. Something that has provided issues on occasion due to old foes from Saturday afternoons in the Nineties being up against him on the pitch. His talent - so far - has outweighed the baggage that he has brought to the pitch. A man who apparently relished the battle off the pitch and clearly enjoys that same dance, once he crosses that white line. A dependable and solid defender who rarely dips below a seven.

3. **The Monk** - Was he religious? I'd have been surprised - if outside of a wedding setting - he'd have ever been inside a church. Did he have a 'Zidane cut' or was ever seen strolling around Muirhouse in a robe? Negative there, again. Did he consume enough Buckfast over a week that would probably be able to keep Airdrie going for a month. Yes, yes he did. Just because he was tanning enough alcohol a week that would've had Oliver Reed putting an arm around your shoulder and saying 'come on, mate, enough's enough, eh?' though, it didn't mean to say that he couldn't kick a ball, like. If Bungalow was the brainless no nonsense centre half. The Monk was more your cool calm and composed Franco Baresi or Davey Narey type. Never one to be phased by what was going on the pitch no matter who it was we were playing and - guaranteed - the only way you ever saw the cunt breaking sweat during a game was alcohol related rather than feeling any pressure from the opposition. Claims that his uncle invented the Burberry checked pattern. No cunt believes it.

4. **Daz** - Young Daz had only got his chance at the start of the season due to Mikey Harris being banged up in Belgium after getting lifted at the Anderlecht Hearts pre season

friendly and not making it back to Scotland in time for pre season training. When word came over just how bad a paggering it was that he'd given one of the Belgians and that he wasn't coming back any time soon Daz got the nod from Jock. Not that Jock was too chuffed about losing Mikey. Good left back, like. Dangerous as fuck going forward. That's probably what the Anderlecht ultra would say too, I suppose. Since he got his chance though, young Benny - called Daz by us because as a newcomer into the team we managed to convince him that it was his responsibility to wash the strips every week - was seen as undroppable. His play out from the back deserves to be seen at a higher level than he was playing at. I wasn't sure if he was going to have the mentality to mix it with some of the brutes that he was going to be facing each week but fair play. Duck to water, like. Maybe a bit too much though as he's a cocky wee cunt who knows he's a decent player and is a bit mouthy on the pitch with it. You want to watch what you say and who to at our level. Because of his youthful arrogance he's been the sole reason for a fair few battles on a Sunday morning but then again. Let he who hasn't instigated a mass brawl on a council fitba pitch on a Sunday morning cast the first stone, eh?

5. **Wullie** - Nicknamed after 'Oor Wullie' on account of the fact that he moved to Muirhouse from Dundee after meeting that Hayley Patterson from Gunnet Court on one of those dating websites. Must've hit it off anyway because he moved from there to Edinburgh to stay with her. Brought his fucking stupid Dundonian accent with him as well with all his 'ehhhs' and 'pehhhs' and that. Something that he repeatedly gets rinsed about from the rest of the lads. Actually, he's a really sound cunt, Cawsey, though, and someone that would do anything for the team or any of the boys in it. One of those utility type of players that if some cunt doesn't turn up on a Sunday morning you can be sure

that Wullie will slot right in as if he played there every week. Good man to have in the side, like. Normal service and everyone reporting for duty though, his place as right back writes itself onto the team sheet. A good lad though and someone that I've always had a lot of time for. Even if he's an Arab.

6. **Terry** - As previously already stated. A shagger. Owns a semi successful window cleaning firm that has a few lucrative contracts across the city although it's always been something seen as questionable over *how* he managed to secure the contracts in the first place. The fact that he's six four, about twenty stone and looks like he did two tours of Nam just because he enjoyed the first one so much *may* have played a part somewhere. Nicknamed Terry after that guy who got kidnapped in Lebanon, Terry Waite. Any fucking time you ask him for a help with something he always says that he can't because his hands are tied. As a football player? *Extremely* limited, I'm not going to be the one that tells him that, though. Logically Jock decided to deploy him in a kind of holding midfield position. The reason, I assumed, was that he would be a big imposing lump in the middle of the pitch that you wouldn't fancy trying to play through. Someone simply there to try and disrupt things rather than influence or put a stamp on the game. Breaking up play, breaking legs. Whatever comes first. Despite the lack of any kind of technical skill to the man, whatsoever, he's undeniably a valuable commodity to have out on the pitch for when it all kicks off. Which it invariably does.

7. **Coffee** - The legend in Edinburgh circles known as the kid who was caught on Sportscene giving John Robertson the wanker signal after he missed that open goal at Easter Road in the Edinburgh Derby. He was only around ten years old or something. Camera caught him perfectly though. Right

at the front of the stand behind the goal. Giving it the old Gareth Hunt hand signal to the Hearts striker like the actor did in the Nescafe advert. It's moments like that, though, which can shape a cunt's nickname for the rest of their life. His was well earned. As was his place in the side. Some engine on the boy. A real box to box player and played every match as if his life depended on it. Weighs in with a few goals here and there which always takes a welcome bit off the load of our boys up front. One of the more quieter ones in the side - despite how his image was portrayed across the whole of Scotland at an early age - although make no mistake. When the time comes for him to mix it out on the field he doesn't go MIA. then again, he wouldn't be getting in the fucking team in the first place if that *wasn't* the case.

8. **Strings** - Well, you already know about me but what you *don't* know is that with over fifteen years service I was Violet's longest serving player. In with the fucking bricks, me. Still waiting on my testimonial though, mind. Initially I'd started off as a full back but Hunter had seen something in me that the previous gaffers hadn't. That being that I was absolutely shite at defending but would give the opposition a torrid time when going in the other direction. You always hear that about full backs where they're described as 'good going forward but can't defend' but every cunt shrugs their shoulders about it as if what can you do about it? Well maybe don't fucking play them as a full back then? Doesn't take Fabio Capello to work that one out, eh? Anyway, big Jock made the switch. Moved me further up the pitch and told me to stay there. That I done more damage inside my own box than anything else so to keep myself out on the wing. Dragging the other players out of position simply by my own movements and positioning. It's always hard when you're talking about yourself but as an honest assessment of myself, as a player. There's no denying that at thirty seven

you're always going to lose a yard of pace. The good players gain one up top though, don't they? As time went on and I found myself not as fast as I used to be. Hunter brought me in from out on the wing to a more central role along with Coffee and Tel.

9. **Rossi** - Our goal scoring extraordinaire and prodigal son who returned back to the side after a three year absence. Not through playing for another side over those years or anything like that. Was more of an 'enforced break' from the league handed down to him from the suits after a match fixing scandal that had rocked the league. It was total nonsense, like. How could a striker be in any position to affect a game of fitba? Maybe miss a pen or something like that but, trust me. Getting a penalty on a Sunday morning in that kind of an environment is not an easy thing to do. I remember joking with one referee during a game - after him knocking back a good three or four stonewallers by then - that one of the other team could've chopped one of our boys legs off with a machete and he would've whistled for it being just outside the box. Three years - Rossi got - just because he'd been spotted talking in a bar with Davie McKenna. McKenna a well known underworld figure whose name continually kept cropping up when the whispers about the attempted match fixing started to surface and the CID got involved. Nothing was ever proved but there's always going to be scapegoats with stuff like that. We only started calling Jordan, '*Rossi*' once he'd came back from his ban, after Paolo Rossi. Jordan took it in the right way. Actually embraced it, in fact, and told me that he thought it was a brilliant 'fuck you' to the league that he was back playing and had been given a nickname linked to a known match fixer. Capable fox in the box striker as well with a sharp eye for goal. I thought the three years out scooping in the pub would've maybe dulled his predatory instinct to sniff out a chance but he slotted back into the

team as if he'd never been away. The only boy in the team that - at the start of the season - you would put your life on ending the season with over twenty goals. And we all need one of those whether you're Muirhouse Violet or Manchester United.

10. **Montana** - If there was ever a fitba player that you'd pray was to avoid being drug tested. Montana would definitely be up there alongside Diego Armando. I knocked all the drugs on the head back in the days when we all used to go to the Rez and Streetrave so at least - unlike most of the team - understood the drug part to him. Didn't fucking understand how he could be up all night and then go straight to Muirhouse Park and play ninety minutes out of his tree, though. Aye, I ken that it's easy to just say get a line up your beak and yourself out onto the pitch and you'll be ready to go but it would generally be someone who hasn't *taken* a drug in their life that would also say that. I remember one match. - The Royal Arms, I think - where he'd been at a rave at Ingliston then a few hours at an afters before turning up to play. He'd been saying that he was suffering from double vision. Depth awareness was all away to fuck. Hunter was having none of it, though. Told Montana to get his boots on and get on the pitch. Soon regretted his decision though when Montana missed that injury time chance to snatch the points when he completely fresh aired it when thinking he was kicking a ball that actually wasn't there. When he's not in a demented state of mind, though, he's a tidy wee striker and has a decent understanding with Rossi even if Rossi takes all of the glory through goals per game average. Montana would score more on the pitch if he scored less *off* it. Something that I've told the boy to his face.

11. **Mr Benn** - Given the name by the lads after the cartoon character one day when Bungalow noticed that he never

had the same rig oot on twice when you'd see him in the boozer. Proper posing cunt, like. Stone Island this - Gucci that. Goes to one of those fancy hairdressers in the city centre to get his hair cut and pays three times the price of any of the rest us. Hardly the type that you're going to depend on to stick his head in where it hurts if he's scared it's going to mess up his hair, eh? Someone who buys white Adidas Predators to play Sunday league and complains when people take turns at booting him up into the air over it. He was only in the side because of Sunny's previous and recent indiscretions, and subsequent immediate ban. At least Mr Benn had a bit of pace that Sunny lacked, when he could be actually arsed using it. We didn't exactly have an infinity pool of talent waiting in the wings for their chance when or if it came around with Violet so when Sunny's position became suddenly up for grabs. Benn got it more by default than anything else. As far as any long term future in the side. His report card most definitely - for me, anyway - had 'must do better' stamped on it.

Chapter 1

Strings

'Now, let me be loud and clear with each and every one of you sat here. Every Sunday when you stick that Violet top over your head, you're representing Muirhouse. For the next couple of weeks, though? You're representing your *country*. You're not just going to be a squad of amateur fitba players but, much more important than that, bloody ambassadors for the nation of Scotland. And, *unlike* the nation of Scotland, when they go out to play in a tournament, we're not just going out there to make up the numbers and be home before the postcards. We're going there to bloody *win*'

Once Jock Hunter - mic in hand - had got himself going, there really was no stopping him. Despite the fact that half of the squad were still running about daft that day, taking care of things - like packing their suitcases - before the next morning's flight. Hunter had sent out the bat signal for all of the travelling Muirhouse Violet delegation to converge for - what was sounding like - one final 'coach to players' pep talk before we all left Scotland, ready to do battle.

I'd known the man long enough to see that he was making a job of hiding the genuine excitement and pride that he had, in anticipation of our trip the next day. Instead, masking it with his whole gaffer persona that he had always tried to maintain when conducting Muirhouse Violet business. He really shouldn't have bothered - on this occasion at least - though. *Everyone* was excited, and there was no shame about it, either. It wasn't exactly every day that you'd find the players and staff of

Muirhouse Violet boarding an aeroplane, heading off to foreign climes on fitba duty.

The - at times - agonising build up had now passed. It was now the eve of us flying out and the whole squad was unashamedly buzzing at the prospect while Hunter was stood there - like some international World Cup coach - trying to keep everyone's feet on the ground over matters.

He needn't have bothered and, considering he'd worked enough years with the core group of the squad, he must've known that half of what come out of his mouth would've went in one ear and out the other where with some it wouldn't have even fucking went in to be able to come *out*. That was Jock, though, and, good or bad, he only ever had the best interests of the team at heart. Had it not *been* for him we wouldn't have even been sat there listening to his pre tournament speech. The man being single handedly responsible for us taking part in the coming together of fitba teams chosen - from the patrons of pubs and bars across Europe - to play in some summer tournament on the Balearic island of sunny Mallorca.

Our manager, secretly entering us - as Scotland's representatives - into a competition, sponsored by some Russian beer company - the absolutely honking Red Bear - whose bottled beer had suddenly appeared one day in The Gunner. The main reason that it had been accepted alongside the 'fine array' of world beers in our boozer, primarily because it was cheap, worryingly so. Without being someone ever likely to take part in The Apprentice, in terms of me having a brain for high level business, I could see that this Russian swally deal was one of those loss leader approaches, just to get themselves some kind of a foothold in Britain, when it came to customers.

Aye, good luck with that, Vlad mate. The minute any prospective customer lets that stuff hit their taste buds that's you *down* a customer, never mind gaining one. Fucking vile, horrible stuff and a possible reminder why you never see Russian made beers kicking about in any boozer you sit in. Still, it did have one advantage. As part of their whole brand awareness approach - being a company whose product would generally be found in select pubs - they were staging a summer fitba tournament where teams from across Europe - representing pubs that stocked and sold Red Bear - would be pitched against each other to see who the champions would be.

The way I'd had it described to me, it was kind of like a Euros but for pissheads instead of the cream of European fitba players. Which all sounded right fucking barry, if you ask me.

Same with the rest of the boys. When you get offered the chance to head someplace warm - like Mallorca - on what will be a near on two week drinking session with your mates, kicking the occasional football about while taking on a whole new set of teams from other countries, - instead of the same old faces every season in Edinburgh - it's not that much of a hard sell, is it? Obviously, the huge sesh, drinking cheap booze in all of those bars and clubs to all hours? Fucking *huge* attraction. Massive. But so was the sporting side to things as well. We'd never come close to playing in European competition and while this wasn't exactly a UEFA approved and fully licensed tournament, it might've well as been with how hyped we all were at the prospect of going toe to toe with players from other countries. Details were vague, going into the tournament. All we'd known was that we'd be drawn in the same group as pub teams from Russia, Portugal and Estonia.

'And you'll have all noticed that everyone making the trip are the ones who earned and deserved a spot. All of you lads sat here who spell commitment in full bloody capitals. None of those chancers who - on hearing about the Violet playing in a foreign tournament - all suddenly started digging out their old boots and shinnies while expressing their interest at getting back playing again. Any more of those cunts came out of the woodwork we'd have needed that British Airways to charter us a flight, eh?'

Jock laughed, along with most of the squad. Well, the ones who were still paying attention. Hunter wasn't wrong, though, about those that you hadn't seen anywhere near a Muirhouse Violet match, only to be over enthusiastic about coming to training in the hope that it got them into the squad, and a chance of going to Spain to play in the tournament.

According to the laws of association football, you're only allowed eleven players to start a match - plus your subbies - so with the best will in the world, fuck knows what you're meant to do with a squad of fucking *forty* to cover a potential two week tournament? A size of squad that would've made Harry Redknapp blush, like. Half of the hangers on that tried to get themselves wedged into the squad? The same cunts that you'd never see at a Violet game during Autumn and Winter but - at the sniff of a jolly away from their wives, girlfriends and family - suddenly trying to make out that they're Thierry Henry.

Give me peace, for fuck's sake.

The 'No WAGs' rule, something that had already proved contentious amongst the squad - although this was more in relation to their other halves reaction to this rule than the players themselves - and, in the run up to the tournament, something that had claimed the five year on off relationship between The Monk - one of our regular central defenders - and his other half and which had also left Rossi's marriage hanging by a thread with him handed the ominous - if a little cliched - warning that if he was to go to Spain then Sarah - his breadknife - wouldn't be there when he returned. Those were the two major ones that I knew about although could've well imagined that with others in the squad, going off to Spain for two weeks was going to cause scars in their relationships that might well have taken a good time to heal.

'No distractions' had been Hunter's orders and - for once - the entire squad were in complete agreement with him over, when it came to telling their other halves about this tournament in Spain and how it was not being treated as some holiday and - as such - there would be no family allowed, while already knowing just how much peaving they'd all be doing out there, minus their wife or girlfriend.

Jock was happy, so were the squad, thinking of the prospect of all the joys a trip to Magaluf would provide, and one without having to worry about things like wives and kids. The actual wives and girlfriends? Aye, clearly they weren't as thrilled about this arrangement as their men were. Well, that all depended on who you were partnered to, I suppose. Han was so non plussed about me telling her that I'd be fucking off for a couple of weeks to Spain and leaving her and Jack to fend for themselves that I'd actually thought that she was deliberately trying to *downplay* her joy at getting some peace from me for a few weeks.

She wasn't the only one who was glad at the prospect of getting some peace, even if my source of calm at the thought of getting away from things for a while weren't anything to do with her. Fuck, she'd been nothing but my rock, that Han of mines, but I could also see why *through me* - and my baggage - that she'd maybe needed a wee break from me.

It had been a bit of a stressful couple of years and I reckon that the trip came just when needed, if potentially a wee bit overdue if I was to be a chooser rather than a beggar. The worries and stresses of making sure you keep your family safe, fed and under a roof in a warm house are something that should always be hanging over you and they were not something I'd been a stranger to for as long as wee Jackie came along. Having those pressures from week to week can get to you now and again, that duress which never leaves and, at times, feels relentless. Life had never exactly been what you'd have classed as smooth. Then throw in the whole unpleasantness - when it came to falling into the pocket of one Mr David McKenna - of ending up in debt to one of the city / *country's* most powerful underworld figures though and soon you're reminiscing over those halcyon days where all you needed to worry about from week to week - and the prime reason for getting out of bed each morning - was taking care of your family.

You know the very worst part about being due a notorious gangster thousands of pounds, starting at the very worrying sum of over sixteen bags and with two years of paying it back through various work put in, still nowhere near to having the debt repaid? You'd think think that it would be the worry hanging over you and your family at being in such a level of debt to someone who could ruin your life by making a six second phone call. For me, it wasn't though.

What impacted my day to day life was that I'd had my freedom taken from me and the fact that no matter what I was possibly planning for myself, be that for earning some money for the family or even a bit of pleasure for myself, like going to the Hibs match or out for a few scoops. When that mobile phone - McKenna had given me and subsequently replaced occasionally over those two years - rang, I answered, and in doing so it generally meant 'fuck me and my plans.'

Utter demoralising, having someone with such a hold over you in your life, like McKenna had with me. A good example of this being that there was a bigger issue in my getting permission to travel abroad for the tournament from this man than I'd needed from my wife. There's your 'freedom' right there.

I'd had enough time to overplay things in my head - since that morning me and Benji left McKenna's scrapyard portacabin. Benji now five grand in debt to my sixteen - and the more I'd thought about it the more I'd became convinced that McKenna had set me up, on the journey I'd made back from Manchester that Sunday morning. Driving with a van full of trainers with gear inside of them. Those traffic cops that stopped me on the way back up from England? With the tentacles that someone like Davey McKenna had - and how far they stretched - it wouldn't have been out of the question for him to have alerted a couple of coppers on his payroll to stop me on the way back and engineer a situation where I'd have given them some free Adidas trainers to avoid any further issue, *just like* how the two police officers had done that Sunday morning. Obviously, knowing that the van was full of Coke, I'd have done just about anything to stop them finding the Ching when the three of us were all staring into the back of that rental van in the early hours of that Sunday morning on the M6.

After the event, though. It had become obvious to me that the two coppers *had* engineered the situation where I would gift them a pair of trainers each. At the time I'd just taken them for a couple of opportunistic officers who - when the chance arises - have their hand out for a freebie. Once I'd been able to stop and think about it, though. I had got it into my head that everything that happened on that journey up happened because it was *meant* to happen, and that none of it had come down to bad luck.

Me - thinking on my feet while desperately trying to avoid being caught in possession of kilos of Cocaine and spending twenty years in jail while losing McKenna his haul which must've been worth hundreds of thousands, maybe even millions - giving the trainers away to ensure I could get back on with my journey to Scotland but in doing so leading to me being - in the not exactly understanding eyes of McKenna -

eleven thousand and two hundred pounds in debt to him. Maybe it was just me feeling sorry for myself or a wee bit of paranoia but I'd convinced myself that what gear was inside those two blue boxes handed to the coppers would have ended up in the hands of McKenna, regardless. Wee bung to the coppers for their work, McKenna gets his Ching back and gains me as a member of staff for an unspecified amount of time. What if it was true, though? Not exactly much I could do about it, like. It was never mentioned in my induction pack but I would hazard a guess that McKenna didn't have a Human Resources department that I could take my complaint up with.

Even if he'd been a complete prick about it when I'd asked about the possibility of some time out, he gave his blessing. To be honest, had he not, there would've been some serious problems between us, because I wasn't missing the trip for the world, never mind McKenna. The break from him - and the, by now, unpredictable nature of day to day life in general - couldn't have come at a much more welcome time.

With the tournament set up seeing that each team would play their three group games inside the space of a week, and the remaining knockout matches all the way up to and including the final taking place over the following seven days. Men of confidence that we were, as well as wishing to milk a trip abroad for as much of its worth as we possibly could, we had taken the vote months before over to schedule a two week trip to Mallorca. Make no doubt about it, we were going there to win but at the very worst and we'd found ourselves knocked out in the group stages then we'd have had an extra week to go on the piss with no hassles like training or playing ninety minute matches of fitba in searing heat to be worrying about.

We couldn't lose, really. Even if we did.

'Now when this tournament begins, it's going to be all about yards. It's the extra yards that someone is going to have to reach for if they want to come home with that trophy on the plane. On this team, we fight for those yards, sometimes a little too literally for my liking. On this team, we tear ourselves and everyone else around us to pieces for those yards. We claw with our fingernails for those yards because we know when we add up all those yards, that's gonna be the difference between winning and losing. Between living and *dying!*'

'Aye, ok, Al Pacino'

The very bronzed Montana sat and whispered to me as he nudged my elbow. Making the same observation that I was arriving at in that part of Hunter's speech to the squad was being unashamedly plagiarised from the famous scene from that American Fitba film. It had only been on the telly the week before so I'd assumed Jock had watched it too and thought he'd bring some Al Pacino energy to his next team talk. As he stood there addressing us, I imagined him to have taped the film when it was on, and how he had watched the scene over and over again, pausing it at times to write down which pieces he was going to steal for his team talk. Jock, so into his impassioned address that he never clocked the pair of us laughing to ourselves.

Montana - himself - who had been visiting a local tanning salon in the build up to the tournament was now resembling someone who had just *returned* from a couple of weeks in the sun. The boy, trying to tell the rest of us that if we had our heads screwed on we'd have got ourselves in for a few sessions ourselves as it would help adapt to the scorching temperatures over in Spain, as well as potentially saving some of us the torture of burning our skin and ending up a traditional British lobster colour. A piece of advice that some of the squad would - eventually - end up wishing they'd taken up rather than replying with 'fuck off ya poofy wee cunt' amongst other similar sentiments - of a dinosaur nature - that cast a less than a flattery like light over the kind of a man found to be visiting tanning salons.

Hunter was too far gone to notice anything.

'Now this is uncharted territory for us all when it comes to foreign teams and match officials and when it comes down to it *none* of us know what we're going into but take a look around you and look at those team mates of yours and remember all of those victories that we've all shared. Now look at the boy next to you. Look into his eyes and you'll see someone who's going to go that extra yard with you. You'll see some cunt who will sacrifice himself for his team because he already knows that when it comes down to it, *you're* going to do the same for him. That's a team, gentlemen. That's the Muirhouse fucking Violet'

Despite still very much ripping Pacino off, it got the response that Hunter was looking for.

That whole room - having given him the floor and the silence that he required - all cheering and whistling at the rousing way that he ended his piece with. To be fair, with the buzz that everyone had about them, so close to the trip and everything that lay ahead for us all. Old Jock could've went on the microphone and said something like 'Fish suppers with mushy peas are fucking barry, eh?' and he'd probably have received the same reception from everyone.

'Now I want to see you all at Edinburgh Airport tomorrow morning. BA check in desk. Six am, half six at the very latest and before you even walk through that departures door. Remember that you've got the weight of not just Edinburgh but Scotland on you. You're representing a whole country and I want to see that in your behaviour and attitude from the moment you enter that airport to the moment you walk back through arrivals'

It was a good - great even - speech, if a little detached from reality. He'd been in charge of this group of men for long enough to know that taking all of them to a destination such as Magaluf, Mallorca and keep them all on the straight and narrow was going to be the biggest challenge of his fitba managerial career.

Chapter 2

Jock Hunter

Only the day before - less than twenty four hours - I'd asked, *demanded* even, for discipline and to show me a professional attitude. Instead - at Edinburgh International Airport - I got a bloody shambles. I'm not sure if there's a collective term for a group of simpletons but if there is then it would've been pretty bloody on the nose of the majority of the squad that I'd had to supervise in the hours before we left for Palma. For lesser managers, the thought of spending two weeks with that bunch of reprobates would've been enough for them to have been back in the house with the telly on before the plane to Spain had even taken off.

Obviously, Jock Cameron Hunter doesn't sit in the 'lesser manager' category, though.

When I got to the airport I was surprised to find that I wasn't the first one there, hanging around the check in area. I'd kind of felt it my responsibility to be there early and ready for the troops arriving so I could start checking everyone off the list.

'Glad you could make it, gaffer'

Montana was stood there tapping at his watch with a big smile on his face, and eyes just as big. Eyes - the size - *no one*, short of a bloody baker, should have at just before six in the morning.

'Fucking *flip flops*?' I said looking him up and down. 'And where's your Violet polo shirt? I told everyone that's what we were travelling in today?'

I thought that the sight of the squad in matching Violet merchandise all walking through an airport - and arriving in another country at the other end of the journey - would've been that extra wee touch of class. Make us look that wee bit official, ken? Through a contact I have through in the Weeg, who has a stall at The Barras, I'd had the team made polo shirts up for our end of season awards, a couple of years before, and had thought that they'd have been perfect for advertising our brand to a whole new audience.

Instead, not only was Montana minus the polo shirt but he was cutting around in bloody flip flops, like he was going to the beach or taking the bins out.

'Honestly haven't seen that polo shirt since the player of the year awards night, Jock. Some, eh, celebrated that night more than others, eh?'

'Aye, I'm sure they did.' I says back to him, without inviting any of the finer details to that.

You could tell that he'd been taking *something*, though. He just had that happy - but mildly manic - look about him. Like I said, people shouldn't be that alert at that time of the morning. I took a wee thought to say something to the lad but decided to leave it. I'd never approved of the boy's drug use. Why someone would want to put that poison into them is something that I will never figure out.

I know that it makes me a bloody hypocrite considering that despite my knowledge of him and the drugs - and my whole anti drugs stance - that I would still pick him for the team, but what was I meant to do? He had been one of our best players for the last two or three seasons. I'm not sure if that was *because* of the drugs or not but well, don't go fixing something that's not broken in the first place. And, anyway. They always say that the best managers pick their best starting eleven. Something wee Montana pissed his way into.

Still wanted to have that word - ahead of a fortnight away and whatever temptations may have been waiting on him - with him but sometimes it's best just to choose your moments. Plus, Strings, Benji, Daz and Mr Benn had now come strolling into the departures hall and in our direction. The four of them stumbling over to us barely awake but exactly how you'd have imagined the squad appearing at such an early time of the morning.

'OH? OH? Fucking polo shirts, cuntos, eh?'

I stood and surveyed the four of them. At least Strings, Benj and Daz were all in sports leisure gear in a mixture of trainers, sports shorts and tracksuits. Benn - ever the show off - had turned up in a matching two set of cream sweatshirt and shorts. With that compass style badge - you'd often see stuck to what he was wearing - fixed to both pieces and a pair of white leather trainers to match. Sunglasses stuck to the top of his head which would've been all and good were it not for the fact the sun wasn't even up in the sky yet when he'd left the house for the airport.

The four of them all just stood and looked at each other hoping that one of the other would answer me on the subject of the polo shirts.

'You were meant to fucking remember me, Benji,' Strings said less than convincingly.

'Bollocks I was' Benji laughed.

Daz kept silent on things while Mr Benn went with a candid reply that was something along the lines of that he would die for Muirhouse Violet but would also rather die than be seen with one of those cheap and minging polos in public.

'Aye, if it was made by that Marble Island you wouldn't be able to stick it on your back quick enough,' I said back to him quick as a flash.

The fact that the rest of them all laughed at this, validation that my patter was up to scratch, regardless of how early it was.

Over the next half hour the remaining members of the squad sauntered into the airport to join the rest of us. Each name getting ticked off from my squad sheet upon arrival.

'Fucking hell, Montana. The state of your eyes, sir?'

I heard big Terry saying, while the two of them stood speaking behind me. Definitely wasn't just me who thought they were on the large side then.

'They that bad, Tel? Aye?' Montana replied back to him. Me deciding to eavesdrop on the conversation while double checking all of my hand luggage as we waited on the last two players to arrive.

'They're like fucking sheriff's badges, M. What the fuck you been up to last night?'

'That's the thing, Tel. Fuck all. Actually went to my bed *early* last night, since we all had an early start this morning. Couldn't fucking sleep though, could I? Too excited about today and the next couple of weeks'

'Aye, but I'm not sure that explains the fact that your eyes look ...'

'Well, that's just it though. It was only when it started to get around back of three this morning that I started to feel a wee bit tired, but with an alarm set for half four. Well, probably would've done me more harm than good if I'd slept for an hour. So I had a wee dab of speed paste, just enough to keep me awake and alert to get me through the whole airport experience and that I'd get a wee sleep on the plane. Was new stuff, though. I'm taking - what I looked on as - a wee dab of the gear but it's strong as fuck. Standing here fucking flying and haven't even hit the runway yet'

'You're some cunt' Terry said. He wasn't wrong either, mind.

At least Montana meant well, about the only nice thing I could say about the situation. Him and his story that morning was just one of many sub plots when it came to the lot of us getting checked in, through security and onto that bloody plane.

Once Rossi and Delaney - a reserve of ours that got himself an unexpected call up to the first team after Bungalow went and blootered fuck out of that ref after he'd given a dodgy pen against us in the Grants Vodka quarter final in the last minute, leading to police being brought into things and, due to the level of violence the big man had inflicted on the poor official, ended up on remand. The fact Bungalow already had a few similar charges over recent years something that the judge took into account which sealed the deal on a wee spell on the inside - arrived, that was the last two names scratched from the list.

It was time to get ourselves checked in.

It had been absolutely yonks since I'd been on a plane to anywhere. Benidorm, eighty nine. Me and her indoors. Don't get me wrong. I enjoyed it. Sun and cheap peave and food. Once I bought the caravan at the start of the nineties, though, our desire for flying abroad pretty much seized to exist.

Truth be told, because it had been so long since I'd flown I couldn't really remember what you had to do to check in but the questions about if I'd packed my own suitcase or if I'd left it unattended in the airport sort of rung a bell. With me being first to check in and not wanting to hold any of the rest up I chose the option of lying by saying that I'd packed my suitcase myself, rather than the truth that I'd had Betty do it for me. The woman behind the check in desk got me on my way soon enough as I felt a wave of excitement rush right over me as I walked away from the check in desk with my boarding pass stuck safely inside my passport. There had been quite a bit of build up to this trip - and what it meant for the team - but, having that boarding pass, it now felt real. I walked away and waited for the rest of the squad to collect their boarding passes so that we could all go through security together.

There lay the fundamental issue, and one that was sure as fuck to surface time after time over the next fortnight. This was Muirhouse bloody Violet. Just because I made it smoothly through the check in process. That didn't mean that the same would apply for everyone else that was following at the back of me.

Problem number one that morning? Come on down.

'Oh you have got to be fucking *kidding* me?'

I heard The Monk shout out as he stood there at the desk, shouted at enough volume that had about half of the massive departures hall looking his way.

'Hang on a second' I interrupted Benji who had been stood with Strings and Montana, the main topic of conversation being that - once past security - the first thing they were doing was hitting the bar. Medicinal before a flight, according to Strings.

When I reached the check in desk I found the apologetic British Airways - aye, none of that budget airline stuff for The Violet although that was more down to juicy friends and family type discount we'd got for the block booking through my niece Kerry, who worked at a travel agents in the town - trying her best not to state the bloody obvious by telling The Monk that he couldn't fly without a passport.

'I had it on me, Jock. You not think that would be one of the first and last things that I'd have checked before leaving for the airport, eh?'

He said, no doubt reacting to what my face must've been like because I hadn't even had a chance to say a single word yet.

'Well where the fuck is it?' I asked, finding my voice while taking The Monk to the side so that Rossi could pass by and check himself in.

He took a wee think about it before his lightbulb went on.

THE FUCKING TAXI! I had it in my hand on the journey to the airport, but I don't remember anything after that. Can't remember putting it in my bag again or fuck all'

'Welllll, what are you waiting on?' I couldn't really hide how pissed off I was with him. We hadn't even got ourselves up the escalator to security and were already having problems, of bloody schoolboy error natures at that.

He just looked at me, clueless.

'Phone the fucking taxi firm and get them to check with the driver if it's there. Jesus Christ, Monk. This shouldn't be as difficult as this'

Stepping aside from the check in desk he got on his mobile to see about locating where his passport was, eventually coming off it again - after a series of calls - with the most sheepish of looks to him.

'Right gaffer, I've got good news and bad news'

'Don't give me your pish, here. Just give me the bad news and tell me what the bloody hell's going on'

The result being that the Monk's passport was indeed sat in the back of the taxi that he'd travelled to the airport in. The real downside to this was that the bloody car was somewhere on its way to Carlisle and wouldn't be back in Edinburgh until about half ten, well after our plane would be taking off.

Hearing the strained exchange between manager and player, the gem of a bird behind the check in desk helpfully chipped in by telling us that - due to the circumstances - if The Monk was to go to their customer services terminal and explain about missing the flight they would get him onto a later flight out to Palma that day, with a nominal fee that would require paying, something that was on The Monk for being such a daft bastard in the first place.

With everyone all checking in and receiving their boarding passes that was about the point where we said our goodbyes to The Monk. Saying how we'd see him in Spain, when we saw him. I almost felt sorry for the boy, that look on his face when he saw the rest of the squad - all buzzing and ready to hit the bar for an early morning pint - all heading off and leaving him sat there with nothing he could really do other than wait the hours and hours on the taxi - with his passport - getting back to Scotland. I asked for professionalism, though. You don't get much more *un*professional than turning up to an airport without your passport. He'd made his bed. We'd catch him in Spain.

I led the boys up the escalator towards security, where I was soon left harking back for the days of minor inconveniences, such as people forgetting their passports.

Now I'm not just saying this like someone does when they're getting their excuses in early before they even tell you something but as I said, I hadn't flown in almost twenty years, so had no clue about how much changes there had been made to airport security since those bloody nutters flew those planes into those towers in New York.

The way yon security boys reacted when they found that I had a four pack of beer in my bag that had gone through their x ray machine? Honestly, not even joking. It was as if they'd discovered someone with plans to hijack a plane and fly it right into Edinburgh Castle, the way they reacted to four cans of lager. Well I didn't know, did I? Almost shed a tear when they took that four pack from me. I'd specifically brought those four cans for drinking in the departure lounge and on the plane. Fuck paying those outrageous airport prices, ken? That was based on my last time I'd been flying out of one so fuck knows what the prices were going to be in two thousand and thirteen, and I didn't want to find out, either.

I'll admit, I probably went over the score a wee bit over four cans, while also showing everyone in my proximity of my complete ignorance towards airport security etiquette in the modern world, but I wasn't the only one.

'It's just four bloody cans. How am I going to hijack a plane with them?' I pleaded while being reminded that I could only bring liquids through security inside containers that held a hundred millilitre and me replying that you don't bloody *get* lager in such small quantities.

Afterwards, when we were all camped up in the departure lounge, Terry was sat there looking absolutely buckled. The reason for this being that he'd been at the back of the queue going into security and word had filtered back over me having my cans taken from me - and the scene that it had caused - which had led to Terry, also apparently unaware of the change in laws regarding what you could take through airport security, tanning his whole bottle of vodka and two litre bottle of coke - by using an empty plastic water bottle that was lying around in a bin - that he'd also planned to take through and drink later.

But I still needed to get myself through security first. Begrudgingly accepting that the cans were gone and that I was now going to get completely rinsed with the airport prices, which you almost think they arrive at by drawing random numbers out of a tombola.

Worryingly, though. As I was finally getting my belongings from the plastic tray on the rollers. I noticed that Montana was being led away by a couple of the security officers, one of them carrying Montana's bag. Stopping what I was doing, I kept watch as they took him away and into a side room.

I tried to get answers from some of the other security that were still stood around but was either blanked or informed that the matter was none of my business.

Bloody hell, we're already missing The Monk - at least for the best part of a day - and now Montana. And depending on *his* situation I couldn't be sure if he'd be joining us *at all*, never mind later that day.

And he only made it by the skin of his teeth, as well. Something like two minutes before boarding started being called. A huge cheer from the - by then - inebriated squad who had made good use of the time available in the bar before getting on the plane when they saw the skulking Montana walking towards them, bag slung over his shoulder.

When pressed by everyone over what had happened and why security had taken him away he just replied that it was down to a misunderstanding but I could tell that he wasn't exactly being straight with everyone. Whatever had taken place and whatever he'd been up to, it would come out. That stuff always did with the squad. Worse than sweetie wifies, them.

Whether one of our main strikers had been up to something dodgy or not, for me, it was very much a case of beggars and choosers. A player that we most definitely were going to need out there in Spain had made it and was on the plane with us.

Something that I could not say the same thing about for Terry. Having sunk so much Voddie and Coke in such a short space of time that he must've come close to alcohol poisoning. Aye, he didn't quite manage to make it onto the plane.

Just like that wee boy in the Home Alone film. We only realised that he *wasn't* on the plane after we'd taken off. Daz admitting that he'd last seen him going for a pish, saying that with all the fluids he'd been putting into him he'd be better going to the toilet before boarding.

By that point, the enthusiasm that I'd had hours before, when greeting the squad on arrival at the airport, had dipped several levels. So much so that when the *seatbelt off* light went on and I heard the shout from a few rows back that Terry wasn't on the plane, the only reaction I could muster to this was.

'Fuck him, he can get the next one with The Monk. Now who's going to bring me a bloody can? You bastards would drive a man to drink.'

Chapter 3

Strings

'Jesus fucking Christ, you want to see the prices inside there, mate'

I shouted towards our table as I brought me and Benji's drinks over on a tray, almost feeling like I'd committed a robbery.

'Fucking three euros fifty for a pint of voddie and coke, and it's happy hour'

I put the tray down and handed Benji over his two pints of San Miguel. One more than he'd expected but when you go up to a bar, put an order in and the cunt behind the counter gives you double of what you asked for, but for the price of half that. Well, you're not going to stop him, are you?

We'd just arrived but sampling the cheap drink offered up during a happy 'hour' that possibly resembles what an hour lasts for on Mars or somewhere but definitely not earth, it was a wee bit ominous. Despite the fact that I was one of the first of us to get wired into the peave - once we'd dropped our suitcases at the hotel - it was still a bit ominous all the same because seeing those prices and how the squad hadn't wasted any time in seeking refreshments upon arrival in Magaluf. I questioned what this same group of men were going to be like after fourteen days of being there.

It was a fleeting thought I had though, very.

By the time we'd got the bus from the airport to the hotel it was around three in the afternoon and soon found that we - literally the whole squad - shared a difference in opinion with Jock Hunter over what our first day in Magaluf was going to involve.

Mutiny would be too strong a word. Overruled would probably be more of an accurate way to describe it.

'Right, lads'

Jock - who had gathered all of the squad in the hotel foyer once we'd all sorted out our rooms and all of that stuff - said, trying to get everyone's attention while looking like some cunt that was sweating more than someone that cleans a sauna.

'We've got our first game in two days time, and your first training session tomorrow. So with that in mind, I was thinking we should go for a wee walk, nothing strenuous. There's a beach five minutes from here so we'll go for a walk along that. We've all been up since the middle of the night so after we've had our tea we'll get an early night ahead of training tomorrow'

The look that came over his face about two seconds after he'd said what he had told me that he'd already clocked the reaction of the squad over what they'd just heard. And that was before any of us even opened our mouths.

'Come on, Jock. Play fair, eh?'

'Naw, man. Let the lads out for a wee swally. It's only still afternoon, eh?'

'Five minutes walk to the beach? It's only a two minute one to that bar across the road, how's that for strenuous?'

The squad began to voice their opposition to his thoughts.

'I'm only saying, lads. If we've come here to win this trophy then it's not going to fall into our laps. You think the other teams here to play in it are sitting in the pubs right now? Probably playing water polo in their hotel pool or out for a run'

He replied, defensively and a wee bit hurt at the opposition he was facing. Generally, we all respected the man, his passion for the team and how much he devoted his life towards it and even if we weren't happy with some of his decisions that affected us, we'd all give him a pass, because it was Jock.

I nodded to Benji to go over and - as his assistant - try and put things into some words that Jock would be able to appreciate. And fair play to Benji boy. What a performance from the man that saw Jock allowing us to all go on our way - him included, the hypocritical bastard - directly to the boozer.

'Look, Jock. Nobody's saying you don't have a point with how you want to plan things out for the team but when does half of this group here ever get the chance to leave Scotland? Most of us - you included - haven't been abroad in years while some of us haven't *ever* been abroad. It's understandable why the squad are as hyper as they are right now. I think that the right thing to do would be to let everyone have this first day to do what they want, within reason, obviously. And they do so in the knowledge that we have training tomorrow, but I have to ask though pal, has this group of lads ever let you down?'

'Exactly!' Rossi shouted out in agreement.

Hunter took a second to mull this over while we all fell silent, waiting on his response, hoping it was going to be favourably because, right then, it really was a case of 'if Hunter sticks to his guns, we riot.'

'Ok, anyone who doesn't show up for training tomorrow, misses the first match. And you know how fitba can go at times. Lose your place, who knows if you'll get it back again?'

Everyone looked around at each other nodding their heads in a 'seems fair enough' kind of way, like they were all complete stick ons for *actually* making training the next day, which they most definitely were not.

'And remember, this isn't training in Edinburgh on a Thursday night. This is bloody Mallorca in the afternoon sun stuff. So prepare to go through hell. I'll be risking death just by standing, pointing and shouting orders at you so good luck to you lot doing the leg work'

Rather than just agree with the wise words that Benji had chosen, he had to get the last couple of bits in, exactly like someone who is in a lofty position and has felt like they've had their authority challenged does.

A win's a win though, and at that time in the afternoon? Training and the whole concept of it the next day felt like a month away for everyone as they marched out of the hotel and across the road to The Arsed Rat.

The boozer, itself, situated on a mini strip that was filled with pubs, restaurants and tourist shops that seemed to be in competition with each other over which one could have the most pre inflated lilos assembled at the shop entrance. I considered how - with us seeing these same shops for the next couple of weeks - it was probably only a matter of time before some wideo from the squad would put their snout out in one.

The owner of the pub was rubbing his hands when he seen us flood the place, though. Could almost see the euros in his eyes when he saw us all walk in, take seats while others waited to be served at the bar. Both inside and out front was full of Muirhouse Violet, it was glorious. While a fair amount of the boys had chosen to sit inside on the comfy looking sofas where Sky Sports News was playing on plasma screens from different angles on the walls. I'd fancied sitting out in the warm, what with me barely ever fucking experiencing such a sensation in North Edinburgh so had told Benji to grab us a table while I sorted out the drinks.

We were soon joined by a much less energised looking version of the Montana that I'd seen at six in the morning back in Edinburgh. While he was holding two pints of lager, his coupon was screaming that there wasn't a chance in hell that he'd be fucking drinking them.

'You alright, pal?' Benji asked as Montana sat down, almost spilling one of the pints before he'd even had a chance to put it down.

'Aye, you're kind of looking as rough as what the majority of us are probably going to be tomorrow before training, only you've managed to get there hours ahead of schedule,' I added.

'What goes up must come down, eh?'

He replied pragmatically before pulling his shades down from the top of his head, taking a laboured sip from his pint glass before telling us that the speed he took - to keep him awake before the airport - had turned out to be stronger than anticipated and it was only by this point that it had started to wear off and, as a result, he was more now resembling what someone who has completely skipped a whole night's worth of sleep *would* look like. The comedown from the drugs couldn't have helped, or the - what felt like in those initial first few hours - unnatural heat we were all experiencing, I imagine.

'Reckon I'm just going to have these two pints and then call it a day, get myself fresh for training tomorrow'

Now the standard response - given the surroundings - should have been 'Fucking nonsense, we're in Magaluf on day one, you're staying out with the fucking lads' but considering he could barely hold his head up before he'd even had a chance to finish a single pint then that hardly pointed towards him being the life and soul of the party as the afternoon turned to evening.

In the end, he only managed three quarters of his first pint. Sneaking off before any of the group - the ones who *would* be shouting for Montana to stay out as part of some forced group fun - noticed him. He did the correct thing. The only alternative, when it came to Montana, would've been him staying out and procuring some more gear which would've probably led to him being up for *another* night, and where would it all end if he'd got himself onto that merry go round? We'd need the cunt on the pitch for these three group games and that wouldn't be happening if the boy was stuck in the middle of some inescapable bender.

Before he snuck off though, Benji and me got the *real* story behind why he'd been taken away by security. I'd simply assumed that one of the airport security had clocked the size of his eyes and thought he'd be worth a pull and given some extra scrutiny. I mean, Montana would've been as well walking through security that morning with a t-shirt on screaming 'I TAKE DRUGS' considering the size of his eyes.

The reality behind matters, however, was a little different, even if still being drug related. When, though, is it not with him?

As he sat there taking an eternity to drink his lager he told us how he'd popped a quarter of grass into his hand luggage before leaving the house.

'Just enough for a wee joint a day when over here, hardly a case of international drug trafficking'

He said, even though I was pretty sure that taking drugs from one country to another was *literally* the definition of international drug trafficking.

'Plus, last couple of times I've been here all I've been able to find was some pishy soap bar which is a fucking liberty considering how close this island is to North Africa. Anyway, wasn't risking ending up with any of that shite this time around, eh?'

He'd apparently hidden his green wrapped in cling film inside his pouch of tobacco. Said he'd read on the internet from other tokers that they used this method all the time when boarding planes. Obviously the security and their fancy x ray machine managed to see the difference inside his tobacco pouch because as soon as he'd walked through the human x ray section he got the tap on the shoulder, and then the grab. And was marched off to a side room where his bag was searched, he was searched, completely.

'The bastards literally made me bend over and part my fucking erse cheeks, for fuck's sake. They might've taken a hundred pounds from me as a spot fine but inside that room they took my fucking dignity'

It was the only time while he sat there that I detected some life to him, even if it was only through a piece of anger stirring up in him.

Obviously, no man wants to strip naked and bend over and show their hoop to a couple of strangers but when you weighed it all up. He was pretty fucking lucky that he'd managed to get away with a caution and spot fine and allowed to travel on his way. It sounded like something that you wouldn't question if you'd been told Montana had been stopped from travelling, and why.

We ended up sitting in The Arsed Rat for near on five hours, four of them happy hour. And - like most that would visit the place during the happy hour that barely ended I imagine - left rat *arsed*.

By this point, food had now taken on being the single most important thing ever known to a human being since records began. Finding a restaurant at eight o clock at night able to accommodate a party of near on twenty people was not an easy thing to do. Or put it another way. Any restaurant that twenty people can stroll into - without a prior booking - and there be space for is probably an eatery that should be avoided in the first place.

Due to this, desperation and convenience won the day, leading us all through the doors of KFC, a wee bit up the hill of one of the main strips.

It was just as well, really. Definitely for the best that a Muirhouse Violet who had been getting wired into happy hour in the boozer for five hours weren't accommodated by any of the restaurants that looked worth going into. Nights would be ruined for holidaymakers, scenes would be caused and strangers insulted, if they were lucky.

This highlighted when that lippy Londoner who was part of some Eighteen to Thirties pub crawl ended up taking a dig from Coffee after mistakingly thinking that he was trying to chat up his bird. Well, that's the laughable part about it, it wasn't even his fucking bird, just someone that he'd been trying to get off with over the crawl and had decided to get defensive over something that wasn't even fucking his in the first place.

I'm not sure how far into their pub crawl they were but fuck me, you could've picked a lot worse group to try and swing your handbag at than a group of cunts from the Naughty North of Edinburgh.

All Coffee had been doing was talking to the girl, having a laugh at his own expense over how pished he was and how he was too far back from the counter to see what there was to eat and was asking her if she'd tell him. Next thing. This cunt in a pair of Charlton Athletic shorts and a Slazenger t shirt comes and squeezes himself in between the two of them while asking her if the boy Coffee was bothering her. Coffee had said that the face she pulled at the boy more showed that if any cunt was bothering her, it was him, not Coffee.

'Nah, I'm not bothering her, pal but any more of your pish and you'll find me bothering *you*' Coffee said as he grabbed the boy's arm and yanked him back out from between him and the girl, Irish I think she was.

'Who the fahk do yoo think yoo are?' He reacted angrily, and very stupidly. Reaching out and pushing Coffee from behind, sending him flying into the back of Sepp, leading to him dropping his phone in what was a brilliant mini example of a perfect storm.

You kind of just watched the next part with half shut eyes while waiting on the response, because of that, there was no doubt would be.

I'd have put money on the red mist coming instantly down and him turning around and ripping the English boy's head off and volleying it straight into one of the fryers backstage in the KFC kitchen. Instead, though, - and I think this was more to do with the busy and bright environment we were all stood in - he was a lot more calm and measured. Whilst the other boy stood there with his arms outstretched like one of those pavement dancing casuals you see that have never swung a punch in their puff. Inviting Coffee to move towards him. An offer which he was more than happy to take him up on. Keeping his cool but now very much in the area of invading personal space.

"Who am I? I'm Coffee, box to box midfielder, eight pints into my night and one of the worst cunts you could ever have the misfortune to bump into on this island'

And with that, he delivered the most subtle but punch packing headbutt right into the boy's nose. I'd never seen an explosion of blood in my life, it was like a water balloon that had been filled with human blood had been lobbed at the boy. His t - shirt instantly covered in the stuff while it continued to stream from out of his nose.

He definitely wasn't so vocal after that. Plus, with Coffee's move being made with a few people for cover. It had been so subtle that barely anyone in the place had even noticed what had been going on. Post headbutt, though, and the mess that it had made of not just the boy on the receiving end but also the tiles of KFC, it was a little hard *not* to notice that there had been an incident. And obviously, there was a few of the obligatory screams from girls who don't even have any skin in the game but can't help themselves during moments like this.

Thinking on my feet, I told Coffee to take himself off - before any Guardia Civil appeared - and that we'd meet him at the bottom of the hill - near the beach - and how I'd sort some scran out for him.

He seemed to pick up what I was saying. Nodding to me before he got himself away to fuck. Unable to resist it, as he was leaving, he stopped by the boy - who by then was holding a bunch of napkins up to his nose - for one final word.

'Two things, ya prick. That lassie there is so far out of your league you're Rochdale Town and she's fucking Real Madrid so stop being a fanny by wasting your night on something that's not going to happen. And two, change your fucking shirt. You're not getting your Nat King off *any* cunt looking like that'

We all sat down by the beach on a wall capable of accommodating twenty radgeys while we fired into some much required scran. But after we'd eaten it? Well that's when the pivotal moment of the night came. Where, as a group, we had to ask the question. We'd had a good scoop by that point. Due to the happy hour element, some of us must've been on about double figures in terms of drink. Now that we'd had something to eat, the question really was - with training scheduled for the next day - do we call it a night or do we keep on going and see what delights the Magaluf nightlife had waiting for us.

Jock Hunter went back to the hotel, the rest decided - quite inevitably - that they'd stay out a little longer.

'I'll see you all at training then'

He said to us all with what was almost a wicked look on his face.

Fast forward to after four - I think - in the morning and me and Benji having to get the night porter from the hotel to come and let us into our room. Not because we'd lost our key or anything normal like that but his assistance was required because two fully grown men - between them - had not been able to work out how to slot a key inside a door to gain entry into their room. Our attempts before giving up taking place over an undetermined amount of time but felt like it hadn't been small. I don't know if he was laughing with or *at* us, but he was definitely laughing as he let us into our room before letting himself back out again but only after benefitting from being in the position of a hotel employee carrying out a task and being rewarded in tips by two people who had been too drunk to get a key in a door, never mind prudently choose work out the acceptable amount of a tip to give someone.

It was only when I went through to the bathroom for a single fish and clocked myself in the big mirror that I was able to appreciate how drunk I was. Let's be honest, we were *always* going to end up going out on our first night and have a wee sesh. That was something that I'd literally taken as fact, no matter what our manager thought about it.

Now, though? The reality of things was that it was the back of four in the morning, and I had training - during what was predicted to be thirty three degree heat - in around eight hours time.

And it was round about that time that the fear truly kicked in.

Chapter 4

Victor Borovskiy

'Ahh, Arben, my friend' I greeted him on my call being answered.

'The Russian, I've been expecting your call. That time of year again, huh?' He replied, the first time I was hearing his voice since we'd last spoken, the summer before.

From time to time we would do business together - although never, ever directly - across the calendar year but business, and life in general, had taken things in a different direction which had led to myself and Kelmendi being virtual strangers to each other. But tradition's tradition. What would society be like if it were to let its national, international or personal heritages slip away?

'It sure is but I must ask, where does the time go? A whole year, gone. In the blink of an eye?' I confirmed while genuinely stunned that it had felt like a year had flown by as I heard his voice again. They say that the later years go quicker, and when you reach those later years you can see why.

'That, I do not know, Viktor but what I *do* is that as long as each year passes and I find myself with more money banked then I do not complain'

Arben's reply showing me the difference between the two of us. While both richer than beyond our wildest dreams, where as I had long since began to take the riches - that came along with the status of oligarch - for granted and was almost blasé of it all.

He - unlike me - seemed to be destined to never forget his humble beginnings. A Tirana street urchin who through his sharp brain and sheer ruthlessness rose through the world of Albanian organised crime, becoming a billionaire in the process.

There was no denying it, however. While both billionaires, only one of us had ever had to fight - and in some cases for Arben, *kill* - for the money that they'd earned. The other was simply in the right place at the right time and friends with the correct people.

You don't choose life, life chooses you. As my dear old babushka used to tell me when something didn't go my way when I was a boy.

'Yes, Arben. There is something rather perverse, though, about the two of us getting even richer each year, but another year older and one year less for us to spend it!'

'Speaking of such matters'

I carried on, seizing the chance before he replied to my philosophical musings. But he cut me off anyway.

'Let me guess? Is this the part where you offer me the chance to make myself even *more* richer?'

I loved the man. He was so straight to the point that he could've been born in the same town as me in the - then - Soviet Union, not, Albania.

'Well it simply wouldn't be tradition if I were to not, Arben' I chuckled down the phone to him.

'What do you say? Same amount as last year?' I asked, assuming nothing other than agreement. Instead, I was met with silence.

'I was thinking, maybe we make things a little more interesting this year, Viktor'

He finally said, breaking the silence.

More interesting? I thought to myself. Almost one year ago I had relieved the man of one million dollars - which had been our general sum that we would stake each year - and he was now saying to me that he wanted to make things *interesting*?

'Tell me, Arben? What do you know that I don't?' I probed, safe in the knowledge that even if there was something, he wouldn't be telling me.

'Oh, nothing. I just feel that this is my year.' He responded, sounding like a classic gambling addict but at complete odds with the wily fox of a man that he was.

This, putting me in a bad position because if Kelmendi was breaking with standard procedure by looking for a possible increase in stake being put up by us, it must've been for a reason. But in taking such an approach, it put me in a place where - despite being cautious of falling into a trap laid out by Arben - I would now need to keep my face.

'So what were you thinking?' I asked, intrigued to see what he had in mind while knowing that whatever he was thinking, I would be forced into some sort of decision in turn.

'Oh nothing too drastic, Viktor. I've heard the rumours about the SEC looking for sanctions issued on you, over your stake in that chemical company over in the states. I wouldn't want to leave you *completely* broke. I was thinking, maybe one point five this year?'

I know he was just baiting me but mentioning my issues with the authorities in America was a low blow. Those Yankees are always threatening to sanction us but they never do. All of that was - as the Americans say - a nothing burger. It was enough for me to be sat there on the other end of the line thinking to myself, fuck this guy.

And also enough for me to arrogantly suggest that we should just round things up to an even two million. It seemed to take him by surprise for a moment, the exact impact that I'd been looking for when in a moment of pique decided to offer to lay down double the amount of money I'd originally intended to, when I'd called his number.

When you take part in a big dick swinging contest, though. Make sure you turn up with the biggest dick, or don't bother turning up at all.

'Ok then, Viktor. Two million it is. I guess, then, the next time we speak we will be discussing Swiss or Cayman Islands bank details?' Kelmendi said, confirming things.

'I look forward to it, my friend, ' I replied, confidently, back to him before hanging up. All that needed said having now been done so.

I'd found the phone call unexpectedly exhilarating, and the most alive I'd felt all day. And this coming on the same day where I'd received - without any quarrel - one of the best - and I mean top three of all time - blow jobs in my life, from a beautiful little Asian call girl who had been brought out to the villa for me.

Without appearing arrogant. When a man has the kind of wealth like, well, like someone such as me. To get any kind of a thrill in life - when being so rich that being rich simply doesn't cut it - you have to go up several levels from the ordinary man to experience feelings of genuine fun.

Levels like wagering bets - in their millions - with Albanian drug lords, responsible for the sale of billions of dollars worth of narcotics across Europe each year.

In the general scheme of things. What really was two million? Yes, clearly an excessive amount for what we were wagering on but that wasn't the point. It wasn't really *about* the money, how could it be when the prize money was nothing but a drop in the ocean to either myself or Kelmendi.

It was the *winning* that was the thrill.

And - regardless of what had given him such confidence - I certainly hadn't made the phone call to the Albanian with pre conceived intentions of losing by the time our business was done.

Life is full of losers.

Mr Viktor Borovskiy, however, is not one of them.

Chapter 5

Sepp

Holy fuck! Hunter said that training was going to be punishing but yet I couldn't help but think that he'd deliberately underplayed things. Or put it like this. If he'd fucking told the squad of Muirhouse Violet just how brutal it was going to be - guaranteed - the whole squad would've handed in their verbal resignation there on the spot and went on the piss in Magaluf for the next couple of weeks. That's what *I'd* have done, anyway.

And another fucking thing. Why - as a goalkeeper - have me do as much running as well? Every bit as much as he had our box to box players who actually *do* some fucking running. And that's without mentioning the black bin bags. I couldn't believe what I was seeing when Hunter put his hand into his Head sports bag and came out with a big roll of bin liners. I spied the Scotmid wrapper going around them which confirmed that he'd actually brought them across to Spain with him, ahead of our training beginning. Seeing his plan, some of the squad objected to the sheer insanity of putting a black bin liner on and running around in such extreme heat.

Strings who before the bags had even came out was looking like he was about to die at any given moment, and that was before we'd even got changed for training - probably not incorrectly - raised the question that wouldn't making people run around wearing bin bags in the kind of heat that Magaluf boasted that early afternoon be verging on potential manslaughter, if not murder.

All he got back was some spiel about how there was more than a few of the squad who were carrying a bit of extra weight - not to mention all of the toxins that we no doubt were riddled with from the night before, and how he'd read that Gazza would always go running with a bin liner on, anytime his weight was starting to get out of control. In doing this, by the end of his session the English midfielder would find that he'd shed several pounds.

'Aye, but it's not much good if we've lost a stone here or there but you're having to make arrangements for getting our bodies flown back to Scotland, eh?'

The Monk - who along with Terry had arrived in Magaluf the night before - shouted out. Maybe having arrived later in Spain than planned but making up for lost time. Again, though. It possibly came across as a wide comment but it was baked in fact.

Of course, though. It had been us who had chosen to completely kick the erse out of things the night before by staying out until - insert each player's own version of events - all hours and in attempting to put up any kind of resistance to training, all it did was make us look like we couldn't hack things, and the reason for this being that we'd consumed too much alcohol the night before.

But us not knowing when to say when in relation to Magaluf and all the delights it offers and our manager being so into things - while I'm sure was also letting out a piece of his vindictive side - that he was risking killing his squad were not two mutually exclusive things.

'Nonsense, these bags never killed bloody Paul Gascoigne and they'll not kill any of you either. Now get them over your heads and let's get cracking'

He said, throwing the roll of bags to Daz, with him pulling one off before passing the roll onto the next man.

Fragile, frail, broken. You could've chosen a whole range of adjectives to describe the vast majority of the squad that lunch time. This was no group of people who were in *any* kind of position for taking part in physical exercise.

We'd made our bed, I suppose. Deep down - if any of us had cared to think about it or admit - training was always going to be brutal but when you're slap bang in the middle of a session with your mates in an exciting and lively destination like Magaluf. Well, fuck training, to be honest.

This exemplified by the blank looks most of them had about them with one of those bin liners in their hand. Wullie literally putting it over him while somehow expecting his head and arms to magically go through the pre made holes that clearly weren't ever going to be there. Standing there in the dressing room with the bag over him until a wee panic attack arrived which saw him frantically clawing at the bag enough to get it off him.

A few pegs down, Rossi stood for a good five minutes trying to separate the bag enough to actually *open* it before eventually saying 'fuck this' and giving up, asking Montana to help him. A chunk of the team - who had got it together enough to be fully changed and ready - just sat with their heads in their hands, unable to face anything, never mind putting bin liners over them. A couple of players were stuck in the bathrooms being sick but you know what? Despite everyone going too far the night before - even the two players who didn't arrive in Magaluf until nearly midnight but who had wasted no time in throwing themselves into their trip - there was not a single player who hadn't arrived for training.

Whether they were capable of actually 'training' training? Well that was a completely different thing altogether.

Was a fucking barry night, though - even if the majority of us were paying for it the day after - and I had to admit that I was looking forward to many more of them before the end of the trip. No taking the pish, either. We were definitely in Espana to win this trophy but you'd have to be having yourself on if you thought that we weren't going to combine that with some absolutely monumental sessions in our down time.

And as we'd always said. A team that drinks together wins together. The next fortnight would be one that was destined to take that ethos to its very outer limits.

Eventually - and with a bit of assistance from Jock, Benji and Pat Doherty our physio whose entire capabilities of 'physio' extended to spraying Ralgex on some cunt if they took a knock during a game or shoving a sponge into a bucket of water - everyone of us were stood there with our head and arms sticking out a bin liner, tucked into our shorts.

'I'm fucking telling you, technology has moved on, Jock. There's this new thing that's been invented to rid your body of toxins. It's called *fluids*'

Strings, still not for dropping things although you couldn't blame him. We were fucking sweltering in that dressing room, which was shaded. What the fuck was it going to be like outside where there wasn't even a cloud in the sky? And then - on top - we'd be taking part in strenuous levels of exercise?

'Right, lads. Let's get out there'

Hunter, completely ignoring Strings as he clapped his hands a few times to rally the troops. Fucking hypocrite, like. Jock was pishing with sweat himself and just about the only muscle *he'd* moved inside that dressing room had been his tongue.

Never mind us in our bin bags, he's not built for standing out in that kind of heat and supervising us. I took the thought as I noticed how struggling he seemed to be with the temperature. At least some cunt get him a hat for standing out there. No sooner had that thought entered my head than Jock was fishing into his sports bag and producing a baseball cap from it. Fucking Jock Hunter, in a baseball cap?! Something no man had seen before. A guy that age, you never really see wearing baseball caps, do you? Apart from Presidents of the United States, and probably Tim Westwood.

This baseball cap was a fucking topper, though, and I was instantly intrigued over where its origins had began, and how someone like him had it in his possession. This big foam fronted trucker cap with the netting over the rest of the head. The design of the cap looking like a seagull had taken several dumps over it with the 'comical' logo on the front that said 'Damn Seagulls.' The type of poor patter that you can wear that could only have been manufactured during a more simpler - and worse patter filled - time. But hey, if it stopped the old cunt from dying out there from sunstroke then who really cared about how funny or unfunny the cap was.

Reluctantly we all made our way from the dressing room and out onto the pitch. On first look, the stadium wasn't much different from back home apart from the fact it had one basic stand - which was above the dressing rooms - but also, and not too dissimilar from pitches in Scotland - a metal pole stretching around the rest of the pitch for cunts to lean on slash get wide with players that stray near the perimeters of the pitch.

It was the same pitch that the matches in the tournament would be played at - with us back there the day after to play the

Portuguese mob - and as we emerged out onto it I clocked some workies who were in the process of putting up some of the banners in relation to that heinous Russian beer company that were putting on the tournament. Kind of gave me a wee feeling of what it must be like for those top level players, like. You know? How they - ahead of a European match - get the chance to train on the pitch that they're going to be playing an actual match on the day after. Probably cunts sticking up the Champions League banners at the same time as well, eh?

'OH, you pair. Forget the bloody ball, you'll not be needing one of those for a while'

Hunter barked over at Rossi and Montana who were casually booting a ball back and forward at each other.

Rossi - with a barely audible 'fuck's sake' - trapped the ball from Montana's pinpoint pass before then launching it off into the direction of the dug outs. Aye, the place had fucking dug outs which wasn't something you could always say about the average Scottish municipal fitba pitch. They were pretty primitive, like. Looked more like greenhouses than they did areas to hold substitutes and staff but still dug outs, which along with the stand at least gave the impression that this was something of importance that we were taking part in.

Not that I planned on spending even a minute sitting *in* the dug outs, mind.

'Right then, boys. You don't need me to tell you how big tomorrow is. We're not wanting to risk any unnecessary injuries so lets get some warm ups done, you know the drill? You switch when Benji tells you to'

It was about the first thing that Jock had said since we'd arrived for training that we'd all agreed with. Feeling - and moving - as gingerly as the lot of us were. Hearing the instructions to do as little as possible such as muscle stretches was a god send. Fuck was it hot, though. I looked around everyone when we were all stood on the spot - gyrating our hips like there were hula hoops spinning around us - and everyone's faces were so full of sweat and hair completely drenched it almost looked like they were all standing under invisible showers. It felt so intensely punishing and at the moment that there was absolutely no enthusiasm for any of the usual taking the pish that would generally run through our training sessions. That there was no patter - *at all* - flying about between the squad told its own story.

We were all in agony, in our own way. While the players were obviously in a world of pain, you had Benji who while not a player was someone who had been one of the last men standing earlier that morning and not fit for taking training. Hunter had fucked off over to one of the dug outs - which was shaded a wee bit - and sat there watching us from a distance.

After about fifteen minutes or something of doing our warm ups you heard the shout from over by the dug outs, instructing Benji to take us for a run around the pitch.

'Take the boys on a circuit run, Benji, son. Ten laps around the pitch, chop chop. I'll be bloody timing you as well, mind.' He sat waving his stop watch at the squad.

That was when the pain really began.

All those pints - and the varied shit that they were being filled with - and the several fast food trips over the night. I felt them all with every stride I took as we began running around the pitch. Jock Hunter might've well as binned the stopwatch because with someone like Benji - who was absolutely hanging - tasked with leading the pace for the rest of the squad it all equalled a couple of steps up from a brisk walk, but even that felt like it was going to snatch your life from you at any given moment. The painful expressions on everyone else showed they were feeling the exact same.

'First one to throw up buys the first round next time we're out'

Wullie said, trying to get a bit of life out of the rest of the lads but we were really all just trying to do our best to hang on and in absolutely no position to use up any of our much needed oxygen, which didn't exactly feel like in plentiful supply. And besides, anyone taking that bet would've been a brave fucking fellow indeed because it could've been any one of us that would've been giving it the old technicolour yawn at any point.

Even just getting to the stage of having done a full lap of the pitch felt like an eternity, and we still had another nine to go after that.

'This is fucking bullshit, like'

Terry - hair like he'd just got out of a swimming pool and his bin liner now completely stuck to his body with sweat said, managing to find the energy while he kept pace. With there being nothing like a shared grievance between people, that had been enough to inject a little bit conversation between some players as we ate into those ten laps.

'I'm feeling like I've maybe pulled my groin' Delaney whispered to me as we ran side by side. Wisely not broadcasting such a concern on the eve of our first match. The cunt only got his place in the team because of Bungalow going and being radge too many times in a matter of months so it would've been a tadge unlucky for the boy to miss out himself through injury.

'Aye, methinks you fucking pulled it last night. Don't think I never seen you slip off with that English lassie that had been all over half the team when we were in The Banana Bar, eh?'

I laughed back while genuinely remembering it for the first time in some sort of a flashback from the night before.

'Well, she was fucking ganting on *one* of us taking her back to her hotel so I thought I'd do my bit for team Muirhouse, eh?' He joked back while also continuing to wince with every step that he was taking.

Due to the abrupt way that our day had all started, which for most had been a case of wake up later than planned and then hooring it to the stadium for training, we'd not had a chance to all sit down and swap memories from our night out but nothing surer. When we did it would have been some night that we'd have pieced together.

The main headlines that I had been personally able to recount, being us drinking in more boozers and clubs than I could actually remember. Thoughts of Coffee breaking that daft cunt's nose in Kentucky Fried Chicken and Terry - who along with The Monk caught up with us once they arrived from their later flight - putting some poor PR cunt on their arse with a right hook because they'd chosen not to take no for an answer as we passed the pub that they were tasked with getting bodies inside. A few of the team fucking off after getting lucky while half of the other team tried like bears all night, without any success. Like all monumental drinking sessions, though. The more you drink the less likely you are to remember anything about it the next day so it was going to take the whole squad putting their heads together for us to recollect all that had truly gone on. Knowing some of the boys in the squad, though. I would've staked my life on there being some examples of behaviour from them over the night that they'd be hoping *no one* had noticed or would remember, by the next day.

'Here, Benj. How many laps has that been now?' Strings shouted from back in the middle of the group.

'Five' The short but sweet reply from the clearly struggling assistant manager. He should've tried it with a fucking Scotmid bin liner over him, eh? See how much of a struggle *that* was. Five laps in and these black bags - over top of nothing but skin - were now fuck all other than a smelly, sticky sweat death trap. Mines was so drenched, the material of the bag was almost fixed to me like it was a *part* of my skin.

'Fucking bollocks it's five laps. It has to be easily seven?'

Strings replied to this. I wasn't sure if - through the potential heat stroke starting to come into play - he genuinely thought this to be the case or was simply at it, trying to finesse his mate and assistant manager.

'I thought it was six?' Daz chipped in. As for me? I didn't even *know* what number we were on. I'd just jogged around the pitch like some drone just hoping, praying and waiting on some cunt telling me to stop again.

We were literally like some group of brain dead hamsters running around their wheel, with no concept of how many times they've done it. Nothing in our heads than to go around and around until stopped.

I think it was lap eight where we suffered our first vomit incident, comically from Wullie.

'Still wanting that bet, aye?' Montana laughed as Wullie stood there bent over, bringing up nothing but liquids. Our resident

Dundonian managing to combine looking at the ground as bile came out of his mouth while raising an arm to give Montana the Vs.

'Had to happen at some point, just glad it wasn't me as I'd have stuck myself in at favourite a couple of laps ago.' Delaney said to me as we concentrated on keeping up our speed, the genuine feeling that the end was now in sight.

'I'll not be convinced that I won't be sick until I'm showered, changed and away to fuck from this place'

I replied, honest as could be. Because - without getting into the thoughts of the others - this felt like hell. Worst training session I'd ever had to take part in, not even any fucking questioning of this, either. We - the Violet squad - were no strangers to *playing* while having had a drink the night before but this was different levels, like. We'd never had to play in such searing heat *or* had been drinking lunatic drinks like pints of spirits at happy hour.

Upon completing the ten laps we were awarded with a much deserved rest break which - for me anyway - pretty much consisted of lying flat out on the ground, spread out like an angel, wondering if I was ever going to get my breath back.

It had barely recovered when I was hearing Hunter - who had camped out in this dug out and wasn't coming out for no cunt - shouting for Benji and Pat to get the cones out.

'Awwww no, please no' I immediately thought to myself. Not the fucking cones. No cunt likes the cones. The brief hope that I'd held that - as goalkeeper - I was going to be taken off to do something else was just that, brief.

By this point, it was now evident that Jock had intended for this session to mirror what we'd have handed to us during pre season. Which - while never not tortuous - was all well and good, but *that* normally didn't take place in over thirty degree heat, while wearing bin liners.

Before we all left the pitch. We'd been put through exercises with the cones, running through some drills, played a mini match between us of twenty minutes each half before then sitting while Jock went over some loose tactics for the next day. Tactics being a hard thing to come up with when playing a team that you have never seen play before in your life, and couldn't name a single player who played for them.

Then again, the Portuguese side were in the exact same boat as us. We had no idea what they were going to have in store for us the next day when we played our group opening match but I'd have been fucking astonished if they'd ever came up against a collective like Muirhouse Violet in their puff.

Whether it had been part of his motivation or not but by the time we were heading back off the pitch for a much needed shower, the thought of a repeat performance from the night before couldn't have been further from the squad's thoughts.

We'd put in some session the night before in the cool air conditioned bars and clubs, but then again, so had we hours later out in the baking sun. And now it was showing. We could barely fucking walk. Some had been sick while various others were complaining of headaches.

Knowing how important that it was for us not to lose our first game, mixed with how emotionally and physically broken we all were over a drinking sesh followed by a much more energy sapping training one. There really was only one option - of a quiet relaxing night - open to us.

As we'd tend to do with Hunter from time to time.

When - back in the dressing room once everyone was all changed - he'd told us that we'd be scheduled to be spending the rest of the day by the pool. A meal at night and then a little piece of team bonding that he'd organised with the hotel, he didn't have anyone arguing against this plan.

First of all, no one had the energy for arguing about anything and secondly, we wanted to make sure we were in peak condition for taking to the pitch against the Portuguese mob.

I wasn't too sure about the team bonding part that was mentioned, though. Knowing that every single time he tried to organise something to pull the team together, it generally led to some of the squad literally trying to pull each other apart.

Once again, though.

I just didn't have the energy to say or worry about it.

Chapter 6

Strings

For a while, at least, it felt like we were a proper squad of football players. Professional stuff, like. All sitting down there as a team at one long table. Eating pasta dishes, big two litre bottles of Font Vella water sitting on the table for the players to share. The chat amongst everyone, mainly dominated by the match the next day and our individual speculation on how Muirhouse Violet's debut in European competition was going to go. For a while, it felt like we were an international squad sitting having its evening meal, night before their World Cup match.

For a while it did, at least.

Obviously, though. Muirhouse is going to Muirhouse and within hours of this cordial meal, where team unity could not have appeared more prominent, we'd descended to the point where some players had taken up arms with bows and arrows and were firing them at each other, with very real intentions of taking cunts' eyes out.

In all fairness to Hunter, he'd meant well. Had kept alcohol off the menu and had avoided going down the predictable route of team fun such as a quiz night - already knowing that it would only lead to arguments - and, instead, had organised with the hotel for them to set up the bows, arrows and targets that he'd spied the kids club using the day that we'd checked into the hotel. Fuck knows how, to be honest, but somehow he had overlooked the fact that putting actual weapons in the hands of the squad - and expecting them to act as adults - was something that was never going to turn out a reality.

Prior to some some of the team going off script and right into cowboys and Indians - well, just Indians, really - the meal had been barry. I had that Spaghetti Carbonara and some beautiful toasted Focaccia bread. Fuck, if you'd shoved a glass of red wine in front of me you'd have thought I was a Serie A player sitting having his pre match meal.

We'd not really needed the prompting - considering how fucked training had left us - but Hunter had insisted that we all have as much carbs as possible ahead of the opening match. Obviously, it was at complete odds with the reality but to look at us, all sitting there eating pasta with bread and pouring out glasses of water and that, it must've made us look like a picture of health. Definitely a case of not everything you see being *what* you see.

Talk soon turned to our opponents. I can't lie, I was buzzing like someone three quarters into their gram of Mandy when it came to the prospect of coming up against a foreign team. For the first time, getting the chance to face off against someone who were culturally different from the standard teams we'd go toe to toe with each and every season.

Ramalde Lutadores, their name which we'd been told translated to Ramalde - a district on the outskirts of Porto - Fighters.

You can imagine some of the comments made by the squad when they heard the translation of their name?

With no YouTube clips or any kind of intelligence on them found on the internet at all - where as, unfortunately, they would find many references to Muirhouse Violet if they'd bothered to have a look, most of them not actually football related though, mind - it really was nothing other than guesswork and speculation when it came to the team who would go up against us the next afternoon.

'I think, technically, they're going to be good'

The Monk said as he poured himself another glass of water.

'Aye ok, mate. Steady on, eh? It's not Benfica we're playing here, for fuck's sake.' Sepp laughed at The Monk coming over all football pundit, taking the fact that they were Portuguese as some form of confirmation that they would be technically good with a football at their feet.

'Naw, you know what I'm saying though, eh? That whole Brazil and Portugal link and how generally players from those countries are good, in a technical sense.' The Monk maintained, even though it was a pretty sweeping generalisation that just because we were playing a team from Portugal they'd be caressing the ball with their feet. I was pretty sure that some of the teams from Portugal had the capabilities of being every bit as shite with a football than a Scottish team.

'They're also pretty good at shithousing their way through matches as well so I'm not sure your point stands up, Monkey Man. Not remember Mourinho's Porto in that UEFA cup final? Never seen the fucking likes of that' Mr Benn entered the chat and someone - still sore from Celtic's loss in the final that season - who clearly *hadn't* forgotten Jose Mourinho's side, and how they'd gone about winning that final.

'Oh gies peace, mate. That final was almost ten fucking years ago, and you're *still* going on about it. Let it go, pal'

Wullie jumped in which - considering an old firm fan was a rarity in our squad - had most of the table backing him up, while taking the chance to have their own wee dig at Mr Benn. As always, he took it like a champ. When you're a fashion victim like he is - and some of the expensive stuff you'd see him in - who plays with a bunch like us at the Violet, you *need* to be able to take the patter that you're going to be subjected to otherwise you're as well not even bother turning up.

'Look, who the hell knows what they're going to be like. Maybe they'll be nothing other than a mob of drunken rockets, just like you'

Jock said this, extra louder so that he had made sure that everyone's attention had been sought, and that he got the laugh he was looking for before continuing on.

'But I'll tell you this, it doesn't bloody well matter what this Portuguese mob are like. We don't need to sit here and think about what or who they are. It's bloody *them* that should be sitting there thinking about the Muirhouse Violet. They're not going to beat you tomorrow. The only way that you lot walk off the pitch having lost is if you've beaten yourself'

'Aye, that or the sun and heat will have completely destroyed us by the time we've reached the twenty minute mark'

I couldn't resist it, even if there *was* factual basis to it. Whilst it was speculation to say that - because we were playing a Portuguese team - we'd be up against a team who were going to pass us to death before sticking each goal scored into the top shelf it *wasn't* speculation to say that the opposition were going to be more, much more, acclimatised with playing in such conditions. Cunts go to Portugal for their holidays, if anything more needs saying on the subject. They also do not go to

Muirhouse or Pilton for their holidays, to hammer home the point.

'I'm not having any excuses about the weather. The professionals play in it and don't moan about it and neither will you. Weather? Tell me the last bit of weather that scored a bloody goal, Strings?'

He waved me away at the mere suggestion of the heat playing a factor in the match.

'Professionals play in it and don't moan about it'

Looking over the table at Daz - someone of a ginger persuasion - my mind jumped straight to the image of Steve Staunton in the ninety four World Cup, standing for the Irish national anthem wearing a fucking baseball cap because the heat was too much for him.

While we finished the rest of our meals, Jock took us through some tactics for the next day and what the whole general game plan was. Normally this would be done with one eye on who the other team were and what to expect from them but with this not being possible, the tactics were based purely on what *we* were going to do, with the understanding that once the match kicked off and we were able to see who we were up against we would possibly then need to adapt our shape and tactics.

I know that he was a pain in the fucking erse at times but - seeing him stood up addressing the squad - it wasn't hard to notice the look of enormous pride he had on his coupon, on the eve of this match. For Jock Hunter, at times it felt like Muirhouse Violet was his life. So fuck knows what he was feeling, leading the team into a European competition. There was never a game I went into that I desperately didn't want to win but, I don't know? Seeing Jock's face, it left me with an even stronger desire to win the game, knowing what it would mean to him. At the same time, you also kind of feared for Magaluf - and its establishments - if we were to win that first match and then went out to celebrate things, which we would do, *if* we won.

'Okay dokey, boys. Time for a wee bit of team bonding recreation time before we call it a night. Mon this way'

Jock Hunter pushed his chair back in under the table and gathered everyone, taking us to an area out by the back of the swimming pool that was lit up.

'Is that fucking archery stuff?' Montana - looking a completely different man from the shell of himself he'd looked like the afternoon before - asked as we got closer to it. Any attempts at asking Hunter or Benji for what 'activities' it was that had been planned for us as part of the whole "operation keep us from the Maga strip" of the night and for some additional information was knocked back as if it was some fucking state secret or something.

'It fucking *is* archery stuff.' He said enthusiastically before I could even reply to him.

'Fucking barry, I'm brilliant at this, was literally in an archery club for a couple of years when I was a kid'

One hundred percent, the most alive and enthusiastic I'd seen Montana without any Class A drugs inside of him.

There were also other positive acknowledgments from some of the squad when it was there in front of them, their recreational team bonding activity for the evening. Normally you've always got those certain cunts that are going to moan for moaning's sake but, really, how the fuck can you moan about getting a shot of a bow and firing arrows into one of those big furry dart boards, eh?

'Well played, Jock. Brilliant idea, pal.' I said quietly to him while patting him on the shoulder as we all inspected the gear that had been laid out. Apparently, when the archery apparatus is used - during normal business hours - there's someone from the hotel who shows you how to fire the arrows and that but, instead, they just left us to get on with it.

Through this - and after a few classic examples of cunts making out they know how to do something when they clearly fucking don't - Montana ended up becoming a makeshift teacher for the first ten minutes. Showing everyone exactly how to hold the bow and where to place your fingers over the arrow before releasing it.

Even all of that slotted into just how the night had been with the feeling of unity amongst the squad, which I think was in part down to none of us dying during training which had left us all with a feeling of being survivors of a kind of sort. Aye, you had a couple of know it alls make a fool of themselves at first with the 'firing' of arrows and they were suitably taken the pish out of, but it was all still in good nature.

It's mad how things can change though, and so quickly.

There had been four targets laid out at the other end and we teamed up into four teams. The ad hoc idea being that whichever out of the four teams who had scored the most points being the winner. Not exactly the stuff of rocket science.

It was quite decent, like. I'd never fired an arrow before in my life, well a *real* one. Obviously I'd fired those plastic ones with the rubber stopper for a tip that you got when you were in primary one at school but nothing as industrial or professional looking as this set up.

If you wanted to be on the winning team then, clearly, Montana was the one man that was crucial to being on your side. I honestly wasn't ersed about winning the competition or not. I hadn't come to Magaluf to win an archery contest. I'd come to get in a hell of a mess for at least half to three quarters of the time, to rattle the cages of a few foreign fitba teams and to come back home with the Red Bear trophy for our cabinet. I ended up on his team all the same, pretty much guaranteeing that I'd be on the winning side, because this cunt was a wizard with the bow in his hands. And you think you know someone as well?

It was later on in the night's competition - by this point it was evident which team out the four had a lead now big enough to be officially out of sight - when cunts started fucking about. Well, *Terry* started fucking about, to be exact. It's not exactly out of the question for someone to do so when engaging in a sporting event where - by that point - they already know they're going to lose. When *weapons* are involved though, maybe, and just my opinion here like, a wee bit of discipline should be more adhered to.

It was during the second last round - by which point the actual *last* round was academic and may as well as been sacked off - and our team had already seen me and Sepp take our shots. We'd not exactly been earth shattering with all of our efforts over the match but hey, at least we'd hit the board on a regular occasion, many others didn't.

The other three teams took their shots which eventually brought things back to us, and Montana. The moment he bent down to pick up the bow from off the astroturf, I saw what was about to happen but yet it all panned out so quickly that I wasn't able to prevent it.

With it being Montana's go, I was standing to the side, relaxed, just about to watch him - no doubt - hit another ten, like he'd done almost repeatedly all night. With him bending over to pick up the bow, I looked to the side - towards the other teams - and saw that Terry was stood there holding his bow - arrow pulled back - with his sights firmly towards us.

At that exact moment, I didn't know that he was specifically targeting Montana, and his erse. If you're standing in the same vicinity of that target then for all you know *you* could be who the cunt is aiming at. Acting on instinct in the moment, I covered my ayes with an arm. By doing so, missing the arrow flying straight into Montana's right erse cheek and the sound of cheers coming from the other three teams.

Having the bow and arrow already in his hand as the arrow slammed into him he acted without thought or reason, but yet I couldn't really blame the boy.

'WHICH CUNT WANTS TO LOSE A FUCKING EYE THEN?'

I'd removed my arm from my eyes in time to see him shoot back up and with scary dexterity slotting the arrow into the bow with it pulled back and pointing it towards all three teams to the side of us.

As you'd imagine, they all reacted - hands in the air - in the way that someone does when a weapon that can be fired at them is pulled out and pointed in their direction.

'Oh, come on, Montana, mate. It was just a wee joke, eh?'

Terry said, deciding to at least out himself as 'the shooter' trying to play down what he'd just done and - I was imagining - without any knowledge just how sore the arrow firing into Montana's Richard Gere must've been. It was all in Montana's reaction to it. I don't think I'd seen him as bammed up in my life as I had in that moment.

'So it was fucking you, aye?'

Montana shouted at him in what I assumed was now going to provide a brief exchange between the both of them. Montana had other ideas, however. Terry was in the process of responding when he found the arrow released and - due to the speed of it - before he'd even realised it found that it had passed between his and The Monk's heads. An inch or two to either side and an eye was definitely being lost.

None of us had expected it. I'd thought that if Montana was going to fire the arrow then it was going to be in the immediate time window of him instantly reacting to the pain of the arrow in his erse. This vital few seconds had passed though so it took me, as well as everyone else by surprise when we saw him release the arrow.

Once Terry - and The Monk - had taken the second to appreciate what had just happened, as well as what *could've* just happened, they both went for Montana. And it wasn't like he was for running in the opposite direction at this, either.

'YA STUPID WEE BASTARD. COULD'VE TAKEN MA FUCKING EYE OUT, YA CUNT'

Terry, screamed at him while a good three or four bodies quickly got between him and Montana.

'I WAS FUCKING *TRYING* TO, PRICK. THINK AN ARROW IN THE ERSE IS A FUCKING LAUGH, AYE?'

There was way too much testosterone flying about and - despite it only involving three people - it was just as well that we had around twenty to put a stop to it.

Things eventually brought to a head by the voice of reason, our gaffer. Telling Terry and Montana that they were both in the wrong with Montana apologising to The Monk while - laughably - saying to him

'I never meant for the arrow to go anywhere near you, pal. It was meant to go straight into that cunt's eye next to you, eh'

With apology accepted by The Monk, that still left relations between Terry and Montana at rock bottom. So as to avoid any further friction I suggested to Montana that he'd maybe be better calling it a night as we were about done anyway. Told the boy that tomorrow was a new day and that it wasn't going to be about him and Terry. It was going to be about the fucking *team* and what we were going to do to those Portugeezers. He saw the sense in this and - with the exception of Terry - said a good night to the rest of the squad.

'You'll need to watch those two as far as tomorrow goes, Jock'

I whispered to Hunter, once things had started to become a bit more calmer.

Whispering back, he told me something along the lines of how many times had one of the team wanted to kill the other and that if he'd had to worry about things like that then the Violet would've put him into an early grave. Completely unfazed by the fact that two of his players - on the eve of such a massive match - had been taking shots at each other with fucking bows and arrows?!

I don't know if it was what I'd said to him which brought the inspiration or not but he broke away from me to get the squad together for one last wee speech of the night.

'Now, what's went on tonight wasn't big and it wasn't bloody clever. If we're here to do damage to anyone, let's make sure it's to the other bloody team, boys. But you know what? I've seen more animation from you lot in the last hour than I've seen all day, training included. *That's* the passion I'm looking for from you. I want you to bring the fucking fury, just reserve it for whoever we come up against on the pitch. Before we all go up to our rooms for the night, though. Know one thing. If we take that fire and energy into tomorrow afternoon's match we'll fucking *walk it* against these Portuguese lot. Right, it's been a long day and I don't need to tell any of you just how big a day tomorrow is so get your erses up to your rooms and your heads down for the night, ok?'

Whether having two of your starting eleven trying to kill each other on the night before the opening group match would turn out to be a positive that could be used to our advantage, well, we'd see the next day.

The day that Muirhouse Violet would introduce themselves to the international stage for the first time.

Strings

Chapter 7

All the speculation the day before about the Portuguese, and what they'd be like to play against? In the end it turned out to be pretty much an amalgamation of every single player's own perception of what they'd imagined. But what I'll always remember them for would be their shithousing. So, so much shithousing.

What is it that they say? Game recognises game.

Considering what took part across the ninety minutes, that Portuguese mob would've had to have been the most grudging of cunts you could ever wish to meet if they hadn't left the pitch thinking the exact same thing about us.

Because if you want to play shithouses with Muirhouse Violet then you're going up against the people who wrote the fucking *book* of shithouse.

They really were a bunch of elite level pricks, though. We'd been able to tell that by the time we'd strolled onto the pitch for our warm up to find them already in their half. Some of them looking over and sneering at the sight of us emerging from the tunnel. Literally both teams' first chance to take a look at each other.

Before I even really appreciated the opponents on the other half of the pitch, I was more struck with how much of a crowd there was dotted around the pitch and already sat in the stand. Turning around to look into the stand I saw a couple of boys from Bonnyrigg, that I'd got talking to in one of the boozers on our first night out. Gave them both a wee thumbs up of thanks which they looked like they appreciated while one of them (Marcus, I think, but I wouldn't have been able to confidently say with a gun to my head) shouted down to me.

'Into these fucking posers, pal'

I'd told them about the game against the Portuguese and that they should come up and give the boys a bit of support from their fellow countrymen. It's one thing to engage in pub talk and make commitments to things - that in the cold light of day - you're never going to follow through with but aye, they were as good as their word. Ten out of ten for the one out the two who had brought his saltire beach towel to give off the impression that there was some cunt in the crowd with a Scotland flag. All in the optics of how things can look at times, eh?

Apart from the random Scots who had learned about the game and - I imagine - had fuck all else to do. The rest of the crowd looked like a collection of locals, those from Red Beer running the tournament and what looked like players and staff of teams who were also there in Magaluf to play in the tournament themselves.

With this not exactly being a big bucks style tournament, it wasn't like there were a series of stadiums that all of the games were being played across. Through this, *all* games were scheduled to be played at the same municipal stadium. And with the tournament now under way, I guessed that we would now all be bumping into players and staff from some of the other teams taking part as we came and went, to and from the stadium.

It was only when I heard Terry say to those nearest to him 'Check these fucking spice boys out' that I actually turned around and clocked the team known as Ramalde Lutadores. Looking over to them and without absolutely no sense of priorities, my initial thought was that they looked like the type of cunts that you wouldn't leave your other half around. Slim, tanned and slick dark hair. Just about the fucking polar opposite of the 'athletes' that they were about to play. Some were standing doing exercises while others were booting a ball fifty to sixty yards back and forward to each other, with running barely required by any of them, when it came to meeting the ball.

They definitely looked the part - fresh and recent Adidas kit template, latest technology when it came to fitba boots and that - and seeing them looking back at us, they weren't too far off what I'd imagined. If they were going by widely used Scottish stereotypes then quite possibly we were looking exactly what *they'd* have imagined.

'Take it they must've been using bin liners for more than one day, eh?' Coffee said, sarcastically, as he looked down at the mini beer belly that was showing through his training shirt.

Culturally we were different but if that wasn't already apparent, you just needed to *look* at them, and then us.

They were of a healthy tan where we - taking Montana out of the equation - were a collection of milk bottle white or lobster red, and nothing in between. They didn't look like they had an ounce of fat on them while we looked every inch a side where - for at least some - their daily diets considered of lager, crisps and curry. Their slick oily hair - without a single strand out of place - while we were either balding, ginger or looked like some cunt with a balaclava back to front had cunt their hair. They were already out exercising and spraying balls about and there didn't appear to be a single bead of sweat on them while we were gasping for air through the heat, simply by moving from the cooler dressing room and out onto the unforgiving, as well as unshaded, pitch.

'Don't you bloody worry about them on that other side of the pitch. Tortoise and the hare, lads. Fucking tortoise and hair. Not think I can't see the way some of them are looking across here?'

Jock said - getting everyone around him - while Benji and Pat made some arrangements on our half of the pitch before we started our warm up.

'They look like they think they've already won the game'

I'd detected the same vibe from some of them as Jock was now standing telling the team. In a way, I couldn't blame them because while I didn't have the first clue on the standard of Portuguese amateur fitba, or what its average player looked like, they didn't look like any fucking fitba team I'd ever had to come up against at our level. I was used to going up against cunts that were as radge and - for half the team - unhealthy as my own team. And in that sense, we must've looked like a right motley crew to this Ramalde Lutadores mob.

Aye, and just wait until the whistle goes and you find what it's like to play against them, I thought to myself as I took one last look across into the other half at them before getting my head down and concentrating on my own stuff. Violet stuff.

'Mind, just a light warm up session. Save the energy reserves for the ninety minutes, you're going to fucking need it, lads'

Benji joked as he launched into taking us through a series of exercise drills while Sepp went off with Pat to do some keeper training. The lot of us meeting up again later for - my favourite part of the pre match warm up - five minutes of Benji knocking the ball into our paths where we would proceed to fire shots in at Sepp.

One of my attempts - where I'd caught the ball by its sweet spot - crashing against Sepp's left post, flying across his goalmouth and hitting the right hand post before flying into the net. The kind of goal that you never fucking score in a match but somehow pull out the bag when you're just fucking about in training.

With ten minutes to kick off, Jock signalled for us all to head back into the dressing room for to get changed for the match, and for one final team talk before we crossed that white line for real.

As we were trooping back towards the dressing room, this just so happened to be as some of the Portuguese players were jogging back to theirs. Going down the tunnel I found myself almost side by side with one of their players and - still carried away with the occasion and not treating it all in the way I would normally on a Sunday - I thought I'd exchange a couple of friendly words with him. Only it never quite hit the heights of friendliness.

Quite a big chap, he was, but pretty much similar to the rest of his team mates. He had already peeled off his training shirt to expose a six pack that you could've broken toffee on.

'Hopefully be a good game with you, eh?'

I said to him, just basic small talk, like. Even if it was something I wouldn't fucking dream about saying to an opponent back in Scotland.

I'd assumed that he would know a wee bit of English. This confirmed by his reaction to what I'd just said to him. He looked me up and down like some piece of shit, enough to have someone back in Muirhouse fucking skelped without them even opening their mouths.

'We fucking kill you out there'

His less than friendly response in broken English but none the less heard and understood loud and clear. To emphasise things, he followed this by drawing his finger across his throat.

'Aye, ok, Jose' I laughed, just enough to let him know that he was fucking working his ticket if he thought coming the cunt like that was ever going to have the impact he'd have hoped for.

Not from the team that he was about to play, anyway.

'Here, pal?'

The Monk - having heard this brief exchange - moved closer, putting a passive aggressive hand on the boy's shoulder. Smiling at the Portuguese lad but with none of that sparkle or shine that you'd normally see from someone's eyes.

'I just wanted you to know, in advance, that when you get carried off with a broken leg, out there on the pitch, it'll have been *me* who gave it to you'

'Wouldn't have been the first limb you'd have broken, mate' I said, laughing and backing him up.

'Yap yap yap, just you keep barking, little doggie' the Ramalde player replied, not taking any of the bait that The Monk was putting out there.

'You British wankers, all you do is talk. If you Scottish concentrated more on football maybe you'd play in a World Cup or a Euros once in a while, huh?'

He had us there, to be honest. France in ninety eight - by twenty thirteen - was now seeming like a life time ago.

'Is it just the Portuguese men who aren't talkers then? Because I couldn't shut your mum up the other night. The things that comes out her mouth at times as well, you'd never be able to look at her in the face again for the rest of your life if you only knew, pal Still a fucking barry ride, though, ken?

No doubt, the combination of the boy hearing this in a second language as well as with a North Edinburgh accent would've made it a challenge for him to understand what had just been rattled off to him, but he heard enough.

'You fucking bastard. If you had any balls I would rip them off you and shove them up your ass' He said as he made a lunge for The Monk. Cue handbags outside both dressing rooms with players and staff from both teams first of all making sure there would be no physical altercations between The Monk and the other boy but through this, inevitably, it then led to a whole series of *new* flare ups between players from both sides.

Eventually, we found all of us shoehorned back into the dressing room with - what I assumed - Portuguese insults being hurled from outside the dressing room along with a couple of kicks to our door from some incensed Ramalde players.

As we got ourselves into our Muirhouse shirts and made our last minute preparations. Jock stood there in the middle of the room with the same smile he'd had on him the night before, after seeing his players firing arrows at each other, with intent.

'Well, that's half my team talk done for me without even opening my bloody mouth. See the arrogance of that mob? Now just think how satisfying it's going to be when they're walking off the pitch having been cuffed by you lot? If you can't win the match for yourself and the benefits a win would bring you, win it just so that those bastards don't!'

'Fucking right, Jock. You'll be carrying me off the pitch in a body bag before those Portuguese hoors have the three points'

A fired up Terry agreed.

'Trust me, boys. These cunts will never have experienced a force of nature like Muirhouse Violet in their fucking life. They're going to shit themselves out there once we get into it, and by then it'll be too late for them' Myself, now a lot more fired up than I'd been as I'd made my way towards the tunnel - following my warm up - kept the sentiment going.

The much more diplomatic knock on the door - as opposed to hard kicks - came from the referee.

Go time. Fucking *show* time.

'Now mind what I went over with you. Keep things extra tight for the first fifteen twenty minutes. I'm not even giving a fuck if their keeper is sitting on a settee smoking a cigar for that first part of the game. Just don't be running yourself out of gas before the game has even got started. We have to assume that this other mob are more used to conditions like today, so we'll need to be cute about how we go about things. Possession's going to be key. When we have the ball, we bloody well *keep* it. Tire the bastards out. Have them chase us. Side and back passes are perfectly acceptable. And when we *don't* have the ball we bloody well get bodies behind it and I can't stress enough about how important it is that we keep things tight at the back. This isn't a scenario where we want to go a goal down and be left chasing the game'

We all stood there in silence listening to him. It was a departure from what our normal tactics would be in a run of the mill game. But this was not a usual game, and it definitely wasn't the fucking match day climate that we were accustomed to. For what it was worth, it was the smart play from Jock. It was down to the players to have the discipline to be able to adapt and play the opening stages in the more subdued manner that the gaffer was asking for. I mean, Jock Hunter asking his team to spray the ball about with passes for passes sake - just so as to keep possession - was the kind of thing that would make someone go 'ok, what's happened to the real Jock Hunter then?'

'Now get out there, do Muirhouse, Scotland and, most importantly, *yourselves* proud'

And with that, the butterflies that I'd had that morning and all the way up to that moment flew away. Replaced by some kind of a fire. I couldn't get myself out of the dressing room fast enough, as was the case with the rest of the team. The noise that we were making, enough to let anyone know that we were on our way.

We were met by the Ramalde players already lined up down the tunnel. With the bad feeling that had already been created between us there wasn't much in the way of friendly faces greeting us as we lined up alongside them.

This beer company going all out with the little touches to try and create the image that this tournament being held was as professional as could be, without actually *being* professional. As part of this. Instead of just strolling out, scratching our arses, casually chatting with each other and - for some - sneaking in one last cigarette until they got to half time. We had the referee and linesmen standing at the entrance to the tunnel while instructing both teams to line up and wait for their cue to enter the pitch.

As we stood there beside each other - barely a metre apart - you could've cut the tension with a knife. You could tell that we were both wanting to look at each other and maybe throw a wee wideo comment the other way, but this was a time where you had to keep your focus on the job ahead. Don't get involved in any pre match distractions.

There's always one, though. On this occasion, Rossi.

'In your Ramalde home, in your Ramalde home.' He sung, and, already knowing what the rest of the lyrics were going to be I didn't know whether to cringe and put my hands over my face, piss myself laughing or join in with the song. With his song seeming to catch on with the rest of the players, I chose the latter option.

'You rake in the buckets for something to eat. You find a dead rat and you think it's a treat. In your Ramalde home'

Obviously, it was a song sung through fuck all other than pure ignorance as I'd have bet my *life* on Rossi having never heard of the area of Ramalde in his life until the night before when we were told the name of the teams we were playing in the group stage.

Ignorance or not, it clearly was understood by the Portuguese players as - without actually laying hands on any of us - they reacted quite negatively to being serenaded by their opposition.

With the combination of Jock, Benji and Pat doing their best to separate us from the Ramalde players. Ironically the Portuguese non playing staff doing the same job of peacemakers. 'Ironically' because once the game would get underway, relations between both dug outs would go on to take a serious dip.

The ref soon telling both captains - stood at the front, leading their teams - that it was time to take to the pitch.

Give the lads their dues as well, they stuck to Hunter's game plan. We showed absolutely *zero* interest in taking the game forward to them. When we had the ball we tried our best to keep possession but that was the thing - as a team, we were hardly known as the reincarnation of Rinus Michels' *total football* - we weren't used to playing that way. We really were more about getting the ball and then it be a case of chhhhaaaarrrrgge. As a result, after winning the ball back and passing it a few times, we'd inevitably lose it again. Even then we were doing all the right things. Covering for each other while keeping things compact and making it difficult for them to get past us.

If the first couple of minutes had maybe seen both teams sharing possession at fifty percent each. By the time we moved into the tenth minute or so, the possession stats would've been telling a different story. Probably more seventy percent, in Ramalde's favour. This, bringing about some arrogance from some of their players. They had this tricky right winger out wide who from the off had been trying to pull off wee tricks and flicks. Stuff that was getting cheers from the crowd which - I guess - only encouraged him further. There was no denying though that if he was to try some of that showboating shite on a Sunday morning he'd be spending his afternoon in the Western General, instead of back at the pub with the rest of his team mates.

It really was only a matter of time before one of us put him up into the air. Almost aptly, it was Daz who took that particular pleasure. Daz being the one out of all of us who had been made the cunt out of the most up to that point. Their number eight gathering the ball and running towards our left back for the umpteenth time. Doing a neat wee feint to go one way before nicking the ball - with the outside of his boot - to the side of Daz who either misjudged his challenge or had simply had enough of the boy by this point.

I don't know, though? There was just something about the way that Daz took both his legs and - then - in a scissor type motion clamped right onto the boys leg which hinted that it may well have been more on the intentional side.

Daz just stood there, apologetically with his hands raised, not putting up any protest as the ref ran over and brandished the yellow card to our full back. Daz couldn't argue, no cunt could. The challenge was more orange card than yellow. Meanwhile this number eight has rolled something like ten times in a row. So far he's almost ended up in Santa Ponsa. Some of his team mates ran over to check on him while some others had ran across and thought about giving Daz grief but the sight of the yellow card coming out seemed to placate them.

'He was fucking asking for it, Strings'

Daz says to me with an apologetic look on his face as we waited on them taking their free kick. Acknowledging that he'd fucked up in getting a yellow card so early in the game (fifteen minutes in?) and now knowing that he was in for a long game, especially with this trickster who was tormenting him and - if he was smart - would double down on that and try to provoke another yellow for Daz. Also, he'd already shown that he wasn't against taking a wee dive here and there - and was *good* at it - which made him all the more dangerous to be up against, while you're on a booking.

The more the game went on, though, the more you saw that he wasn't the only one who was partial to a bit of simulation out of their team. An incident midway through the first half where one of their midfielders performed a worse dive than fucking Greg Louganis. Trying to con the referee into booking Coffee for a phantom challenge and then when no card was produced half a dozen players crowding around the referee.

At least Louganis picked up a bit of a knock, eh?

This incident brought a bit of light comedy to the match as it ignited some animation from both benches. While the Portuguese player was being treated for an injury that he didn't have - The Monk and Wullie hanging over him giving him grief about his shameful cheating - I was treated to the sight of Jock Hunter and the Ramalde manager - some boy who looked half the age of Jock standing in a crisp white polo shirt with the club badge on it and who had been holding a note book all half, taking notes occasionally - going head to head, literally. The Portuguese manager throwing his book down onto the ground while him and Jock exchanged alternative views on things. Heads pressed against each other while literally doing as much as they could without throwing a kick or punch at each other.

Benji filled me in later on what had been said but it was along the lines of Hunter having seen one dive too many before eventually erupting. Marching over to the edge of his technical area - still feels mad saying things like that in connection with a Violet match, like - and began shouting at the Ramalde staff about what cheating bastards they were and telling their gaffer to sort his team out. Their manager not taking kindly to such accusations of being cheats - even though he'd probably taken part in training them *in* the art - and saying 'to fuck with technical areas' by coming over and entering the Muirhouse one. Apparently he'd told Jock that we were fuck all than a team of water carriers and hammer throwers. From there, they traded insults until both being pulled away. Already having enough on his plate *on* the pitch, the ref swerved the whole thing and left them to it. A more jobsworth of an official would've had them both sent to the stand.

With the extreme heat, even in the technical area, that wee outburst must've worn Jock out because you never heard him again for the rest of the half, and you *always* heard Jock Hunter throughout a match. The old cunt kind of reminded me of that keeper Aberdeen used to have - Theo Snelders - who, regardless of how many thousands were in a stadium, you were always able to hear shouting to his defence.

I don't think any one of us appreciated it at the time but Daz getting his booking - and igniting a bit of on pitch needle between the players - changed the half. Instead of keeping the ball and trying to do something with it, Ramalde were too busy getting involved in personal battles on the pitch with our players, which we absolutely lapped right up. Now we were playing at a level where we were at our most comfortable. Some of their players who had strutted about the pitch like they were Figo or Rui Costa for the first twenty minutes were now looking all kinds of rattled through some of the - mostly off the ball - treatment that they were being given. Not that their players were shy about dishing out their own certain brand of the dark arts either, mind.

The sound of the half time whistle - when it went - was one of the most beautiful and sweetest things I have ever heard in my life. Over those forty five minutes it had felt like we'd had to fight two battles. One against Ramalde, the other against the heat. Walking off the pitch it was - by then - clear which of the two teams were comfortable in playing in temperatures such as - on the day - thirty two degrees heat. We'd only played forty five minutes but walking off the pitch looked - and felt - like we'd just had to play ninety minutes, extra time and penalties, in Doha.

Their only problems - judging by their coupons - was that they had clearly expected to be in a winning position by that stage of the match. I'd say that we were good value for being even, though. Aye, we'd not really troubled their keeper other than a couple of hopeful shots from distance through Montana and Rossi. But it wasn't like Sepp had been peppered with attempts either. The team - for the best part - had done our job and, as far as the plan was, the second half was going to be one where we were going to take the game to them in a way that - considering how the first had gone - they weren't going to expect.

As Jock said as we left the dressing room again for the second half.

'Show these arrogant bastards that for water carriers and hammer throwers, we can kick a bloody fitba too, eh'

If the first half had been largely uneventful - for a Muirhouse Violet match - then the second couldn't have been more of the opposite. All of the belief and positive thinking that we took to the pitch with, completely extinguished in the first minute of the second half when the referee had awarded Ramalde a penalty in a move that - completely catching us cold - had stemmed from kick off and ending with their striker flying like he was Superman in the box with a Sepp lying there on the ground, having come out to meet him. Our central defence caught completely flat footed with the boy waltzing right through to receive an - admittedly - naughty as fuck threaded pass from one of their midfielders.

Was it a penalty, though? Of course it fucking wasn't. Even from as far back as I was I could see, Sepp taking his arm away right at the moment where the striker was attempting to round him. It was the oldest trick in the book for a striker in that type of position - one on one with a keeper - but the ref bought it and there was fuck all we could do about it. Well, I say that there was fuck all we could do about it but that's not strictly true. As well as me, our whole back four had been able to see Sepp pull his hand away - and the boy dive - and were right over to the Portuguese lad, sitting on his arse in the box holding up an imaginary card - I assumed - looking for Sepp to be sent off. Maybe the ref was going to send him off, technically it would've been the correct call - if he gives the penalty - but the sight of two Violet players (Delaney and The Monk) dragging the Ramalde striker up from the ground, via the material of his shirt possibly distracted him, as did the predictable rushing in of Portuguese players to protect their man. Sepp was off the hook and in place to face the penalty.

Through the course of the first half it become more and more apparent that number eight was their star man. Don't get me wrong, there were a few others on their side that were silky and you could tell were players, alright. It was no surprise though when we saw number eight gathering the ball for the penalty.

He's got to save this, I thought to myself, because there was no way I fancied us having to come from a goal behind and win the match under such circumstances. My ideal scenario had been to sneak a goal and then get that bus parked up as soon as possible, while doing as little running as possible. Of course, though. For that scenario to happen we'd have to be actually *creating* chances.

Sometimes, though. Just because a team is hitting you with its best, it doesn't mean that it'll be automatically *for* the best. Case in point being that with all players standing impatiently outside the box on the kick being taken and the referee putting everyone out of their misery by blowing his whistle. This fancy dan decides that now is the time for him to take a Panenka.

Something that Sepp read all the way to the point that when he gathered the ball, it was done with such casual ease it could've been kicked toward him by his two year old son.

'Ha ha ha ya stupid wee prick'

Terry was right in the face of the boy. Big Tel, in his element.

'What the fuck was that?' Daz running past him adding while waving his hand back and forward past his nose to indicate the smell of how bad the pen had been.

'WEY-HEYYYYYY'

The Monk shouted, jumping into the air - behind the number eight - and coming back down with his arms crashing down on each shoulder of the boy. One hundred percent copying Martin Keown at Old Trafford that time.

Instead of running to offer protection this time, his team mates were less than pleased, at him. A few of their players with sour coupons spitting Portuguese in his direction. The boy looked like he wanted the ground to open up and swallow him. He had the crowd laughing at the penalty, the piss absolutely ripped out of him by the opposition and fuck knows what grief from his team mates over his fannying about with his penalty attempt.

Still, it was a lucky escape. Any other of them took it and they'd have likely slotted it away and left us in the shit. I'd like to say that we learned the lesson from that and set about turning the tide as far as how the second half would go, but this is Muirhouse Violet we're talking about here, remember?

Around five minutes after this, we had the tensions between Terry and Montana - from the night before - boil over when

Montana erupted over the lack of service Terry had been giving him. I'd noticed it in the first half, sometimes it was glaring. Even when the *only* pass available to Terry was to Montana, he wouldn't make it. Montana throwing his hands up each time and moaning away to himself. Eventually he'd had enough when he'd actually snuck into a dangerous position that could've put him in on goal, if Terry would've only passed the ball to him.

Fuck knows what the other side thought about things when Montana pulled down the back of his shorts - exposing his erse cheeks, one of them wounded - while shouting to his team mate

'If it's any cunt who shouldn't be passing to the other it should be fucking me to you, ya cunt. Where's *your* fucking wound, Mr Wronged'

I'm not even going to pretend that I know *all* of the finer details to the laws of fitba but, anyway. Montana took a yellow card from the referee for showing his erse. I suppose that seems fair enough. I mean, if you get booked for taking your top off and that?

'COME ON, BOYS. KEEP THE BLOODY HEAD OUT THERE. THIS MOB ARE THERE FOR THE TAKING'

Hunter's voice filtered over and onto the pitch.

It didn't fucking *feel* like they were there for the taking. Whilst the game had descended into what might have been classed as 'bitty' it was done so where we weren't really laying a glove on them. The amount of diving they were doing was starting to get old. This reflected by the yellow cards that we were beginning to tot up. The majority of them not even fouls, which only added to the general frustration of things.

When we lost a man around about the seventy minute mark, that was the signal that our tea was out. Quite understandably, by that point of the match we were literally breathing out of our erses. I'd been happy to notice that Ramalde weren't looking so fit as the fiddles that they'd done in the first half either, though. Just because you're used to extreme heat doesn't have to mean that you enjoy running around like a dafty for seventy minutes, I suppose.

Once more, though. It was the shithousing that was our undoing. Typically, it all came from a move that was meant to be a positive for us and something that might've brought about a goal. While both sets of players were jostling for position before Coffee whipped the ball in, I clocked one of the Portuguese defenders punch Terry in the kidney. Now I'm not sure which kind of Shaolin Monk taught move it was that the boy had caught Tel with but the big man went down like a tonne of bricks, rather than react with an elbow to the boy's face as I'd have normally have predicted from him.

'Fucking penalty, ref!' I shouted, instantly. There was fuck all else you could call what I'd just seen. It was clear as day. We'd been given nothing all day by this Spanish referee. He'd bought every piece of shithousing that Ramalde had produced into the bargain. Here was a legit penalty for us, no diving, simulation or engineering a situation to take place. Instead, it was a literal assault on one of our players.

With Terry on the ground in front of him, the Ramalde defender leant down with faux concern and while down there taking the opportunity to rip various hairs from Terry's legs. This being the spark that Terry needed for him to spring to his feet and take his knee firmly into the defender's balls, leaving him in a crumpled mess as he let out a blood curdling scream.

The main problem in all of this being that the kidney punch had been something that had taken place off the ball - with so many players making moves at once - while Terry's part that he played was something that *everyone* had witnessed.

The red card was inevitable. An - justifiably - incensed Terry was appealing to the referee, trying to show him via the medium of international sign language that the number five who was still on the deck - holding his nethers - had punched him. Tel lifting his shirt up to show the mark around his kidney.

Obviously, he was wasting his time. Referees simply don't reverse decisions like that. As incensed as he was, he left the pitch a lot quicker than he would've done if the same scenario was taking place on a Sunday morning. Can't blame him if he was just glad to get away from that searing heat. I'd have been happy with just ending the game there and then and taking a point, to be quite honest.

Their number five was quick enough on springing back to his feet once Terry had been given the red card though, mind.

'Your fucking card's marked, pal'

The Monk wagged his finger in the grinning Portuguese defender's face. A smile that you could've put your fist right through, had you not still twenty minutes left to try and get a result. Twenty minutes that were - in all likeliness - going to be completely backs to the wall while trying to keep them and their extra man out and sneak a point. When it comes to group fitba, aye, a win in your first game is fucking barry but ultimately, just don't get beat and leave yourself with one foot in the grave before you even get to game two.

'I'll wipe that fucking smile off your coupon, ya prick. You'll be smiling when the first aiders are carrying you off the pitch with a broken leg, eh?'

Delaney got involved, shoving the boy who was now playing the choir boy with his hands behind his back, offering no retaliation. All for the benefit of the referee, of course.

Once the match restarted, things went kind of as expected. Ramalde - with their extra man - started trying to press home their advantage to get the breakthrough. As we'd tend to do, though. When suffering some sort of an on pitch injustice, like Terry's sending off. It tended to galvanise us, as a team. Suddenly we were able to run that extra yard. Cunts putting their bodies in front of shots that they hadn't been able to for the previous seventy minutes. They were dictating things, our only real hope being a counter attack now and again, but due to this mission that we were now on. As much of the ball as they had, they were being severely restricted when it came to what they could actually *do* with it.

Apart from that, as good as our word, we made their number five's life complete hell for the rest of what was left of the match. Our players systematically taking it in turns to assault him, within the card system laws of the game. Between us, we worked out who were on yellows and who weren't, equalling who had a free pass to have a go at their defender.

And it was through this that for the first time all game, we caught a break.

In what had been one of our rare forays into the Ramalde half of the pitch we ended up being awarded a corner which had looked to me like their defender had cleared the ball out for a throw, before it had crossed the whole of the line. Normally, with the protests that came from him - and a few of his team mates - and how passionate and insistent they were with the linesman and referee you'd have automatically have sided with them, simply through the appearances of matters. The only thing about that though was that this was how Ramalde had been the *whole fucking game* - claiming for decisions that weren't there's to claim - so their behaviour was nothing out the ordinary. Personally, I was just happy to let them waste what was now precious minutes as we moved into the last ten.

Finally accepting the decision, both teams began getting into position for Mr Benn - who had been standing over the ball for a few minutes watching on as the assistant referee to the side of him took pelters from the Portuguese - to take the kick. All the mini battles between Muirhouse and Ramalde in the box as we tried to make sure we were all where meant to be when the ball arrived in. There was no way the ref - and assistants - were going to be able to keep track of everything. As long as he was looking in *my* direction, that really was the only thing that mattered.

Their number five was standing shouting something in Portuguese to the rest of his players in the box but looked like it was of an organisational nature. Spying that no one was picking me up, he moved the few steps across to me and with the advantage of the blind side of the ref, linked arm with me, so as to stop me from making a run and getting the jump on him.

Since he'd got Tel sent off - I mean, some would say that Tel got *himself* sent off, what with the kneeing the boy in the cojones and that - we'd made his life hell to the point that the arrogant smirk that he'd carried about him - following Terry's red - had descended into a permanent scowl. He'd been kicked, elbowed, snidely punched, forearm smashed, stamped on and - like any human being - was showing signs off someone who'd had enough.

Perfect.

When we were linked arms, I thought I'd try a different tact with him. Couldn't physically touch him after the flying elbow I got in on him earlier in the match when we'd both been jumping for the ball. Nothing in the rule book that says you can't *speak* to the opposition though, eh? Well, there maybe *is* to be fair but if the ref doesn't hear you say it then it simply might've well as having not happened.

'Tell you what, Jose. Your sister, mate? What a fucking barry ride she was. Are all Portuguese girls as dirty as that? Was telling the rest of the team about her and now they're talking about running a train on her'

I said loud and clear - and in my best pronounced English as I could, so he'd understand me - softly into his ear as Benn swung the ball in, but while we were both tethered to each other.

Well the cunt just flipped his lid at this. Unlinking his arm from mines and letting me make an attempt at meeting the cross. That's all I'd tried to do, get an edge on him in what could be a key moment in the game. And it had worked, my words had rattled him enough so that I'd been able to get myself free from him. The punch to the back of my head was just a fucking bonus ball.

I barely felt it. His fist lightly brushing against me but felt enough for me to go down like a sack of spuds, screaming out loud in agony while - the Violet players who had seen it - were screaming out at the referee for the penalty.

Fuck these cunts, I thought as I lay on the ground holding my head. We'd had all game of this kind of pish from them so why not give them a bit back? I done a few rolls for effect - that their number eight would've been proud of - while number five stood there with a look about him that told you that he knew he'd fucked up.

The ref confirming this by whistling and pointing to the spot to the obvious joy of our players and the obligatory protests from some of the Portuguese. There was absolutely ride all wrong with me but - even with us having been awarded the pen - I kept up the act. Figuring that considering I'd had a 'head knock' it would be justification enough for to get Pat onto the pitch and me get a wee drink of water off him, along with the amazing feeling of the wet sponge squeezed into the back of my head to 'soothe my injury.'

As their number five walked off the pitch, there was a coming together between him and Jock Hunter - who was still aggrieved about his behaviour earlier on in the match with Terry - which then brought the Ramalde manager out of his area again. Luckily - for Jock - the number five wasn't for taking too much of the bait. If he'd been up for it he looked like he could've put Jock six feet under without breaking sweat. He passed our manager and stood at the tunnel entrance to watch the penalty. Meanwhile Jock and the Ramalde manager were having a rematch of what had gone on in the first half. This time, however, the ref having felt that he should do something about it.

Running across to the two of them and in classic European football referee style, showed them both a red card, no fucking about or questions asked. It was a high tension moment. When we *finally* got the chance to take the penalty, if scored, it could well have been a match winning moment. We weren't getting the chance to actually *take it* though, because of the theatrics of our own manager. The look on his face, the almost offended features etched on him because a referee was sending him off.

I think it was more a case of the ref not wanting to waste any more time so made the decision to send them both off so that he didn't have to get into the who said and done what part of it all. Nice straight and clear red card, solves everything.

None of this could've been helping Montana, who had grabbed the ball as soon as the referee had blown his whistle. The longer you have to think about it the more chance you'll miss, they say. All the shithousing that the other team has the chance to pull on you. Snide comments in your ear. Keeper dancing about on his line, trying to psyche you out, persuading you to hit it to the side they *want* you to. All of that shite.

'Just don't fucking Panenka it, ya cunt, or *you'll* be getting fucking Panenka'd about the dressing room after the game'

The inspiring and supportive words that The Monk had for Montana as the ref rejoined us all, ushering whoever was still left in the box out of it so that we could *finally* take the penalty.

With there not really being much in the way of home or away fans in the stadium, there wasn't really much examples of anyone trying to put Montana off when he was about to make his run up. More a kind of silent anticipation than anything else, including the players. Some of our boys couldn't even watch and had turned their backs, looking down the pitch towards Sepp, and for his reaction as and when it came. To offset this, there was the comical sight of Jock, the Ramalde manager and their number five all standing by the tunnel watching, despite them all having been given their jotters, and not exactly having enjoyed the best of relations with each other.

Just fucking score, I repeated to myself in my head like some mantra as the whistle eventually blew and Montana began his run up.

Their keeper - trying to get into Montana's head - had been deliberately standing more towards one side of the goal instead of dead centre as they waited on the ref signalling for the kick to take place, but even after the whistle, he *still* stayed in that off centre position. Who knows, like? Maybe that stuff works on other cunts and has them going for the direction that has less space to aim for, instead of the obvious side that he's leaving open for you, the one that you could drive a bus through.

To Montana's credit. The keeper could've been stood in the centre of the goals and he was never going to save it anyway. Montana - taking up the keeper's invitation to hit it towards the big gap that had been left - hitting the ball with such perfect positioning that the ball hit the inside *of the side* of the net. Their keeper's dive woefully a day late and a euro short.

It's fair to say, we as a team erupted. Couldn't fucking catch Montana who had wheeled off to celebrate, mind. Half of us probably ended up with a stitch *chasing* the cunt, as he made a bee line for the dug outs and tunnel. Solitary finger up to his lips to their number five who couldn't resist bending down and picking up a half drank water bottle and lobbing it at our striker. The bottle - whilst not hitting Montana - was made good use of. Coffee pouring its contents over his head before throwing the empty back at their player while we made our way back into our own half.

The celebration had caused more drama by the tunnel area with Jock taking exception to the boy throwing the bottle at his player but by the time Ramalde were taking centre it looked like things had been sorted out. All three were now missing from the tunnel area and - I'd assumed - back in their dressing rooms. It wasn't until after the match that I would learn the realities of things in that Jock had taken a two litre bottle of water and whacked their number five on the head with it which then provoked the Ramalde manager into kicking Jock in the shin. The fracas only coming to an end via the help of random well wishing members of the crowd who had been forced to leave the stand to stop the madness. I tell you, the stuff you get away with when you don't have one of those grassing bastard fourth officials, eh?

The remaining minutes of the game were an exercise in doing the simple things, well, *simple.* Effectively giving up any pretence of looking interested in scoring a second, and, instead, putting every body behind the ball. Ramalde managed to carve a few chances out for themselves but - to me - it had looked like the penalty had gutted them.

Regardless of that. In that heat, every minute felt like an hour. It was all I could think about, hearing that final whistle go. Considering all of the drama that had gone on in the second half, there should've been no surprise at the amount of added time the referee was potentially going to come up with but even so, when I heard seven minutes being mentioned, it felt like some cunt had shanked me.

Exactly like those Portuguese fannies would've done had they been in the same position, we time wasted our way out of those seven minutes. Drawing fouls from their frustrated players while in no rush to take the free kicks then awarded to us. The last three minutes or so, spent out by the corner flag where - at times - it felt like a free for all between the Violet players trying to shield the ball and the Ramalde players in how they were attempting to retrieve it from them.

When the full time whistle eventually went, there were no rapturous celebrations from us. We were literally too knackered for any of that caper. All of us flopping down onto the pitch in the exact same way as we'd have done had we *lost* the match. As for the losers? The Portuguese boys didn't take things too kindly. When it came to shaking hands after the match, they weren't interested. Shooing any attempts away from our boys while in some cases they just flat out blanked us. Classless, cunts. There were words exchanged as we went down the tunnel but I think both teams were so fucking drained that nobody had it in them to cash any cheques that they may have wanted to write.

Jock Hunter had come out when he'd heard the shouting outside the dressing room, to get us all inside before anything escalated. Didn't do so without having one last dig at their manager before coming inside and closing the door.

'Aye, you maybe hadn't heard of Muirhouse Violet until a few days ago but I doubt you'll fucking forget about them now. Get it right fucking up you and the rest of your nasty pieces of work'

It was novel, hearing *our* manager describing another team as a nasty piece of work, I'll give Jock that.

'Fucking top of the group, ya bastards. Yaaaassssss'

Daz shouted as he took a stray ball and booted it against the wall. About taking Delaney's head off in the process, neither of them caring.

Technically he was right. The Russians and Estonians were next up so with the expectations being that the Russians would win - and by a few goals to spare - we would be sharing joint top with them in a couple of hours time. We'd already been told by this point that the Russians had been a permanent fixture in the Red Bear tournament which, I suppose, made sense, with it being a Russian beer company sponsoring the thing. Apparently they generally came with a strong team and if they weren't winning the competition they were going far in it each year.

Had we been professionals, we'd have showered, changed and then taken our places in the stand to sit and watch the two teams that we were going to play over the next week, more specifically the Russian side who were now thought of as being our rivals for finishing top of the group, now that the Portuguese had been disposed of.

We weren't professionals, though. Not even fucking close, eh? We were a bunch of radgeys from Edinburgh who had just played our first match on the European stage. A *major* test - as a team - in a game that had everything. On pitch violence, top notch shithousery, drama, missed and scored penalties and red cards.

The *only* thing in our minds - as far as afternoon activities that day - involved finding somewhere with an extended happy hour. We had some celebrating to be doing and to such an extent that if I'd known in advance how it was all going to turn out I would *one hundred percent* have stayed behind and watched the Russians and the Estonians.

Chapter 8

Viktor Borovskiy

'They did *what?*'

If it was not for the fact that my close circle and security detail would not have dreamed of yanking my chain and that whenever they called me, it was always strictly business. I'd have thought this was some attempt at a light hearted joke.

'They finished a moment ago, boss. You asked for to be updated as soon as it was over'

The ever compliant Valery said, probably thanking his lucky stars and all the planets too that he had been able to deliver this news via the medium of a telephone call. He'd worked for me long enough to expect a negative reaction to the topic of the call.

'But, how?' I asked, not that it really mattered, in a mix of disbelief but rising anger.

'Theyyyy, ummmm, simply weren't up to the task, I guess. Big shock'

The non committal reply back.

He was treated to the sound of me repeatedly slamming the phone against the coffee table.

I was fucking pissed at the news, majorly. So sure of things - in advance - that I hadn't even *planned* for this outcome. This was meant to have been the *easy* part and something that would not require any contingency plans. Well, that was the idea anyway.

'So what would you like done now, boss?'

He asked, once the noise had stopped.

I thought it over in my head, like a chess player. Trying to see a few steps in advance, and where things would be sat by then.

Because I was already now behind.

'Find the Scots, that shouldn't be too difficult a task for a man with your capabilities'

And there was no joking when it came to Valery's capabilities. A man who years ago had found that there was a lot more money in being part of an oligarchs security detail than it was working for the state, in his previously held special forces position.

'When you find them, you know what to do'

Chapter 9

Benji

I fucking told the boy that it was a bad idea, but he wasn't hearing it. So worked up by the combination of beating the Portuguese and then the repeated trips to the bar during happy hour.

'Come on, Benj. It'll be a laugh, eh?'

Normally when someone says to you that 'it'll be a laugh' it - in my own experience - is almost a cast iron nailed down pledge that it won't be. And by fuck, was Strings' idea of stealing a pedalo, taking a bag of cans onboard and the two of us heading off out into the sea about as funny as a boot in the fucking balls.

If I hadn't been as mortal as I was myself, I'd have been able to talk him out of it and - in fairness - my warning of two cunts who were steaming drunk, and had further replenishments on them, going out onto the water being a bad idea was only a brief one before - with Strings already taking his seat inside one - he had me saying 'Ah fuck it' and joining him before we got the pedals into action. The boy in charge of the pedalos - lining that wee section of the beach - only clocking us when it was too late to do anything about it.

'We'll square you up when we get back to the shore, pal'

Strings shouted over to him while the guy shouted various things - insults I assumed - in Spanish when he realised that his initial 'come back' plea was being completely rubbered by the pair of us.

'We are top of the league say we are top of the league we are top of the league ...'

We belted out at the top of our voices as we pedalled our way out to sea. Can each, held up in the air triumphantly for everyone who was lying around and stood on the beach, or playa as the Spaniards called it. I always liked to try and pick up a wee bit of the local lingo when outside of my usual surroundings. Plus, you never know when that wee nugget of information might come in handy?

Once we were far enough out, we eased off on pedalling so much. Allowing us to float - and gently drift - while sitting having a fag and a beer, spraffing away to each other the biggest amount of drunken pish going.

With the environment we were in and how warm, sunny and beautiful it all looked. The sea itself sparkling like it was full of diamonds. One of those moments where everything coming together is just the perfect mix.

Strings, seeming to appreciate exactly this, managed to find a piece of clarity in between the absolute nonsense that he'd been slavering since the third round of happy hour.

'You know what's been the best part about the past few days? Not the getting away and having a good old fucking scoop in the sunshine with the lads. Isn't the buzz of taking on an outfit like those Portuguese cunts today and beating them. And neither is it anything to do with getting some time away from the wife and son'

Strings said, looking out into the distance but giving me the impression that he wasn't seeing anything anyway, so far away deep in his thoughts he was.

'Well, considering you've written off just about every potential reason for why the past few days have been so good, what *is it* that's made it for you?' I asked him as we continued to - by then - leisurely pedal.

'Fucking, McKenna's phone. The fact that I haven't had to have it glued to me for the past couple of days. I mean, the cunt could go weeks without ever calling it but just the knowledge of *having* to keep it on you - and in doing so offering you a daily reminder of how fucked you are - and that at some point, it's going to ring. Honestly can't explain how good it feels to not have to be carrying it here in Spain'

'Aye, fuck him,' I supported my best pal. 'Let McKenna call it all he wants, you're off the clock, for a change'

'To be honest, he could call it all he likes, Benj. It's sitting in the kitchen drawer anyway' he said pissing himself like you'd expect from a drunkard like him at that point.

'I'll drink to that, mucker.' I responded, throwing my empty can into the wee region in the middle of the pedalo that we'd deemed as being an adequate make shift bin before fishing out a couple more from the bag that we'd ingeniously tied to a hook on the side of our vessel so that we could keep our beers cool.

'Get that down you' I insisted as I pushed a can into his chest, forcing him to take it from me.

'Don't mind if I do, senor' he said, taking it from me but - enjoying the coolness against him - leaving the can there before transferring it from his stomach and around to the back of his neck. Cracking it open - eventually - and, having not given it that vital couple of seconds to settle, watched about a quarter of the can come rushing out of it all over him.

'Fucking liability' I laughed at him.

Taking his first swig out of the new can, he broke out into another round of *we are top of the league*, me happily joining him.

The consideration that by that time of day, the Russians had maybe won their match by two clear goals or more and us actually *not* top of the group, something that neither of us had any thoughts on. And like any fitba fan will admit, never let facts get in the way of a good chant when you're buzzing about a result.

I'm telling you straight, though. Maybe I never kicked or headed a ball out there but I'd never been prouder of that group of players than that day. We were no soft touches ourselves and it had been said by many that we were the team that they hated playing against, mainly through our 'win at all costs' philosophy, and the depths we would stoop to to *get* that win. But these lads from Portugal were like us, times ten.

Some would've maybe said that all we'd received had been a taste of our own medicine but that Ramalde were way fucking worse than us *at* our worst. You'd never see us diving, for one thing.

Seeing us deal with all of that provocation from an opposing team and *still* have the mental strength to be the bigger men - Terry, excepted, but even then, no cunt could've blamed the boy for his reaction that got him sent off - and grind out a win. It was one of those moments where it makes all the hours you give up for the Violet worth while.

The boys had rightfully earned their day out on the batter, something Jock couldn't and wouldn't have grudged. Hunter being the only one out of us who stayed behind to watch the other two teams in our group play.

The rest of us - once showered and changed - couldn't get away from the stadium quick enough. Setting up camp at The Arsed Rat to begin with. It's funny how things happen in life that affect you which in turn leads to something else, though. Case in point being that it was only because the chef for the boozer hadn't turned up that day which meant that there would be no scran on offer for any patrons of what was fast becoming our go to boozer. This meaning that when Strings and me fancied something to eat - the combination of playing ninety minutes of intense fitba in that heat and then getting wired into the pints of Voddie and Coke leaving Strings in a bit of a state. Something food would've at least helped with so - forced by the chef situ - we had to leave the pub and go looking for some fast scran from somewhere else.

Obviously, this didn't go to plan because instead of sitting inside a bar or restaurant, eating a fuck off burger or a bucket of chicken, we were in the sea on a white pedalo with cans of beer and absolutely fuck all in the region of food.

'Tell you what. This is the fucking life though, eh?' He slurred, while appreciating his lot. 'Just floating out on the water, sun on your back, no cunt nipping your head wanting something from you'

I couldn't disagree with the boy. Rarely would either of us find ourselves enjoying such peace and tranquility but out there floating about on the water we had everything you could've asked for. Sun, peace, your best mate and beer and fags. Still could've done with some scran, like, but that would be addressed when we made it back to dry land. For now, I thought. Just enjoy what you have.

I took a big swig out of the can before shoving it into one of the wee cup holders the pedalo had - which I thought had been a nice wee feature - and positioned my head backwards, closing my eyes and just simply sitting there, soaking up the almost therapeutic sun that was beaming back down on us.

When the unmistakable feeling of the pedalo bumping hard into something came, it was only *then* that I'd even realised I'd fallen asleep. Opening my eyes in a panic, like you do when you're disturbed from an unplanned snooze, only add the panic because you were sleeping and have woken up *in the sea*. I looked to the side and Strings was probably resembling whatever the fuck I was. He'd fallen asleep too. Easy done when you've had a few ales and are laying (or sitting in our case) about in the sun. Probably not advisable when you're sitting on a light craft floating about the Balearic Sea. Well, not without at least one person being awake, anyway.

'The fuck's just happened' A confused Strings looking at me asked where if he'd just looked in front of him he'd have seen what had brought both of afternoon naps to an untimely end.

Without any guidance from either of us, the pedalo had drifted wherever the mood had taken it. Coming to, and trying to get myself up to some kind of speed - despite being as confused for those first few seconds, exactly like Strings was - I'd managed to establish that we had crashed into some small island.

'Fucking pheeeeew. The bang that the pedalo made I thought we'd crashed into a speedboat or had killed some poor cunt out water skiing or something'

Considering the more grim possibilities, crashing into a small inhabitable looking island - having both fallen asleep at the wheel - was an end result that you'd have gladly taken.

'Mon, we getting out and doing a wee bit exploring?' Strings not so much asked while he tried to get the pedalo into a position were we'd be able to jump out of the front of it without having to get our feet wet.

Exploring? When I say that it was a wee island I mean that there were probably bigger islands on top of balding men's heads. Before even getting out of the pedalo all it had looked to consist of was lots of bushes and - judging by the noise - fucking loads of crickets.

'May as well have a wee deek around the place, since we've ended up here, eh?' Strings - now already on dry land - coaxed me out of my seat to join him. Making sure to hold the pedalo before taking the wee bit rope that was attached to the side and tying it to the root of a big bush at the edge of the island.

The 'deek around' due to how small and - mainly - inaccessible the island was only took us around ten minutes before we were back at the pedalo again. Hardly the stuff of Columbus, like.

'We better get ourselves back to shore, fucking starving here' I said, as I made to get back into the pedalo. Strings agreeing but suggesting that we take a sit down for a minute and have a smoke before getting going. Pulling out his packet of Regal King Size and offering me one before shoving another in his mouth, lighting it, and then passing me his Clipper.

Both looking at the tiniest speck in the distance - each of us guessing, to be Magaluf - that was our final destination, we - now that the buzz of the alcohol had let the sleep interrupt it - sat ruing the decisions that we'd made hours before. It had been a barry laugh on the way out but the return journey now looked fuck all other than a pain in the erse.

We were only meant to have sat there while we had a cigarette but I'd long since pinged mines into the water and we were both still on dry land. Talking about what a night it was going to be, following the result earlier on in the day. We weren't wrong, though. Before even travelling out to Spain you already knew that had we won that first game, then Magaluf was going to fucking know about it, you best be sure of that.

It was a shame that me and Strings would go on to miss it. A damned shame.

It was when we were talking about which club we'd probably end the night in. That was when I started to smell the smoke, then hearing the crackling noise to accompany with it.

'THE FUCKING BUSH, STRINGS'

I screamed at him. Looking over his shoulder, around four metres away from him was a bush that was on fire, and looked like it was in the mood for spreading.

Cue the two of us panicking like fuck for a couple of minutes in terms of what to do. Water water every where and not a drop to put a fire out, is that not how the song goes?

In that exact moment, I suppose it didn't matter and wouldn't be able to undo things but my mind went to Strings and how - while I know what I'd done with mines - I'd never seen what he'd done with the butt of his Regal.

'GET THE CANS FROM THE PEDALO, QUICK'

He screamed out with more urgency than I'd ever seen him display on a fitba pitch.

Decent quick thinking from him, had we not already drank all of our beer. This, something I hadn't been aware of until jumping onto the pedalo only to find a collection of empties.

'THERE ISN'T FUCKING ANY'

I shouted back at him while freaking the fuck out as I watched - what had only been one bush at first - the fire begin to spread.

I quickly untied the pedalo from the root it was fixed to and got Strings back on board with orders to pedal like fuck! As we made our way from the island, looking around, it was clear that this wee part of land wasn't going to stand a chance. Everything on it was so dry - probably hadn't seen rain in fucking months - that it was a virtual tinderbox, if anyone was daft enough to come along and start a fire on it.

This was bad, though, *really* bad, I thought to myself. We've really fucked it this time territory. Aye, we'd done a few things in our time, I'm not denying that for one minute. Setting fire to an island in broad daylight in another country, though? No, this was a new one for us and as far as I was concerned. Unless we could get ourselves back to the mainland of Magaluf - and able to disappear ourselves into all the tourists walking about the joint - wherever the fuck Magaluf actually *was* then there was always going to be a chance of some cunts clocking us out there in the water, and putting dos and dos together and getting cuatro.

'That was you with your snout, eh? Did you fucking ping it to the side of you?' It's not too often me and Strings will be at each other like that but what a fucking idiotic thing to do.

'Might've done, can't really remember now. It's that hot just now though, pretty good chance that it just went up by itself, eh? You know how those forest fires start in Australia and America, like'

Aye, mate, I thought to myself. This wee island that had existed for fuck knows how many centuries just happened to go up in flames at the very same time as two pissheads had been cutting about on it.

And it really was going up in flames. We were a wee bit away from it by now but looking around at it you couldn't not notice the massive flume of black smoke that was going up into the air along with the colour of the flames that were completely at odds with the greenery that the place had boasted before we'd visited it.

Unfortunately, if it was hard not to see for us, that meant the exact same for others. Specifically, the local police. One of their boats rounding us up when we were aimlessly trying to make our way back to Magaluf's mainland. With how far out the island was, - and how unusual it would've been for anyone on pedalos to be as far out as that - it wasn't hard for the police to draw their own conclusions on things.

Initially shouting at us in Spanish through a loud speaker fixed to the side of the vessel before realising that they were talking to two clueless cunts from Scotland and switching to English. None of what they were spraffing good, either.

Especially the bit that involved us being under arrest and how we were to now get on board their boat.

The fact that me and Strings would now no longer have to risk still being out stranded in the Balearic Sea by night time and or us being spared having to pedal all that way back to shore was not much of a consolation, if I'm being brutally honest.

Chapter 10

Strings

How unlucky can you get, though? You burn down an island - that's not the unlucky part - and are clocked by a police marine unit near the scene of the crime, who are only there in the first fucking place looking to catch drug smugglers?! Even the coppers appeared to be a little underwhelmed by the crime that they'd arrested these two foreigners over. Not fucking embarrassed enough to just put us back where they found us, though, mind.

Apparently, the island that we'd slept our way to had been known for traffickers dropping gear off at, so had been the target of the police's attention, sitting miles away on their boat staking out.

Like I said, how unlucky can one get? Couldn't it had been another island that cunts were stashing their gear, leaving me to set fire to a different one in relative peace? Just one of the questions that I repeated on a loop as I spent that night in the cells.

Tell you what, though? If there *was* any fucking gear stashed in some of those bushes on that island, it wasn't there anymore because - by the looks of things - after me and the Benji boy visited the place it was left looking like some cunt had operated a scorched earth policy on it.

Now I'm not going to say that - the unlucky aspect of the police catching us and how they managed it aside - I never played a part in things myself, because I did. I'll hold my hands up to that. I just didn't with Benji when he asked me. He's not fucking stupid either though.

The ironic thing is that, aye, I pinged the fag to the side of me - as opposed to it going in the water - but in doing so I actually thought I was doing the *right* thing. It's not like we'd been throwing our empty cans into the sea as we floated along. No, we were being respectful, eh? Fucking, friends of the earth, so we were. So when it came to me wanting rid of my snout. Aye, my natural instinct was to just toss it into the water in front of us but I had the mental image of it floating around in the sea and how it wouldn't be right to pollute such beautiful blue waters. So, instead, burned a fucking island down. Sometimes you just can't do right for doing wrong, like.

The other thing was - not that it made me feel any better about things, mind - that one of the Spanish coppers was telling me that radge drunken tourists and party animals were always accidentally setting fire to some of the wee islands dotted around the Balearic. Cunts having BBQs along with a healthy peave, that kind of stuff. Proper recipe for disaster, like.

'You are not the first and you will not be the last. The mistake you made was *which* island you set fire to'

I thought back to that sign that we'd seen on it, when we were having a look around. The one that was all in Spanish but seemed to be telling any cunt that was interested that no trespassing was allowed, or something to that effect. Next to it, another sign with a fucking massive no smoking logo on it saying non fumar. We never really took much notice of either, especially the second one.

Of course, though. Can't just engage in a wee spot of accidental arson. Nah, I had to go and set fire to the one place in the whole of fucking Espana that the precious Cotofanga plant grew on. This main sticking point being the difference between a firm talking to from the police, and me and Benji spending a night in the cells, being up before the judge the next day.

It was all a little confusing to me because I was still half pished which was mixing with tiredness setting in from all of the fitba, drinking and over exposure to the sunshine, but the way it had been briefly explained. The Cotofanga plant only grew in a select amount of places on the planet - the Balearic Islands of Spain being one of those few areas - and enjoyed some kind of privileged - as well as protected - status, environmentally speaking.

Like, how can you get lifted - not for arson or anything that would've appeared obvious - because you destroyed a plant? I've known a few cunts in the past that got charged for *growing* plants. Never for destroying them though, mind. I actually laughed at first when we were told the extent of how much trouble we were in. Laughed in that way you do when you're sure some cunt has just said something to you that you've already taken as an unserious statement. It's the part when they don't laugh back at you that's the downer though, like.

What a difference a day makes, like that song says. In our case, not even twenty four little hours. Only took us less than twelve to go from the highs of beating those shithousing Portugeezers and landing up in a Spanish cell, alongside three other tourists and one of the locals.

Our 'friends' for the night being a Scouser in a blood stained white Tommy Hilfiger t shirt with a face that suggested he'd taken a heavy paggering off someone.

'If that's the state of you, being the cunt that's been lifted, I can't even begin to imagine what the other boy looks like'

I tried to joke with him, figuring if we were all in there for the night then me and Benji should at least get on terms with them.

The Scouser just laughed, uttering 'Fucking Spanish bizzies, la' before the penny dropped.

'Oh aye? Fell down the stairs, pal?' I replied, once I was on board.

Dez- from Huyton - who was in for putting a bottle of beer over a bouncers head after he'd been thrown out of a club. Despite his reasons for being inside. The boy turning out to be quite sound and funny as fuck. And if there's something that you need when you're sitting in a cell, it's a laugh. Because they're generally in short supply. Not much to laugh about though, I suppose.

Other than him there was Quinn - out of Belfast - who was absolutely fucking mortal. I know the cunt was Irish but there was no need to go to such lengths to reinforce national stereotypes. He claimed that he'd not done anything and had just been grabbed for no reason and huckled into a van but it was hard to imagine someone as drunk as he was *not* having done something of sorts. Whether he could remember doing it? Different proposition altogether, like. He was in those three quarter length trousers that can't decide if they want to be trousers or shorts and some Irish hurling team's - Leinster - shirt that I'd never heard of. To be fair, I hadn't heard of *any* fucking Hurling team, not just his. He wasn't a bad lad, just completely ruined and pretty early on I'd come to the conclusion that - for the advancement in group relationships - it would be better if his post swally mindset kicked in and he fell asleep.

Penz, this cockney kid who could've only been twenty years of age at a push. Sitting there in not much more than a pair of white Fila tennis shorts. Telling the two of us that he'd been caught in the middle of a pure kleptomaniac sesh while in the local Lacoste boutique earlier on that day. Happy enough to admit to the rest of us that he'd been caught bang to rights. Saying that he had planned to take it back home and sell it. Some old school casual energy from the kid. Stealing the labels abroad to take back to Britain and sell it. I didn't bother with the labels so much by that point in life but could appreciate his hustle all the same.

Finally there was 'Paco' who spoke decent English which was just as well for him otherwise he'd have been shut out of the whole conversation. Something telling me that asking him for 'dos cerveza' probably wasn't going to cut it in such a setting. Big fucker, Paco, so when he told us that he was in for battering fuck out of his wife, none of us were interested in pulling him up about it. Telling the rest of the group that he broke her jaw after he'd read a couple of text messages which indicated that she'd been shagging someone else.

You should've seen all of their faces when we told them why *we* were in there with them.

Dez and Quinn just pissing themselves laughing while Penz just issued us with a sincere 'fuck off' in disbelief.

'Fucking tourists. What is it with you and fires?'

Paco sat there shaking his head like it was a story he'd heard many times before that night.

'But why are you in *here?*' he asked.

'For something such as that you would really only receive a talking to and, depending on which police officer, possibly a beating or you having to bribe your way out of things, but not a prison cell'

He seemed so assured about what he was talking of but then again, he was a local so you'd think he'd have been more up on things than the rest of us.

'Well, look, Paco,' Strings answered.

'See Quinn sitting here? Well hours ago, me and Strings were in that ballpark level of inebriation so when the police caught us. I'm not sure either of us really clocked half of what was going on or being said. One of the officers, though, said that we'd been unlucky enough to burn down an island with special plants on it, or something to that effect'

Paco's face changed after getting the additional information supplied.

'Oh'

All he said before following up with

'You two fucked up, amigos. You burned down Chuleta Island'

Neither me nor Benji knew this to be fact. It was hardly like we'd jumped into the pedalo with our map and compass, setting pedal for Cheleta Island. Instead, if it hadn't been for the island you have to question *where* the fuck we'd have ended up by the time one of us had woken up. Ibiza?

Paco went on to explain that - if we'd burned the island that he thought we had - there was a protected plant that grew on it. Something that was almost a miracle in its being as nowhere else in Europe had it in their country. It was like a 4D David Attenborough program as Paco told us how there was these juices that was found *on* the plant that attracted a butterfly called a Penguina - due to it's unique colour scheme which was that of a penguin - which was almost extinct. And because of all of this - and how cunts are always looking to protect something or other, probably to justify the extravagant wage they're probably being paid, - it was an island that was meant to be protected under all kinds of Spanish environmental laws.

'*Now* I understand why you are both here' he affirmed while giving us a serious look. As if he wasn't the cunt who had put his wife in hospital who was looking at us saying this.

'Fucking sound, eh?' I turned to Benji, giving him an ironic thumbs up. 'Not only did we burn down an island but we probably wiped out a species of animal at the same time. A right two for one, eh?'

I said, while having the nagging feeling - now that I'd had something that came close to an explanation that made sense put to me - that I'd actually *seen* a couple of mainly white - with added splash of black - butterflies flying about on the island.

'We?' Benji answered, flashing me a glare to express just how pissed off he was at me, with good cause, I suppose.

Obviously, Paco could've just been spinning us a big yarn to keep himself amused while we were in there. That was something we'd find out the next day when we were taken to court, as had been explained to us when we were being processed into the police station.

'Are we going to get a fucking stretch for this, Paco, mate?

Benji, looking heavy stressed, asked our new Spanish acquaintance. I was fucking bricking it on what his reply was going to be. The more I found out about what we'd done, the worse it all seemed to get.

After working out the cultural differences when it came to lingo, and use of words for certain things, and Paco knowing what a stretch was in our country, he gave us his verdict, eventually.

'Have either of you been charged before in Espana? His question to our question. The both of us shaking our heads. Paco's face immediately lighting up at this.

'Ahhh, then you will be ok. You will get a fine and be back on the street tomorrow, no worries, my friends.' He said, waving his arm around as a form of expression while telling us the good news.

'Well thank fuck for that, eh?' I breathed a sigh of relief. It was the first of me seeing Benji show some sign of his usual self, too. I think - because of the drink - I hadn't really attached too much importance about being lifted, figuring that the Magaluf coppers must spend half their time throughout the summer, lifting British tourists so me and Benji getting huckled wasn't going to be too much of an inconvenience. Once the drink started to wear off, though. That's when you start to see different viewpoints, when a bit of hazy clarity returns.

Now with a relative degree of confidence that we weren't going to end up in the fucking pokey. Thoughts turned to life on the outside of the police cell that we were in.

'That's training fucked for tomorrow though'

I said to Benji, already assuming that it was going to be impossible to get carted off in the morning to Palma and put in front of a judge and us get ourselves back to Magaluf in time for the start of training.

'And with that, bang goes my chances of playing against the Russians'

I suppose I should've really been concentrating on the short term and the problems that existed there but I knew that if I didn't make training then chances were, some cunt was going to take my place. While aye, we had a starting eleven that - if all fit - pretty much picked itself, no team can operate on the bare bones. There were a few candidates for my position. My guess. Bobby Brady. Tidy wee midfielder who'll put in a shift for you that were it not for the silky but industrial skills of yours truly would have seen a lot more minutes for Muirhouse Violet.

But that match against the Portuguese had been the greatest moment I'd experienced in a Muirhouse shirt - pissed all over any cup win we'd had as far as I was concerned - and it had been like some kind of elite level drug, and I wanted more.

'Fuck, the rest of the boys? They'll be wondering where the hell we disappeared to,' Benji said, completely ignoring me.

'You serious?' I asked in disbelief.

'It's fucking Magaluf we're in, and we're Muirhouse Violet. Even by tomorrow morning and we're not making training cunts will be writing us off as having went somewhere for a drink, after getting the food that we didn't have, and then the rest of the day going sideways. We were hardly the picture of health when we staggered out the boozer looking for food'

His face looked like he was beginning to appreciate the sentiment.

'Trust me, we'd need to be gone for a full forty eight hours before even one of them started to think about maybe going to the police. Would you, for any of the others, if you lost *them* for a day? Because I fucking wouldn't'

I suppose - at the time - you just had to take the positives that were there, even if there didn't appear to be many of them. We weren't going to be getting banged up for one thing so our 'Banged up Abroad' episode was down the swanny. That was a good thing, though. Didn't much like the sound of the fine that Paco had said we'd be getting hit with but he had kind of shrugged it off like it was nothing so - following the local - I thought nothing more of it. Fuck all more you *could* do, with a trip to see the judge booked in for the next day.

Fuck, how I wish we'd just went and found some food, earlier on that day, though. Obviously, it would've avoided the whole unpleasantness that followed but not just that. It had meant that food had ended up pretty much taking a back seat. And you know what it gets like when you've had a good drink, eh?

One of the Guardia Civil - a few hours into us being there - bringing Benji and me a roll that you could've taken and smashed fuck out of the officer's skull with that had 'cheese' inside it that *couldn't* have been real and a nice refreshing warm plastic cup of water to wash down such a delicacy. It all still got tanned though, like, while I hated myself for how much I enjoyed it, so ravenous I'd landed myself.

Sleep eventually came to us all, once we'd done talking and it had started to get late. Not that it was the best night's sleep you were ever going to get in there, mind. The blue plastic tray - that looked like it would've been a barry sledge during the winter - we were all given, hardly a king size bed with memory foam pillows, like.

Hours later, we were rudely woken by an officer, bringing us breakfast. The irony, but also, ultimate paradox of - I'd guessed with it being early morning - the breakfast being the exact same fucking thing that had been served up for supper. The paradox being that the roll was fresh as a daisy and no longer the weapon that it had been the night before but to offset this, the cheese appeared even *less* believable than it had been the night before. As previously, though. It was demolished all the less.

It wasn't long after that where the six of us found ourselves all put into handcuffs and led out into a van that looked a wee bit like a Securicor one, different branding though, like. The Spanish version, eh.

Having had all the hours the day before to get to know one another, we all sat having a good laugh on the way to the court house. If you didn't know any better you definitely would not have thought it was six men on their way for sentencing in front of a judge. Paco was cracking us up, slagging fuck out of the two officers sat in the back with us and then translating what he'd just said into English, so that we could get the chance to poke fun at the coppers too. They weren't happy about this, as you'd imagine.

It was only when the van stopped and those back doors opened for us to get out that the nerves began to kick in. The court house - architecturally speaking - was beautiful and looked like some place that you could see some revolutionaries storming in some film or something, overthrowing their government and that. We were taken into a room where - not long after - some appointed English speaker - I wasn't sure if they were a lawyer or not as they never asked us for any money - joined us and explained what the process was going to be that morning.

Mainly the judge speaking in Spanish and this young boy in the suit who was sitting talking to us would translate whatever was being said. Looking at our paperwork to see why we were appearing in front of the court - and seeing that there wasn't anything complex about it - he advised that it would be a simple procedure and that all we'd need to do on our part was to confirm our names when asked and to state our guilty plea. He would do the rest.

Obviously, if we'd had money and had been back in Scotland, we'd have had lawyers on the case straight away but with it being Spain not to forget having fuck all in the way of 'lawyer money' to throw around, we didn't really feel like we had a choice other than to admit that, well we're not even sure *what* we had admitted to, other than that the island hadn't been on fire when we arrived and that when we left it was going up in flames. Effectively we were admitting our guilt but - because of this - that now meant that we'd be taken care of sharpish.

He left the room again for a while, telling us that with us both being tried for the same crime we would be appearing in front of the judge at the same time, and that we were scheduled for around two hours time.

The room practically emptying over that period. First Dez, half an hour later Quinn - who looked like he was absolutely hanging, post sesh - being called for. Eventually it came to me and Benji.

While we'd been sitting around in the room, we'd speculated about our fate, or specifically, how much of a fine we were going to get. It had been a struggle for the both of us to get together enough funds to bring out to Magaluf to provide for enough mammoth drinking sessions and the required scran to go with. There had never been a consideration that we'd need to factor in a court fine into our budget.

Based on absolutely no knowledge of how these things went in our own country, never mind a different one altogether, we'd estimated for something around two hundred and fifty euros each, seemed fair enough, like.

Without actually admitting my guilt outright to Benji, my offer to pay his fine could easily have been taken as an admission of some kind of wrongdoing.

When we were eventually taken up to the see the judge, for the best part, we didn't have a fucking scoob what was going on. You could tell that the big man wasn't happy with us, though. The way he was looking at us and talking in a raised voice that - depending on if you had a headache or not - could've almost been classed as shouting. Funnily enough, the English speaking kid in the suit appointed by the court wasn't much for translating most of it. Maybe trying to spare our feelings but sometimes you really don't need a translation when someone is giving you a look like that belligerent cunt was from his lofty position.

Some of the translation that we did get, though. Was really just along the lines of a mix of what the sea coppers had told us and then what Paco had added.

'You are responsible for an environmental disaster which the whole world will be aware of. Something that will reflect badly on the island of Mallorca'

One of the things the boy *could* be arsed passing on to us.

'And you should be held accountable for your crimes, to the full extent of the powers that I am permitted'

That's what all the judges say though, eh? I thought to myself as he continued ranting at such a speed it made your average

Spaniard sounding like they spoke after tanning a bottle of vallies. Maybe *that* was why the kid wasn't translating as much as he was, eh?

You could tell that from his body language, the judge was in the process of wrapping things up. Squeaky bum time, like.

'So I will be fully enacting the environmental protection law for mainland Spain, the Balearic and Canary Islands of two thousand and eight'

Aye aye, aye. Just get to the part where you tell us how much we're due and we can get out of here, I thought. Stifling a yawn that I never wanted to come out with. Not then.

Before saying the next piece of translation, the wee boy in the suit kind of just looked at me and Benji. When he gulped before he spoke, I can't speak for Benji like but I knew we were fucked.

'One thousand and five hundred fucking euros, *each?'*

I said, stunned, to an equally trance like Benji as we walked free from the court and out into the blistering heat. I felt numb and couldn't even remember the moments after - being issued with our release paperwork and instructions to pay the fine within twenty eight days - that had taken us to the outside of the court.

It would be accurate to state that neither of us saw *that* coming.

'What the fuck are we going to do, Strings? We didn't even bring that amount for peave and food. We don't *have* one thousand and five hundred euros between us to pay for ONE of our fines, never mind two. What are we going to do, mate?'

He looked like he'd had his stomach ripped right out of him while - on my side - it kind of felt like I'd been subject to some kind of similar disembowelling.

There's always a way out of things, though. Fuck, the life I'd had. If I hadn't sussed that valuable lesson out in life at an early age fuck knows how long I'd have lasted.

'We do what we always do, Benji. We go stringing'

I said, trying to sound confident but also while knowing that this was not a town I'd had the luxury of scouting out first of all, and established where its weak spots were. One thing for sure, though. It wasn't going to be short on puggies. Thank fuck I always carried my 'apparatus' with me. My old faithful stringer sat back at the hotel in my suitcase.

'Now let's try and work out how the fuck we can get ourselves back to Magaluf and pray that the anecdote we're going to have for Jock will be enough to save us from the hairdryer treatment'

Chapter 11

Strings

'That is just a bloody outlandish enough story to be true'

Jock Hunter stood facing us, in the hotel bar, on our eventual return to Magaluf after our slight diversion, via Palma.

'Aye well if you don't believe us you'll probably read about it in next month's science and nature journal'

I said, trying to see the funny side of it but - after that hefty fine that had just been dished out to us - there wasn't much to laugh about that day.

Predictably, the rest of the squad that were sitting there - detoxing from the night they'd had, celebrating the first group game win, and then the torture that followed the next morning with training - did nothing other than laugh like fuck. Sepp saying that he'd heard a couple - in a boozer he was in at one point - talking about how there had been a fire somewhere out at sea on an island.

'Didn't fucking think it would be you two though, for fuck's sake.

'We all thought that you'd went for a drink somewhere and that we'd catch you up later on. But we didn't and then we, obviously, ended up in a blaze ourselves so finding you wasn't exactly top of our priorities,' A barely alive looking Terry said whilst sunk into a bar sofa.

'Well, you've given me a decision to make for tomorrow's game against the Farleys. You've played under me for long enough for me to at least be upfront with you on that, Strings'

Jock's final parting words before he departed the bar lounge, off for his afternoon siesta.

Once he was gone, though. The rest of the lads filled us in on the stuff that we'd missed out on, while otherwise removed from things.

'So, what did we miss?'

I asked as I was bringing back a couple of ales from the bar for me and the Benji boy.

'Well, training for one thing' The Monk replied first of all, clearly resenting the fact that he'd just been put through some more fresh hell - hours before - while I'd missed out on all the fun. Hey, if the cunt had wanted I'd have gladly swapped place with him, if he'd thought that somehow he was the one out of the two of us who had ended up with the shitty end of the stick.

The others that were sat about all kind of looked around at each other - when it came to my question - in the way that suggested that we'd missed out on *something*. Of course we had, that was a given. Those mad bastards weren't going to go out after winning the first game and it *not* ending up as eventful in some way or other.

'Well, what then?' Benji said to them. Noticing - just like I was - that there was definitely something they had to say. 'Spit it out, ya cunts'

Cautiously, Coffee looked around the bar to see who was sitting close by, and if anyone was listening in on us. With it being mid afternoon the place was almost empty, apart from the few lone husbands and fathers, who had left their families outside by the pool while they snuck in a cheeky refreshment in the nice air conditioned - as well as shaded - environment of the hotel bar.

'You're not going to believe this, lads, but last night. Six of us were sitting in The White Horse having an ale when this Russian cunt - along with a couple of boys - came up to us and sat down beside our group. I was literally about to ask what the fuck he thought he was doing. I mean, who the hell does that? Put it another way, if I seen six players from Muirhouse Violet out on the piss, the fucking *last* thing I'd be doing would be walking right up to them and sitting down as if I was *with* them'

'Yet that's exactly what the fucking Farley did,' Rossi said, cutting in.

'Sometimes when someone shows such massive cojones and with a display of audaciousness - like he did - it can knock you off your guard a bit. That was kind of the score with this boy. He'd already taken a chair at our table - big warm smile on his coupon - before any of us had even got the chance to ask 'and who the fuck are you?'

Mr Benn said, giving his version of events before adding. 'Took a few minutes to clock that he had a couple of 'mates' hanging close by while he spoke to us. A Farley's Rusk but, give the boy his due, spoke better English than any of the six of us'

'So what the fuck did the boy want?' I wanted them to get to the point. I'd expected anecdotes from them. Tales of bad behaviour and carnage. Who'd made cunts out of themselves over the night and what it was they'd done to deserve such status awarded to them. And the first one they were giving us was about some man sitting down to join them at their table when they were having a drink.

'So anyway,' Coffee grabbed control again before going on to tell us *why* this stranger had joined them.

'You guys played good today. Ramalde were an excellent side, but even with one man more than you, I guess they were not good enough'

The first thing that he'd apparently said to them all, at least confirming that he'd sat down with them in relation to the game earlier on in the day.

'I thought he was simply some cunt who had seen the game earlier on, clocked us out on the batter later on that night and just wanted to say how good we'd been,' Montana said, in that - at times - naive and from another planet way that he'd often be.

'Yes, that's because half of your waking hours you have some kind of fucking narcotics running through your veins.' Terry - still not exactly mates with Montana by then - said sarcastically before adding 'Any cunt with a semi functioning brain knew that there was more to it and that he was trying to butter us all up'

Montana was about to say something back but decided against it.

'Nah, the fact that the boy was Russian had me a wee bit suss from the off. Ken? With us having a Russian team in our group and that. Plus, if you'd seen this boy, Strings. Hardly looked like a fan boy, or even a tourist just out on their night out. Looked more of a businessman than he did someone out on the piss. And anyway, how many fucking Farleys do you see in Magaluf on their summer holidays?' Rossi chipped in again.

I couldn't help but feel that they were doing a lot of talking but without any fucking substance to it whatsoever.

'Is there an end to this story, aye?' I said irritated although being brutally honest. If I hadn't just received the level of fine that I'd been given hours before I may well have been less susceptible to irritation towards anyone in my line of vision.

'You better fucking believe that there is.' The Monk laughed, the rest of them joining in. Leaving the obvious two in the group sat there like spare pricks.

Through the six players that were all there at the time - and their separate accounts that they were chipping and interrupting each other with - Benji and me were finally brought into the fold when it come to what this Russian was wanting with the boys.

He'd sat there, telling the boys how impressive they'd been against Ramalde, before adding that the same could not be said for his fellow countrymen, FC Zavorovo.

'I didn't even know who the fuck he was talking about, like. Even if it had sounded like I was meant to,' Montana admitted.

Zavorovo was the name of the Russian side in our group. I recognised the name straight away because the first time I'd been told their name it reminded me of that Scottish singer, Lena Zavaroni. You know how the human mind works and that, eh? Couldn't tell you a song she'd ever sung to save my life, but her name had always stuck.

Picking up on the context of what the Farley had said to the rest of them, it literally had me thinking of what the score had been in the game after ours for the first time since we'd got on the ales the day before, but from what I was hearing, it didn't sound like things had gone too well for the team that we had next up in the group. It had been assumed that they would win - at a canter - but now sounding like that outcome hadn't come to pass.

Apparently, the boy had then entered into some small talk over how Muirhouse and the Farleys were playing each other next and how bad a spot it would leave Zavorovo, if they were to lose against the Violet. The Russians and Estonians playing out a one all draw in their opener. The boy wasn't wrong, though. Lose to us in game two and it was more than likely going to leave them having to beat the Portuguese to go through. We, on the other hand, would be through to the quarter finals - with one game to spare - *if* we were to get a result against them.

'Fucking kid you not, Strings. While he's talking about the state of our group - and Zavorovo's prospects of getting out of it - he pulls out this wad of dough, enough to choke the obligatory, like. The boy himself, coolness personified and fuck all like what you should be when you pull a move off like that,' Terry said, massive fucking smile but looking like he barely believed what he was telling us.

'Takes this fucking king's ransom and placed it right down on the table in front of us. It was only then that I think any of us clocked what this was all about, and why this random Farley had been so interested in talking about a group in a beer company fitba tournament that pretty much the only cunts that knew about it even taking place were those involved in it'

Coffee said, having once again had a wee look around to see who was clocking anything before continuing.

'As calm as fuck, this boy just looks around the six of us - who were all looking at the money instead of him - and says to us that we can consider that a token of goodwill on behalf of the businessman that he represented. It was all done in such a suggestive, but as less incriminating as possible, way'

'Cunt then just stands up as confident as you like and wishes us a good rest of the night while telling us that if we were to make sure that we 'took it easy' against the Farleys when we met each other he'd be back to see us and that what he'd left on the table we'd find was just a drop in the ocean'

The Monk retelling a wee bit of it from under the nose of the next man. Like I said, we got the story from all directions.

'What did the cunt look like?' I asked.

'How much did he leave on the table?' What was on Benji's mind.

Smart casual. Gucci loafers, dress trousers and a polo shirt. What had looked like Russian military tats on his arms, neck that was thicker than Mike Tyson's, a crew cut and a nice wee scar under his eye.

Sounded a splendid fellow.

Three thousand euros, the answer to Benji's.

It wasn't hard to find the irony in while we were sitting in a police cell waiting on a court appearance that was going to result in a collective fine of three thousand euros, some of our squad were visited by a stranger and literally *given* that exact same amount of money. They're definitely right when they say that the world works in mysterious ways.

At that point, neither me or Benji even knew what had then happened to the money - after the Russian departed - but, even if the boys were still in possession of it, Benji and me had known this group long enough to know that appealing to their sense of good nature, and for them to help us out with our fine money, would've been an exercise in wasting time and energy in addition the insulting of intelligence.

'So, what did you do with the money?' I asked, whether I was going to get my hands on any of it or not, I at least wanted to know the position on where the dough was.

'I've got it in the safety deposit box up in my room,' Sepp affirmed with a wee wink.

Now that they had shared all of this with Benji and me. Inevitably, I wanted to know their thoughts on things. It would've been the saddest day going, the day Muirhouse. Violet were paid off to lose a game of fitba. Going into ninety minutes intending to lose was simply something that was not part of our DNA. You know how money can change things, and people, though? I mean, I barely knew too much of the situation but - given what had happened to me away from the team over the past few hours - even *I* had a devil and angel on your shoulders scenario. The angel clearly disgusted at the mere thought of us letting the Farleys beat us in the second game while the devil on the other shoulder was going 'hang on, Strings, mate, hear me out. You're in the shit - financially - with the Spanish authorities and, for whatever reason, you've got some business man who is willing to pay a pretty price to make sure you lose your match.'

'So now that you've told me this, *what* is it that you're telling me now?'

I wanted their thoughts on what came next. In a horrible way, personally. Whatever their thoughts on the way forward was going to be. I would be on board with. Fucking hated myself that I wasn't sitting in the position of taking the moral high ground of there being no other answer to the question other than 'fuck the Farleys and fuck their money'

This, being the fucking Muirhouse Violet boys, I don't know why I'd even questioned how they were feeling about things.

'Well the way I see it, if some cunt is daft enough to lay down three thousand euros on a table, in front of a group of people he's never met before and not agree terms on anything before walking away. Who were we to stop him, eh?'

Big Tel said with a mock innocent face, a few others all agreeing theatrically.

'Obviously the boy can fucking bolt though if he thinks that we're going to let this Zavorovo beat us tomorrow night'

The Monk said, looking around everyone to make sure their was no wavering from anyone on the subject.

'We're not a team that you can buy but we're definitely one that if you're fucking stupid enough to leave three grand in their possession then you're not going to be seeing it again, eh?'

'I take it Hunter doesn't know about this?' I asked which was kind of obvious really but needed to know all the same.

Terry laughed, 'Well, that was the thing. Once the Farley left us and we got talking about what had just happened. Obviously we weren't going to take the cunt up on his offer, we knew we had two choices. Choice number one being that we take the money he'd given us and split it between the squad, help make our money go further when we're out here and how it would be only right that the whole team got a wee share of it. Not exactly a life changing sum when evenly split but would still pay for a couple of nights out for us all. Choice number two was that we tell Jock about this illicit offer made to his players which leads to him doing something fucking moronic - but in his mind more of a noble act - like handing the money over to the police and reporting the incident to the tournament organisers.

'And obviously, choice number one was what you ...' I tried to say before three or four of the players all at once replied with an

'Obviously!'

I was ashamed of myself that - due to my own sudden desperation - without even being sure of how much I'd personally pocket out of things, I hadn't been against us taking a dive in the match. Considering all that I'd put into being a Muirhouse Violet player the thought of me wishing us to lose a match was the kind of thing that would bring an instant *syntax error* in my head. It was more a case of me still reeling from my earlier court appearance than any real desire on my part to throw a game of fitba.

By fuck, was I proud of the rest of the boys, though. Showing that pure Muirhouse spirit of taking thousands of pounds from some cunt - as some pretext towards a bigger pay day afterwards - in relation to a spot of match fixing, but with absolutely ride all intention in following through with any of what was now possibly being expected by this supposed businessman with - clearly - a vested interest in the outcome of an amateur fitba tournament.

'Aye, if these fucking Farleys think that we're turning up tomorrow to have our erses felt by them then they're going to be in for a surprise,' Montana said to mass agreement from the others.

I highly doubted that I was going to be involved in the match anyway, so was going to be as powerless to affect things out on the pitch as the mystery businessman who was about to find out that he'd thrown thousands of euros down the drain.

That part, though, was something that was niggling at me. From what the lads had said. Some hard as fuck - but passive aggressively nice - looking lump appears out of the blue and hands them all of that money, leaving them without having even coming close to pressing any of them for their agreed compliance in what he was asking them to do. Instead, just ups and leaves with the suggestion of what he *wants* them to do.

People generally aren't as naively stupid as to go about doing something like that. Acts such as this are normally carried out by someone with an extremely large amount of arrogance, confidence and expectation.

How was this businessman - or his representative - going to react when this Scottish team ended up not playing ball, as they were expecting, though?

My guess was that they probably wouldn't be too chuffed, like.

Chapter 12

Strings

Predictably, I was benched for the match against Zavorovo. Jock taking me to the side back at the hotel - before he officially announced the team - to take me through his decision. Which, while disappointing to hear what I'd felt was going to be the inevitable, I'd appreciated the gesture from him.

'Look, son. It was you that put yourself out of the side, not me. You know that you'd be in the starting eleven but I can't have the rest of the squad thinking that I play favourites. How's it going to look to everyone if you spend a night in the cells and roll up, hours after everyone has already been put through their training which, after the night they had, I assure you none of them enjoyed, and you *still* make the starting eleven? So I'm putting you on the bench, Brady's coming in for you and you're wise enough to know the score, there. If he doesn't give me a reason for you going back in the team against the Estonians then he'll keep his place'

It was gutting to receive the confirmation from the gaffer, even if I'd already prepared myself for the very real possibility of it happening.

I was pleased for Brady, in a hope he has a stinking performance or gets himself sent off - to get me back in the side - kind of way.

Earlier on in the day Ramalde had beaten - the impossible to pronounce - Hiiu Club Sporting, two nil and, technically, were sitting top of the group, at least until us and the Farleys played each other. Due to the flying start we'd had in game one, we already knew that if we won this next one we were through and - while still having one last group game left - in doing so would've afforded the boys a wee bit of an extended drinking time before the business end of the tournament began and when we reached the quarters. Who was really going to give a flying fuck about the Estonians - and that final match - if we were already into the hat?

This person who had been so desperate for the Farleys to beat us that he'd throw thousands of euros at it? Desperate must've been the word for it because it wasn't like this team from Russia were a bunch of mugs. Something we found, when we came face to face with them.

While the Portuguese looked like they would try and ride your wife the minute that your back was turned. The Farleys looked like a bunch of Ivan fucking Dragos. Proper cyborgs, like. When I took a look around their squad there was a wee part of me that was *glad* that I'd been dropped for the match because it looked like it was going to be a bruising encounter.

These boys - carrying the reputation they apparently held as far as the tournament's history went - were, following the embarrassment at not beating the Estonians, surely going to react like wounded animals. Where - as far as their opponents went - they'd be facing *general* animals.

The main part of Jock's team talk before the match focusing on how he anticipated proceedings to be more of an industrious affair. Reminding us that we wrote the fucking book on getting through matches that were more physical than they were skilful.

'Just try to bloody keep it within the laws of the game. We're not going to keep winning matches if we can't keep eleven players on the pitch'

The banned and dressed in his going out clothes Terry doing as much as he could to look down at his trainers during that part.

With us enjoying the luxury of playing our second match at half seven at night, and the temperature being distinctively cooler than the first match, Jock instructed us to revert back to usual Muirhouse rules and just 'go for their throats from the off.'

Giving the players their credit, they carried out the instructions to the letter of the law, short of causing any actual physical harm to any of the Zavorovo players' throats. Two nil up after ten minutes. A beautiful one two between Montana and Rossi, sending Rossi in on the keeper who - with a delightful wee dink over him as he dived at Rossi's feet - put us one up. This causing a wee bit of an argument between two of their midfielders, the pair of them having to be held apart by their own team mates while - laughably - their strikers waited - with hands on hips - on kicking off. Needing their team mates to *stop* kicking off before they did.

Seeing this going on, the team smelled blood. As soon as they got the ball back - following the restart - they immediately took the game back to the Farleys, resulting in a second a few minutes after Rossi's. This one a wee bit less easy on the eye than the first had been but hey, a goal's a goal. As long as the ball crosses that white line then who really gives a fuck how it did?

The Monk, bringing the ball out from defence sprayed it across to Daz who - with back to his marker - kind of flicked it past the Russian with a very tidy wee pivot, leaving his marker in no mans land. Daz sprinting down the wing before sticking in a lethal cross. Montana ghosting in between two of the Zavorovo players with the intention of knocking it into the net with his head. Montana - despite his excellent movement as the cross was being delivered - completely mistiming his jump though and instead of the ball hitting his napper, it kind of hit his chest, but was enough for the ball to find its way into the net regardless.

The Farleys, obviously knowing they were deep in the shit at two goals down so early in the match, were all appealing for handball but they were fucking at it. There was nothing wrong with the goal, and the officials agreed.

The scenes on the pitch between the players were matched every bit as enthusiastically by all of us on the bench. The game had just started and we already had one foot in the quarter finals.

'If this boy who was lobbing thousands at us to lose the match was wondering how it was going to pan out tonight, he's probably got his answer by now'

I whispered to Terry, while Jock was out on the touch line, barking orders for the team to keep the head - as well as their shape - and not slacken off.

'Aye, if that's a team who have went out to earn themselves some extra pocket money for themselves by getting beaten then they've got a pretty funny way of showing it'

'KEEP THE BLOODY HEADS, NOW. NO SWITCHING OFF'

Hunter stood there tapping the side of his head to the few players who were even bothering to look in his direction.

Muirhouse Violet, as it was to turn out, *did* switch off. Barely managed another attack for the rest of the first half as the Farleys threatened to overrun them. Sepp coming to the rescue with three genuine world class saves to keep the score at two nil by the time the referee was blowing the whistle for half time.

It was maybe different because I wasn't out there on the pitch but this Zavorovo looked to have been the complete opposite of the Portuguese team. Practically no shithousing from them whatsoever. Just a proper fitba team, whose only interest was to try and win the game through their skills mixed with their clear athleticism that they possessed. If we looked like we'd came right out of the pub then that mob looked like they'd come freshly out of some processing plant, following their completion. Apart from that first ten minutes, it had been like we'd been playing eleven robots, that looked like they could run all day.

'Back to fucking basics out there, now. We get back to that then we automatically make things harder for them. Scoring those two quick goals like we did was the worst thing we could've done if that's the way you then react'

Hunter, taking his usual centre spot, pacing around while he spoke, tried to prepare the team for going back out. Despite it being a night game, it was still warm enough to feel it - if you were out there running around - and the players all sat there guzzling from water bottles as Jock bellowed out the instructions.

I know it makes me sound like a right cunt but - while obviously happy that we were two up - I hadn't exactly been too upset at Brady having a bit of a mare in the middle of the park. Getting bullied by the Farleys in his area of the pitch and wasteful when in possession. Hearing Hunter calling him for everything any time he made a mistake? Absolute music to my ears.

As had been the case at the start of the first half, we took the game their way. Forcing a couple of corners that came to nothing and a shot from Montana that caused more danger to the grass it skimmed along than it did to the Zavorovo keeper who had all the time in the world to scoop the ball up.

Soon after, the Farleys took control again. And the for the most part for the rest of the game, not let go.

Following Brady giving away the ball - while we were under intense pressure - too many times, Hunter decided to send me on with half an hour left. Putting me out to warm up five minutes before but without it being a will he won't he scenario.

'Get yourself ready for going on, Strings. I need you to bring a bit of composure out there. Someone that can put their foot on the ball and make the right passes'

'Then I'm your man, eh?' I said as I leapt out of the dugout and went for a wee jog down the side of the pitch, doing my exercises as I went.

'Well played, Brady pal,' I said as he left the pitch but you could see it written all over his coupon that he knew he'd not had a good game. With Jock and his man management skills, it was assumed that he'd have been telling Brady about how he'd had to wait on his chance coming around and now it was here, and how it would now be down to him to keep his place. Going by Brady's body language - walking off the pitch - he already looked like he knew he wouldn't be in the starting eleven for the third group game, and the second one wasn't even over yet.

I was only on the pitch two minutes when their hulk of a number six welcomed me to the game by putting me about six feet in the air, getting the fucking ball before doing so which left me lying around in agony - worrying that I might have to go off - and we never even got a free kick for it. Pat ran out with his Ralgex and his magic sponge and used both for effect before leaving me back up on my feet and hoping I could get through the next couple of minutes and shake off the pain I was going through in my left leg.

Instructing the rest of the midfield to play around me for a moment which gave me the chance to start to run things off. Once I had, I managed to make a stamp on the match. Ensuring that we kept the ball for longer and winning it back when we'd lost it, but - by then - I was only one player. The majority had played the whole of the match and while it wasn't in the same kind of heat as the previous game, it was - ironically, probably due to the cooler temperature - a much more high tempo match, which would've sapped the energy somewhat.

Meanwhile, the Farleys looked like they were going to be able to run all night, and had the bit between their teeth when it came to trying to squeeze us enough to result in us conceding.

They were getting closer and closer with each attack they made. Hitting the woodwork twice and Sepp - like the first half - pulling off a couple of worldies. The second one, with the ball looking like it had already passed him, where he stuck his arm *behind* his diving body to palm the ball out for a corner, a save where he had the Farley shaking his head in disbelief while wryly smiling as he shook Sepp's hand, after helping him to his feet.

You knew it was coming though, it was just a matter of *when*. The goal coming from the most route one approach you could possibly get. One of their defenders booting it up the pitch towards our box. The Monk jumping to head it but the ball skiffing off the side of his napper and falling right at the feet of the grateful Zavorovo who ran on and tucked it away before Sepp could even get a chance to react.

Following the goal - for the first time in the match - there was some static between both teams. The age old argument where the team scoring wants to retrieve the ball in an attempt to get it placed on the centre circle spot so that the game can be restarted within a window of time that they prefer. I've never seen the reason for this kind of commotion in a game of fitba. All the fights, arguments and cards that get dished out just over that one scenario. Let the cunts place the ball on the spot if it makes them happy, you can *still* take as long as you want before you actually take centre, for fuck's sake. Plus it winds them up even *more*, which is another bonus on top.

Anyway, we had that same scenario going on. With the ball beating Sepp. Wullie was the first player to make it to collect it. Holding onto it like a mother with her baby while the Farleys desperately clawed at him to prise it away from him. A couple of Muirhouse players then entering the goal, pushing and shoving the Zavorovo players. The ref - obviously a shitebag - doing fuck all other than repeatedly whistling at everyone, without actually daring to come near any of them. The afters finally being brought to an end when Wullie had had enough of the frantic attempts to get the ball from him.

'Want the ball, aye? Well here you fucking GO'

He said as he took the ball and booted it as far from the park as he could. He was probably going to take a yellow for that but the Farleys all turning around to the referee in protest sealed the deal. Sometimes a yellow card can be classed as a good one. Just for wind up purposes - as well as being funny as fuck to stand and witness - I was prepared to put Wullie's into that category.

Still, though. With them scoring - and with a good twenty minutes left - it had definitely put the feline in with the flying rats.

They were going to be relentless for the rest of the match, fuck all surer. While us? We were on our erses. The combination of drink, train, play, drink repeat now looking like it had caught up with the lads. I'd only played ten minutes or so and was feeling it so fuck knows the hell that the others were going through.

For a brief moment I thought to myself - with Zavorovo clearly in the ascendancy - what would happen if we were to end up running out of steam and losing the game and whether we would end up getting all of the rest of the money that had been promised if we didn't win. Unlikely, considering there had been absolutely zero sign the whole game that we had been a team trying to engineer anything out of the match other than a win for ourselves. Like I said, though. It really was just a brief moment before I reminded myself that we weren't going to fucking *lose* the match, and that if we could just keep hanging on we were going to be walking off the pitch as quarter finalists.

The more minutes that ticked away the further the Farleys became desperate, which in turn made them that wee bit less dangerous although if they had the ball near our goal - which they did a *lot* - then they were always going to be a danger.

Just like the end of the Ramalde match, we'd pretty much resorted to having every man behind the ball. The only plan being to make life as difficult for the other team to get past us, rather than having any aspirations of getting in behind them.

Yet - almost as if they had an extra couple of players - they were still getting the better of us, whether it was down the left, right, through our middle or over the top.

I'll be honest, as we moved into the five minutes of injury time - Wullie's fucking about with the ball coming back haunt us there - when I saw their boy out wide on the right deliver the cross right onto the nut of their big blonde number nine and the ball hitting the net, my erse collapsed. On the balance of play you'd have to have been extremely biased to have suggested that the Farleys hadn't deserved it. If you'd claimed that they'd done enough to *win* the match you would hardly have been laughed out of town, either. We'd scored two goals at the start of the match and then done basically fuck all else from that point. They deserved the equaliser, even if it was extremely galling to arrive at the time it did.

Only, with our heads down, - knowing that it was probably the last bit of action the game was going to see - while the Farleys celebrated wildly. A couple of us noticed that while the referee had indeed blown his whistle, it wasn't for a goal.

Standing there making a pushing motion to indicate that their big man had committed a foul on The Monk in the build up to the goal. It was one of those decisions that a ref comes away with that makes no sense at all, to anyone. When a team isn't protesting for a decision, but the referee gives them one anyway, that's generally when you know that there wasn't a decision to give in the first place.

You could say 'those wacky foreign referees, eh?' but in reality, we all know that the Scottish ones are every bit as fucking radge and incompetent as their European counterparts.

Plus, if The Monk had been fouled before the goal there was not a single chance that the boy wouldn't have had something to say about it. Chances are he'd have been fucking chasing the ref around the pitch, had the goal been given, following him being fouled. That he hadn't said a single word was all I needed to know on the subject.

While you can't have blamed them. The Farleys - once they realised the goal had been ruled out - went a bit over the score. Laying hands on the referee as they surrounded him. The linesman nearest to him coming running onto the pitch to try and give him a bit of back up and quickly wishing he hadn't. As if those two Mr Bean looking cunts were ever going to be able to handle those cyborg CSKA Moscow ultras looking beasts screaming abuse at them if it came to anything of a more physical nature.

By the time the moment passed, the Farleys were missing three players, all sent off. The referee then choosing *not* to add the further minutes that had been taken from the game with all of the arguing and simply letting Sepp take our free kick. The moment the ball left his foot the ref then blowing the full time whistle. The match official - doing away with normal tradition - sensing what may be about to come, turning on his toes and running from the pitch, with a couple of the Zavorovo players in hot pursuit. One of their subs, taking a wild kick out at him as he was sprinting past, - fortunately for the ref - missing him by inches.

The Farleys that were left on the pitch, though? As classy as the Portuguese players hadn't been. Aye, obviously they were gutted at losing - especially when it had looked like they'd snatched a draw at the death - but were still men enough to stand there and shake hands with all of us.

We'd been completely outplayed by them but somehow had managed to edge it and were now officially through to the knockout stages. A feat that Jock Hunter took extreme pride in reminding us that was something that our national team had never managed to achieve in their puff.

The chatter back in the dressing room being not on our likely opponent in the quarter finals but where we were going first for a drink, because if the team had celebrated the win against the Portuguese like they'd won the Champions League, then actually *qualifying* for the quarter finals would merit something even further on from that still.

Jock's warning that we still had one group game left and how we needed to finish top to ensure that we played one of the second placed teams from one of the other groups, listened to by the squad and then entirely ignored as plans began being hatched for the night ahead.

Ironically, considering who we had just beaten. The bill for the night of excess and exuberance we were going to go on to enjoy, would all paid for by the mysterious benefactor with his Russian bag man.

Sometimes, things just write themselves, eh?

Chapter 13

Sepp

There are walks of shame, and then there's *walks of shame*. Fucking muggins, here, he chose the latter. I suppose 'chose' wouldn't have been the entirely correct word to use, because no one - and I repeat *no one* - would've chosen the scenario that I was part of. The morning after, trying to make my way back to the hotel.

Like a lot of times in life, - before the fall comes - things had been going well. More fucking well than I'd been able to remember in years, too. I don't know? Maybe that should've been the red flag for me right there, but was just having too good a time to realise it.

Once we left the pitch, having seen off the Russkies, we couldn't get ourself into the centre of Magaluf quick enough. After a rapid change back at the hotel - and into the old dancing shoes - it was time for our new team ritual, before we left for our night out.

On the first day, Wullie had bought this baseball cap from a tourist shop that had a hard plastic half pint balanced on either side with two connecting tubes that merged into one. This single tube going into your mouth. The cap, itself, had 'Foam Dome' written on the front of it. A truly horrific hat - fashion wise - but one that had its uses, and you had to give it that. The prime one being that we would fill up each half pint and every one of us would down them, via the conduit of the tube. Passing the hat from player to player as we all chanted while we watched our fellow team mate suck those half pints dry. The first time Montana - who would be the first to admit that out of the rest of us, he was the one who wasn't as much of a drinker. *Drugs?* A completely different thing, though - stuck that hat on and, cheered on by us all in the you better not fucking stop, ya cunt, kind of way, managed to take both half pints before promptly turning to the side and - weirdly - looking like he'd immediately brought it up, only for it to look about ninety nine percent foam. Fucking foam dome, alright.

Anyway, with the hat being passed around and 'muchos' San Miguel used up in the process, we were ready to hit the strip. What a fucking feeling, as well. Heading out with something actually meaningful to celebrate over, instead of the simple fact that we were in Magaluf, loved a swally, and there were a shit load of places that could accommodate such patrons.

I hadn't the first clue what to expect when we flew out to Spain to kick a ball around. Didn't know if we'd get there and find out that we were way short of the expected standard. But there we there, already through with a game to spare, and what a fucking buzz it was for the lads. Kind of gave you a wee bit of pride that you just never quite came close to, on domestic duties. Aye, there was definitely that wee feeling of representing the country you came from that was undeniable.

There was no road map before the tournament began which could help you plan your way through it. Even if there had been one, it wasn't like you knew anything about the teams in the other groups anyway. Because of this, we weren't giving a fuck if we finished first or second. We were the fucking Violet and would take on whoever they wanted to send our way in the quarter finals.

The night couldn't have began any more different, compared to how it then progressed from there on in. Terry - in what was an excellent wee bit of advance planning - had taken it upon himself to book the whole squad a table at that fancy looking restaurant. The one with the massive, but expensive, steaks that we'd passed every night which - while never looking like it could sit all of us in any case - was one felt - by many in the squad - that its prices sat on the high side, and not one for suiting many people's budgets for over there. For this meal, and the peave for the rest of the night we'd be knocking back, though. *This* would be all courtesy of the radgey who'd dropped three bags right into our laps.

It was a meal of champions and - that night - that was *exactly* what we felt like. On a personal level, I'd played a fucking blinder against the Russians. You can always tell you're playing well by the reactions of your team mates, and some of the saves I'd pulled off, they were rushing to congratulate me as if I'd scored a goal up the other end. Aye, that's when you know, like. To double down on that, though, and actually have one of the Commies coming up to shake my hand, *because* I'd saved his shot? Not normally the kind of on pitch behaviour you'd find from an opposition player back in Edinburgh, I can assure you of that.

To be fair, mind. That followed what could well have been the best save I'd ever pulled off in my career. It almost defied logic. The ball was past me, and when you find that the case, generally there's absolutely fuck all you can do. Somehow, though. I've managed to still get a hand on it to divert it wide. Obviously, there was an element of luck about it. You can't exactly cut about saying that you meant to save a shot when the ball is behind you and you can no longer see where the fuck it is. You make your own luck in our game, though. I'd acted with the speed and instinct of a cat, and however the fuck I'd managed it, I'd kept it out.

I know that things were overshadowed by them getting that goal chalked off in injury time but as far as I was concerned.

That save was the moment that clinched us the win. Not that I'm one for tooting my own trumpet, mind. Who knows, though. With that save coming and still a wee bit of time to go there's no guarantee that we'd have even *drawn* the match, which would've left us in a wee bit of a sticky position going into the last game.

Aye, best just get the business done in the first couple of matches and relieve yourself of all of that stress about last group games, and all the permutations that you can end up going over when it comes to potential outcomes for the teams involved.

The fucking meal was the absolute fucking berries, though. Probably one of the only times in life where we were all able to sit and look at a restaurant menu and not give a flying fuck what you chose, knowing we weren't paying for it anyway. The cover story - as far as Jock Hunter was concerned who was out with us for a meal, before heading back to the hotel for a night's kip - we'd fed our coach was that since this was a team celebration in relation to Muirhouse qualifying for the knockout stages of the tournament, as a show of respect towards our manager, we had decided that dinner was on the team.

Bless, the old bastard. He was well chuffed by the gesture. If only he'd have known the reality of things, eh?

'Aye, just you pick whatever you want, Jock. It's all on the boys. No way would we be sitting here - six points out of six - in European competition without you behind us. We just want to say a wee thank you and let you know that none of what you do for the team, from the sidelines, ever goes unnoticed'

Terry said. You could've almost called it a warm and touching moment, had you not already known that he was gaslighting the fuck out of Hunter to cover up for the fact that we'd been 'gifted' an amount of money that was directly related to an attempted bribe of his players.

What someone doesn't know, though. As they say.

Soon as we polished off our desserts - oh aye, none of this one course pish for us that night. Starter, main *and* a dessert. You know you're in a posh establishment when their profiteroles are shoved full of vanilla ice cream instead of the usual squirty cream - it was a case of let's fucking *gooooooo*. Despite treating him to the best meal that he'd probably had in his puff, Jock was left with no choice but to issue us with the - by now - standard warning about us not going too far over the score, and how anyone who missed training would be out of the team.

'He's not fucking joking either.' Strings - who'd had a few glasses of wine over the meal shouted out a little loud for the rest of the restaurants particular liking. His use of industrial strength language drawing either looks of daggers or audible tuts from those sitting eating around us. Strings either not caring or didn't notice.

I don't think any of us *cared* for Jock's warning before departing for the night either.

Coffee's rebellious musings - after Jock was away and we were squaring up the bill - that 'what if *none* of us were to turn up for training?' and what the fuck would the gaffer do then, an interesting theory that was worth looking further into, as far as I was thinking. The longer the holiday and tournament dragged on for, the more chance that we might be brought to that stage. Because it wasn't like this group of footballers were going to suddenly get *fresher* as the two weeks elapsed. Only progressively more and more rough.

Having mistimed things, we were in the process of trying to pay for the bill while at the same time had a round of drinks arrive. Agreeing to tan them as quickly as possible so that we could get out onto the strip and make a mischief of ourselves.

When the drinks were put down on the table - out of the blue - Strings stood up and started doing that banging on a glass with a knife thing that you see cunts doing when they want control of the room, so they can speak. It was hardly immediate - and was never going to be with the assortment of boys sitting at this long table - but once the silence arrived he then launched into a mini speech.

'Now, while we've got these drinks in front of us, I just wanted to raise a toast to that man over there'

- motioning his glass in the direction of me, everyone else's heads turning my way -

'If it hadn't been for some of the world class saves the boy pulled off tonight we wouldn't be here tonight as fucking quarter finalists'

This bringing a loud cheer from everyone with added bangs on the table with fists before they all grabbed their glasses and joined Strings in standing up and - to a man - all raised their glass and shouted 'TO SEPP' before taking a drink.

'Awwww fuck off with your birthday card pish'

All I could say, a wee bit embarrassed by the attention this moment brought.

I think it had probably been one profane word too many - accumulated over the course of the whole meal - but shortly after Strings standing up to give his speech, we were asked if we wouldn't mind leaving. Something we did, respectfully, without any causing of a scene.

There was no need to ban us. Barring any phenomenal amounts of money dropping unexpectedly into our laps, we wouldn't fucking be able to afford to come back anyway. After we'd departed 'Los Caracole' we started at the top of the hill of the strip and worked our way down. Getting progressively MWI as the hours passed. No fucking joke, halfway down the hill. We were sat in the - can't remember the name of it now - boozer and this cunt walks in with a chimpanzee hanging onto him. I knew I'd had a few by then but even so, couldn't help questioning if I was seeing things.

I soon realised that this was the boy's hustle. Take an obscure animal out with him round all the bars and get cunts to pay him for a photo with it. You had to admire the optimism of someone going with that kind of a gig, when practically every single person in the room had a camera in their pockets, now called phones. Can imagine he must've coined it in back in the day, before technology came along and fucked things for him.

I actually felt a bit sorry so - despite having the chance to just have one of the boys take my picture when I was holding the chimp - made sure I put some money his way. Obviously, there was no chance that he was walking into that boozer, finding us all in there half pished, and not being called over. He probably wished he'd just swerved the whole thing. His chimpanzee *definitely* wishing that he'd done so.

The chimp - inevitably - being everyone's focus of attention and I think, after a while, it got pretty pissed off with all the touching, stroking and being passed from pillar to post, as you would do. As things tended to transpire with us - if allowed enough time - matters all went a bit tits up in the end.

We'd all had a go at being passed it where it would wrap its arm around you - it was fucking reeking by the way - giving you a cuddle or would just sit there like you had your kid on your lap. Things going wrong by the time that it had been passed to Montana.

The chimp sitting on his lap and making a cheeky wee grab for Montana's Vodka and Red Bull.

'Awwww, you wanting a wee swally, pal?' Are you the same chimp that was pals with Edmundo, aye?'

Montana asked while he reached over to pick up his glass, bringing it up towards the chimp's mouth. Even then, I not even for a second believed that Montana was actually going to feed the chimpanzee his drink. You could tell that he was just messing about. Well, that's the way I took it, and I'd known the boy for a while.

The Spanish owner of the chimp, however, had never seen Montana before in his puff and had no clue what the boy was or wasn't capable of doing. Because of this he went fucking tonto at the sight of the glass of alcohol going anywhere near his pet's mouth.

'NADA NADA NADA'

He yelled at Montana while making an attempt at getting the chimp back again, although - inadvertently ended up with a few Muirhouse lads between him and the chimp so it wasn't as easy as just reaching over and collecting it back from Montana.

Well, you know how they say that pets can sometime feed off how the adults are behaving? This must've applied here because - what had been an otherwise well behaved, if a little cheeky, ape - following the Spaniard losing his shit at Montana. This - in turn - provoked a reaction from the chimpanzee.

The fucking thing was screaming its head off, you know when they do that thing were you can see just what a heavy load of teeth they're packing? Montana was fucking bricking it and didn't quite know what to do. His problems eased a little - a lot - by the fact that it then jumped right off his lap and was now without any supervision at all. Now we had a problem.

The chimp, resembling one of those parkour gadgeys as it jumped from table to bar before making a leap for an overhead wooden fan. Screaming its fucking head off as it went round and round before dropping to the floor.

The guy with the chimp looked like he didn't know what to do first. Continue to berate Montana, or catch his - now on the loose - ape. For the general safety of everyone in the heaving bar, he chose to run after his hairy pal.

Fuck knows what history man and chimp had. For all we could've known, it had been just waiting on this day coming along, so it could be free of being taken around the pubs and clubs of Magaluf every single night of its life. Can't think of anything worse than being consistently taken round an environment like that, and not having a drink.

Whether it was one of those domesticated pets that were serf like enough to be happy with the captivity that was their life or not, it wasn't for going back to its owner. Eventually slipping out the front door just as a couple came through it. The chimp running past them and brushing against the woman's leg - once she saw what had just rushed past her - causing her to let out a shriek. Honestly couldn't class it as a scream, like.

'Thank you, you fucks'

The parting words from the chimp boy as he looked over our way before running out of the bar, chasing after his mate who was now experiencing the true meaning of 'the wild.' The Magaluf strip.

'What the fuck's the boy expecting, eh? Take something like that around boozers where there's obviously going to be pissed up cunts like us? Fucking recipe for disaster, that'

A clearly on the defensive Montana the first to say anything about what had just happened. The rest simply thinking that the episode had been nothing other than funny as fuck. And that thankfully none of us were needing any trips to hospital to treat any bites.

'Imagine the scenes right now - outside - with it running about the strip. Jumping into KFC for some food and then across the road to that Bambino's for an ice cream?'

Rossi, laughed.

Apart for anyone outside on the street that were to find themselves in the line of vision of this radge as fuck ape bolting towards them, it was hard not to laugh at the thought of the carnage it was going to cause - until caught - in such a busy part of town.

After that, it was time to hit the club. We'd already agreed that we would go back to that club 'Fuego,' which we'd landed in the night we'd been celebrating the win against Ramalde.

'You'll love this place, Strings' I stood telling the man who had missed out on our previous visit due to being locked up.

'Barry tunes and cheap drink, what more could you want, eh?'

This working out to be a complete waste of time because - over the course of the night's drinking - the bouncers had decided that some of our group were not getting in because of being too drunk. In terms of how MWI you are, when you're at a level where a Magaluf doorman says that you're too mortal to gain entry. *That's* an indicator that you've been having a pretty fucking good go at things.

Through our leave no man behind group mentality, the door staff of Fuego were told to ram their club right up them as we decided to try one of the other clubs available to us. Eventually we landed up in what was probably the town's most upmarket and expensive of places - BCM - but the main thing had been was that the bouncers had no problems with the various states that we were all in as we rocked up those stairs to enter for the night.

The place looked well impressive and - as far as nightclubs go - was fucking massive. Bigger than anything I'd ever been to back home. Wasn't too much into that rave music that was being played and neither was I a fan of the price of drinks, considering everywhere else we'd ever been to were almost fucking paying *you* to drink their booze, so cheap it was. Still, that night really wasn't coming out of our own pockets so I wasn't too fussed about the drink prices, more of an observation than anything else.

Regardless of the entry price and how much the drinks were, the place was fucking rammed. We kept ourselves upstairs but looking down onto the dance floor it was the proverbial sardines scenario.

We'd maybe been in there for three or four drinks - just standing around spraffing and having a laugh - when I got the tap on the shoulder. I'd always found in life that taps on your shoulder were never for a good reason. Always some cunt wanting something from you and the fact that it comes from behind you - and you don't know who's tapping you - leaving you at a wee disadvantage before you even get around to finding out *what* they're wanting. This time, though. I was pleasantly surprised by it.

Expecting it to be one of the club security telling me to stop being so animated - or something to that effect - I turned around to find a smartly dressed man - for a Spanish resort nightclub, anyway - in a suit with open necked shirt standing there.

'Would you like to come with me please, sir?'

He shouted into my ear over the thumping beat that was pounding out of the speakers.

Come with him? Who the fuck *was* he, never mind if I was just going to up sticks and go with him? At the very least, when someone asks you a question like that - in a setting such as a night club - they're normally showing you some form of identification.

We were in a good mood, that night, and I'd seen no reason to risk spoiling it by being nippy with the guy so tried to be diplomatic with him.

'What do I need to come with you for, like? We going somewhere?' I asked, a wee bit suss because he had a foreign accent and even though we had the music to contend with, it almost sounded like the accent had been Eastern European, or somewhere like that.

'There's someone who would like to meet you'

His cryptic reply before he took a gentle grip of my arm and manoeuvred and positioned us just enough so that I could see my way into the VIP section of the club. From inside there, a woman was sitting in a booth by herself with a wee smile on her face as - seeing the both of us looking in her direction - she gave, what felt like for me more than him, a wee wave.

'What? *That's* who's wanting to meet me? Her, there?'

I asked, not in a bad way, mind. It was dark and she was sitting a wee bit far away for any high definition assessments of her but even so, she looked tidy. Even from the distance she looked tidy, but quite a bit older than me. No exaggeration when I say that she was possibly *double* my age of thirty one but if not then she was easily twenty years older.

At that moment in time? When there's a beautiful looking women - sitting on her own in the VIP section of a club so, by definition, must be loaded or a celeb - sending one of her minions to get your attention. Well, tell me how you're not going to bite after that?

Made sure all of the boys knew where I was going, before I fucked off, though. Just to rub it in.

'I'll just leave you peasants here while I fuck off over to VIP, eh? Have a good night if I don't see you for the rest of it, eh? Don't wait up for me now'

I gave Strings and Terry a wee wink as I left with the boy in the suit as we walked across to meet the big bouncer - guarding VIP - who, after a few words exchanged, unhooked the velvet rope to let us enter.

As I got closer to the smiling woman - who maybe it was the drink and my deluded sense of worth but had felt like she was undressing me with her eyes - I could see that aye, she was definitely closer to being double my age but still looked good for it. You see birds *my* age round my way that looked older, for context.

'Hello, I'm Anya. I hope you do not think it forward of me but I have been watching you across the room and thought you might like to join me for a drink. Would you like a glass of Champagne?' She nodded towards the bottle of Moët that was sitting on the table in an ice bucket.

'Hello, Anya. I'm Colin but everyone calls me Sepp. Pleased to meet you, I'd love a glass of champagne, thank you very much'

I said back to her as I formally shook her hand, entering charm mode. If I'd thought the boy had been Eastern European then I *knew* that the woman was, both by her accent and then what her name was.

Apart from the fact that she was sitting in the VIP section of a nightclub - with people doing her bidding at the click of a finger - she was obviously someone with money. You could also tell this by what she was wearing. Those high heel shoes with the red soles, garish but ridiculously expensive Versace blouse, Chanel handbag sitting on the table and jewellery that looked like the Royal Family would ask to borrow for some of their elaborate shows of wealth. I knew the next thing to nothing about perfume but she even *smelled* rich.

I have to say, from the moment that I left the lads to go to VIP, they were obsessed with what was going on over there, leaving them unable to think about themselves.

I couldn't help smiling when - prompted by Anya - I reached for the bottle of Moët, topping up her glass first before filling one for myself, knowing that all eyes were jealously fixed on me.

'Why you smile?' She asked, me having had no clue that she'd been watching me in that way.

'Well, it's not every day for me that a beautiful women requests my presence for to sit and enjoy a glass of champagne together,' I responded, like the silver tongued devil that I had in me, for when it was worth bringing out.

The pleased but bashful look from her at this, showing me that I'd hit the spot with the remark. Assessing the situation, she'd been as blatant as to request me to sit with her, so I didn't see this being a one drink and then parting ways kind of deal, if I didn't want it to be.

And what really can I say? Aye, I'd had a decent swally by then so *any* advances from women would not have been dismissed, within reason. *This* was a different level, though. This was fucking sugar mummy stuff. Beauty and the beast, like. Her and all her wealth and me who does a bit of sparky work off and on, cash in hand. Two people from completely different worlds. That was maybe part of the attraction for her, though. These rich types surround themselves with so much of the same people that it has to get boring after a while not being around *real* people with decent patter. There was also the - not to be ruled out - potential aspect of her 'thing' being a *bit of rough* and if that was to be the case - for the night - then I would've been quite happy to play that part.

Not that the patter side of things was much good in that situation with her. Due to the cultural differences of someone from Moscow and another from Muirhouse, my wit would've been lost on her. I couldn't even speak in my normal way, never mind crack the jokes. Instead, having to speak slowly and clearly for her so that she could understand. This in itself prompting her to say just how much she loved my accent and how she found it quite sexy, running her hand up and down the inside of my leg as she said this. Deliberately making sure that her thumb would brush against my cock and balls before sliding back down my leg again.

Oh aye? It's like that, is it, eh? I thought to myself, pleased. It was probably signposted for me by the fact that the woman had spied me out of a crowd of others and 'called for me' but now she was just being outright blatant about it. We sat drinking champagne, flirting and chatting with each other for around an hour. Me making sure to raise a toast towards my ever onlooking friends on the other side of the velvet rope each time my glass was topped up with Moët.

When she'd asked me what it was I did for a living - already assuming that I was never going to see her again after that night - I took the advantage of reinventing myself right there on the spot by telling her that I was a marine biologist, which I immediately regretted having done so just in case she was then going to ask numerous questions on the subject. On her side she said that she did not work but that she did not need to. Obviously - from the wealth that she was displaying - she must've had a whole story that could be told with regards to where the money had come from, but it really wasn't important in any case. Luckily - when I'd told her about my made up position - she showed no interest in finding out more about it.

The only thing - after an hour of the two of us guzzling our way through a large bottle of Moët - that she appeared interested in was *me*, but not in any kind of a deep and meaningful way. Her hands had began wandering much more blatantly than she'd initially sat doing so. During the early part of getting to know each other.

Kind of tipsy and with inhibitions at a low, she had now moved onto rubbing at my cock through my trousers under the table. Purring in my ear at the feel of it growing to her touch.

It's mad how much difference appearances can be, though. Just say I'd been in The Gunner and some old dear in there in leggings and a pair of crocs - sitting with a bottle of Sweetheart Stout on her table - wanted me to join her while she sat fondling my valuable. Simply wouldn't fucking happen. Could *not* happen. Yet switch scenes and have someone just as old but dripping in wealth and class and I was all fucking over it.

'Why don't we leave here and go somewhere where we can be, more alone?

She said, taking this moment to cheekily give - what was now fully hard - my cock a squeeze.

Please don't suggest my place please don't suggest my place please don't suggest my … All I could think of there and then. The room that me and Wullie - after several days of being in it now - shared looked like a tip, and smelled like one to go with.

As it would turn out, I couldn't have fucking dreamed of where the two of us were going to land up. It certainly wasn't the fucking Magaluf Park Hotel, anyway.

Agreeing with her that, yes, we should maybe look at making our departure from BCM. With an excited look on her face crossed with the naughtiest of look in her eyes, she summoned over the man in the suit that had introduced me to her before issuing him with the orders to

'Have the car prepared'

None of this, go and sort out a taxi for us or fuck all but a proper fully in control instruction such as that.

'Yes, Mrs Borovskiy'

He said as if she was the fucking queen of England before shuffling away to carry out his order.

'We get a another bottle of Champagne for taking back with us, yes?'

She asked.

Well, aye. As long as I'm not going to have to fucking pay for it, knock yourself out, I thought as I nodded my head. Calling over one of the club staff and whispering into the girl's ear. A few minutes later she returned with an even bigger bottle than the one that had been sat in the ice bucket that we'd been wiring into over the past hour or so.

Can't help but admit that I felt *the fucking man* - after the suit had come back to tell Anya that the car was ready outside for us - when the two of us walked from the VIP area past all of the Muirhouse boys as I carried that big fuck off bottle of Moët in my hand. Telling them that I would see them at training, even if at that moment I didn't fully believe that to be the case.

When it came to player's positions in the side. Being goalkeeper was something that could be used to one's advantage. Aye, there was Danny Irwin who was already there waiting in the wings but even Jock would've admitted in private that Danny was only there as a back up keeper because *no cunt else* wanted to play in that position. The fact that I not only fancied playing in goals but was actually not bad at it made me about as bombproof as you could possibly get when it came to making the starting line up of the Violet.

At that time, though. I couldn't have cared less about Muirhouse Violet. I was off for my hole with some rich, glamorous and not exactly shy Russian. Life's all about priorities and - right then - that wasn't so much the thing that was sitting top of my list. Other than going back to this woman's gaff and giving her the message, I didn't *have* a list of priorities.

We walked out of the club with arms linked like we were some actual couple.

'I cannot wait to get my hands on you, my Scottish hunk' she whispered in my ear before biting on my lobe as we walked down the stairs of the club towards - which I had already assumed to be her car - the Range Rover with the blacked out windows.

I was right. The boy in the suit, opening the back door for the two of us to get into before closing it behind us. Him then jumping into the passengers seat before the driver - who hadn't moved or said a word on us getting in - drove off.

I hadn't the first idea of where we were going. And with this Range Rover having a sound proof compartment that - at the touch of a button - separated the back from the front seats. I was too busy getting fired into this exotic women to have even bothered trying to notice.

'You and me will have naughty night, yes, Scottish man? She said as she bit on my bottom lip and pulled it away with her before letting go.

I practically *guarantee* it, I thought to myself but stopping short of actually telling her so. When you'd drank as much peave as I'd done over the night, you're better off not making any fucking promises to the women you're going home with. Just in case things fall out of the realms of your control, like.

After a while I - looking through the darkened windows - saw that we were on the motorway. Signs pointing for us heading in the direction of Palma. Something had told me that she was never going to be staying in some package deal hotel, just from her looks alone. I don't know, though? I figured that she probably had some villa up in the hills or something. Didn't figure Palma, though.

And I *definitely* didn't picture that - instead of the villa I'd conjured up in my head - we were heading back to a fucking YACHT. But there we were, driving down onto a marina with us pulling to a stop right beside this vessel that looked like it was bigger than five houses put together.

There was definitely *something* to this women, though. The fact that stood outside on the marina decking outside the yacht was some tasty looking cunt with a walkie talky, whose job looked to be fuck all other than just to stand outside it and keep guard. Once we'd got out of the car and made our way the few steps towards getting onboard. This boy - not Russian, maybe Israeli if I was going to guess but that wasn't really my area of expertise - with the walkie talky kind of bowing his head slightly at Anya as we passed him.

'Mrs Borovskiy'

'Ari'

I issued a friendly 'alright, pal?' While also passing, which drew a wee non committal nod from him before we disappeared onto the boat. Before doing so, she said something in Russian to the boy in the suit from earlier which had him coming over to stand with the one that she'd called Ari.

I'd had no idea just what it was that she'd said to him but with the way she was gripping my hand, and leading me towards the inside of the boat, it looked clear that *she* had plans. For all I know, she was telling everyone outside that she wasn't wanting disturbed for the night.

I think my jaw dropped when I first set eyes on the inside of the yacht. Luxury? I'd never seen the fucking likes, and it wasn't even a *house*. It was like a more tasteful Tony Montana gaff, turned into a yacht. Although I was destined not to see too many of it. When we entered I couldn't help but mention how amazing it looked. She - asking me to open the new bottle of champagne while she went to fetch a bucket and ice - told me of some of the rooms it had, such as a gym and a cinema room.

All I would end up seeing out of it would be - I guess you'd have classed as - the living room, but mainly the bedroom.

Before we reached that point, though. There was something that I'd picked up on a couple of times now and - at the risk of blowing a night of sex, right when it was about to kick off - I felt I had to bring up.

'Anya? A couple of times tonight I've heard someone call you *Mrs*?' I asked while taking a sip of the freshly opened Moët.

'Oh *that*? Please do not trouble with this. Yes, I am married but no. This no problem. My husband and me? We have an, *agreement*'

'Oh, like an open marriage?' I replied, assuming that she would've known what this was. She didn't, which meant I had to then explain it to her.

'No, not really.' Her reply, once knowing what she was replying to. 'I do not love him and he does not love me but it is complicated. It is a society thing. Sometimes, people stay together, but not *for* each other'

'Ok, but there's no way that he's going to come back to the yacht and find you and me here tonight?' The main question I had to meet her with. I was still trying to get my head around having sex with a - fully up front - married women but mainly, I didn't want to have to deal with any drama from her husband. No time for that shite, like. Apart from that, though. I was drunk and I was horny and *that* - for some - can be a dangerous cocktail.

'No, no. He is elsewhere,' she assured me as she slid up closer on the sofa in the living room before - after a glass of the new champagne - suggesting that we go through to the bedroom.

By the time we'd moved from the darkness of the club to the darkness of the car to the eventual brightness of the inside of the yacht, I'd been able to see that I'd misjudged things a wee bit, when it came to what age she was. Seeing her a lot more clearly now, I'd have doubted that she was a year younger than sixty five which while, aye, was verging on the territory of maybe you shouldn't be having sex with someone who was already mid thirties by the day that your mum was pushing you out into the world.

But by then, I kind of felt, what's an extra five years difference, eh? It was weird how we had went from a nightclub to a fucking super yacht but yet in doing so - getting a proper chance to see her - her sense of being glamorous had dipped a couple of levels. Not enough to not give it to her tight, though, mind.

We barely made it into the bedroom - size of bed in there *easily* double the diameter of my king size back home - before clothes started getting ripped from each other as the pent up sexual aggression that had been built up from across the night began to simmer over.

Seeing her body in the flesh - which backed up her apparent age - was a wee bit of a shock to the system for a moment before I was able to somehow recalibrate myself and get myself right back in the mood again. My idea to light some of the various candles that were positioned across the room and dim the lights, definitely aiding things further.

Away from the visual side of things, though? Barry as fuck, like. This Anya had turned out to be every bit as filthy as she'd come across as promising earlier. As far as *I* was concerned. I didn't let the lass down, either. Gave her *exactly* what she was looking for and once again, no blowing my own trumpet there.

Besides, I had *her* to do that for me, eh?

Nah, she was one of those talkers during sex. Something about that foreign accent drove me fucking wild too. Plus, with her talking, you kind of knew where you stood if you were hitting the spot, so to speak.

'Ohhhhhhhh Colinnnnnn, if you fuck any deeper and harder you fuck me all the way into afterlife, baby'

She screamed out loud at one point as I had her bent over, slamming it right fucking into her. Just for the most briefest of moments I couldn't help but have the rest of the squad pop into my head. Them back in Magaluf eating a McDonalds - absolutely mortal - on the way back to the hotel having had fuck all in the way of joy with the other sex. And here was me, giving it tight to a fucking Ivana Trump, on her super yacht.

Fucking tremendous stuff, like.

After going round a couple of times we both - contented - passed out naked on the bed. Mallorca a place where you could easily do so without ending up brass monkeys with nothing covering you. So much so that it was hours later before I woke up, her still lying there in the way that she'd ended up, after she'd had her second orgasm.

Fuck me, though. The difference between the before - when you're mortal through tanning a couple of bottles of champagne and horny as fuck - and the after, where you wake up with a sore head and turn to the side and see the granny that you've just had a night of passion with.

Self loathing is such a real thing.

My head was fucking splitting and I was trying to piece things together. Obviously, I had a naked Anya lying on the bed so that part - and meeting her in BCM - wasn't hard to remember. Neither was the sex which I can't say I never enjoyed it because it was fucking tremendous but at the same time I wasn't exactly brimming with pride over, when it came to self reflection.

Then I remembered about how we'd come all the way to Palma from Magaluf and how I now had the hassle of getting myself back. Maybe she'd be sound enough to fix me up with a ride back, I thought, but then again, I wasn't sure if I wanted to *be* around for when she woke. Even looking at her face - compared to what I'd been looking at with all her make up on in the dim lighting - she looked almost dead compared to the face of a woman who at one point in her life I'm sure was extremely tidy but who time had also caught up with. Even if I'd wanted to stick around, though. There was no guarantees that I'd get a lift back and - as I began to quietly get dressed - the only real certainty was that I only had coinage in my pockets, which probably wasn't going to be enough to get me back to base camp again. Because of this, I doubled down on that whole feeling of shame side of things by deciding to have a wee rifle through her purse. Taking another wee look over at her on the bed, to make sure my moving about hadn't led to her stirring before opening up the black Dior purse that she had sitting in the Chanel bag. Inside the purse, I found the polar opposite of coinage. No notes less than fifty euro notes sitting inside there. I figured that I would easily be able to get a taxi from the Marina and back along the motorway to Magaluf for less than fifty euros, but took a hundred from her, just to be on the safe side.

Hey, there were hundreds more inside there. I could've completely taken the piss but decided not to although I'm not sure how much that was based on the knowledge that while she would've only *possibly* have missed the two fifty euro notes that were missing where she'd have *definitely* missed the NO notes that were sitting in there, because I'd pinched them.

Once I'd got the notes safely into my hipper and placed her bag back where it was, I decided that I would just let myself out, and leave her to wake under her own time. This wasn't one of these occasions where there would be a repeat performance between each other. While I'd one hundred percent been star struck a bit the night before with the attention I'd been getting and from someone drinking champagne in VIP sitting decked out in expensive clothes who took you back to her super yacht, the stripped down aesthetic reality of things were *not* so glamorous.

The ultimate in an exhibit a, lying right there on the bed.

As - what I thought would be seen as a nice touch - I was about to leave, I took one last walk over to the bed and grabbed the silk sheet from the bottom of the bed to put it over her. Thinking that when she woke and found I'd gone, but that I had showed care in putting a cover over her it would have at least shown a little example of gallantry from me. Aye, the very same cunt who had just been dipping into her purse.

As I took the sheet to cover the Russian woman, though. I took one last look at her. And *that* was when it hit me, something that might've appeared obvious when I'd woken, had I not woken with such a confused and splitting sore head.

She wasn't fucking *breathing*. And the colour of her from head to toe was just a bit, off. Any plans for sneaking off without having any awkward morning after conversations were now put on hold while - in a sudden bout of panic - I grabbed her shoulder and started shaking her. Repeating her name around half a dozen times in a row. Letting go of her shoulder, she just kind of flopped back onto the bed again.

You always see those on the telly checking people's wrists and then looking solemnly up and saying that there's no pulse. Tried to do that and couldn't get anything so then moved to pressing my hand against her heart to see if I could detect anything. There was nothing.

She was fucking *BROON BREED*.

In some kind of a flashback - mid panic - I got the memory of a clearly in the moment and loving it Anya screaming that if I fucked her any harder or deeper I was going to send her into the afterlife. Fucking hell, be careful for what you wish for, eh?

And I *did* give it to her harder and deeper, the more she sexily provoked me, because *that's* what she was wanting, practically fucking *telling me* to when not implying it.

Surely fucking not, I thought? I'd had a full on sex session with someone close to seventy - and fuck knows the state of their heart - and wake up the next day to find them croaked? Surely

I couldn't have rode the poor woman to death? But that's exactly what it was fucking looking like from where I was standing.

I was plunged into Nam. Do I phone the police and if I do, am I grassing on myself? Do I tell the security detail that she had looking after her - one of them who looked like he'd been moonlighting on his annual leave days from Mossad - and if I do, am I going to end up taking a couple of bullets to the back of my napper and dumped in the sea?

My head was too fried from the night before to fully remember everything I'd done in the yacht but I had a half hearted attempt at getting rid of any sign of my fingerprints from across the living room, bedroom and bathroom. I hope they can't take fingerprints from people's body's because there probably wasn't a part of her that I *hadn't* touched the night before, just one of the irrational thoughts I was getting when I was hurriedly trying to facilitate my exit.

As I was about to leave - and I don't need anyone to tell me how wrong this is - I thought about the *rest* of the euros, that were sitting inside her purse, and doubled back on myself.

Five hundred and fifty euros that were remaining inside there taken out and shoved into my pocket. This based on the fact that this woman now no longer needed them where she was.

Popping my head out of the yacht, I could see that the sun had come up by now. The two men stationed at the marina beside the yacht were still standing there. The Range Rover, however, gone.

Just act normal, for fuck's sake, I told myself as I staggered down the little walkway to get myself back off the boat. Maybe it was purely down to how much money she had but normally women don't have 'security detail' so - in my mind - it's specialists that you hire when you're putting a security team together. The type of cunts that would smell a rat from a mile off, if there was one to smell.

I think it was a help that as I walked down the little runway it gave them a chance to see that I wasn't even sobered up yet. They'd seen us disappear onto the boat with a family sized bottle of Moët, and I'm walking back off it a little worse for wear.

The pair of them chuckling at the sight of me while I was doing all I could to prevent myself from looking like I'd just seen a ghost although, in a funny way, that's *exactly* what you can end up looking like if you've drank too much peave.

'She's, eh. Wanting a few hours extra sleep, know what I mean, boys?'

I tried to front things out, giving them a wee suggestive wink.

'Ok, ok' The one in the suit from the night before - who by now was also holding a walkie talky - said to me in a way that suggested that he wasn't giving a fuck whether she was or she wasn't.

And with that. In some fugue like state I managed to get myself away from the marina and somehow find a taxi to get me back to Magaluf.

The thoughts on the journey back being not so much had I or had I not just committed manslaughter on that poor woman but, what was now going to follow on the subject?

Because it goes without saying that when her dead body was discovered. The last known people to have seen Anya

Borovskiy alive - her security detail - were surely going to mention the fact that - the night she died - she hadn't spent it alone.

Chapter 14

Viktor Borovskiy

Problems problems, fucking problems. Why always problems, I ask?

It had only been a matter of hours - and I was still processing things over - since I'd been told that the match hadn't went as planned, and I mean *planned*. Those fucking insolent Scottish bastards, I screamed down the phone at Valery as he gave me the kind of news that I had already taken as granted would be the opposite.

It had all been - to my blissfully unaware state - cut and dried to the point that the *only* expectation I had was that at some point over the night I would receive the news that Zavorovo had beaten this team out of Scotland called Muirhouse Violet. The only blank that required filling in was what the scoreline would be.

Those dumb fucking Scots. A man with the appearance - not to mention presence - like Valery walks in on them and hands them a pile of money - *my money* - while advising them of what his expectations were going to be, moving forward. Following such an interaction, the tendency would be to carry out the instructions that the man had left you with, no? Surely anyone with the tiniest of modicum of how the real world works would have known this?

Instead, the Scots had decided that they would simply *steal* from me. Which, naturally, was never going to be the wisest of moves to make. You don't steal from an oligarch, *we* steal from *you*, not the other way around. Understand?

I was in the middle of planning out what kind of message I'd have liked sent out to this team from Edinburgh when the phone call came through to me from Yevgeny - one of her assigned security detail - and by the time the phone call had come to an end. Suddenly, enacting revenge on a team of thieves over the quite paltry sum of three thousand euros, it now didn't seem as much of a priority for me.

Fucking Anya. As much of a pain in the ass to me dead, as she'd been alive.

This I don't need, my first thought when I'd received the call. Telling me that her body had been found on our yacht. No feelings of loss, heartbreak or devastation that a husband should be immediately struck with, upon being told that their wife had passed away. Because - by then - she really was nothing other than a wife in name only.

I didn't love her and she sure as hell did not love me back, something that we'd made each other well aware of over recent years as we grew further and further apart to the point we were almost strangers to one and other. Why not divorce then? The question that you're probably asking yourself? Sometimes things are not so simple when you have a wife who doesn't love you but loves the *lifestyle* that you can provide. Yes, you can still divorce, under such circumstances. But *not* when your wife knows the kind of secrets that Anya did. It was as complicated as it was political.

Options other than divorce?

If I was to have her killed it would not have played well back home in Russia, and I knew it. And for that reason, she was untouchable. No bomb that could blow her up and no window that she could fall out of. Despite the fact that we hadn't slept together for years and barely even spent the night under the same roof as each other, she was in no hurry to go anywhere. Happy to dine out on my vast wealth as we lived out life, mainly apart.

Yes, we would be seen together on the nights where we would be *expected* to. Gala dinners, award ceremonies and state functions back in Moscow. But it was all for appearances sake.

The Kremlin were not too crazy about any of the Russian billionaires creating negative headlines, while living outside of Mother Russia, so Anya and I played the game. I'd seen what happened to those who didn't and ended up on the wrong side of the state and the next thing they know they've 'fallen' out of a window or brakes had 'failed' on their car, and it wasn't going to happen to me.

On the surface of things. We were just another successful rich Russian couple. One of many based in the West. Scraping below that, however. On the same day I was receiving one of lifetime's greatest blow jobs from that Asian call girl, Anya was probably fucking the pool guy. She always *did* seem to have a thing for men a lot younger than she was.

And now she was dead, and I was going to have to take care of the aftermath. Deal with police, press, have her funeral arranged and - personally - the worst part of all, play the grieving husband in public.

When the rather stressed sounding Yevgeny called to tell me the news, that Anya had been found unresponsive in bed. Other than the realisation over just how much problems this was all going to cause. I really felt nothing, to the point that I felt guilty over *not* doing so. Pure emptiness. I'd met her at a dinner party when we were in our twenties and we would go on to be together for over two thirds of our lives, up to our mid sixties. That, not exactly an inconsiderable amount of years in someone's life.

I should've felt *something*. Some cherished memory from the past out of all those years but with how strained things had become over recent years, *those* memories were the ones that were more fresh, more raw. Harder to see past to get to the more fonder recollections of her and I that would've still been buried deep somewhere into my mind.

'What should I do, boss?' Yevgeny, asked while I lit up a second consecutive cigarette.

'What do you mean by 'what should you do?' I asked before taking a medicinal extra long draw on the Marlboro.

'You are the first person who knows, boss. The first call I have made on discovering her'

While it was right that I should've been the first to know, regardless of the relationship that our 'marriage' now was. But now procedures would need to be followed, as much as I cringed at the thought of them all.

'Well now you call the emergency services to report what you've just told me. When the police arrive tell them that I am on my way, I'll have Igor drive me to the marina'

'And, what should I tell them if they begin to ask questions?' A clearly shaken Yevgeny asked.

'Then you tell them whatever it is that you know' I answered - exasperated by how much of an amateur this so called professional security operative was sounding - before face palming.

'Actually, hold on, Yevgeny,' I paused for a moment.

'Is there anything else that I *need* to know, before you tell the authorities?'

I already knew that this was not just going to be a simple case of man loses wife / man buries wife. *This* was going to be news in both the West as much as it was back home. As little as I knew about the situation, I could already see how it was going to look.

'Anya Borovskiy - wife of Russian billionaire oligarch - was found dead on the couple's super yacht 'Prosper and Conquer' in Palma, Mallorca'

Already knowing how the West covered news stories like this, they would inevitably be drawing their own conclusions over how suspicious this all sounded. It sometimes appearing that those in the West simply didn't understand the concept of how death comes to us all, and that it doesn't *always* have to arrive wrapped up in a conspiracy theory.

Any other women dies on a yacht, it would not even be questioned but when it's an oligarch or his wife who dies, then clearly there would have to be something darker to it.

The news would also raise eyebrows back at The Kremlin. It was never a good thing when one of their many prominent billionaire businessmen - making their mark outside of Russia - were spoken about in less than glowing terms. I'd already had the issues with the American financial authorities which had seen me regularly spoken of in the Wall Street Journal. And now my wife just happens to die?

There was a conspiracy theory all pre made, completely outwith my control. There would be speculation on the American news networks that - due to my problems with the authorities - a 'mistake' had just coincidentally happened to me, likely sponsored by the FSB, as a message sent to me to stop bringing unnecessary attention towards The Kremlin. None of it true, of course, but I also knew how the game was played, outside of Russia.

None of this, I needed.

'Emmm well, you should know that she was not alone for part of the night,' Yevgeny said, breaking the silence in a hesitant way, not wanting to be the one who told the boss that his wife had been likely fucking someone that night. *This* changed things.

'Ok, then you *don't* tell the authorities everything that you know, understand?'

He let me know that this was understood.

This additional information changed things in a big way. Due to how Yevgeny had said she'd been found, I highly doubted that the person she'd been with had been her killer, but - with details so thin on the ground at this early point - it couldn't have been ruled out. It, also, was possible that the person that she'd been with had simply been someone that she had picked up at a nightclub, a practice that she was no stranger to. And with the security that we had manning the yacht anytime either of us spent a night on it, most likely the person had boarded along with Anya at some point.

Regardless, this information would not be something that was going to be made public. I would find out more about that side of things in due course but until then I wanted it kept from the authorities.

Conspiracy theories aside, a man of my stature and reputation simply did not the world knowing that on the night my wife had died, she had been with another man.

'You tell them that you saw her get on board the yacht at whatever time you seen her do so - but that she did so alone, if asked - and that you found her hours later dead. I'll be over soon to deal with things. If there are any signs in the yacht that two people were there. Two glasses, used condoms, *anything*, then you clear them up before the police arrive, ok?'

'Ok, boss'

I heard him say as I was hanging up.

'Fucking Anya,' I said out in frustration, knowing what the rest of the day - and beyond - was now going to involve, all because she'd had to go and fucking die. Some would call it selfish, from my now ex wife.

Getting over to the marina - after a quick shower and change - I found myself arriving there after the Guardia Civil but before the doctor and ambulance had got there.

Who looked like the detective inspector; greeting me on my arrival, shaking my hand and thanking me for coming so quickly, while also expressing his condolences. Thanking him while admitting that I was still in shock at the news, I invited him on board, while instructing Yevgeny to get us some coffee. Purely for effect - once on board - I asked the inspector if I could take a look at Anya's body. I had no interest in looking at the dead body of the woman who was only my wife in name but I'd felt that it would've appeared unusual if I *hadn't* asked to see her.

'Si, si,' he replied, telling me that she was lying in the bedroom. Him allowing me this moment in private while he sat there with the coffee Yevgeny had brought out to him.

While in the bedroom and after taking a brief look at Anya. I hadn't been able to look at her as my wife and life partner in years so seeing her lying there, no longer of this world, it almost felt like I was looking at a stranger. I could only stand to look at her - lying under a white silk sheet - for a second before I had to look away again. Not really wanting to - but for the sake of my curiosity - I lifted the sheet up from her to see if there were any marks or bruising to her, but there was no signs of anything from what I could see. Seeing her naked body, like that, it made me think of what that body had been like forty years before. She was the one that everyone wanted but chose me. That seemed so long ago right there, though. Fuck, it *was* long ago.

Taking the time inside there, I used it wisely to scan the room for any evidence that might've been there which would've suggested that Anya hadn't been alone that night. Anything that Yevgeny may have missed when clearing the room before calling the emergency services. I suppose it didn't quite matter by that point, anyway, because I'm sure that the police had all been in and taken a look at her, and the surroundings she was found dead in.

I went back through to the living quarters and rejoined Inspector Padilla who dealt with me in the way that I could not have seen him doing so had he been sitting in a slum high rise on the outskirts of town, with a dead body lying in the next room.

'Would you be ok to answer some questions, Senor Borovskiy? only if you feel that you are up to it. I appreciate this must be a very difficult moment for you'

'Sure, Inspector. I will be happy to tell you all that I know,' I replied, taking a seat to face him and then a sip of coffee. Damn, for ex special forces, that Yevgeny really could make a fucking good cup of coffee, the thought popping in while I took my first sip.

'I still cannot believe that she's gone,' I said, putting down the cup again. 'I've known her for much more of my life than I haven't.'

'Si, it must be such a shock,' the inspector empathised with me.

Just as he was getting his notebook and pen out to begin, the medics arrived, them interrupting me and the inspector's chat as we showed them through to the bedroom. You could see just how impressed all of the emergency services were with the opulence of the yacht. It was written all over their faces but they were also in there through a work capacity so knew that they could not express what they were feeling. Even the inspector couldn't hide it when he entered behind me. None of this mattered, of course, but it's the little things you pick up on during these moments.

Me and the inspector stood at the edge of the bedroom while the doctor performed her formalities. Checking Anya's pulse before removing the silk sheet to check her body as she entered into some Spanish, in the direction of the inspector. Respectfully, when he noticed that the doctor was going to pull the silk sheets away, he grabbed my arm to pull me to the side, so that neither of us would be facing the bed, and the cold stiff body lying there on it.

'What is the doctor saying?' I asked the inspector, reasonably for a husband who has just lost his wife.

'Let us go back through and leave the medics to their work and I shall tell you.' He ushered me back through out of the bedroom. My heart - for the first time - feeling some small morsel of sadness while we passed a medic carrying what looked like a body bag.

While we sat back down again, the inspector told me that the doctor was of the opinion that Anya had been dead for less than twelve hours and - on initial viewing did not appear to have died via any blow or puncture wounds and with no signs of a struggle and on initial findings appeared to look like through natural causes. I really had no idea why I had felt the need to act my way through various things that he said to me - while playing the husband, *playing* being the operative word - considering I'd had nothing to do with her death in the first place but when he told me that it looked like she had died peacefully in her sleep and of apparent natural causes, I let out a contrived sigh of relief, telling Inspector Padilla that it was of some small comfort to me that while she had died, it had been a peaceful passing. Something that we would *all* choose, for when our time comes.

'Now if we can just clear up some questions that are purely standard in a case like this we will be on our way, I appreciate that you will have much to do. I also believe the medics will be taking Anya off board shortly'

Of course, the answer. Any question he cared to ask, my conscience was clear.

'Can you tell me where you were last night, Senor Borovskiy?'

The directors cut version for him could have been that I went out for dinner around eight o clock and - just around the time I was paying the bill - I was informed that the team I had been banking on winning me two million, and had engaged in bribery to help this happen, had lost their latest match and for the rest of the night had sat stewing and plotting revenge on those who had stolen from me. Instead, I went with.

'I had dinner at 'Pancho's Grill' in Santa Ponsa with some associates, before being driven back to my villa where I spent the rest of the night until going to bed. Sleeping right up until I received the call from one of my wife's security detail, - Yevgeny - the one who found the body and called you'

'And when was the last time you saw your wife?' the next question to follow.

Three nights before, my answer. We'd went out - on one of those taking her with me for the optics - to dinner with a Madrid construction magnate - Santiago Parejo - and his wife, in Palma.

'And is it usual for you and your wife to have spent such an amount of time apart?'

He asked, a little intrusive for my liking but a question I was happy enough to answer.

I assured him that - due to the nature of my many business interests - it was completely normal for me to have to go days at a time without seeing her before - trying to make a joke out of a bad situation, like people do - adding that the pair of us had only recently been stuck on the same yacht as each other from Nice to Palma and how we couldn't wait to see the *back* of each other by the time we reached Mallorca.

The inspector laughing at this, telling me that he was married himself and *understood*. The pair of us then laughing as I said

'Ah so you know the pain of marriage too, huh?'

This small light moment lasted for the exact limited amount of time it was intended to with my face dropping again a second later, I assumed in quiet reflection.

'And do you know what Mrs Borovskiy was doing last night? Her whereabouts?'

I answered with the stock reply that I'd already agreed with Yevgeny on - which he'd been instructed to feed back to everyone who was on duty the night before - that, after thinking about in the shower, I'd called him back to advise on.

'While I hadn't been in touch with her last night, her security detail have told me that she did not leave the yacht yesterday evening. As you'll appreciate, when you reach a certain level of wealth, you can become a target for kidnappings. We don't go to any country without our security. Of course, you will be free to talk to them in addition to myself, should they be of any help to you'

'Gracias, Senor Borovskiy. We will question them but being honest with you, and this comes from someone who has attended to all forms of deaths, there is nothing about Mrs Borovskiy's death that appears to be suspicious. No scenes of a disturbance and no apparent injuries to her. It does not appear to be an investigation that I can see taking up too much of your time. I appreciate time is precious to a businessman, such as yourself, si?'

I dryly laughed at this before telling him that he really didn't know the half of that, even though it was nothing but lies.

When you reach my kind of position in life, one of the whole *points* of getting there is the being able to have others do the things required, so that you no longer have to. You just collect the money at the end of it. *That* is the point, otherwise there really isn't one at all.

Soon it was my time to ask some questions to *him*. Mainly in connection with how long the body would be held onto, so that I could have the arrangements made to have her flown back to Russia. *Another* inconvenience. Not the actual arranging for a body to be flown from one country to another. Once again, another task that could - and would - be delegated to someone else to arrange. The inconvenient part, that I was now going to have to disrupt part of my summer by now flying back to Moscow for a funeral.

'Ah, si. I understand the need for to have your wife's body. It will be released as soon as we can for you. In an event - such as this - where there are no suspicious circumstances surrounding her death, there will be no need for a post mortem, as far as my assessment.

Now *this* I was pleased to hear of. I wasn't sure but I'd had the impression that a post mortem would possibly show that she'd had sex in the hours leading up to her death. This would add a complication to matters that I would've much rather avoided.

'Thank you, inspector. It is very much appreciated. I have so many things to arrange and the transportation of the body to another country is but one of them'

This appeared to spark the inspector into action. Standing up telling me 'of course, you will have many arrangements to make, I should let you get on with them'

Me standing up to meet him as we both shook hands again while he thanked me for my cooperation. Handing him my business card, I told him that if there was anything else he might need, he could reach me through one of the numbers on there.

As we were standing, the medics walked past us carrying Anya, zipped up in the black bag, on a stretcher. Despite the fact that you can be married to someone for decades, which leads to the two of you hating each other. You still *had* something with each other at one point. There was no hiding the sharp stab of pain to my heart as that body bag was carried past on its stretcher.

'Be strong, amigo'

The inspector reached out - having seen the look on my face - and squeezed my shoulder before telling me that he would let himself out, and quiz Anya's security before leaving the marina. While they could easily have told the much more juicy story of her being out the night before and picking up another man, where they came back to the yacht - done whatever the hell they'd got up to - only for the man to leave, and hours later Anya's death discovered. A version of events that would have had the police opening up a whole new different type of investigation, and one that I wasn't interested in taking over my life. Instead, Padilla would be fed a line that involved Anya Borovskiy not having left the yacht for over twenty four hours. The *rest*, that stayed in house.

Privately, I'd been told that she had left a Magaluf nightclub with a younger British man. They'd spent several hours on board 'Prospect and Conquer' before he left again in the morning. From what I'd seen with my own eyes, this man hadn't harmed her. It was possibly nothing other than bad timing that he should be with her the night that she died, or maybe there *was* more to it?

If we were to find out that - in fact - he *had* harmed her, and that he was the reason for her death. *Then* we would go about things, but in our own way. In house and without any police involvement. Obtaining the security camera footage - for one example - from the club Anya was sitting in 'on the prowl' to see who she met that night - and then left with - would hardly be an issue in obtaining, should it have been felt as required.

Once everyone had left the yacht, I sat there and tried to take stock of the whole situation, and everything that I was going to have to face for the rest of the day, which had now been sabotaged.

I had important calls to make, notably to Anya's one remaining parent and to some of my key members of staff, issuing them with their instructions as to how to deal with this 'problem' that had now occurred. And - it went without saying - once news began to break of the death of Anya Borovskiy to the wider world, I was going to have media from both the Western news networks and the state sponsored ones back home, reaching out for quotes. It was going to be a crazy twenty four to forty eight hours and, frankly, a pain in the ass. Almost the *only* positive being that - through the insurance policies that we had for each other - Anya's death was a lot more of worth to me than her life and because of this I was now about to become richer by the figure of hundreds of millions of dollars.

Perspective can be a strange thing, however. There I was, having lost a wife and in doing so gaining hundreds of millions of dollars in the process.

Yet, sitting there inside the yacht alone, - and taking my first pause for breath since Yevgeny had first called me that morning

- out of all the things that I *should've* been thinking of. I was, instead, pondering just how cocky Arben Kelmendi must've been feeling, with his Albanian team sitting with four points and the so called worst team in their group still to play, while *my* representative in our personal bet were in the very much precarious position of second bottom, with only the one point. I didn't know if I was more angry at the Scots for stealing my money or the players of Zavorovo for not having it in them to win both of their matches under their own means, but the combination of things had left my bet - which meant more to my pride than it did to my bank balance - in a bad spot.

Looking at where things lay. The Scots were now through but, away from them, the three other teams in the group could all technically reach the next phase, but for Zavorovo to make it, they would have to win - the following day - when they played the team from Portugal. Not only that, however. They would need to win *and* pray that the Estonians - who had kick started this whole shit show in the first place - did not better the score of my countrymen, when playing the Scots.

After winning their first two games - and despite stabbing me in the back - I had faith that Muirhouse Violet would do enough in their game. When it came to Zavorovo, however? I did not have as much confidence.

The reports that I'd been given had been that they hadn't actually played badly in either of the two first matches. *Devine intervention* was how I'd been told when it came to the reasons why they had managed to avoid at least one win. Being told that on any other day they could've won both games against the Estonians and the Scots. Maybes and could've beens were no good to me.

While it been put across to me that it appeared only a matter of time before Zavorovo's luck changed and that they'd get a result which was more in tune with their performances, they only had one more chance for things to fit into place. And this was too risky for me. I could not just let chance play its part. I *needed* a win for Zavorovo. So played all the cards that I had open to me.

Before picking up the phone and calling Galina - Anya's mother - to tell her the news about her daughter, I made one quick call before doing so, to Valery.

'Sorry for your loss, boss.' He said on answering. Curiously, any of our security detail that were close enough to me and Anya - and had been with us for any length of time - would've already known that our marriage was nothing but a sham, and that ninety nine percent of the time they'd never had to guard us when we were together and that they were effectively a two unit set up. So for to hear them express their condolences - in the way that they were to me - felt a little hollow. Respectful, towards their boss, but hollow, considering what they *knew* about 'The Borovskiys.'

I thanked him while taking a moment to think of how long it was going to take before the condolences I was going to receive from people in the coming hours and days would begin to grate on me.

'So, Valery. Clearly the plan with the Scots did not work'

I said, letting him know that - despite the death of my wife, business would continue - I wanted to speak to him on other matters.

'Yes, it did not. What would you like me to do about them?'

It wasn't exactly an unusual question. Someone had wronged me, and under normal circumstances, would pay for such insubordination. But there really were more important things at play than arranging retribution over an amount of money that I make more by standing and taking a piss.

'No, forget them, for now. They may yet still come in handy'

The thought that technically the Estonians were still in with a chance of qualifying, so leaving the Scots unharmed - ahead of playing their last match - had seemed a logical thing to do. In any case, I had other - more important - work for Valery.

'No, I want you to find the players of Ramalde - ahead of tomorrow's match - and you throw *more* money at them than you did the Scots, but this time you leave the players in no doubt over what will happen to them if they *don't* comply with our request that they lose the game. You tried to play nice with the Scots and they took a liberty as a result. There will be no liberties this time, Valery. Take four of the baddest looking members on our detail with you, as a show of strength, and get it through to these Portuguese fuckers that they can be either very rich by the end of the group stages or they can be very dead'

It should never have come to pass - over an insignificant football tournament that was going on under the whole world's noses - but these amateur players from Portugal were about to be made an offer that countless Colombian police officers and state officials had famously been also pitched to them by one Pablo Emilio Escobar Gaviria, back in the eighties and nineties.

Plata o plomo

Silver or lead.

I assumed that the Ramalde players would make the right choice, given their extremely limited options.

Hanging up on the call to Valery, I then immediately looked up babushka Galina's number, to make the call and tell her that her only daughter had died through the night.

Just one of the many things that I was dreading facing over the coming days that had now been forced on me.

Chapter 15

Strings

What really can you say about that last group match other than if you turn up to a play a match pished then you can't really claim to be surprised if *pish* is what you see out *on* the pitch. It really was one of our worst ever ninety minutes as a footballing sporting club. For perspective, it rivalled that time Leith beat us six nil when the word had got out that there would be Edinburgh police in attendance, specifically on the look out for some of our players who'd had outstanding warrants out on their name. This leading to Jock having to put out three quarters of the young team from the MCF to play the game, due to our core group staying away that Sunday.

Back to present day, though. As you can imagine, Jock Hunter wasn't too chuffed, and neither should he have been. The night before, he'd offered us an inch, but - of course - we had to go and turn that inch into the equivalent of a fucking marathon.

'Now, and this is only because of how well you've done up to this point, I've decided that I'm going to give you all a bit of leeway tonight'

He'd said at the end of our tea. Which was usually the signal for him to head back to the hotel to get some sleep. He'd only been 'out' with us all once since we'd got there - that first night - and couldn't hack it and ended up back at the hotel before even the witching hour. It's no game for an old man, though, tackling the pubs and clubs of Magaluf. Before leaving for the night he'd told us that he was allowing us all to stay out and have a couple of drinks to relax and unwind before our last game of the group. Fuck knows where he got this fantasy from but he had told us that he expected us not to take the piss and that we would all be back to the hotel in time for us to get a good sleep, ahead of the game against *Hiiu Club Sporting*.

'Fuck it, we're already through, anyway'

The common theme that came up against any suggestions, when it came to going back to the hotel at what might've - definitely not by Hunter, though - been regarded as a *decent* hour.

By the time you've got to four in the morning - and still out - you've kicked the arse out of it that much that it really doesn't matter what time you go back by then. That whole best to be done for stealing a sheep than a lamb line of thinking, eh?

I think - in the end - the most sleep any of the squad managed had been about three hours, and even they were in the minority.

'These fucking Estonians have won a watch today and they don't even know it yet,' I said to Benji as we sat near the back of the minibus as it took us up to the stadium. Because, not to be defeatist or fuck all, it went without saying that it would've taken the ultimate in delusion to have ever imagined up Muirhouse Violet coming away from the match without anything other than nul points.

Looking around the bus at everyone. Some players sleeping on the journey, others looking white as sheets - despite having had several days in the sun by this point - while the rest, still evidently pished, sat joking around. The scent in the bus was not pleasant. You already had the heat inside there. Mix it with the strong smell of alcohol - that was radiating from most of the group - and the reprehensible stale smell of burps and farts from near on ten men. If some on the bus were already barely hanging by a thread on being sick, the collective musk from the squad present on the bus would've done the job of seeing them over the finishing line.

Clearly, we were not fit to play a game of fitba. This confirmed when we took to the pitch against the - nothing more than - workman like Estonians. Afterwards, when I was looking back at the match, or what I had been able to remember. It had been a chance missed because even if we'd went home three or four hours earlier then I'm sure we'd have still had enough about us to deal with them. There was nothing special about them. Just a team of jobbers bereft of any skill but - with the possibility of still going through, however slim it might've been - with something to play for. They also, however, did not look, move or play like a group of players who had been sitting in The Banana Bar belting out that KC and the Sunshine Band song, 'Give it Up' at five in the morning either, unlike some.

The result of this mismatch - by the time the referee mercifully blew his whistle for full time - a four one win to Hiiu Club Sporting. What a fucking red neck, like. Humped by a team from Estonia. For any of the players who had been still drunk at the point of the whistle going at kick off, getting rinsed in the way that they'd just been would've been enough to sober the cunts up.

It's fair to say, none of us really turned up, even if some tried their best, which wasn't close to being enough. I'm not one to point fingers or fuck all - especially when we were pretty much all in the same boat - but Sepp had an absolute stinker.

Considering he was the one player out of us who - at least - didn't have to run around the pitch *plus* the form that he'd carried into the game, following his heroics against the Farleys. The boy had a complete mare. I'm not saying that the Estonians wouldn't have still beaten us anyway but the fact that we were beaten four goals to one, and that he'd gifted them three of the goals wasn't lost on me.

Even before the game he was a wee bit off but then again - in our own way - so was everyone else. The three that he was responsible for were absolutely soft as shite goals to give away. Their first, fucking slower than a week in Saughton getting down to their striker's shot, the ball slipping under his body and into the net. Their second, without even looking, he passed the ball out from the back *right* to their winger, who didn't have too much of a task lofting the ball over the edge of the box loitering Sepp. The third one - which made it three nil to them - in the second half where he completely fresh aired a clearance, leaving one of the Estonians - who had been hanging about on the off chance - with fuck all else but a tap in. It was like our keeper was miles away. On the pitch along with the rest of us but - at the same time - with a mind in another location.

'Probably thinking about that posh VIP totty that he'd been riding the other night,' I said to a disgruntled Daz as we walked back to take kick off, again.

When they made it four - this one, only the churlish could've attempted to lay the blame at Sepp's feet - I just wanted the man in black to blow the whistle and let us get ourselves to fuck. There was more than just them getting the win at play, though. You could tell by the way the Hiiu players had went pure radge on the fourth going in, as opposed to the steely and determined reaction they'd had to the third, and Sepp's wrapped in a bow gift they'd just capitalised on.

The difference to them in being four goals clear of us - compared to the three - pivotal to proceedings. Our game had followed the Ramalde and Zavorovo match which had seen the Russians finish up three nil winners. When we'd been told this we'd all speculated if the win had been *financially incentivised* considering we'd played both teams and didn't see that kind of a gulf between the two of them. It was something that we'd never know or not. What it *did* mean, though, was that - with Zavorovo now sitting second on four points behind us - if the Estonians were to go through, they would need to beat the group leaders by four goals or more. Highly unlikely, what anyone with an interest in the tournament would have predicted ahead of Muirhouse versus Hiiu. They didn't know which version of Muirhouse Violet was going to turn up for that final group game, though.

And yet, there they were. Four goals up, opposition's heads up their behinds while looking like they'd never seen a football in their life. Of course, though. As dogshit as we'd been over the game, we had to go and blow it for the poor bastards. I think the realisation that - and beyond any of their wildest dreams going into the game - they were literally *through* to the next phase of games. They - normally - had no right to be four goals up against a team like us. When they'd found out that the Russians had won, and given the goal difference a decent bounce at the same time, you'd not have blamed them for already thinking that the jig was up.

Reaching the unthinkable of being in a winning position that was going to see them qualify, it kind of fucked with their heads. They'd played like men possessed, intent on scoring those four goals - which they'd never have come close to had it not been for Sepp, mind - while keeping the back door locked from us making their task harder by scoring. That fourth goal was the moment where they seemed to collectively decide to hold what they had. Given the heroics they'd pulled off over the match, you couldn't have really blamed them for suddenly becoming a little over protective.

How rattled we all were. Some seriously needing sleep, others alcohol. All Hiiu needed to do for the final stages of the match was to keep coming at us, and they'd have been as good as gold. Instead, through giving up possession to a team who - mentally - didn't really know what to do with it. They had to suffer the sight of Coffee's thirty yard shot that was one more out of frustration - because he'd looked around him and found that hardly any cunt had bothered to make a run to give him options - than it had been a measured and skilfully placed drive.

'Ah, fuck the fucking lot of yous lazy bastards, then'

He screamed out as he looked up and then dug out what had to have been the best goal of his life. Delightfully kissing the underside of the crossbar as it hit the net. Without question, the best goal of Coffee's puff, and completely meaningless.

Only, it *was* to the Estonians.

Our consolation goal proving to be the difference between them going through to the quarter finals, and not.

Proper dead weird vibe to the sound of the final whistle, though. You know? In the game of fitba, the aim of things is to score more goals than the opposition and if you do, then it's job done. You won, the others didn't. Generally something to be chuffed about after putting in a hard shift for ninety minutes.

But, instead, the Estonian's coupons were fucking tripping them. Fuck knows how gutted they must've been, like. So near but yet so far, as they say. That gut punch feeling of having something within your grasp, only for it to slip away from you in the cruelest of ways. Still, if you're going to go out of a tournament, make it by way of the screamer that Coffee had scored.

It felt like a wake, as the players all shook hands out there on the pitch. The Estonian's tournament hopes were dead and on their way to the morgue while at least half of the Muirhouse contingent looked like they should've been *lying* in one already.

We had the farcical sight of Coffee - who, at the time, hadn't understood the significance of his strike - apologising to the crestfallen Hiiu players for his goal after learning *why* the other side were so pissed off about the humping that they'd just dished out to the other team. Telling them that if he'd known - the margins - he wouldn't have even had a dig at goal. Comically trying to pass the buck by telling some Estonians that if only some of his team mates had been 'ersed supporting him' he wouldn't have *had* to fucking shoot in the first place.

Some of them seemed to appreciate the sentiment and his sense of fair play - if you could call it that, the Farley's definitely fucking wouldn't have, for one thing - but all looked like they couldn't wait to get off the pitch. I was with them on that, big time.

Soon as we got back to the hotel I was going straight to my scratcher, with the plan of sleeping as long as I possibly could, regardless of what time of day it was and whether I missed out on a night out with the boys or not. It was always going to reach this point for us all - under our own clock - where you'd kicked the erse out of things so many times that now your body was stepping in and taking over. By the looks around the dressing room as we sat there after the match, I didn't look like I was going to be the only one removing themselves from Magaluf for a period of time, for some R and R.

On the way back in the bus - reflecting about the group we'd played in and how it had turned out - I couldn't help but think if stuff is already planned in life and how there's not a single fucking thing you can do about it.

Days before, Some boy had attempted to bribe us into letting another team win. We took their money and then said fuck you, Oleg. Yet, by the close of play, it was *us* who were the difference between the Farleys going out of the tournament and on their way home, or joining us in the knockout stages. We - despite being still drunk or easing into a real time hangover - had been the kingmakers, as they're called.

I laughed at the irony of how it had all turned out and hoped that this so called big businessman, the one that thought he could bribe Muirhouse Violet, had managed to see the funny side of it all.

Chapter 16

Benji

Fucking Joseph Strings Carson? Best mate, aye. That doesn't mean to say that the boy didn't drive you up the wall at times. Up the wall? The daft cunt could drive you up the side of the bastarding Empire State Building.

Aye, we had Muirhouse business to contend with, but away from that part of things. Magaluf was *meant* to be a holiday, an escape from everything back home. Which, again, I shall refer you back to Strings.

Things were only worth escaping from back in Scotland because of the small matter of the debt that we'd found ourselves in with probably the *one* man in Edinburgh that you really did not want to be due dough to. That being a long story which could've easily been condensed by saying that my best mate had picked the wrong establishment for us to go and steal money out of, from the puggies. This error leading us all the way into the pocket of McKenna - which at the time seemed to be a better option than being put six feet under by those psychotic brothers from the West Coast - and approaching three years, still inside it.

I didn't have anywhere near as much to pay back as Strings did, but that wasn't the point. What I was still due was *enough*. Being due Davey McKenna a pound would be one pound too fucking many.

The amount of hustling that we'd both had to do just to be able to scrape the funds together to travel to Magaluf? And even then, we'd both needed to seek permission from Davey McKenna to let us go. Actual adult men having to ask for permission from some cunt else, just so they can go away on holiday? I know - unless you work for yourself - that, technically, most have to get permission to go on holiday but me and Strings weren't most cunts. We didn't have bosses to submit holiday forms to while crossing our fingers that no one else in our departments had got there first. Only, with McKenna, it kind of felt like you *did* have a boss. Hard times, like.

So you could imagine how thrilled I was with Strings burning down that island, and getting us both huckled by the Spanish 5-0, eh? That fine, too? Well harsh, if you ask me, although of course I'm going to say that when I'm on the receiving end of the financial penalisation. Still, one thousand five hundred euros still seemed a little excessive. Call me paranoid if you like but I left the court that morning with the feeling that we'd had our pants taken down, on account of us not being locals. I'm no dafty, like. I ken the crack when it comes to locals and tourists in some of those destinations around the world.

The locals are left in the awkward position of liking the money that tourism brings but not so much the dickhead behaviour that they have to put up with from the tourists that are *bringing* the money. Bit of a catch twenty two for them, I suppose. I mean, being Scottish. You're used to seeing drunken fannies but I reckon if I had to put up with the sheer volume of how many you get in Magaluf I'd probably smash fuck out of a tourist or two on a daily basis, if I was one of the locals.

What really could you do though other than pay the fine? An act that wasn't going to be an easy thing to do for either of us.

Aye, the 'holiday' part was something I'd looked forward to every bit as much as the fitba side of us being there. And now -

thanks to Strings - that part had been kind of sabotaged. It wasn't even as if I was asking for much. Just a chance to have a good scoop with the lads in the evening and to just lay by the pool - the next day - and do as little as humanly possible before going out and repeating the exact same steps from the night before. And now - instead of catching some colour about myself and soaking up this thing that we don't see too much in Scotland but is called *the sun* - I'm having to go out and about town with Strings looking for 'opportunities' with regards to us pulling in some money that we could then hand directly over to the Spanish Government.

Steals from the Spanish / give to the Spanish. It was an uncomplicated but also a *very* complicated strategy.

As much as I resented Strings for putting us in this position in the first place - placing financial pressures with international countries while robbing me of my leisure time - things could've been worse. He - at least - had a means for making money which was one up on me, short of robbing a Banco Santander. Because of the bond between him and his dad, Strings' *stringer* was never far from reach. Even though he wasn't coming out to Spain to 'string' he'd still brought the device with him in his case. It was a sentimental thing, I suppose. Made him feel closer to his dad, something like that.

That time in Blackpool when we'd been rumbled by those Eastern Europeans that ran the amusement arcade as to what we were up to and all the trouble - and risk - Strings went to when it came to getting the stringer back the next day?

'We ready, then?'

Strings said, moving his stringer back and forward in front of me like some hypnotist. I'd been sitting in the lounge having a beer waiting on him coming down from the room so we could get going. I wasn't in the best of moods as I looked out of the big windows from the lounge and into the large pool area outside. All the guests lying out on sun-loungers and messing about in the pool.

Should be me, I thought, well disgruntled about my lot. Instead, we're off for a walk to find viable options for places to string from.

This, first of all was risky in itself. It was not how we worked. We didn't just go into the first place in Scotland that had a fruit machine and get to work on it. There were many facets to the stringing game and *every one* of them had to be adhered to, if you wanted to subsidise your week to week life while also remaining free of police and or hospitals.

The - mostly - meticulous way that Strings would plan where we would put in a bit of graft. Usually taking several visits to an arcade and sitting in there for hours, making a show of using one of their machines while all the time observing everything about the inner workings of the place.

Camera positions, do they move or are fixed? Number of staff and if that number is consistent each day. How busy the places get and - if so - at what time are they at their busiest, because if there's one thing you can't do, it's string a bandit when there's cunts on either side of you sitting firing their coins with the queen's head on it into the puggies that *they're* using. Need a bit of space to work, like. So much things to take into account when it comes to the stringing life but the main message had always seemed to be that you didn't rush things. You only robbed from a puggy when you felt that you were absolutely positively safe to do so.

And there we were, on foreign territory in Magaluf with only a week to go to 'win' three thousand euros. With the clock ticking, we didn't *have* the luxury of being able to not rush things.

'You got a game of fives on, aye?'

I asked, clocking him, now changed into a Hibs away top, Scottish national team home shorts and a pair of Gazelles.

He just flashed me the v's before calling me a 'fucking wide cunt'

'Aye, let's get this over with,' I answered him, standing up, grabbing my shades and hat while hoping that the two of us would be returning back to the hotel again later on, instead of ending up *back* in that police cell that we'd been in only days before.

We *did* make it back to the hotel - several hours later - but it could hardly have been described as a successful day at the office.

The one and only place that - after a much more shortened security assessment from the two of us - Strings put himself into action was an Irish pub called Blarney Rubble's. It wasn't busy enough to make stringing a little iffy but not too quiet enough for the pair of us to have stuck out while in there. If you can't blend in with the surroundings while committing robbery in broad daylight then you're not going to last a fucking crack.

Counter productive is how I'd have classed the visit to the Irish pub and - in itself - it showcased the major difference between stringing from an Ayrshire amusement arcade on a dark and cold November afternoon and - on holiday mode - sitting in a Magaluf boozer in the middle of summer. Probably the most notable part being that Ayrshire amusement arcades don't serve you up ice cold San Miguel on draught. Aye, it can't be denied. Stringing and drinking simply do not go together.

Over the course of our time inside there, Strings managed to take out near enough three hundred euros. Not the biggest amount in the world and definitely not exactly making a dent in the three bags of sand that we were due the Spanish, but you've got to start somewhere, eh?

The main problem was that *out* of that three hundred euros, we drank fifty euros worth, spent another twenty five on food and then - after six pints - Strings had got himself into some alpha male thing with this English boy in relation to one of those machines with the punchball that registers how hard your punch is. This was right at the end of our 'work' and when finishing our last pints Strings had stood and watched him having a go on the machine.

'Thought you were meant to punch the thing, mate, no feel it up, eh?'

He just had to say it, didn't he? Why couldn't he have just observed the boy's punch and then left it at that? This comment, bringing Strings to the English lad's attention which led to a fifty euro bet being laid down on who could punch the ball the hardest. Both getting one punch each.

A sober Strings wouldn't have made the comment and neither would he have risked fifty euros, that he'd literally just sat and earned. But it was what it was. I could already tell - just going by appearances, mixed with how well I knew my best mate - that it looked like Strings was making a bet that he was never going to win. And I wanted to say so, but didn't wasn't to make a cunt out of him in front of this other boy, so, as a result, had to back my man.

'Trust me, Benji boy, we'll make more money from one punch than we'd have done sat for another hour at that puggy'

He said, confidently, to me after watching the English boy give it a decent punch and landing a respectable score of three hundred and twenty seven.

'Well you know what you need to do, lad,' I said, wishing him luck.

Luck wouldn't have even been enough for him, as it turned out. Strings punching a way off two eight four, leaving the guy standing there with a shit eating grin on his face and hand out waiting on his fifty euros.

Out of three hundred euros gained - over around four hours - we'd then given away almost half of it in some shape or form. And now, we'd had too much to drink to move onto somewhere else and try our luck. As much as our need for money was there. We weren't about to take leave of our senses by going about town half pished and on the string. We'd have been as well as just handing ourselves into the police and save them the petrol money in coming out to collect us, had we carried on.

We headed back to the hotel again, richer than we'd been when we'd left it hours earlier but hardly close to being a fruitful day of events.

We still had a week left.

If there was one thing that our first day of stringing in a foreign environment was to teach us, it was that to be successful we had to be more disciplined than we'd ever been before.

Which pretty much translated as we needed to stay away from the fucking peave, while working.

Walking back to the hotel - half pished - we resolved to do better on our next outing.

Chapter 17

Sepp

My mind had been in a spin, since I'd left that marina, and a Russian woman lying dead on her yacht, ridden to death. The whole scenario just played around and around my mind on a loop. I saw her dead body when my eyes were open *and* when they were shut. I couldn't escape her, or it. Pure heavy fried the brain, like, though.

And paranoia? Don't even fucking start with that stuff. My only real experience with that - until Magaluf - had really been when I'd been younger going to the raves and that. If I was coming down but was still in the rave I used to think that cunts were pointing and talking about me, that kind of stuff. Strangers, like. Obviously it was the comedown from the Eckies but just you try to tell yourself that at the time and see how far you get. Just like I was going through in Mallorca, from the moment I clocked that she was brown bread and onwards. You can *feel* the paranoia but can't get close to being able to persuade yourself that that's all it is, and that your mind is just fucking with you.

If only it were that simple, eh?

Maybe then I wouldn't have fucking shat myself anytime I saw a police car driving along the road. Slipped off to the toilets whenever I caught sight of the obligatory Guardia Civil coming into any boozer we were sat drinking in while they done their nightly checks about the bars to make sure no one was up to no good in there.

Even *without* cunts in police cars or uniforms, I was still struggling. All it took was for you to be in plain clothes and cast a look in my direction for me to get a sweat on, on top of the one the Spanish heat had already provided. The amount of holiday makers that - through nothing other than unfortunately looking the wrong way - I'd decided were Spanish C.I.D, or whatever equivalent that they have in Mallorca.

All during the day and night, just waiting on that tap on the shoulder, closely followed by me being led handcuffed to a waiting car. Waiting to take me away so that the whole *process* could get started. It was inevitable.

You know you're fucked in the head though when you think - at least - a hundred times a day about just handing yourself in to the Feds to get your ordeal over with. Obviously, I'd always manage to talk myself back out of that thought straight away but that also didn't mean that I would wind up back thinking the same thing again ten minutes later.

Rock and a hard place, and no mistake. Hand yourself in and go down that road - wherever it takes you - or stick to slowly going off your fucking head.

My plan - if you could call it that - was just hope that it took the authorities longer to find me than I had days on the island. Not like *that* would save me, either. Because sure as fuck that kind of thing follows you to whatever country you move on to. That Interpol and Europol, sticking my coupon on their databases and radge stuff like that.

It wasn't exactly going to be hard to find me, either. Fuck knows, I'd thought enough about it, from all angles. One of the woman's security boys tells the police that me and her had met in that BCM. Coppers go there to get the CCTV camera footage from that night - and put a face to the mystery Scot - then while in there ask a few questions and some grassing cunt tells them that a massive group from Scotland were all in there that night, celebrating winning a game of fitba.

If any law enforcement weren't able to work things out from there then they'd obviously be in the wrong job. As far as I was concerned, it was that easy. Or was it my *paranoia* that was of that opinion? Nah, it made sense. I'd watched enough episodes of The Bill to see how your Don Beech's of this world formed an investigation. He's probably a bad example though as he was hardly a fine upstanding member of Sun Hill but you know what I'm saying? You get a lead, follow up on it and if you just so happen to be as lucky as to get a picture of the person of your interest, along with the intel about the fitba side of things. Well, you could have the cunt locked up before your siesta time.

If I'd been just some random out for the night, seeing if I might get lucky with someone, only to leave with Anya - felt weird even saying her name as I didn't really think I knew her long enough to refer to her by name so familiarly, following her death - then even with the CCTV images, I'd have just been another tourist and it would've been needle in haystacks stuff. How many other Scottish men were in Magaluf at that exact same time as me? I rest my case.

Of course, I had to be there under different circumstances, though. One that left me a lot more traceable.

Look, the sex? Aye, it was rough and it was filthy but it wasn't like some risky asphyxiation stuff gone wrong, like the boy in the news who had the rope around his neck and was found in a French maid outfit and an apple in his mouth or fuck all. I'm not a fucking weirdo, eh? Nah, she was fucking begging me *'harder, harder you dirty Scottish man.'* Well, what the lady wants, the lady shall have, eh? And, aye. It *did* get pretty rough at times, like I said, but not anything to endanger anyone's life. But then again. I'd never shagged a woman that old before, not even *close* to anyone that age. So I could well have been endangering her without even knowing it.

She was already old looking - but good for it - when we were sat the VIP having a scoop of champagne but by the time we got back to that yacht, she seemed to be ageing by the fucking minute. I never did find out what her age was, because it went without saying, I couldn't ask her. Wished I'd found out though although the only way I was going to find that out - after the event - was when reading about myself in the papers where the tabloids were fucking nailed on to quote her age. They love all that stuff. By the time the rags got hold of the story it would be told to the world as some gold digger murdering the poor cow for her yacht when the reality was that all I wanted was a wee seat in VIP - to wind the rest of the team up - and my Nat king at the end of the night.

Fuck's sake! I've dished out enough sore faces to cunts that deserved one over the years but someone who could commit premeditated murder. Come on, eh? Even if I *was*, you think I'd be daft enough to try, with security like that Mossad motherfucker only metres away from me outside?

Getting back to the hotel - that morning - from Palma where I'd eventually catch up with the rest of the squad was tough. Because you can imagine what they were all like? Watched me sat there with some glammed up woman draped in designer labels - and we're talking fucking *top end* designer labels - while we drank champagne in the VIP section of a club before us leaving them all to it, disappearing into the night in a Range Rover.

Questions were always going to be getting asked, as soon as they saw me the next day. That's just the code of the man.

Wouldn't have mattered if it had been some girl from Huddersfield who'd had too many drinks and now just wanted a Big Mac and then some sex that I'd went off with, I'd have still got the - ironically - Spanish Inquisition. That I'd left under much different circumstances than that, only adding a whole lot more spice to things.

And they wanted *details*.

Which I gave them, up to a point. Had to put in the acting performance of a lifetime while telling them about the night before and all we got up to, because internally I was in bits. It was only hours ago that I was waking up next to a dead woman. A pensioner if we want to be specific.

But there I was regaling the team with tales of blacked out Range Rovers, Mossad guards, champagne bottles bigger than that wee man from the Austin Powers film and sex on a super yacht. It's fair to say, they were envious. But I tell you what, though. I'd have done absolutely fucking *anything* for it to have been Terry or The Monk - or any cunt else for that matter - who had been sat there holding court, telling the tale.

I couldn't wait to get away from them all and go back to my room, so I could drop my whole bravado like act. Just to be on my own and try to process things.

Training that day got fucked off, which - naturally - fucked *Jock* off but my head wasn't in it. I had that 'I'm the keeper' card tucked away and I really didn't want to ever come across as a prick by playing it - like, saying to the rest of the team, look at me and how indispensable I am - but that morning? I couldn't have given a single fuck about training, the upcoming match, the tournament, *the lot*.

While they all trained out in that - yet again - blistering heat, I sat in the hotel room trying to get my head around things.

Her man. He popped into my head, did he know by now? I must admit - after the way she'd explained how her 'marriage' worked - I'd never bothered with minor details like the fact that she was married. Lesser men would've done. Well, *better* men. Due to the size of the living room (?) of the yacht there were a few pictures hanging up and there was one that I'd assumed was him and her. Some old - could've been maybe older than she was - boy. Russian as well, or something to that effect.

'Forget him' She'd said as she clocked me sitting looking at their picture. And then she started to unzip me, and forget him I did.

Was fucking remembering him the next day, though. Did he know or not? Going by how things were between them, maybe I'd done him a favour? On the other hand, though. Maybe he was the other way and heartbroken about it? If there was a direction that I could approach thinking about it from, I'd find it.

I couldn't fucking stand it - the amount of things coming into my head - so I necked a couple of the pills. The ones that I'd brought over with me for the bad back I'd been suffering from, leading up to the tournament. One of those daft as fuck things that don't even make sense. I was sitting on the couch when I pulled it, for fuck's sake. Only reached for the remote and something snapped. I'm sure Rio Ferdinand injured himself from his sofa as well, so I'm in good company. Anyway, those Codeine filled beauties always done the trick and took the pain away when it was at it's worst. They also happened to make you super drowsy when you took them so I figured that a couple of them down my yak would've at least blanked my nightmare out for a while.

Fucking blanked me out, right enough. I didn't wake up for around *twelve* hours - Wullie told me later that he'd tried for about five minutes to wake me up, before everyone went out for the night - which by then all the team were out for the night.

It was the evening before we played the Estonians and - as far as I'd last known - the boys were going to be sacking the whole no drink before a match rule. I thought about texting one of them to see where they were and arrange to catch up with them but within minutes of being awake, I was right back to where I'd been, pre pills. Not exactly the mood you'd want for going out to have a good time with your mates?

Instead, I chose sitting up most of the night going out of my mind as I'd thought of all of the variables there were to the *situation* I'd walked away from, back on that yacht. I was still up when I heard some of the team getting back to their rooms, Wullie - struggling to fucking walk - eventually coming through the door. Barely able to even speak three joined up words to me before flopping back on his bed and passing out. I took his trainers off and moved him into a position that wouldn't be possible to be sick in his sleep before going back to what was the longest night I'd ever seen in my life.

I'd pulled the 'I'm not training and you'll still not drop me' card when it had come to training, but I wasn't going to be able to pull that for the actual match itself. Fuck, you should've seen the absolute state of the passengers inside the bus taking us out for the stadium. You couldn't make it up. *I* was the only person sat on that bus who wasn't either suffering from a bad hangover or still at the drunk stage, yet every single one of them - no matter how rough or ill they were - were in a better position to play ninety minutes than me.

Mentally, I wasn't fit to play a game of fitba, and oh how it showed, once the action got underway.

Talk about a fucking blooper reel, though. Howler after howler in a performance that could've had its own Christmas DVD out, with Danny Baker or Nick Hancock, taking the pish out of me.

When we'd arrived at the stadium it was discovered that the Russians had won three nil which meant that whatever happened in our game, we'd be finishing top of the group so - technically - it didn't really matter when I dropped clanger after clanger. Didn't feel like that at the time, though. Especially with the grief that I was on the receiving end of from my less than impressed - but in their states, *easily* irritated - team mates.

One of the key tasks for a goalkeeper is to be keeping up with what's going on away from them, spot any incoming danger and be prepared for it. There were times the Estonians literally had a shot - going past the post or above the bar - before I'd even known they'd done so. Snapping out of things enough to at least be able to appreciate that I then had a goal kick to take.

'Fucking waken up, Sepp,' The Monk came running over to me before I took the kick. I was awake, no worries, there. I just was somewhere other than on the pitch with the rest of the team. And I'm not going on the defensive here when I say that I still made *some* saves over the game, but the three mistakes I made - for their first three goals - would be the ones that would stick out the most. Goes with the territory of being a keeper, like.

When I fresh aired the ball for their third goal and their striker - laughing as he did so, at me - gratefully accepting the gift given to him and putting it away while the keeper meant to be guarding the goal lay flat on his back, I wanted to walk off the pitch there and then. We were like a man short with me in the team so why not make it official, eh?

Instead, I stuck around to concede one more although *no cunt* could've ever blamed me on that one and if anyone tried to we'd have been going for a wee roll around the pitch. Like the rest of the team - but for completely different reasons - I couldn't wait to get off the pitch quick enough, as soon as that whistle went.

The ninety minutes had completely passed me by, although I wasn't the only one out of the team that could've had that accusation aimed at them. Everyone remembers when the keeper has a howler, though and always forgets the midfielder who loses the ball fifty times a match or a striker who's too lazy to make runs to get himself in a position to even get a chance of a shot at goal, never mind actually *have* any.

'What the fuck was that out there, ya cunt?' Terry initially tried to have a go at me - once we were back in the dressing room - before he was drowned out by the rest of the boys, which was decent of them.

'Look, Tel. We were all out until fuck knows what time this morning. Cunts stotting about blootered right before kick off. Sepp's no different to the rest of us, eh?'

Strings said, admirably speaking up for me and fighting my corner.

'Aye, only he wasn't *out* last night' Terry replied, trying to keep it going. Hungover to fuck and wanting something or someone to take it out on.

'Aye, right enough. You never came out last night, did you?' Strings - having been countered - said to me before that smile of his crept onto his face.

'*There's* your fucking answer then. Haw, Jock? Make sure this cunt gets fucking hammered before the quarter final. This fresh as a daisy stuff doesn't seem to work on him'

Strings taking the heat out of things there and then. Good cunt, Strings, though. Type of boy who rarely *has* a fucking pound but if he does he'd give it to you if you needed it more. Always backs his mates up, doesn't mince his words either and what you see is what you get, unless you happen to be the owner of fruit machines, obviously.

'Just an off game, boys. It's happened before and will sure as fuck happen again in the future, I'm just glad I got it out my system before the quarter final.' I tried to front things out, while not even knowing how - or where - I'd *be* by the time the quarter finals rolled around.

For now - following the final game of the group - it really was going to be a case of letting the paranoia truly begin, while trying to act as normal as I could around the rest of the team. This not always possible when scenarios would throw themselves up such as the team deciding to go *back* to BCM because - once more - they'd been knocked back from clubs that had been - originally - more towards the top of their list for the night.

The mere mention of going back there, enough to send me into a flap. Through the paranoid thoughts living rent free in my head, as soon as it was mentioned about BCM I instantly conjured up a scenario of us being in there *exactly* when a few coppers would come in - with my picture from the CCTV - asking any of the people in there if they'd seen the man in the picture.

Aye, fuck that, I thought. I'm not going to make it *that* easy for them. Taking myself back to the hotel that night and letting the rest of the team get on with things.

Had a wee moment of clarity, walking back from the strip, though. I *knew* that my reasons for not going to the club with the rest of the team were top grade irrational. Clarity was something I could've done with in spades.

By the time I'd got back to the hotel - so deep in thought I'd been that I'd actually walked *past* the fucking place ten minutes before so had to double back the way I'd come - I'd self coached myself into adopting the 'no news is good news' approach to things.

Whether I'd be able to keep that attitude up? Different question altogether but with the quarter final coming up in a couple of days, I *needed* to make sure I had my mind right.

Because while I might've got away with things in the - as good as - dead rubber match against the Estonians, I definitely wasn't going to be given a pass if I put in a repeat performance, once we got into the whole knockout phase part of proceedings.

We'd been told earlier on that day that we'd been drawn against *The Saint George,* a team from Bermondsey, London.

And it would go without saying that the difference between making an absolute cunt out of things against a team from Estonia and putting it into my own net during a - in what would inevitably be hyped up by our own players as - Battle of Britain?

Absolutely fucking *massive.*

No one was going to be able to be posted as missing that day with *everyone* needed at the top of their game. According to Jock, the team from England were like a southern version of ourselves, only less skillful - although you could never rely on the truth, if Jock thought otherwise - so we already *knew* that we were going to be in for a war. Aye, as if that wasn't taken as a fucking given anyway as soon as we found out the team - and nation - that we were drawn against!

In the mean time. I just needed to keep myself from going insane, thinking about riding some old lady to death *and* from ending up in a Spanish police cell.

Chapter 18

Strings

It was one of those days where you didn't need to set an alarm for getting you up in the morning. You were already lying in bed awake before it came around. I lay there, thinking of the match we had ahead of us later that afternoon, and my chance to stick on the old Copa Mundials once again. I was buzzing, completely filled with adrenaline. And that was before even getting out of bed. It had a cup final feel about things. Then again, it was against the English. It fucking *was* a cup final.

Meeting up with the rest of the squad for a psychological style team breakfast that Jock had arranged us to have at Jimmy's - a Scottish pub not far from the hotel - it was apparent that I wasn't the only one buzzing and in that whole frame of mind. Montana *buzzing* in a different kind of way. Fucking wish I'd had a pound for every time the radge bastard had turned up for one of our games, like he was that morning. I'd have had enough money to not only cancel my debt with McKenna but *buy* the cunt out and have him be *my* lackey.

There had been two different stories flying about when it came to him, one that he supported, the other that he denied. There was the very real possibility that - once the team had went off to sleep that night - he had slipped out, banged some Class A's into him while in BCM until sun up. This theory, met with full denials from him. *His* 'theory' being that some German bodybuilder that he'd got talking to by the pool the day before - Montana telling him about the match with the English coming up, shared enemy and that - the guy, Montana going at great pains in his story to make sure that we knew he was from

Frankfurt, having offered him some Ephedrine, telling Montana that they would put a wee bit of extra zip into his performance.

'Fucking ephedrine?' Wullie laughed before speculating if that was the same drug that got Maradona thrown out of the World Cup.

'You get pulled for a drug test you'll be on your way home, lad. A modern day Willie Johnston, if you will,' Terry - as always - had his opinion on things.

Not that we were playing in a tournament that took itself as serious as to have designated drug testers, Jock Hunter didn't miss the chance to have his say.

'Listen, if they were to drug test that dafty, bloody ephedrine would be the *last* thing he'd be worrying about showing up,' he said, looking disapprovingly at Montana, clearly not buying his 'a big boy done it then ran away' line of defence.

Weirdly, had it been any cunt else who had broken curfew before such a big game, the rest of the squad would've been fucking raging at him but - after years of it - we'd been so used to Montana turning up before a game absolutely wired after being up all night but with an ability to *usually* put in a performance that we kind of just accepted it. I say 'usually' because the boy had obviously had his moments out on the pitch while in his drugged haze.

Things like fresh airing the ball because he was seeing double - going for the wrong ball, the one not actually there - to shoving a couple of lines of Ching up his hooter in the bogs at half time because he'd felt like he was coming down during the first half, and that it was affecting his performance, only to go right back onto the pitch for the second half - flying on those two lines of gear - and commit one of the more dangerous of kinds of over enthusiastic 'strikers tackle' which saw him seeing red and removed from the second half action almost as soon as it had begun.

Hunter - tapping into the whole patriotism of the day - had decided that breakfast in a Scottish establishment would be an appropriate start to things. I had a wee laugh, thinking about teams like the Italians and Germans and what *they'd* have as a pre match breakfast, while we sat there tucking into our cultural delights such as square sausage, haggis and tattie scones, washed down by glasses of ice cold Irn Bru and cups of Scottish Blend tea.

Funnily enough, Montana wasn't too keen on the sausage, haggis and tattie scone element to this breakfast but found no shortage of takers when it came to relieving him of what he hadn't touched. When reminded - by Hunter - that there was no way he'd be equipped to play ninety minutes in a match - that was nailed on - that was going to be full of high intensity from start to finish it took a happy medium coming through Montana agreeing to get some fruit into him and a protein shake from the wee smoothie shop that was on the other side of the road from our hotel to placate Hunter.

'Just don't make me eat *that* stuff'

All that Montana was really concerned about.

'Wonder what the other mob are up to right now?' The Monk speculated before adding that they were probably doing something similar to us, only having a 'full English'

'Those cunts like to make out they invented the concept of a fried breakfast,' Coffee opined, which I'd assumed was not factually based although let's face it. If there's *any* cunt who's going to come up with the concept of making the most important meal of the day your most unhealthy - by frying it - then you'd like to have thought that out of the two nations to attempt it then the bookies would've had the country of Scotland as odds on. Wouldn't bet against the Sherman Tanks being in with a shout either though because any country that accepts pizza for breakfast is definitely for the watching.

I was on the fence whether Jock's idea for us to have breakfast in a Scottish pub - covered in Scottish fitba, domestic and international, strips that holidaymakers had pinned to the walls and ceilings along with various felt pen scribbles, signatures and messages on them - had been a master stroke or an error in judgement. It was easy enough to see what he'd been aiming for. Get the lads hyped up for the game while instilling some passion for our land of birth. He'd never done this for any of the other matches so he was clearly looking to inject some Scottish pride into us for that particular day. It *is* possible to *over*hype someone, though. Just ask anyone who has ever tried to get a bairn to bed when it's all hyped up on E numbers?

We were already playing a team of cockneys, how hyped did the man want us? And that was before he'd told us about the match being mentioned back home in the Evening Times the night before. This only because Jock *himself* had put in a call to their fucking sports desk from - Magaluf - to tell them about it, figuring the whole Battle of Britain aspect could well have been something that would've grabbed their attention. Which it most certainly did.

'So if you didn't already think that you were representing your city and country, you bloody well do now. The amount of people who haven't even seen you lot kick a ball once but will be wanting you to win today, simply on principle, because of who you're playing'

'Well, we'll *need* to fucking win now because if we don't we may as well not go back home, eh?' Rossi said, not exactly one hundred percent in jest.

Unlike the previous three games, where we were hardly fit as fiddles, anxiously waiting to arrive at the stadium to get on with things. This time around, we couldn't get up there quickly enough. There were two quarter finals scheduled to take place that day. One afternoon match and one in the evening and despite having to play in the much more relentless conditions of the afternoon, it was better that way because I don't know what we'd have all done if we'd had to kick about in the hotel, waiting on evening coming around. Nah, we couldn't fucking wait to get up there. We had urgent work to attend to.

When the bus pulled into the stadium car park there were already a couple of mini buses parked. Looking like they'd just arrived before us with men piling out of it while some boy stood at the back getting all their bags out.

That's got to be them - The Saint George - I thought to myself. they definitely looked like a group that were there to play a match and since we were the only other team due to play, I got the number four after adding the obligatory two twos together.

First impressions on them? I thought that they looked like they'd all starred in that Ross Kemp programme, Britain's Hardest Pubs. But then again, so did we. It promised to be quite an event. Of course, it didn't much defuse that with their being a few less than friendly words exchanged between the two sets of players, once all off their busses.

Wasn't even us who started it, mind. The second I heard one of them say 'Jock cunts' I knew there wasn't going to be any turning of blind eyes. Terry right over to the boy who had said it, telling this walloper how old and weak his patter was but how it would still be enough to get his head ripped off. As tends to always be the case, the boy who'd said it looked like he'd seen a ghost, once his words had provoked a reaction. Him only recovering his composure *once* enough people had got between him and Terry.

'Oh fahk off you sweaty cunt. I'll see you out on the pitch, you mug'

He wasn't the biggest out of them by any stretch which I suppose was the reasons for the bigger mouth to compensate. Could only have been five six five or seven. Inspiral Carpets style bowl cut that looked like it hadn't been washed in months and a set of teeth that made Shane McGowan look like he was one of the 'after guys' off a toothpaste advert.

'Aye, you keep talking wee man. Going by the look on your team mates' faces, even *they* know you're talking pish,' Tel said, cooled down a wee bit and showing a much needed bit of maturity. Maturity being a key asset we'd be needing in spades over the game, if we wanted to finish the match with the same amount of players that we started it with.

I'd also heard someone shouting 'Fahking junkie wankers' at us which I'd thought of as a bit of a weird insult as - without ever having lived there - I was pretty sure that London Town must've had a strong and thriving Heroin community. Cunt watches Trainspotting once and thinks - because we're from Edinburgh - we're all on the fucking skag, eh?

Away from that, there were other words shared between both teams but nothing that threatened to spill over into something more serious. After all, we had the *whole game* for that caper, eh?

By the time we'd reached the dressing room, half the team were now fired up over something they'd heard or seen moments earlier. And they'd hardly been what you'd have looked on as calm before that point.

'Fucking Sweaty Socks? Cockney rhyming slang pricks'

'Did you see that big cunt with the skinhead and the face that looked like both his cheeks had been slapped with an oversized salmon? Putting up the fists?'

'That lump in the Tachini tracksuit, telling me that he was going to break my legs out there'

Of course, all the Muirhouse players had acted nothing other than angelic during the exchanges outside and there was no possibility of the London team now sitting in *their* dressing room voicing off about similar things said in their direction!

Jock Hunter - watching everyone caught up in the rage that they were in - just smiled while rubbing his hands together before announcing - to whoever could hear him over top of their own moans and gripes.

'Well there'll be no need to gee up the lot of you today, eh?'

And he wasn't wrong, either.

Fuck cup finals or league deciders, I'd never wanted to win a match more in my life, and I'd been one of those who had tried to be focussed enough to not let the baggage of *who* we were playing become a thing? It was hard not to get swept up in, though. It's like any derby match, I suppose. You can try and play things down and say you're not going to get worked up or fuck all but the day the match arrives your whole attitude changes, and there's nothing you can do about it - apart from taking a couple of Vallies - other than be carried away by things.

'Now, no capers during the warm up. Just blank the other team out in their half of the pitch. As far as you're concerned, they're not even there. Keep that bloody pent up aggression for the game'

Jock's wise words to the team before we all ran out pre game, for our warm up.

Obviously, there was a wee bit of sniping between a few players - closest to each other by the halfway line - but apart from that, we ignored their presence as much as possible. Their fans, though? Aye, bit of a different scenario, there. Congregated behind Sepp's goal, a decent sized mob of twenty (ish) loud and lairy in England tops and union jacks wrapped around them - that kind of vibe - standing there already getting fired into carry outs. As we'd find over the match, the more bottles and cans they tanned, the worse they'd become.

Me and Montana choosing to see the funny side of things to the way they'd greeted us when we took to the pitch.

'WANKERS, WANKERS, WANKERS, WANKERS'

I gave them a sarcastic thumbs up before putting my hands in the air and giving them an applause. Montana blowing them a couple of kisses before we both turned our backs on them and went for a jog. Naturally, not every Muirhouse player reacted in such an easy going way.

The Monk, turning to the crowd and - once they'd stopped singing - asking one of them if he was including his own mum in the song, or was it a case that she'd just taken that extra bit of shine to The Monk.

'Cahnt,' the lad erupted, looking like he was up for invading the pitch and having it with The Monk before being held back by some of his mates.

'It's not worth it, Bal. Leave it, fella'

'Well, you know where I am, ya wee fucking gimp,' Tel said, arms out like he was Christ the fucking Redeemer before getting on with his warm up.

It's funny how - when you have that wee bit of fire in your belly about something - the heat didn't dominate things pre game. Maybe we'd just managed to finally get ourselves acclimatised by the fourth match but personally, I didn't think so. The distraction of the whole circus of the day, enough to give us something *else* to focus on, other than how fucking hot it was. Heat comes from different ways, though. While - somehow - insulated from the warmth of the sun up above. It was going to be *impossible* to escape the white heat from what was taking place on the pitch.

We got back inside for those final ten minutes before kick off to get ourselves match ready while hydrating for the forty five ahead of us.

Jock didn't fuck around with his final parting words before we left to - as good as - go out to war.

'Now with these lot being English, I'm expecting more of a British style of play from them so as far as today goes, it's Muirhouse Violet rules applies. Just go out and play your game, like you would do against any team of bams we'd face on a Sunday back home. Which means you do as much as you can possibly get away with when it comes to the laws of the game, because you can be bloody sure that's what *they'll* be doing. Don't be getting drawn into anything with any games they might want to play. Just go out there and look after yourselves - and your team mates - but don't go picking up any stupid cards'

I agreed with pretty much every thing that he'd said, *apart* from the subject of yellow and red cards. *Those* - as far as I could pragmatically see - were going to be collateral damage.

'Aye, we'll see what we can do on that last part, Jock, but I don't think any of us can go making any promises there, like'

I joked, - well, *said* it like a joke, at least - trying to get a wee laugh out of everyone to take the edge out of the tension filled dressing room. It was a waste of time, though. The whole starting eleven were literally pacing about the room waiting on the call from the referee.

The fucking national anthems, though? I'll be honest, when they played them - out of the world's shittiest set of stadium speakers - that first game against the Portuguese team. I thought it was a nice wee novelty. Had never stood in a row on a fitba pitch - like the mens international side - while Flower of Scotland played. For the next couple of games I'd never treated it as serious and had seen it as fuck all other than just procedure. This was different though. It tends to be the case when God save the Queen is followed by Flower of Scotland, though.

By the time the anthems were over and done with, if you weren't ready by that point then you shouldn't have been on the pitch, and I think that would've applied to the Bermondsey boys as well. Was near on a cut scene from Braveheart - our reaction - when the song came to an end.

As for the pre match handshakes? Waste of fucking time. The referee instructing us to walk down the line of the Cockneys and shake hands with each other. Instead, you had some of them who were turning down the chance to shake a Muirhouse player while some of us just walked down the line - facing forward the whole time - as if there wasn't anyone standing there to the side of them. There were more sneers and snide comments made to each other than handshakes.

What a backdrop for a game of fitba to start off with, like.

We were - as you'd expect - in our fucking element and - running off into our half - absolutely ganting on the whistle going to get things underway.

It came soon after and I can only describe the opening scenes to the match as physical combat. The referee - having maybe done his history homework - deciding to take the approach of letting each team assault the other as many times as they liked, without any cards being produced. They say that's what the good refs do in matches like between two teams with 'previous' or some kind of agenda but I don't think it makes them out to be higher beings. All it means is that they're someone who knows that if they bring out a card in the first couple of minutes then they'll need to keep going after that, and the game will soon turn into a farce.

Both teams didn't fuck around though when it came to the clear pass that the referee was giving everyone. Things only calming down when one of their midfielders committed a deliberate trip from behind on Daz. With it being right under the nose of the ref too - and how obviously intended the foul was - he really *had* to book the boy. Their number six moaning his puss off at the ref, stating how many things others had been let away with yet *he* ends up booked, and missing the point completely in stating so.

I mean, he wasn't wrong, about all of the other examples, even if his version of events was rather one sided. Neglecting to mention that they had a central defence that looked like the fucking Mitchell brothers and who had been systematically taking it in turns to 'upset' both Rossi and Montana while conveniently bringing up Sepp jumping to collect the ball and kicking out at their striker karate style and Terry - in a very much premeditated fashion - elbowing their number eight bang in the coupon while protecting himself from an incoming challenge. Terry's elbow - admittedly - quite nasty. Saw the boy coming in towards him, and was ready. Drew blood from his mouth, the lot. Had to go off the pitch for a few minutes and on his return was pointing at Tel and mouthing off at him being next.

Terry - as always on a fitba pitch - completely unfazed by this. Only winding the boy up even more. This was just one of many vendettas that had already been achieved. I had my own thing going with that wee cunt from outside the stadium. The boy with the bowl cut. A right nippy wee bastard to play against who just would not shut his fucking mouth. We'd already fouled each other a couple of times in that first fifteen but in fairness, there were mini battles going on all over the place.

Once the madness of that first fifteen had passed, a bit of fitba broke out, to our misfortune. Should've been a foul anyway - the way their striker had backed and backed his way into Delaney - but when he managed that deft wee flick on, his partner had read it all the way and was put in one on one with Sepp and easily finishing, we were one down.

Due to the layout of the stadium, it allowed for fans to move around it, which meant that the mob that were there to support the cockneys were simply going to be behind the goal that their team were shooting into. Looking towards the goal, I could see Sepp picking the ball out of the net while one of them was as close to him as possible - shouting something at him through the nets - while around him, his mates were spraying beer all over the shop.

'Fucking come on now, Muirhouse'

I clapped my hands, going round most of the team as we made our way up to take centre. I didn't like how the heads seemed to be instantly down the moment that ball had hit the net. It was like all of that fire and fury they'd had had been extinguished in a single moment.

'You'll be back sitting in your shitty little council estate house looking for your next fix while we're playing in the final, mug'

Bowl cut boy winked to me when we next came up against each other following the goal.

I tried to just ignore him - and not play into his hands of taking my concentration away from events on the pitch - but still couldn't resist replying to him that if he can't even afford a fucking haircut and, instead, has his mum do it for him then I wasn't imagining that the cunt lived in fucking Mayfair himself.

'Jock cunt'

The weak as piss come back which achieved nothing other than producing a wee laugh out of me, as I ran past him to keep up with play.

Wasn't fucking laughing when they made it two nil with around five minutes left of the half. Filed under 'fuck all you could do about it' but a dagger to the heart all the same. Would you believe it but it came through my nemesis in the middle of the park? The absolute *last* cunt out of their eleven players that I'd have wished to have scored a goal, if you could call it that.

He'd got away from me in the centre circle, leaving me chasing after him. I'd not picked up a card by this point so thought it might be a good time for me to take a 'good yellow' for the team, but didn't quite get there in time. The boy taking a shot - which wasn't even that good of a connection - which The Monk stretched to block, but in doing so the ball hitting the inside of his heel, sending it off into the opposite direction of the flat footed Sepp who could do fuck all else other than watch the ball roll into the net.

The Saint George player celebrated this as if he'd scored a recreation of Zidane's goal at Hampden or some equivalent. Bit of a red neck, like. Still, two nil was two nil, regardless of how impressive or shitty the ball had crossed the line.

The dressing room at half time wasn't a pleasant place to be. I'd never seen Jock go so fucking mental at the team before. Normally he would refrain from going so far because of the very real chances of someone having had enough and decking him. That day, he didn't seem to care over the risks of speaking his mind, fully.

The team were angry with Jock, answering back at him. Angry at each other, laying blame on each other for incidents that had taken place in the half, and, ultimately, angry at themselves for now being in the position they were. This was our big day, and we were blowing it. You couldn't really have done anything to prevent either goal. One should've been a foul for us and the other? Well, you can't do fuck all about deflections. Of course, the whys and hows didn't really matter, sat there at half time. All that really mattered was that we were in a massive hole and it wasn't going to be easy getting back out of it, and if we were on the verge of fighting with each other during the break then we had *no chance* in the second half.

Taking to the pitch to the sound track of *Ingerllund Ingerllund Ingerllund,* courtesy of the mob who had now changed half and stood behind the other goal. I'd love to have said that we were like a team transformed and one that had the opposition on the back foot from the off, as a team two down *should* approach the first five to ten minutes of the second half.

As teams a couple of goals up tend to do, the English were less adventurous in the second half. What they had they preferred to hold, by the looks of thing. This giving us a bit more of the ball but as the minutes ticked by we weren't looking like knowing what to do with it. Obviously, the half was littered with fouls as well which put a stop to any real flow to things. Proper stop start. They foul us, some pushing and shoving, maybe a card comes out. We return the favour. Repeat to fade.

It was around the seventy minute mark that things took a turn, sadly not involving us sticking one away into the onion bag.

One of these fannies - behind the goal - had decided that it would be a good idea to lob one of his empty bottles of San Miguel at Sepp. The oblivious keeper of ours - with back to goal - feeling the bottle scud off the back of his head. Due to us going up the other end of the park at the time, it was only Delaney who had clocked Sepp going down, and the brown bottle lying beside him. But he wasted no time in letting everyone know.

Screaming at the ref to stop play while running towards Sepp to see how he was. With the whistle going, the team - en masse - ran down to the other half of the pitch. And it all got a bit fucking mental after that. Some of our players were in amongst the fans behind the goal, hand to hand combat. One of their fans had ran onto the pitch - with fuck knows what plans he'd imagined up in his head was going to go down - only to turn on his heels with Terry hot on them, eventually the big man taking a well timed swipe at the boy's legs which was enough to take him down spectacularly, and then came Tel's carefully placed Predator boot to the boy's coupon.

The Saint George players finding it unable to resist getting involved themselves - and through this and how they'd used their names - confirming that the lads behind the goal were indeed their mates. In amongst this. Sepp's now sitting up, with a head knock being out with the skill set of Pat's magic sponge applying and Ralgex spraying capabilities.

Miraculously - and I felt that this was purely down to there being so many things happening at once - the referee didn't even produce one card when, in reality, he could've easily brought out enough to officially end the match. Referees, eh? Either sending you off for something innocuous or letting twenty two men off with taking part in a riot. Some cunts, them, like?

Due to the capers going on all around and how long it took for a Sepp - who really could've and should've been subbed - to get himself match ready again, it took an absolute age before we re-started the game. Coffee tapping at the imaginary watch on his wrist to the ref, reminding him how many minutes had been wasted. Our midfielder being waved away by the ref in a way that I couldn't decide was through arrogance or through it being so obvious that aye, time would clearly need to be added on.

I'd hoped that Sepp taking a bottle to the nut would have been some kind of catalyst to get us fired up enough to go right at them for the last part of the game, but apart from a couple of half chances we never threatened.

'They're going home, they're going home they're going, the Jocks are going home'

You heard coming from behind Sepp. Hard times, like.

When we reached the ninety minute mark and the referee indicated that there would be eight minutes added on, the cockneys were apoplectic, but they were fucking at it if they didn't believe that it had been an adequate enough amount of time to be added on. They definitely weren't fucking moaning when they were swapping kicks and punches with our players during the melee that Sepp's bottling had provoked.

One of their midfielders was still trying to moan about it when he was disposed, in his own half, near the halfway line, by Daz who, - and fuck knows where the quick thinking came from after such a draining hour and a half, mentally and physically - looking up, ingeniously shot for goal. Having clocked that their keeper had also been out mouthing off at the ref for such an extended amount of injury time being awarded.

We could do fuck all other than just stand there and watch the ball go over him, while hoping it was going to dip enough under the crossbar. Time seemed to slow down, watching it fly through the air. But, fuck me, what a beautiful sight it was when that Adidas Tango dropped into the net.

'Have that, you Inspiral Carpet looking muggy little cahhhhhnt'

I turned to my mate - who had been only a few yards away, also watching Daz's strike - and said in a questionable Cockney accent.

It was only a glimmer of hope, but it was more than we'd had as the team slipped into injury time. Scoring two goals in eight minutes after having gone through an energy sapping ninety minutes was the tallest of orders. But in Muirhouse, we're taller.

Our equaliser - controversially - coming in what was technically the tenth minute of injury time and effectively the last kick of the game. The Saint George taking centre and the ref immediately blowing for full time. Before this had happened, though. We'd been blessed with the funny as fuck sight of the Cockney team's manager running onto the pitch going absolutely fucking radge over the fact our second goal had come outside of the eight minutes awarded.

'Where did you get those fahking extra two minutes from you dago wankah?'

Words that would be enough to see you sent to the stand, which he duly was. The piss ripped out of him by some of our players while he was 'removed' from the field by some of his back room team.

Through - a rare - Terry's equaliser, coming through an almighty scramble in the box that had seen several players make half arsed attempts at either scoring or clearing, that finally saw the big man getting a firm enough connection to steer the ball through the sea of bodies and into the net, we had achieved the improbable. Two goals in injury time, against the *team* that we'd scored them? What a fucking feeling, like.

We all know how the game of fitba goes, though. If a team is two up only to blow that lead, and especially in the dying moments of the match. You all know who has the momentum out of the two sides on the pitch, and who the more likely winner is going to be. Psychologically one team's heads have gone and the other's have got all kinds of top notch endorphins flowing through them.

The only real flaw in this thinking - which on any other occasion would ring more true - was that we were absolutely fucking knackered. We'd never had to play more than ninety minutes and even then, that had been *enough*. Equally, the English team were in as bad a spot. Let's face it, pub teams - in general - aren't built for one hundred and twenty minutes at the best of times, never mind in the Spanish afternoon.

As a consequence, the following thirty minutes of extra time were a non event. Two teams on there erses so much that even their desire to maim and insult each other had pretty much evaporated. No one likes things to come down to penalties - apart from sadists and neutrals - but the longer that extra time went on, the clearer it was that we were heading for them.

While not looking forward to the pressure cooker of what the pens were going to be, I was just glad to hear the ref blow the whistle for the end of the additional thirty because I literally couldn't run anymore, barely anyone on the pitch could, to be fair.

When it came to the pens? As they say, it's a horrible way to lose a game of fitba. And things didn't exactly get off to the best of starts when Rossi skied his attempt over the bar, to the delight of the crowd who had torn it around to the other goals the moment that they'd clocked the ref take the logical decision of taking the kicks into the ones that they *weren't* stood behind.

The cockneys scored with their first penalty to go one up on us. This piling a wee bit of extra pressure on the amount that was already kicking about on yours truly who stepped up to take penalty number two. Miss it - and then they score their next - and we'd almost be as good as done, before we'd even got started. Trying to focus but unable to *not* look at the Londoners behind the goal all trying to put me off, one of them literally bending over and - having pulled his shorts down - showing his arse. Even with all of that nonsense going on, I still slotted it easily enough. Giving their keeper the eyes, while sending him diving the wrong way.

In those moments - when your team has just scored *their* penalty - all you want to do is see the other side make a cunt out of their next one. The English boy didn't, though. Taking the easy route and blasting it straight down the middle with - the already committed to diving - Sepp having to watch it fly into the net, putting them back in front, two one.

Next up for us, Montana. I thought about the fact he'd been out the night before and hadn't been to bed - because he was working his fucking ticket if he thought I'd bought that ephedrine off a bodybuilder pish - and had now played a hundred and twenty minutes. How was he, mentally? Was he up for this? He looked nervous, standing with hands on his hips as he waited on the signal. You know how sometimes you just need to look at a player's face to know he's going to miss his penalty? Written all over Montana. And to be fair, he done his best, *to* miss it.

At the end of his run up, he managed to slide right as he was connecting with the ball, kicking one foot with the other and sending it in an unintended direction high to the keeper's left. I assumed it was over so when I saw the ball clip the inside of the postage stamp and end up in the net, was breathing a major sigh of relief.

Montana, turning back to the team - all stood at the halfway line watching him take that long walk back - taking his two hands and making the top corner sign with them, with a look on his face as if there wasn't ever a doubt he'd notch, even though he *knew* how lucky he'd got. Fucking camouflage couldn't have hidden it.

These bastards weren't for missing any though. Putting away their third with as much ease as the first two. Sepp hadn't come close to any of them.

By our fifth penalty - Wullie cleverly putting the keeper on his arse before even striking the ball - we'd done all we could do. It was all on one man now. Unfortunately for us, a man who may or not have been seeing double for the last hour or so. Kind of like playing Montana in goal after he's come straight from the club. Sepp had been insistent on playing on even though he could easily have been suffering from concussion. I'd felt that some of this had been down to how badly he'd played in the previous game. Even told him as much while he was recovering. Told him it wasn't worth it - risking his health - playing on, but he was having none of it.

One of their Mitchell brothers stepped up to take it with a look of urgency, like he just wanted to get it over and done with. This showing when the whistle went and he wasted no time in his run up. Hit it well, like, and to one side. He didn't really do fuck all wrong and it was all to do with the unbelievable save that Sepp decided to pick out, right at the very moment it was required. Us - redeemed, for now, at least - going absolutely tonto up at the halfway line while Sepp in a he who laughs last kind of way turned around to the knuckle scrapers behind the goal, giving them the *shhhhhhh* sign and being showered with beer for his impudence.

Which brought us into sudden death. Before the game I'd have thought there would've been more chance of *sudden death* coming through one of the players keeling over in the heat, but here we were.

Daz, one of those on the list but after the first five and - obviously - hoping that matters would have been taken care of before being called on was up next but considering the coolness of how he'd taken his goal earlier on, there was no surprise when he sent their keeper the wrong way to put us ahead for the first time in the shootout.

'You're fucking missing this, by the way'

Terry shouted at their midfielder - the big lanky sub that had come on as a substitute when one of their players who was already on a yellow was getting himself close to an upgrade - as he started making his way from the centre circle.

He, in fact, did not miss it. Instead, delivering the best penalty out of any player yet. High and measured towards Sepp's top shelf.

'You were saying, you muppet?'

He said, when he'd made his way back up. Fair play to the boy and there wasn't much Terry could say back. But sometimes you can say something without opening your mouth, eh?'

Coincidentally, Terry himself now up to take his.

'Don't go bottling it or anything, treacle'

The lanky boy said, which you couldn't blame him for jumping all over, once he saw who was up next.

To a chorus of whistles and boos - behind the goal - big Tel ran up with man on a mission like purpose and - feigning towards shooting to the keeper's left - stroking it in the net to the right, keeper already committed and unable to do anything about it.

With it all being such a high pressure situation, there had been a lot to take in and because of that I'd never clocked that my mate - who we'd enjoyed the ding dong with all match until both tiring - hadn't taken one yet. It was only when I seen him beginning to leave the halfway line that I realised.

'You sure you've got enough energy to even make it all the way down there to the penalty spot? I don't know, you look kind of fucked, like'

No reaction from him. No bites, not even a look back. He was fucking bricking it.

'Go on, Col my saan'

One of their players shouted after him but once more, all we saw was the back of him. And it was *still only* the back of him that we saw when we broke into the - unnatural amount of energy shown for men who minutes before could barely move a muscle - sprint from the halfway line, making a beeline for the Sepp who was on his knees looking up to the skies.

The bowl cut headed hoor had elected to go down the middle but Sepp had managed to get a leg to it, enough to divert the ball over the bar.

We'd fucking done it. It had been an ordeal at times but we'd done it. We were in the semi finals. *Who* we'd be playing against? At that moment in time, that really all was irrelevant to us.

On our way towards Sepp, I couldn't help but ruffle the boy's bowl head on the way past him while offering him a 'better get the jet ready to take you back to the palace, pal' before continuing on and jumping on top of the already growing pile of bodies, with our goalkeeper at the very bottom of it.

By the time we all got off the top of him the poor cunt - our hero - was barely able to fucking breathe. Maybe our celebrations had been a little excessive and exuberant - or maybe they hadn't been *enough* - but by the time we were all back on our feet and looking around, all we could see was the backs of The Saint George players, as they disappeared down the tunnel.

Bit of a lack of class - from them - I thought to myself before remembering that if the boot was on the other foot there was not a fucking chance Muirhouse Violet were going to stand there and watch all those wild celebrations, just so they could shake the hands of the team who had done fuck all other than kick and wind them up all game long. Even their fans - who I'd have expected a reaction from - had filtered away without even a whimper.

What a feeling, though and one that if we were to eventually reach - and win - the final, I wasn't sure would be able to be replicated again.

We'd earned our place in the semis and not a single person could have argued that we didn't deserve the piss up that was coming to us for the rest of the day, but how we'd had to work for both.

After the event, I was happy to admit just what a horrible match it had been to play in, and how horrible a team they'd been to go up against and if it had been true what Jock had said - about them being an English version of us - then I could see why half the teams - back in Edinburgh - absolutely detested playing Muirhouse Violet.

Jock, who had stood there waiting to shake each players hand as they left the pitch - biggest smile I think he had ever cracked in his entire puff - was reminded by me that he would need to get back on the phone to the Evening Times and let them know the match report.

After all, we were local and national heroes. And even if we weren't, I sure as fuck *felt* like one as I made my way back to the dressing room.

Chapter 19

Strings

After the - almost unrivalled as a Muirhouse Violet player - high of the day before and the - by now, obligatory - tortuous training session that followed, it was time for me and Benji to go to work. Because simply through our night time drinking habits, we'd been haemorrhaging money between us. And it went without saying, that not insignificant fine we'd had - handed down by the judge - wasn't going to fucking pay itself.

'Mate, you think I'm thrilled to be going out for the afternoon working when I should be out there on a sun lounger sleeping off training?'

My reaction to *that* look from Benji, followed by the sigh, when I'd grabbed hold of him to get going. The same look and sigh he'd given me the last time.

'Aye, and whose fault exactly is that?'

He got up from the table he'd been sitting at, having a pint of fresh orange and lemonade while fucking about on Facebook on his phone.

I chose to ignore the comment, couldn't exactly have bitten, could I? Sometimes you've got no choice than to let things fly.

'Well, up to you, Benji boy. You can sit there bringing yourself up to speed with where cunts that you don't even fucking like have 'checked into' or you can come out with me and try and get us out the hole we're in. I'm just not sure how much understanding you'll get from the Spaniards when you tell them that you don't have the dough for them because you were too busy seeing that Sandra Burnett from Pilton was telling the world that she'd arrived at Asda'

He had a point, but so did I and it was probably best left at that.

We hit the street with one firm plan for the hours ahead. No alcohol. That last time turned out to be a complete waste of an afternoon. Aye, maybe we came back with a wee bit extra coin in our pockets than when we'd left the hotel with earlier that afternoon but it was hardly a life changing amount, and was, in fact, a drop in the ocean in relation to how much we were due the government. The bit that grated the most was that we'd spent more money while out 'working' than we'd come back with in profit. Aye, I probably shouldn't have taken on that boy - when it came to that punchball machine bet - but that all comes back to us peaving while we were meant to be switched on criminal professionals.

With it being a case of stringing in new territory - in a foreign country - I was way out of my comfort zone. Trying to act on the same instincts that got me by back home, when out putting in a shift, but when you're in another country. Sometimes what works in one place doesn't always have to mean it's going to be the same result somewhere else. Us landing up in that Blarney Rubble's wasn't *because* it was a boozer, it was because of the placement of the puggy inside of it. As we'd been walking along the street - doing a wee bit reconnaissance - *no* establishment was deemed off limits. Desperate times equals desperate measure, though, as they say.

Soon as I saw the layout of that Irish pub - and the advantageously placed puggy - I knew we'd found our first place to get started in. Obviously didn't bargain on the amount of food and drink we'd buy while *at* work in such a tempting environment. You learn by your mistakes, though. Something we'd intended to do when it came to our next attempt.

We walked along the street discussing plans for the day.

'You know how I work, Benji boy. I'm fully behind that whole look before you leap proverb. Don't go into anything with eyes half shut. Never string a place upon seeing it for the first time. I take my time but it - generally - always pays dividends for us'

None of that, anything that could be denied by Benji. Take away that *issue* with the Weegies years before and I would've had an, otherwise, unblemished record.

'I'm not saying you don't, mate,' Benji said defensively as he passed me a smoke.

'No, I *know* you're not, Benji but what I'm saying is that with five days left before we go back home, I'm, *we're*, going to have to think outside the box when it comes to where we're going to find puggies to string. We don't have weeks for me to case out joints before deciding to make a move on them. We need *instant* results, while we're not even in our own country'

'Aye no pressure, eh? We've kicked the arse out of this holiday so much …

'Had a fucking good time in doing so, though, eh?' I briefly interrupted before he continued.

that we're already having to keep an eye on our money for the rest of what's left to go, so that we can still get a decent swally every night, along with life's other necessities like nicotine and food. But to the side of that, a problem that *most* people experience when they come away on their holidays, we - into the bargain - have got to pay the fucking Spanish authorities three thousand euros, and we don't have a fucking cent of it. *Think differently?* Aye, you're not fucking joking there, lad'

This new - desperate - approach to doing business saw us inside the Iberia Sol hotel, one of your more up market Magaluf hotels. An establishment that you'd have thought almost the fucking *last* place you'd think of to go and steal money from, but that was kind of the point.

I'd had the brainwave when thinking about a trip with a group of pals to Ibiza in the early nineties where - despite there for ten days - I'd made a cunt out of things after the first weekend and had used up a farcical amount of money within those first two days on drink, drugs, clubs and taxis back and forth to Playa den Bossa from our base in San Antonio. Regardless of having two of the greatest days and nights that I will never remember, it *did* leave things rather sticky for the rest of the holiday, so corners would need to be cut, if identified.

One of them had been a wee hustle I'd managed to pull off by literally walking into one of the more upmarket hotels near us - composed to the fucking two star apartments that *we* were living in - and bold as brass - just had a go at seeing if I could get breakfast in there without paying for it, thinking that - to any untrained eye - I'd have just appeared as a holidaymaker, staying at the hotel. Fucking cinched it, as well.

Due to the type of hotel it was, it had security dotted around all over the place and one stood directly outside the large dining room. I remember, walking towards him - looking every inch the *patron* with my shorts, flip flops and shades on while carrying my beach towel under my arm - thinking that this was the point where I was going to be rumbled or - at the very least - be asked to show my key or provide my room number.

Instead, though, getting to those big doors the lad in the beige uniform lit up with a big smile and opened the door to let me walk straight through.

'Buenos Dias, senor,' he said, smiling with a nod.

'And a buenos dias to you, hombre,' I gave him a thumbs up as I strolled in, where I was able to fill my boots with all kinds of breakfast related goods. Fry up stuff, continental, fucking omelettes made to order. Absolutely tremendous stuff, like.

Seizing on this, I had thought it sensible to be extra pally with the security boy on the way back out - couple of croissants for later on, shoved into napkins and hidden in my pockets while there was a selection of fruit tucked up inside my towel - figuring that I was one hundred percent coming back there for a scran again.

Getting the boy's name and telling him mines, wee bit of fitba talk while we were there - he was a Valencia fan - and I told him to have a good day and would see him later on about the hotel. It's all how things appear at times. The other security guards in the place? Any of them see me standing there having a good laugh and bit of craic with 'Emilio' and they're automatically likely to be less suspicious of me.

After that morning, I ate at the Balearic Boutique for breakfast - stealing enough to cover lunch - and at tea time for the rest of the holiday and not one single person said a thing about it. I mean, half the time the fucking door was opened by a smiling security guard, literally *allowing* you to come in and steal from them. That stroke of genius from me literally saved my whole holiday.

With that kind of entrepreneurial energy in mind, I decided that the two of us ducking into the large scale hotel complex might well have been one of my better ideas. Busy place, lots going on, many areas for any hotel workers to be looking after. I'd said we'd need to be thinking outside of the box and this was an example of that. In theory, I'd thought it had been a good idea. In theory.

The reality of it though was that while I had enjoyed the goodwill of what was probably the world's worst security firm - back in Ibiza - where as here in Magaluf, the security inside the Iberia Sol were a different beast altogether.

The guy on the door at the entrance to the front lobby was good as gold but after him it was fucking jobsworth city. First of all there were too many security stationed around for my liking although - once we'd found our way to the bar, where there existed a wee games area with a couple of puggies, Sega Rally car game that you actually sat in the car, few other arcade games, pool table and foosball table - we found only one to be standing around inside there.

Trying the friendly approach, I said a wee hola to him as we entered the bar but was given one back that suggested he really couldn't be ersed reciprocating but thought - since it was a holidaymaker of the hotel - he probably should. Because of this, his hello couldn't help but come across as less than warm and welcoming.

I tried not to take this personal and let any paranoia creep in. Instead, preferring to take things that he'd have replied in the same way to any other patron of the hotel, like he'd done to me.

Men of our word, we ordered a couple of cokes from the bar and made our way across to the games area. In theory - aye, there's that expression again - the place was perfect. With it being a bar - instead of a money making business like a real amusement arcade - there were barely any cameras for to be worrying about having Benji standing in positions to block them out. Mind you, when you've got that many security walking about a hotel complex, where's the need for *cameras?*

We got off to a good start, as well. I'd managed to pocket a good hundred and fifty euros inside the first twenty minutes. We'd not even drank half of our glasses of Coke before I was transferring all of that coin into Benji's bum bag. Hardly the height of fashion, I know, but I'd thought them the ideal accessory for going out stringing in a country where actually *wearing* one wasn't going to stick out.

Thinking on his feet - although I'm not sure if this was anything to do with the weight that he was having to stand about holding up in front of him - he asked the guy behind the bar if he needed change in return for notes. This being an offer the barman was pleased to accept. Me not moving from the puggy while watching the scene of Benji tipping out all of those coins onto the bar and assorting them into easily countable piles for the barman to inspect before swapping notes for them. I think that was the first thing that started to draw attention to us. I suppose it doesn't really matter *what* the reason for having attention drawn towards you is. If you're up to no good, you have attention now on you, like we did there inside the Iberia Sol. Over the next hour and a half - over a couple of cokes - I took out another three hundred and fifty which had been a decent couple of hours all round and something that had at least produced something - in a monetary way - that resembled a bit of daylight, when it came back to paying our fine.

'Five hundred euros down, only another two and a half thousand to go' I said to Benji as I was about to move over to the other Puggy and give that one a go, figuring I'd already pushed things further than I should've done with the first machine as you could travel the world a million times over and never sit and watch someone sit and win that amount of money from a puggy, in such a short space of time. Unfortunately, the security guard in the bar - who with fuck all else to do than stand and watch us - just happened to be in the position of watching this take place.

I'd always preferred to go with the jacket wedged into the coin dispenser part of a puggy - to disguise the loud noise of pound coins crashing down onto hard plastic - when back home on regular business but over there in Spain, that wasn't something open to me. Due to this, *every* cunt in the whole bar heard each and every win and coin drop out of the machine.

I'd just sat down at the next puggy when - in a kind of urgent whisper - Benji warned me to put my stringer away because the security boy was coming over to us.

Without turning around, I popped my stringer away in my shorts pocket and replaced it with a one euro coin in my hand, for appearances.

'You are very lucky today, senor?'

He'd positioned himself to my right side while Benji stood there on my left.

'Aye, aye I suppose you're right, eh? Sometimes it just goes your way, eh?'

I tried to pass off his comment even though I'd felt that there was more to it than a simple observation from him.

'These machines? No no no. They never give luck like that, amigo, never. I stand and watch people play them almost every day of my life, but no *luck* like you'

It left me really wanting to say to him 'aye, and your point is?' But I wasn't really in any kind of position for such attitude. I was stealing from the property and the man literally hired to prevent that kind of thing was right beside me, apparently questioning my good fortune.

'See, pal. That's *exactly* why I've moved onto this machine now. Was only a matter of time before the old luck ran out, eh?'

'And let me guess, you move on to *this* machine, and your good luck will continue?' He asked, but with a tone to it that I wasn't liking the sound of.

'Well, aye. That's the plan, like. Either that or I spunk the lot of what I took out of that one and put it into this one, mind. Can't rule that out either.' I tried to play things cool, but it never worked.

'No, senor,' he said, moving in closer to me so what he was about to say next was not going to be overheard.

'What the *plan* is that you give me half of what I have watched you 'win' since you came in here, instead of me having the Guardia Civil come straight over and arrest you for stealing'

'Wait a minute, here,' Benji jumped in. 'The boy sits down and plays a gambling machine and because he's winning you want half his winnings or you're calling the police? What kind of an operation is it you're running in here, like?'

He'd said it out loud and - apparently not seeing what I was seeing in front of us - I instantly grabbed him, telling him to keep his mouth shut.

He wasn't for letting it lie, though.

'What are the police going to lift him for, like? Being in possession of good fortune?'

Confident as you like, though. The security guard - answering the question but not through looking at the person who had asked it - looking directly at me and answering 'well I'm sure the police would be able to find the *reason* quickly enough when they get here, don't you?'

I don't know. It was possibly as simple as it was. He'd watched people play - and lose, mostly - that machine all day with wee pay outs here and there but - as is the way the fucking things are designed to function - generally more money going in them than coming out, something I'd bucked the trend on in a big way that afternoon.

'Well, just imagine what your bosses are going to say when they find out that you called the police on some guests, only for them to be innocent. And that's without us even talking about your attempted bribery'

I tried to style things out. Dangle the prospect of him losing his job all over this and hope that it would be enough to bring the boy back into line. Those that have actual jobs, it seems to be the biggest fear that they have in life - losing theirs - so I'd thought - aye, different country and that - the same rules would apply in Espana.

If I had attempted to intimidate him into backing down, it had failed, miserably. Him just sneering at me before replying

'But *are you* innocent, though?'

It was said with such certainty and - being in possession of the knowledge of what we'd been up to over the past couple of hours - something that had left me with not much in the way of an answer.

'The fact that the two of you think I am so loco to not know what you have been doing, it makes me want to take *all* of your winnings, never mind the half that I am asking for'

And right there, I sussed it all out. After a few quick - and publicly noisy - wins, and then Benji showing everyone the *extent* of the winnings, by exchanging the coinage with the barman. This cunt on security had been watching us - with a suspicion of what we were up to - letting us build the pot higher and higher before swooping in. The boy wasn't stupid, like. *That,* you had to hand to him.

Coming in closer to me to the point that he was talking directly into my ear - for clarity - he then went on to tell me that he knew *exactly* what we'd been up to and had stood and watched us doing it before asking me if he thinks scamming puggies had been something that people only did in Britain?

Fuck

While Benji stood there to the side of me - clueless - this security guard decided to give me a very brief but concise history of how - years back - Gypsy settlers in Mallorca had introduced, to the island, the concept of taking money from slot machines while - technically - not ever putting any money *in*.

'*Now* do you believe me when I say that if you do not pay me what I want I will have the police brought to the hotel. I cannot lose. Either I get a 'tip' from you and your friend or the police come, arrest you for fraud and I get big pat on back from my manager for being good at my job'

He said this with such self assurance, I wanted to fucking deck him. After what happened on that island, though. We were about the *last* people that needed anymore police involvement, because it would have been a given that two tourists being hauled up in front of a judge - for two separate reasons - was going to result in them probably not being released so easily, compared to the first time.

Feeling absolutely defeated and almost like I'd been playing a high stakes game of snakes and ladders and I'd just landed on a snake, after climbing several ladders on my way. I turned to Strings and told him to fish out half of what was in his bum bag.

'But, Strings, for fuck's sake, mate? The government? Our fine?'

I think he must've heard the words first and seen my face afterwards because any protests from him were instantly dropped when he seen the look on my coupon, and how rattled I'd most likely appeared. It's one thing to accidentally set fire to a piece of land but to go out with the *intention* of committing a crime - with regards to having my stringer on me - would, in my opinion, have been well frowned upon.

Back home in Scotland I'd have been classed as 'going equipped' and it wouldn't exactly have been a stretch to imagine that the Spaniards would've viewed things a similar way.

Tourists of all shapes and sizes always end up in trouble with the law when they're in Spain, normally all drink related. And they tend to get treated as such, and not looked at in the proper criminal sense. Just some dafties who done radge stuff when MWI. *Me* on the other hand, nah. I was just going to look like a criminal, which couldn't have been a good look. Coming to another country with intentions of carrying out crimes, even if, technically, that had *never* been the intention when I'd flown out. You know how that shite would end up being painted, though? Could just see the prosecutor

'So, we are being asked to believe that Mr Carson travelled alllll the way from Scotland to Mallorca - in possession of the apparatus required to carry out the crime - but had never intended to use it, while there?'

It wouldn't have looked good, however you wanted to try and dress it up.

'Now, I assume that neither of you are guests of this hotel so I will not expect to see you in the bar again, si?'

The guard said as he took the notes from me - looking around the room before quickly sliding them into his shirt front pocket - which I was now taking as the point where we should leave.

'It was a pleasure doing business with you'

He joked while ushering us both away from the second machine, before I'd even had a chance to test it out to see what fruits it could've brought.

As we were walking out of the bar, he went onto his walkie talky and said something in Spanish - which I'd taken to be in relation to me and Benji - this being the case when the security guard - who had greeted us with such a warm welcome when we'd arrived - was standing on the look out for us, to make sure that we left as planned.

'I can't believe that we just got shook down by a jobsworth security guard.' Benji said, taking his frustration out on a bairn's dummy tit - which had been lying on the ground - by booting it twenty yards against the quarter panel of a car, parked outside the entrance.

'Aye, he wasn't a jobsworth, mate. He was a leech who knew what the fuck we were up to from the minute we started winning'

I felt truly depressed as I went on to explain to Benji that our *craft* was something that had transcended the United Kingdom and was, in fact, an age old practice brought to the island by those ingenious travelling people who - if there was a way - would always find an alternative strategy towards approaching something.

'So does, that mean that this whole fucking island *knows* about cunts stringing puggies?'

Benji asked with a fearful look on his face which was matching how I was feeling inside. His face and the sinking feeling in my stomach both tracking with the fact that our only way that we had open to generate finances from had now become a lot more complicated.

'I'm not sure, Benji. Could've just been that he was more streetwise about things like stringing puggies. I was too busy trying to avoid the fucking cops being called on us to find out if this was generally known around town or not. Maybe with him being in security it was just one of those wee nuggets of information that he'd gathered over the years, eh?'

I speculated, but that's all it was, speculation. I didn't know what I didn't know but what I *did* know was that raising the money required, inside five days, with - potentially - half of Magaluf looking over our shoulders while we did it was going to be one bastard of a job to pull off.

Regardless of how desperate things were, I wasn't about to abandon my rule about pushing my luck, not that I'd had that much back inside the Iberia Sol. The possibility of almost being lifted for stringing had rattled me so much that there was not a fucking chance that we'd be moving on to try somewhere else that afternoon.

With around two hundred and fifty euros or so pocketed - which at the time felt like *two* - we headed back towards our hotel, heads down and with tails between our legs while we discussed the very real prospect - given the amount we needed to come up with while put against how many days we had left to raise it - of us not raising the dough required, and what consequences were going to follow as a result.

Chapter 20

Sepp

I'll be honest, when I saw the two shady looking fuckers pull up beside me in the street - in that BMW, - I thought it was the moment that I'd been waiting days on coming around, *finally* arriving. As it turned out, I couldn't have been more wrong. Thought I was a stick on for being taken away and done in by them, as part of some gangland assassination.

Not even fucking close.

I know they say that time's a healer and *that* was something I'd had a wee bit more of - since the night of the trip to BCM and the whole shagging someone to death unpleasantness that followed - but without getting carried away or fuck all, it had only been an extra few days I'd had to get my head right.

Felt I'd found redemption - when it came to making up for the last group game and my shocker I'd had in it - against the Cockneys by walking off the pitch as the hero, having saved the vital sudden death penalty. Have to be honest, though. Even during that - a Battle of Britain and a quarter final, at that - I was *still* caught in those dark thoughts. I'd found, though, that as the days passed I was managing to cope with things better, even if it was only minimally.

Just because I was coping with things, though. That didn't have to mean that I wasn't still expecting to end up in handcuffs, or worse than that. Still, every day that passed without either happening to me was classed as a win. The human mind can do that thing where it can lull you into a false sense of security, though. You know? No news is good news, and that kind of stuff. While I could've adopted that viewpoint I wasn't quite there yet. The superstitious side to me, chipping away while nip nip nipping at my brain with the thoughts of the moment I started to believe that I was out of the woods *that's* when I would find otherwise. I don't think I could've handled the high and extreme low that scenario would've brought, so decided I'd just sit tight, there in the woods.

I can't overstate the *relief* that when I was asked to get into the car, it was to offer me a bribe, instead of being driven somewhere to my death. Obviously, I'm a Muirhouse boy. Rarely leave the place so it's not like anyone could ever label me as 'well travelled' so when this handy looking boy - in broken English - asked me to sit in the car for a moment, I'd already taken it that he was Russian. Add to that, one of them had already got out of the car and was on his way to ushering me in, - like I didn't have a choice in the matter because really? What adult gets into a car with strangers? - and I don't think anyone could've fucking blamed me for how I was seeing things.

Even though it felt a million miles away from a scenario that I should've been laughing at, I almost did. Near enough started pissing myself - with relief - right there beside the two of them when it dawned on me that these two lumps weren't anything to do with what had happened on the yacht. They weren't even fucking *Russian*, for one thing.

Didn't exactly help though that their English was absolutely brutal although, fair enough. They could've said far worse things about me when it came to being able to speak *their* lingo, because I wouldn't have even been able to issue you with a hello or a goodbye in Albanian. Exposing my ignorance, I wouldn't even have been able to point at the country of Albania on a fucking map if it was to save myself, but what was *important* at the time was that the people in the car I was sitting with were not Russkies.

In the limited way that he was capable of putting things across to me, while his mate - who had been in the driver's seat when they'd pulled up on me - sat on the other side of me to complete this intimidatory sandwich. This boy with slick backed black hair, just as dark bushy beard and a pair of Ray Ban's that never left his face - without any fucking about whatsoever - just pulled out a wad of notes and started counting one after the other.

What the fuck is going on here? I thought, rather than ask. I mean, it wasn't like this cunt was someone that was due me money and had spied me on the street so thought he'd just square me up or fuck all?

'You, goalkeeper'

He said, having stopped counting out the euros, them all now in one of his hands.

It was only then that I tippled onto what the fuck was happening. Still didn't know the three quarters, mind, but seeing someone counting out a pile of money and then mentioning the position I played for Muirhouse - and thinking back to what had happened to the boys earlier on in the holiday - I started to realise where this was all going.

'Aye, Muirhouse Violet, pal'

I confirmed, taking a wee look to the boy on the other side of me who had fuck all for me other than a *what?* look back in my direction.

'Tomorrow, you play not so good, ok?'

He said, thrusting the money into my hand. Given no chance of not taking it. It looked a decent amount but I wanted to know how much there was, so started to count it. Two thousand euros. Tidy. Fucking wish the cunts had paid me that and given the same instruction before the game against the Estonians, mind. Proper cashback, that.

'Lalo's Bar, good. You, not so good, yes?'

He said this with the name of the pub that we were playing in the semi with his thumbs up and then - when turning to my part - turning them down. Cunt must've thought he was fucking Julius Caesar or something.

'Awww, no, pal. I'm part of a team, like. Can't be taking a wee bung and sell my pals out, eh?'

Didn't have a fucking clue if the boy could even understand any of what I'd said or not but - and this was maybe more because I wasn't in a group with the rest of the boys while this was going down - was at pains to let him know that I wasn't wanting the money from him. Don't get me wrong, like. I wanted the money, of course I fucking did. But I didn't *want* it. Not from these intimidating bastards, I didn't.

He just waved my protests away.

'Do not worry about this. I bring more after the game'

He grabbed hold of my hand that had the euros in it and clenched it hard before letting go and nodding to his boy on the other side of me, who opened the back door to let him and me out. Under any other circumstances you'd have had to drag me back kicking, biting and screaming out of that beautiful air conditioning inside the Beamer but - all things considering - I was extremely happy to be back out in that scorching heat.

What's it with cunts trying to bribe you over here? I thought to myself as I shoved the notes into my pocket. Fucking hell, if it was like that half the time back in Edinburgh none of us would even need to worry about getting up for work in the morning.

Had only went for a walk to try and clear the dark thoughts that had been creeping back in that day. That's what they say, eh? Go for a long walk and help clear your mind. I'd done not bad with training but it seemed the minute we were back to the hotel - and now with the rest of the day ahead of us - I started to think about the obvious. Thought I'd go for a long walk and clear my head, and returned two thousand euros richer that afternoon.

When I eventually returned. Stopping off at the occasional boozer on my walk - there and back - it led to me being gone for hours. By the time I *did* meet up with some of the rest of the team, I found out that I wasn't the only one out of us who had landed themselves two thousand euros richer.

Starting from the back - other than me - both The Monk and Delaney had been 'approached' in the same way and left with the same basic demand. Just play shite, to paraphrase the Albanian boy, like.

Other than the keeper and central defence. Both Montana and Rossi had also been compensated for something not even done yet.

'Smart move, from them. Take care of the defence and the strikers and you're in with a good shout of affecting the outcome of a match,' said a Strings who - over the course of the conversation - if I hadn't known better I'd have thought that he was a bit pissed off that no cunt had offered *him* any dough. Poor bastard deemed academic in the whole scheme of things.

'But why do we keep getting offered fucking bribes, though?'

I asked, again, only this time I had an audience. Not that anyone had a clue as to the answer.

'It's not as if it's small amounts they're dishing out, either. Especially with these Albanians, eh? Fucking *dwarfs* what we got the first time. That, in the end, only really paid for a couple of barry nights out for us. Ten grand's a different thing altogether. I say we just split it, it's going to work out around five hundred euros each'

Strings voiced his opinion. I couldn't help but have a wee laugh at him. Not only has he decided that we should split the money - of which he wasn't in possession of a single cent of - but has already worked out how much money *he's* going to make out of it.

'Well, if there's one thing, and let's face it, wee bit of a pattern emerging here. If we've got Russian and Albanian goons trying to bribe us by the thousands, then sure as shite there's some cunts up the chain making a *lot* more than that. Why they're willing to go betting such high stakes on a match involving pub teams? Well I'm fucked if I know, cause there's got to be easier ways of making a bit of cash than depending on a bunch of weapons like us'

Tel answered, completely ignoring Strings - and what he'd suggested with what we should do with the euros - to his visible annoyance.

It made sense, like. You bribe someone then it's because there's a bigger picture to things. A greater good. When it had just

been the one time, it was kind of a novelty and through it also
being a Russian boy who had given the group the money - and
a Russian team we had to play - we didn't immediately take it
as "match fixing" match fixing. Could've just been about
Russian pride and how they wouldn't be able to go home if
they didn't represent on the big stage. What with it being a
Russian beer company sponsoring the tournament and that?
You know how those Russians can be, like?

It wasn't until the *second* bribe - plural - that we were able to see
things from a different point of view.

Certain people were clearly needing specific teams to do well in
the tournament, just not Muirhouse Violet apparently. Our part
was to be fuck all other than caught in the crosshairs of other
people's plans.

But that's not to say that we couldn't - and did - profit out of
the drama of it all.

'So what we going to do with it, then?'

The Monk asked the rest of us, even though options were
limited when it came to the money.

'I already said what we should do'

Strings tried again but was shouted over the top of by Rossi
who - with this kind of bribing being done more on a personal
nature than the group one previously - said that the two bags of
sand he had on him was nothing to do with anyone else. I
reckoned he was on the wind up but if he hadn't been then he
was given a dose of reality by the look that Terry flashed him,
alongside the threat that if he just so happened to miss any easy
chances the next day against *Lalo's Bar* then it would've been
assumed that he'd went against the team.

'Fucking right'

Strings said, agreeing with too much in the way of enthusiasm, trying to make sure that he was going to pocket something out of it.

'Pooling all of that together, and, like we did last time, putting it towards nights out? There's *too much* money and not enough days left to use that on nights out. I say we just split it, minus Jock, obviously, and it should probably see us all go home at the end of the holiday with a bit of cash in their hipper, and who, at the start of the trip, could've fucking predicted *that?*'

Benji gave his thoughts on things. He was right, like. We had the semi final the day after and - if things went our way - then the final a couple of days after that, and us on the plane home to follow.

'See, that's what I've been trying to say!'

Strings, predictably, jumped on this line of thinking. Logically, there wasn't really any other way for us to do it. Clearly we weren't handing it back, we couldn't even fucking do that if we'd tried, something some of us *had*. Giving it to Jock would've been a waste of time because that daft old cunt would've went and handed it over to some rep from the tournament who - not believing their luck - would've pocketed it for themselves.

It really all came down to *how* we would use it up, and as much as I loved a piss up with the squad. The thought of a *ten grand* session - with the playing staff of Muirhouse Violet - scared the living shit out of me. Dividing the money between us seemed the smart thing to do. And it's not like there wasn't a few of us who were starting to get a bit light on our bank balance, after over a week there.

Strings seemed especially happy with his payout which, considering his troubles with the Guardia Civil, you couldn't really have blamed him.

As for the semi final itself, against the Albanians of Lalo's Bar, and how we all viewed it, coming up the next night?

Well, put it this way. It wasn't us who had asked to be bribed in the first place, was it? We were nothing more than just innocent bystanders, caught up in someone else's business. Fuck all to do with us, eh?

As far as the Muirhouse Violet boys were concerned, they had a semi final to win.

Chapter 21

Viktor Borovskiy

If you ever need a reminder on just how much you miss home - or in the case of myself, *not* missing home - then all you need to do is return back there. Fuck, I could not get myself back onto the G-6 and into the air above Moscow quick enough. Inconvenience now over and on my way back to Mallorca to resume the summer. Fuck that shit, what an *inconvenience* to have thrown your way.

One moment you're enjoying oral sex from some of the most talented sex workers in the business before then going for a swim in your pool, lapping up the summer sun. The next? You're thirty six thousand feet in the air, transporting a dead body back to its homeland to lay the woman to rest. At the whole risk of sounding like the world's worst person, it had been an unwelcome spanner thrown into my summer plans.

I don't know what I'd have done without having been able to delegate pretty much *all* of the funeral plans to my personal assistant, Mariana. By the time the jet touched down at Sheremetyevo - and I, well, I suppose, *we* were met by the waiting delegation - Mariana had planned a complete funeral for me. I felt almost as if I was a DHL worker, crossing trans international with a vital piece of cargo that was required for an important event. In reality, I was a little bit more than just a courier.

Getting into the backseat of the limo, nodding to Dmitri, - one of the firm's drivers and a face I hadn't seen in over a year - as I got in, I took Mariana's call. This coming through at the very moment where my cell had decided that it now knew which country it was in, and which network I could piggy back on to use. My assistant calling me as soon as she was made aware that I had arrived in Russia. Telling me of all the final arrangements that had been made while I was in the air.

The name of the funeral directors that Anya - now lying in the back of the Mercedes van that had been parked behind the limo - was to be driven to, ahead of the funeral. Which church the service was to be held at, - and where my now deceased wife would be buried - this, something that I had left between Anya's mother and Mariana. Somehow, it hadn't felt it appropriate that I take a leading role in where she was going to be laid to rest. It was hardly as if at some point there were plans in place for me to be buried beside her, once I finally passed. Mariana confirming that the news had eventually been picked up by Russian media which ensured that - on the day of the funeral - there would more than likely be a press pack, covering the story. I had nothing to worry about, despite how our later years were between each other. I had instructed Mariana to ensure that Anya Borovskiy's send off was to be a lavish affair, in all ways.

I wanted the occasion to reflect on how Anya was as a person, so thought a funeral that was grand, opulent and - to the visible eye - *very* expensive would be appropriate. With how many millions I was going to gain in Anya's passing, it was *her* who was paying for the luxurious looking affair anyway. No one needed to know that, however. To any onlooker it would be made to look like how an oligarch would pay his last respects to the one person who had been with him for most of his life. Even in her death I found that I still had to play the optics game, for the rest of the watching world.

I couldn't get it all over and done with soon enough. Citing 'business,' I arrived the day before the funeral and had a slot scheduled back again at Sheremetyevo for leaving Moscow in the early hours of the day after it.

As for the funeral itself? Hundreds came although I did not reach the status of being a billionaire by being a stupid man. I wasn't naive enough to not know that there were several in attendance who were there *just* to be seen. Although in that sense, I guess they weren't so different from *me?* Their reasons were different from mines, however. At least six different Moscow based businessmen taking the opportunity to let me know just how sorry they were for their loss, before giving it the required amount of minutes that - in their minds - they thought appropriate before asking if I would have time to listen to what projects they were in the proposal stages of, and if I would like to invest. The fucking nerve of some people.

Leeches, and that is without even mentioning the astonishingly crass disrespect shown by that fucking British investigative reporter - Brian Glazer, someone who had crossed paths with me over recent years, be it articles written about me or the persistent interview requests from him - who had shouted as I got out of the car to walk into the church for Anya's service.

'Is it true that Anya Borovskiy died under suspicious circumstances? Would you care to comment, Viktor?'

I did not even give the man the satisfaction of looking his way, never mind answer his question but what I *did* do was - from inside the church - relay a message for some of the security detail outside to make sure that Glazer was to go on to have a very bad day, in whatever shape or form that turned out to be. Generally, I liked to allow my security to have some *creative license*, when it came to aspects of their jobs.

Babushka Galina - Anya's sole parent - and how devastated she was on the day of her daughter's burial had left me feeling nothing but a fraud. I *should've* been in the same state as Galina, under normal circumstances. You cannot cheat your feelings, though. Over the day - hiding from everyone behind my sunglasses, which were near to permanently fixed to my face - I had tried to carry myself with a quiet dignity. Accepting everyone's expressions of how sad they were over what had happened, while eluding anyone's attempts at forcing any further conversation out of me. Galina, however, displayed every inch the haunted grief stricken look that a parent has when having to bury one of their children. At times she wasn't even able to hold herself up out of just how broken hearted she was. It pained me *more* to see Galina in this way than it did for us to be burying her daughter.

While I could not have said the same thing for Anya, I had always had nothing but fond memories of her mother. A mother in law who genuinely appeared to like me more than my *own* mother had.

Before I left the wake, Galina and I sat at a table - away from everyone else eating and drinking in Anya's memory - talking with each other. Sharing memories and stories of the woman whose coffin we had just watched be lowered into the ground, just hours before. It had been the exact kind of conversation that I'd tried to avoid the whole day. For me to have thought back to all of those cherished memories would have been to have reminded me of the times where I had truly loved the woman, and that part of me still did, and always would. *That* approach did not suit my narrative, which was to continue focusing on the more recent years, where we were man and wife in but name, and through my continuing to pay for her lifestyle. It was this approach which had allowed me to - almost - breeze through what should have otherwise been one of the saddest and traumatic things to happen in my life. If I started from that other angle, though. That would be where emotions might come into play.

For Galina, though. I was happy to play along. It was the first time of the day where she was not a complete mess of an old lady and the fact that she could sit there and talk about old times - and not burst out crying - was an improvement. I had actually been in the process of trying to attempt to say my goodbyes but once she began speaking - in the way that she did - I could not deny her. After we were done, I left soon after. I had shaken enough hands over the day, heard the same platitudes so many times that they had lost all sincerity or meaning. Anya was now in the ground, after all. There was not much more required of me.

Before leaving I reminded Galina that I would be in touch with her - once the attorneys had been through Anya's will - and that whatever left to her I would see to it that she received it as soon as possible. When I said this to her I was not ruling out the fact that Anya - so self centred at times - may not have even left anything to anyone and that if this turned out to be the case then I would have just magicked up a life changing amount of money that I would send to Babushka Galina, while *telling* her Anya had left it to her.

Babushka looked at me with shock, as if she had never considered or planned for this, which I suppose *did* make sense. If you're supposed to die *after* your parent, then why put your parent in your last will and testament?

Regardless, Babushka Galina would be looked after.

The short time I'd been back had reminded me just how lucky I was to have the *world* as my playground, and not stuck there in Russia. So while I could not have ever offered Babushka weekly visits to take her to the supermarket for her shopping, I at least wanted to ensure that whatever years she had left were more comfortable than she had ever known.

When I was back at the hotel, winding down from the day with a few glasses of Scotch and brief sleep before leaving for Sheremetyevo for the flight, I received a call from Valery with - considering the day it had been - what was the first bit of light relief I'd felt since arriving in Moscow.

Zavorovo had beaten the French team from Marseille in their quarter final match and were into the semi final against *Camparo's Bar*, a drinking den in San Sebastián, Spain.

I knew that I could rely on Valery to make sure things would go smoothly, following the whole shit show surrounding the attempted bribery of the Scots. With that not exactly going to plan, he'd been instructed to change his terms and conditions, when approaching players representing anyone who was scheduled to play the Russians of Zavorovo.

It had worked, like a dream when it came to the third group game. The team from Portugal rolling over and dying, in return for a generous fee. I must admit, it takes a lot to make me laugh but when I had learned that - even through throwing out all of those thousands of euros out in *incentives* to the Portugal team - it had taken the Scots to score a single goal to ensure Zavorovo made it through to the next phase, I laughed out loud. How more fucking ironic could you ask for? They steal my money from me and then do me a favour - a *huge* favour - days later, without me even requesting one. Because let's face facts, if I was requiring someone do me a favour, the Scotsmen would have been sitting at the very *bottom* of the list.

Before leaving Mallorca. Valery had been instructed to repeat his actions - with the Marseille based side - only, with it now being the quarter final stage, to increase the amount appropriately, as an extra sweetener although to - once more - go to great lengths to explain to the players that there would be a second option open to them, if the Frenchmen did not wish to accept the money offered to them.

Now hearing that this policy had paid off once more, and that there was now just a semi final in the way of Zavorovo and a place in the final. Kelmendi's boys also still there fighting for the cup and very much now a case of things beginning to heat up, as far as our gentleman's bet went.

'I probably don't need to tell you what your next move is, Valery, do I?'

I said, on hearing the news, and who would be up against the Russian representatives in the tournament in the next match.

Valery just laughed before asking for confirmation on - with it now reaching the semi final - what figure of increase on the amount that he would go on to offer the players of Camparo's Bar that I wanted to sign off on.

It was the day after I'd arrived back from Moscow when I had the same man call me to let me know that - to neither his or my shock - Zavorovo had steamrollered their Spanish opponents five to zero in what had been such a blatant one sided match - according to Valery - if it had been *professional football* there would surely have been some scrutiny drawn, with regards to some of the curious mistakes that were made by Camparo's Bar. Valery laughing out loud while he described an own goal that they scored where their defender had hit the ball towards his goalkeeper with such ferocity it would have taken three goalkeepers to keep it out. I admired the player's commitment to making sure that he did not receive a bullet in the head, even if he surely did not need to be so direct about things?

So they had made it to the final, with a little assistance from myself. Thoughts then turned to the *other* semi final, scheduled to kick off early evening. A game that was as close to a nightmare scenario as I could possibly find.

Lalo's Bar from Tirana, against my old friends, Muirhouse Violet from Scotland.

A nightmare scenario as in bribery had paid off in such a big way that getting Zavorovo into the final had been relatively simple. *Whoever* made it through to the final - I already knew - would be untouchable. Kelmendi's Albanians? I would not begin to even insult Arben's intelligence that I would be able to pay off his countrymen to throw the final. And the Scots? Well, I already knew where *they* stood on matters. Only a fool would go back to a group - who had already pocketed three thousand euros of your money - and offer them thousands more to lose the match. What is it that they say about the definition of madness?

No, whoever it was that would join Zavorovo in the final. It would be a corruption free game of football and truly down to which team would be the greater fighter on the day to determine who would be the champion. I couldn't help but feel that it would have been almost poetic if it were to be Lalo's Bar who made it to the final match, with regards to the sub plot of the alpha male orientated bet between Kelmendi and me.

Lalo's Bar against FC Zavorovo. Albania against Russia, and Arben Kelmendi versus Viktor Borovskiy. And besides, I'd had the Albanians watched and the intel received had been that Zavorovo would be able to handle them, *if* they were to meet.

Later on, early evening just as I was waiting on Oleg preparing the car to take me into Palma for the night, I received the update on how things had gone in the other game from Ari, one of my ex Mossad security detail and - for the last year or so - someone who I'd had protect Anya but with him not really having much in the way of work in that specific area, - or was ever likely to in the future - had been put to work elsewhere. The life of a member of Viktor Borovskiy's mini army, huh? One day you could be guarding a husband or wife from potential kidnapping from serious and organised criminals and the next? Watching a game of football with a hot dog and a Coca Cola.

While Valery had been given the job of watching over Zavorovo against the team from San Sebastián, earlier in the day. Ari had been issued with the task of hanging around the stadium, to find out the outcome in the second semi final. He called me - as instructed earlier that day - the very moment the final whistle sounded.

He must've been real close to the pitch too because, before he even got a chance to say a word, I could hear shouting and celebrating in the background, and couldn't help but notice that I was hearing *British* accents.

The Scots had won two goals to one, after extra time, and it seemed that they were intent on telling the whole of Magaluf.

When Ari told me the scoreline, bittersweet was the only way I could describe emotions. Kelmendi's team were out of the tournament, and, with that, so was his chances of winning our bet. To counter this good news, however. If *I* was to win our bet, then Zavorovo would have to win the final. And to do that they were going to have to go out and win against the *only* team that had beaten them in the tournament so far. And - with Kelmendi's chances now in ruins - being the only person who could win the bet. My viewpoint on things was that if I didn't *win* the bet, I might as well as had lost it, but if there was one thing for certain. This team, Muirhouse Violet, weren't going to make things easy for me *or* FC Zavorovo.

'Ok, Ari. Good job. You can take the rest of the night off and I will be in touch with you tomorrow,' I told him, having taken a moment to digest the news he'd called with but now ready to hang up.

It possibly was not in the best of taste, considering I'd only buried my wife two days before, but I had dinner in Palma planned and then - afterwards - a visit to one of the city's best kept secrets, Momentos Tentadores. A *very* exclusive gentleman's club, where the girls there are just waiting to cater for your every need, and I do mean *every* need. With Oleg sitting outside with the engine running - and admittedly more thoughts in my head about the Momentos Tentadores part of the evening than the more pressing dinner appointment that I needed to be at - I said goodbye, ready to end the call.

Ari stopping me before I got the chance.

'That is not all though, boss. The team from Scotland? And them reaching the final? I think I may have found a way of making sure that Zavorovo will win the match'

Chapter 22

Arben Kelmendi

'JUST WHO THE *FUCK* DO THESE FUCKING BASTARDS THINK THEY ARE?'

I screamed in the face of poor Bujar. One of my very most trusted men but someone who was simply in the wrong place at the wrong time. Pieces of spit had come flying out of my mouth when screaming at him - so enraged I had become - and had landed on his beard. I'm not sure if he even knew this or not but I was not about to interrupt the tirade that I was unleashing on him to comment on it.

I had not taken the news well, as one does when they are used to getting what they want *when* they want it. But it went a lot deeper than that.

What is a man without his reputation?

I'd had the Scots paid off - handsomely - with the message being put across to them that there was not going to be any other option open to them than to allow those useless fucks from Lalo's Bar an easy passage into the final.

AND WHAT? THEY GO AND FUCKING WIN ANYWAY?

Did they think that I was just some insane philanthropist who paid people to go around throwing money at random football players from other countries?

I guess I was too much in the red zone - and I rarely ever found myself at a *ten* - for any real sense but the most pertinent question I found myself asking was, what kind of people accept money from the Albanian mafia, and then do not keep their part of the deal?

I think it was *them* who were the insane ones, not me.

'Ok, Bujar. I want reprisals and I want them *tonight*. Round up all of the other men and go looking for the Scots around Magaluf. If you found them as easy as you did, when throwing away my money, then you'll find them just as easy tonight. Maybe Lalo's players will not be playing in the final now but I want you to make sure that you leave as many Scottish players in the same position as you can'

This was a literal command, and the type that would have had Bujar nodding his head and on his phone, calling on reinforcements, while already on his way out of the door.

Instead, he hadn't moved. Still standing there with my spit having now dried its way into his dark beard. I'd known the man long enough to see that he had something that he wanted to say but - given how much of a rage he'd had to stand and watch me put on display - was hesitant to do so.

'Can I just say something, boss, and it is said while *also* saying that, of course, I will be happy to carry out my orders?'

I motioned for him to continue, intrigued to what he had to say. When you're used to yes yes yes all of the time, it can sometimes be a novelty when you come across something different to that.

'The way I see it. Yes we *can* go out tonight and give the Scotsmen some instant payback, but then, there is your bet, with Borovskiy?'

With a great deal of logic to it, Bujar's thoughts on things were that with the Scots due to play against Borovskiy's Russians, it may have been slightly counter productive to go out and attack some of the Muirhouse players, and leave them out of the final. *This* then automatically increasing Borovskiy's chances of winning the bet we'd struck before the tournament had begun, with FC Zavorovo coming up against a much weakened Scottish team, inflicted by the Kelmendi clan.

Clearly, he made good sense. If I wanted to increase the chances of avoiding having to pay out two million euros to Borovskiy, then I should've been putting the players of Muirhouse Violet up in the most expensive health spa available in Mallorca until they had to leave for to play the final. Not hatch plans to brutally injure them in ways that would be left down to Bujar and his boys.

But sometimes, things are more important than money.

Principle, pride and reputation being just three things. As logical as it was from him, I was in disagreement with Bujar on this one. Which, of course, meant that we were *back* to the original instruction that I'd given him.

'These Scottish fucks may not have heard of Arben Kelmendi before, or the risks of taking his money and not delivering. They will now, and *that* lesson given to them will be much, much more satisfying to me than winning or losing a bet against Viktor fucking Borovskiy. Now go, Bujar. And call me when it's done'

Chapter 23

Strings

Well as for the night? It started off barry as fuck, taking on - and beating - the Albanians. You'd think that starting your early evening by reaching the final of a European tournament, it would then be the signal for a night you'd never forget. Which, I suppose we *did* get, just not in the conventional way that you'd think a 'reaching a final' celebration would result in.

The fitba part of the evening was fairly straightforward. Well not quite *straightforward,* as we'd had to go to extra time before seeing off *Lalo's Bar* from Albania but even though the game went on for longer, I'd never had the feeling that we were ever in any danger. The Albanians, a team who were extremely limited when it came to any kind of skill - by half time I was asking the question of how the fuck a team like that had managed to reach the semi final - but I was convinced that most of their players were roided up to fuck, and looked like they could've ran all day if they'd needed to.

Putting a team like that up against the players of Muirhouse Violet who were as flat as the fucking Netherlands, it kind of evened things up a little. Enough to at least see us having to play another half an hour before a Rossi 'fox in the box' effort in the second half of ET - and just when I was starting to worry that we were going to end up with *another* penalty shoot out - took care of things.

Our flatness on the day - as far as I was concerned - was the combination of us playing too many games of fitba in such a short space of time, while being on what had felt like a never ending bender. Eventually the body starts talking to you, though. Couldn't have spoken for the rest of the boys - even though their performances spoke *for* them - but by the time we moved into the second half I'd felt like I had barely fuck all left in the tank. You know when your petrol light comes on but that you can still drive for another seventy miles before the tank runs out? It had felt as if I was at the 'better get to the next petrol station as quick as possible before the fucking car konks out' part of proceedings. It didn't look like I was the only one, either.

Don't get me wrong. Even that first game, all the way back when we played the Portuguese on day one. Even *that* had been a struggle to get to the end of, due to us having to play in such heat. That heat had never gone away since but - as a team - we'd managed to master *how* to play in such climate. The semi was different. Aye, the heat was there, of course it was, but it really was like I was running on fumes. Almost felt like fucking crying when The Monk smashed the ball against the crossbar - from a header - as a result of a Coffee corner as we were heading right into injury time. I thought the reprieve of having to play another half an hour had eventually come. Can't even describe the anguish I felt as I seen the ball rattle the bar, and end up being headed away by one of their defenders.

Still, though. The lads dug in and got the job done. I don't even know *how* we managed to celebrate in the way that we did when the ref ended proceedings. Most of us could barely stand by the time of the sweet sound of that whistle but when it sounded it was like the Albanians had been handing their steroids out to the lot of us. More energy displayed in the on pitch celebrations than we'd managed during the actual match itself.

Jock - who despite kicking every ball from the side of the pitch had clearly not used the same energy that we had - came running onto the pitch.

'Did I not bloody tell you lot that we were going to the final, ya beauties?'

He said while going around us all. You couldn't help but buzz off Jock's happiness. We were happy - and proud - ourselves, mind. It's just that for Jock Hunter, *whatever* we did on the pitch with a Muirhouse Violet strip on, it always felt that wee bit *more* to him.

It was only when he started shouting about us reaching the final that I was able to stop and fully appreciate it. Aye, we were playing in a semi so I'd obviously known just what was at stake from minute one but when it got to the survival of the fittest part of the match, you really were just trying to do whatever it took to emerge from things as the winner.

Now, though? As we danced about that pitch singing. Cunts on each other's shoulders and all kinds of capers. *That's* when things sunk in. We'd come over from Edinburgh with not a fucking clue who we were going to be playing against, and what levels of skill these teams were able to play at. We'd had some ups and downs and the shift that we'd put in through all games was something that no cunt could question. Had it not been for the constant peaving and unhealthy eating I reckon you'd have actually been able to have seen a visible difference to all of our physiques.

Five games inside two weeks - and with a sixth now on the horizon - is a run that they wouldn't even ask a professional team to play, never mind a team at our level. We'd have ended up going back home and cunts not recognising this new svelt looking Violet, had we not went on the biggest bender we'd all ever been on as a team.

And on the subject of the bender that was now into its second week. If we'd been smart, we'd have taken the warning - that our bodies were trying, screaming at us, actually, to give us during the semi final - and maybe took things easy and just put our feet up between then and the final, which ironically was going to be against the same Farleys that we'd played in the group stages. I'd thought that they'd been a decent side - when we'd played them - and we'd been a wee bit lucky to beat them, so wasn't that surprised to see them make it to the final. Neither was I scared of them though, mind.

The smart thing to do - following the semi final - would've been to go back to the hotel and have a quiet one for the rest of the night and give ourselves the rest that our mind body and soul were crying out for.

I'd fucking *loved* to have seen someone suggest to the players of Muirhouse Violet that, after reaching a cup final and a European one at that, they should have a night in, though! Anyone coming with that would've met a stiff resistance in amongst some choice words thrown back at them. And I would've been one of them, laughing at the suggestion that we didn't go out and celebrate. I'd even go as far as to say that if there is ever a day that the Violet reached a cup final - domestic *or* European - and the team *didn't* go out on the piss to celebrate, then I hope I'll have retired by then because that would be a Muirhouse Violet that I simply would not be able to reconcile with.

The real irony is that, while our bodies were screaming for some rest and a decent amount of hours sleep. If we hadn't gone out that night then *none* of what followed would've went on to happen. That whole sliding doors stuff, eh? Han had made me sit and watch that film with her one night. Total rom-com pish, like, but still left me questioning life and how if you do - or don't - something, what then follows after that? Well by not taking the stay in option - and the option that wasn't really an option at all - it then led to the darkest day in the history of Muirhouse Violet, on what should've been its greatest.

After getting the old 'Foam Dome' hat ritual out of the way, we started off across the road at The Arsed Rat for a few before hitting the strip. We'd had a few wins to celebrate over the years but could not remember a time where the full team were as buzzing as we all were that night. The lot of us would've fucking rivalled Montana on any of his Class As. High as kites, we were. You can't beat a night out like that, though. Everyone all in the best of moods while we also had that whole 'team' mentality thing going on alongside things. If there had been any beef between certain players - and this was Muirhouse we're talking about mind, beef between players was unavoidable due to us all being out and out radges - then it was put to the side that night. Proper one for all and all for one, like.

The vibe was good, beer extra tasty and the tunes fucking banging. Fuck knows what it must've looked like to anyone walking along the strip and saw us sitting at the tables outside Bingo Bangos, singing our hearts out to Sympathy for the Devil, the *woo woos* included. Half of us pissing ourselves while attempting that part.

Coincidentally, like a Rolling Stone, while out on the drink each night, we never really ever stopped long enough in the one boozer to gather any moss. Usually a couple of drinks and then on to somewhere else. Those introductory free shots, *always* an incentive to move on to another bar. There were about half a dozen or so of the team who had ordered food, while the others were getting a bit restless and at the point of wanting to head up the strip a bit.

'I'll text you to see where yous are, once we've had our scran'

Rossi agreed with Terry as we all got up to leave. A decent idea, *especially* since we didn't know where we were going ourselves. Most likely the first place that had a tidy looking girl offering free drinks, to have the honour of leading us into the bar she worked for.

Being towards the back of the group - talking with Benji about how if we had any sense we'd be in our hotel room saving the money that we were contributing to keeping the Magaluf nightlife in the black - I didn't know who or what had been the reason for us heading into a bar - that we'd not yet frequented on the trip, about the fucking *only* one, like - a wee bit up the hill but it was appearing that we were giving 'Mandy's' a try.

After the customary free shot of disgusting - but try turning it down - Sambuca had been dealt with we all got our *real* drinks in and - with the place already packed - stood about inside having a scoop while listening to the DJ. He wasn't as good as the one back where we'd been, like. Too much of that dance stuff for my liking. I used to go to the Rez back in the nineties but hadn't really been into the music as much as everyone else. Was just one of those deals that all your mates are going out and getting fucking melted on drugs and you not really wanting to miss out on it, eh?

I wasn't the only one out of us who wasn't as impressed with the tunes.

'Ibiza's fucking that way, eh'

Terry, shouting over to the boy who was too busy trying to mix to even clock Tel. Head down staring at the decks with one half of a headphone wedged between his shoulder and ear.

Apart from the music, though, things couldn't have been more perfect. We were in a European fucking final and - as a group - on top of the world. Patter flying back and forward between us all. Piss takes aplenty but in the good way that even the target can't help but laughing alongside. I genuinely could not have recalled a time where things - as a Muirhouse Violet player - had been as perfect as they were in that moment, and on that night in general.

All of this exposed for just how fragile it all was the moment Tel got that text and opened it up to have a deek at. His face visibly changing - from the man who was in the middle of ripping Montana over one of the girls that he'd went away with a few nights before - in front of us in a split second.

'COME ON, WE NEED TO GET BACK TO THE OTHER BOOZER'

He shouted to the group while putting his - near to - full pint down on the bar before bolting out of the place. Not exactly helping with us being half pished, confusion reigned. Apart from all rushing out of Mandy's right behind Terry, we didn't really know *why*.

This was mainly because even Terry didn't know.

GET BACK HERE ASAP. EVERY CUNT!!

All that Daz - not Rossi - had typed out in the text and sent.

Running - for a consistent period of time - after mass alcohol consumption is not an easy thing to do, but we just about managed it. Actually managing to run *faster* by the time Bingo Bangos was coming into view. By that point, it was all too clear that something had gone on back there. And judging by the fact that there were three ambulances, two police cars and a van, it looked like there had been a major incident. There were more fucking lights flashing on the street than inside that BCM.

You couldn't help but have a bad feeling about things, seeing all of those emergency services, and all the rubber neckers who were standing around watching on. That feeling only getting worse with every step, revealing more of the carnage up ahead.

One of the three ambulances taking off with sirens and flashing lights just as we were reaching the bar. Initially - the ambulance - finding the pissheads walking along the middle of the road a hindrance until everyone realised what was going on. The ambulance soon taking on the look of Moses parting the Red Sea. You never like to see an ambulance in such a rush to get its passenger to the hospital, though. I hope the poor cunt's alright, whoever it is, I thought to myself as I saw the white van disappear from sight.

Once we got to Bingo Bango's, it was fucking chaos. First of all I noticed that The Monk was sitting being tended to by a medic, who was wrapping a bandage around his arm while he sat smoking with his free hand. This, then leading to me trying to do a head count. Apart from The Monk, I could only see Daz at first.

Still in the process of finding out what the fuck had gone on I could only assume that some of the others - who had last been seen waiting on their scran coming out - had either now been lifted, or worse. They were in one of those three ambulances.

I eventually clocked Mr Benn - his prized Stone Island Marina t shirt that he never stopped fucking talking about - covered in blood, from his face by the looks - standing talking to one of the Guardia Civil, but that was it. Three out of the six weren't there.

This wasn't good.

'They fucking all came from nowhere, like'

Daz shouted cryptically to the first of the group of us to arrive, completely out of breath from the sprint from the other boozer.

'Fucking snide, cunts, too. Brought weapons with them.' The Monk - still being strapped up from whatever injury he'd landed up with, the dressing being on before we'd arrived - shouted over to everyone before going on to acting a bit of a wideo with the medic who - only doing their job - he was accusing of wrapping the bandaging around his arm too tightly.

'*Who* did? And where the fuck's the rest of you?'

I asked Daz and or The Monk. Daz looked still in shock while The Monk looked more angry over whatever had taken place in our absence.

'Fucking Albanians'

The Monk shouted across to us with a vengeful look on his coupon.

'In the ambulances'

Daz grimly replied. The look on his face telling me that things were bad.

'That one that took off before you got here, Delaney's inside it. They fucking *stabbed* him in the chest. Couple of times, like. I'm not sure how bad it is but the medics didn't fuck about getting him out of here when they arrived at the scene. The boy didn't look too clever when they were taking him away on the stretcher, though'

'Fucking *stabbed?*'

I replied, trying to process all of what was going on. It was only up close to Daz that you could see that he had blood running from a burst lip and a couple of fresh scratches on his face. Compared to Delaney, though. He'd had a fucking right stroke.

Thoughts then turned to the others, and why they were in the *other* ambulances. The whole thing was a fucking mess. With the sheer numbers that we were out in, it was difficult to remember who had went to one pub and who had stayed in the other one, so for a moment I didn't even realise which of us were *in* the ambulances. Despite intel being on the thin side, it was looking like Wullie was in one with a suspected broken leg and - in the other - Rossi lying with what, The Monk had shouted to us, had appeared to be a serious head injury.

'Aye, a fucking hammer to the head will do that, eh?'

The Monk followed up with before then - impatiently - asking the medic if she was done with him, wanting to come over and fill the rest of the boys in about what horrors had gone on. The way Daz and The Monk told us - an animated Mr Benn still engaged in talks with the Guardia Civil - I was kind of glad that I *hadn't* been there but at the same time couldn't help but feel that had we carried a bit more strength in numbers then three of our team might not have ended up with serious injuries on their way to hospital.

'Fucking shitebags had knives, hammers and baseball bats, three cars of them as well, mind.' The Monk described the scariest of scenes while - collectively - we all jumped out of our skin as the ambulance parked beside us, that Rossi was in, sounded it's siren, as it began to pull away from the bar.

The full story being that the six of them were sitting there eating their scran and three full car loads of Albanians had pulled up. A radge looking mob all piling out and going straight for the Muirhouse boys, although - looking around the bar - there had clearly been some collateral damage handed out to some innocents sat in there too.

'We tried to face up to them as good as we could but it all happened that quick'

Daz - unnecessarily - tried to offer some form of defence over the fact that our boys had evidently taken second prize.

'Things escalated that fucking quick I was trying to punch one of them with one hand while I still had my burger in my other'

The Monk said, working himself up until he felt pain in the bandaged arm, wincing when feeling it. Must've been sore - whatever was under the dressing - to make that hardy bastard show his pain.

'It was fucking chaos for a good couple of minutes. Cunts getting tanned all over the place. Bats being swung, knives slicing through the air and that fucking radge cunt with the beard with the claw hammer? It's probably a blessing how tight it is in here that the bastards didn't get much room to swing some of the tools they'd brought,' Daz continued painting the worst sounding scene you could imagine.

'Obviously wasn't unconnected to the semi final, like. The cunts kept shouting about how we'd upset Arben Kelmendi and *this* is what happens when you do that'

'Does he not play for PSV Eindhoven, naw? Full back?' The Monk - sparking up another smoke - attempted a wee joke but it really wasn't the time for anything like that. Not when we had one player with stab wounds and another poor cunt who'd had a hammer to his head. Those two making Wullie's suspected broken leg - due to a good half dozen strikes from a baseball bat by all accounts - seem like a minor scratch.

'Doesn't mean to say that all of them walked away without a scratch on them, mind'

The Monk said, before looking around him and clocking the coppers who were now finishing up with Mr Benn, - who I noticed was looking down at his t shirt, pointing it out to the copper while shaking his head - lowered his tone for the next part.

'Did you fucking see me shove my fork in that cunt's eye? Boy's stumbling about screaming with the fork *still* stuck in him, fucking class, like'

'Was that you? I seen the boy with the fork but didn't know where it had came from,' Daz said, shaking his head at The Monk before adding that it really was a case of every man for himself and that if the Albanians had thought nothing of bringing the toys that they had then they couldn't complain if we'd been inventive with what was at *our* disposal.

We would be able to go over the reason for why a hit squad of Albanians had come looking to inflict as much damage possible to the Violet, later. But it wasn't going to be hard to look ourselves in the mirror and recognise that we'd brought it on ourselves.

This, no comfort at the time. With two players who - for all we knew - were on their way to hospital with life threatening injuries. *That* was the only thing that really mattered.

Not who was to blame and certainly not that we were now going to be missing three first team players from the Red Bear Beer cup final.

The cup final? That night, I would've doubted if a single player were in the position of giving a flying fuck about it, and I'd have been well disappointed to learn if any had.

I know that Shankly was on the wind up anyway with his whole fitba being more important than life and death thing, but while we stood there, assessing the aftermath of the attack from the Albanians, and how brutal it had been - as well as how shocked to the core it had left the group - it really did highlight just how much pish the legendary Liverpool manager had been talking, when he gave that famous quote.

'We're going to have to wake up Jock'

Benji said, looking at his watch, knowing that by that time, the old man would've been well down for the night. Benji boy was right. This was one of those *exceptional circumstances* where you definitely woke the gaffer up, like when something happens in America during the middle of the night and they have to 'wake the president.'

Thinking on my feet, I told him to go back to the hotel to wake up Hunter, while I said that I'd sort out a couple of taxis to take a select group of us to the hospital, to be there for the three lads currently on route.

It would be a long night - and morning - and not the kind that a team now in preparation for playing in a big cup final - with any aspirations of winning it - would find themselves a part of.

But, once again.

That night, at least. Fitba - despite being the sole reason we were even *on* the fucking island in the first place - was the very least of our worries.

Chapter 24

Sepp

What a fucking state for an amateur sporting organisation to get itself into, eh? Pocketing thousands of euros in bribes to lose a match they were never going to, provoking a sickening retaliation that had left three of our players lying in hospital, and in a bad way.

By this point of the morning, I didn't know if any cunt had died through the night or not. Obviously, the whole squad couldn't have all rocked up at the hospital expecting to be able to see any of the three boys taken in. Instead, Strings organised a couple of taxis to take some of the team through to the hossie, with the promise of any updates texted back to the boys, as and when.

Delaney, out of the three, the one who apparently was drawing most of the concern from the doctors, even though it could've been worse for the boy. Apparently, if the knife had been an inch to the left it would've been in his heart and it would've been buenos noches and adios amigo to the poor fucker.

Any hospital updates - for me - were now at a close. My phone being one of the first things that the Israeli looking boy had asked from me when him and a similar looking private soldier entered the hotel room, closely followed by an old man. I recognised him, though. It was *him*. The fucking husband. I already knew - when I saw the boy from Mossad, who had been looking after the yacht that night - that I was in the shit, and that things had eventually caught up with me. Like I'd convinced myself they would.

I'd actually thought that it had been one of the other boys from the team, when I heard the knock on the room door. Put it another way. If I'd had *any* fucking idea of who were waiting on the other side, I wouldn't have opened it with such haste and enthusiasm.

I wouldn't have opened it at all.

But I did, and now I was in this thing.

The old man closed the door behind him and suddenly - with four people inside of it - the room was feeling a touch claustrophobic. The extreme panic that I was going through, either the cause of or the contribution to.

'Sit, sit'

The old boy said, as - with both arms - parted those two huge goons as if they had weighed eight stone, taking himself to the front, and face to face with me. The person who had killed his wife. I didn't feel much for sitting down as I saw that as a vulnerable position to put myself in, with them all standing over me. Aye, as if I was going to be able to handle one never mind *both* of the Russian's bodyguards, anyway. Standing up or sitting down, it wasn't going to matter a fuck in the end.

With the environment that it was, though. I done as told. The old man - who soon introduced himself as Viktor Borovskiy and on first appearance did not carry the look of someone who had come face to face with his wife's killer - grabbed one of the two chairs that the room had and dragged it over beside me, sat on the bed. Sitting down, he fixed his eyes on me, like he was weighing up his next words - or actions - before breaking the silence.

'Now you may not know who I am but I most definitely know who *you* are, and that recently you took something that belonged to me'

Well she's not fucking in here, I thought to myself when hearing his words. It - out of all the ways he could have approached the situation - was a novel way of putting things. I'd taken something that belonged to him? Well, one thing for sure that I *hadn't* taken had been her fucking virginity. Aye, she sure had a funny fucking way of behaving like she was *O.P.P*, like.

I just sat there silent, trying to meet the man's glare, but couldn't help straying to the hulks behind him.

He clicked his fingers back and forward like some hypnotist trying to bring his participant back into the room again. It did the trick.

'Forget them, it's *me* who is talking to you, not them'

I should have went on the default setting of defensive - from the moment the accusation of taking something that belonged to the old hoor - and been sitting there on the bed asking who they were, why they had forced their way into my hotel room and how this must've been some big misunderstanding. But there were *no* mistakes made, here. These three were *exactly* where they were meant to be and to try and put on some big act that they weren't, would've only wound them up. And from where I was sitting, if there was one thing I probably should've avoided doing - right there - it would've been to insult them in *any* kind of way.

All those days where I'd pondered who was going to catch up with me first. Bizzies or people more personally connected to the situation, in a personal way. I'd thought so long about it and yet still hadn't been able to work out which scenario was the more preferable out of the two, and now here I was confronted with one of them, and about to find out which way it was going to go although, understandably. I'd feared the worse.

You kill some woman, who's married to a man of extreme wealth and power? You really cannot be surprised by any blowback that comes your way. And how, sitting amongst that menacing atmosphere there in the room. Aye, it fucking well blew, alright.

Instead of offering a firm denial that I didn't have a fucking scoob what he was on about, I tried to make an attempt at going down the bargaining stage. Not that I could possibly ever have anything of interest to a fucking billionaire, mind. The key word there was 'tried.' Couldn't get any words out and was all ums and ahs until the old boy put his finger up to his lips to signal for me to stop.

'Tell me, how old are you?'

He asked, before telling one of the goons to get him a glass of water. The man taking a strip of pills out of his jacket in anticipation of receiving the drink he'd requested. Knocking back a couple of of them as I told him what age I was, while trying to work out the relevance of the question.

'Hmmmm, thirty one?'

He seemed to stop and work out the calculation in his mind before going on to tell me that him and his wife 'Anya' had celebrated their tenth wedding anniversary by the time I'd been born.

Being the nervous wreck that I'd been pretty much from the moment I'd snuck off that yacht, the mention of her name - as well as *who* was sitting there speaking it - was enough for my complete fucking opposite of a poker face to show him that I knew he wasn't just telling me a wee nugget of information, as part of two people getting to know each other.

I just kept silent. I didn't think I had much in the way of words to say in any case but had been told to keep my mouth shut, and wasn't in any mood for going against orders handed to me. I couldn't help but feel that - despite this calm demeanour of the man and how civil it all was - this all ended one way. One of them putting a couple of bullets in my head via a silencer, allowing everyone else on my floor to sleep blissfully through the gangland style execution that had taken place in the hotel while they'd snoozed in their beds. But there was always that wee - no matter the tiny percentage it was - chance that it might *not* happen. And as long as you have a chance at something, it should always be enough to keep you going.

Maybe he's here just to find out about that night, maybe they won't *actually* kill me? I tried to tell myself, *convince* myself, even. Maybe the old boy just wanted closure so that he could move on, eh? A lot of people need that when they lose someone in less than straight forward circumstances. I was thinking that I had a grief stricken husband in front of me, someone who had been married for longer than I'd been on the planet. Only for me to then subsequently grow up to then bring their decades long marriage to an end. I was guessing and second guessing at a rate that far surpassed the speed of how the man spoke.

As far as I could see, there really was only two reasons for him - and his men - to have gone to the trouble of tracking me down, as pin point as right to the door of my hotel room as if they'd used GP fucking S. Either they'd visited to do away with me, or there was this other option that I was trying to tell myself, that he was here to fill in the blanks of what had taken place that night. Not for the first time in life, I was well off the pace with things.

'Now, a man with what you must have on your conscience? You may have wondered why the Guardia Civil have not arrested you by this point? *Or* why you and I have not sat down earlier and had this little chat?'

I *may* have? For fuck's sake, it had been almost all I'd thought of since I woke up next to a dead woman.

'Well, aye, I mean, like, I was ...'

I was just saying words but not coming close to forming any kind of a meaningful sentence.

'It's ok, it's ok'

He said, weirdly in a friendly soothing manner while he reached over and patted my shoulder. Definitely not the behaviour you'd expect from the man who you'd recently made a widower.

'To answer that question, I will answer in reverse. I have had to take the dead body of my wife back to Russia for her funeral so, as you can imagine, matters such as this take up one's priorities. As for the Guardia Civil? Well, the decision was taken that we did not *want* to involve them, we wanted it to be dealt with in house, as they say. As far as the police think, Anya spent the whole night on our yacht, alone. Of course, we both know that the security cameras at the club where you met her, as well as the on board cameras we have on the yacht, would tell a different story?'

The fact that someone has the chance to have the police lock you up easy as pie, and don't take it, because they want to deal with it themselves - as the man had just sat and told me - can *never* be a good sign. Not for the person sitting in the hot seat, in the middle of things.

I wanted to sit there and tell him how it had been *her* who had come on to me. That he had one security guard who literally was the one who propositioned me on her behalf. *Needed* to express that she had been the driver in it all. Aye, obviously, I had then went on to ride her senseless afterwards, mind.

I couldn't sit there and say - to a man who's just buried his wife - that his now deceased Anya was a bit of a goer. Some things you can't do and one of them is speak ill of the dead, *especially* when you're sitting in earshot of someone who was married to 'the dead.'

And anyway, would he have even believed me if I'd tried to explain? It could've just come across as someone trying to say anything to save their skin, and in doing so only make the situation even worse.

'My initial thought when I heard the news that Anya had passed, and that she had been found dead after spending the night with someone? I chose violence. I actually told Ari there, behind me, to go out that morning and find and kill you. But then I calmed down a little, and called it off'

HA, so I was fucking *right* when I was going out my mind in those first forty eight hours, following the Russian wifie's death.

One nil to Sepp, eh?!

'I decided that, after returning from the funeral, I wanted to see you first. I wanted to look the man in the face who had killed my wife'

I cringed inside at the use of 'see you first,' with even further emphasis on the word *first.*

'Time can offer a little, what is the word? *Perspective*, yes, that's it. I went from instantly wanting your head on a spike, to wishing to sit, cordially, in the same room with you, like we are right now'

I'll admit. I didn't have a fucking clue what the hell was going on by this point. Were they going to clip me or not?

'Look, mate. I'm not going to sit here and bullshit you, Mr Borovskiy, you're clearly too intelligent for that kind of stuff, so I wouldn't even think of insulting you with lies'

I finally found some kind of voice and unless one of his security pistol whipped me, I wasn't stopping.

'Aye, I was with your wife that night. Gen up, pal. She told me that you had some kind of an 'understanding' though, where yous could ride anyone that you wanted. Your man Ari, there, eh?'

I pointed at the big Mossad boy.

'Wasn't as if he was stopping me from getting on the yacht that night when I was getting out of the Range Rover. Actually, there wasn't much in the way of questions from any cunt in your security set up, like'

'Yes, but you are overlooking one key part to an open relationship approach, between a married couple'

I didn't think I had, as it had all sounded so simple in my head. You're married to someone, but you could ride other people if you wanted to. Fuck all complicated about that, is there?

'Most open relationship couples? Neither of them normally end up *dead* at the end of the night'

Aye, that fair shut me up, like. I *had* planned to say that there hadn't been any monkey business or fuck all and that while, aye, we'd had sex with each other, we were both alive the last time I'd remembered. I just sat there and kept my mouth shut, though. I'm not sure it would've helped, anyway.

'But let us not dwell on such matters, eh?

He said, I could not have been in more agreement with this.

'There have been some, let us say, *developments,* since you left my wife Anya lying dead in our bed last week, and after having some time to reflect, I feel that I may be as willing to extend enough charity to you that would mean the Guardia Civil remaining oblivious of your name and face, or the three of us leaving this room today with you on your way for your *next* sexy time with Anya. Not that you *deserve* such goodwill, of course'

Who the fuck *cared* about what I did or did not deserve, I was more interested in this chatter from the boy that involved me not being killed or huckled by the police.

'I would very much appreciate this, Mr Borovskiy. I really did not mean to kill your wife'

I offered him, sincerely, while sneaking in what I'd meant to say earlier but putting it across in a lot more eloquent way than I'd probably have managed, while I was talking and couldn't stop myself.

I wasn't fucking stupid either though, mind. *No cunt* takes the trouble of finding out which hotel I was staying in and staged what would've been the equivalent of a dawn raid, all just to tell me that it was a case of forgive and forget. You're clear with me and I'll make sure the coppers don't find out about you, so you're golden, lad. Nah, that didn't even make sense and so while he was talking in what sounded like a lot more promising way for me, I was waiting on the 'but.'

'Would that work for you? You return back to Scotland at the end of your trip. No troubles from Guardia Civil, no troubles from Viktor Borovskiy. That is good, yes?'

Well, aye, of fucking course it was, but he already knew this.

I nodded my head while never unlocking eyes with the man. I was by no means out of whatever woods I was stuck in but I couldn't help but think of Rossi, Delaney and Wullie. Were they dead or alive by this point of the morning? Well, obviously, Wullie was good, even if he'd be leaving Mallorca with his leg in a stookie. My phone had went a couple of times with text messages and missed calls, could hear them going off inside Ari's pocket. As each missed call passed I was sat there secretly hoping that by me not answering anything, this would've led to someone finally coming to the hotel room looking for me.

'Well let us talk. You are a smart man, Sepp, and will already appreciate just how big a favour I have decided to do for you. For what you did, to my Anya. The love of my life? You should be rotting in a Spanish jail cell or found floating in the Balearic Sea'

Here it comes, I thought. And I wasn't far wrong, mind.

'Likes I said, mate. It wasn't on purpose, eh?' I tried a wee bit of counter to what he'd just said, which, for the most of it, had sounded grim as fuck, in terms of scenarios that were possibilities, if he'd seen fit to make reality. It didn't matter what I said, anyway. He was already on his way to saying what he was going to anyway. What he'd literally came to my room with the *intention* of saying.

'As you'll appreciate, a favour like this, would require you doing one back for me in return. It would be only fair, after all, yes?'

Once he'd started dangling my freedom in front of me, this was *always* coming, and I was glad for it. Considering the alternatives, anyway.

'Yes, Mr Borovskiy,' I replied. For some reason - from the moment he'd walked in and introduced himself, I'd been inclined to refer to him in such a formal way - I'd found myself talking to the cunt like I was back in high school in one of my classes.

'I appreciate such goodwill shown to me and if there's anything that I can do to help you in return then just say the word'

It didn't matter if I said this or not, it was going to be the requirement anyway. Regardless of this, I continued rattling on to the old billionaire gadge.

'I'm not sure what someone like myself would be able to do for you, though, eh? A man of your reach and power and that, and me? Just some man in the street, sparky by trade, from an area of Edinburgh that you wouldn't have even heard of. And it's not exactly like you need a tap from me which is just as well because I'm probably the fucking *last* cunt to be looking for a wee loan of money off. Fucked if I know how I'm even going to last the rest of the trip before running out of dough, never mind lending any out. Wouldn't be much of a bodyguard either, hardly a candidate to be part of your private army and work some of my debt off to you, either? Fuck, my head can't even get its head around driving a car on the other side of the road so you wouldn't want me as your driver and *you* wouldn't last very long *with* me as your driver'

I was just rambling like fuck in that way you do when you're nervous as fuck about something, and can't stop speaking even though there's absolutely fuck all of substance as to what's coming out of your mouth.

'Oh but on the contrary'

He said, holding his hand up to stop me from the torture of having to put up with any more examples from me of why I was probably the *last* cunt that he could've done with needing a favour from. It would have almost been easier for him to just have me done in and by fuck, it wasn't as if me - head in bits - was sitting there like a complete fucking rocket, *giving* him reasons for to not want me to carry out a favour. Don't get me wrong, I'd told him that I would do anything he wanted in return for taking the spotlight from off of me, whilst giving him *tonnes* of examples where he should strike off from actually asking me.

'It's *exactly* because of you coming from a part of Edinburgh that, until very recently, I haven't heard of. It is the *only* reason that you are sitting here alive or not in Palma jail. Now correct me if I am wrong, but some of the intelligence my men found out about you was that you are a goalkeeper, here in Magaluf to play in a tournament, is that so, yes?'

Chapter 25

Benji

'We're proper fucked, eh?' Strings sat there with his head in his hands. As is the Muirhouse Violet way, and opposed to *any* other group of people in the fucking world, even the words *'We're proper fucked, eh?'* were ones that always required narrowing down some more.

Were we fucked, as in a group of players who were going to be flying home in a matter of days with some of our contingent going to be on the plane in the hold, in a coffin?

We're fucked, as in we'd flown out to Mallorca to play in a fitba tournament and had - somehow - made the final but were now approaching the match in one day's time with three of the first team one hundred percent going to be missing - two of them looking like they had no chance of even being able to fly home on the same plane as the rest of the team - from the eleven that would play in the final while - also 'we're fucked' - the rest of the players had been drinking for almost ten days straight while playing a gruelling ratio of games to days alongside the bender?

We're fucked as in an Albanian death squad - following orders because we'd not lost the semi - could ride up on us at any point and hand out a bit more of what they did last night to our boys, and leave us there in the hospital as more of a fixture than a visitor?

We're fucked, as in we don't have a single bit of energy left between us due to being up all night, pacing the halls of Palma

Hospital, waiting anxiously to find out the varying conditions of our three mates, and if all three were going to make it through the night?

It was none of these - very real - examples. Strings, instead, speaking more *personally*, when it came to just the two of us, and - while, aye, managing to avoid being brutally attacked by Albanian radgeys and staying out of a Spanish hossie bed - the more pressing issues we had.

'Well, what's the scores on the doors?' I asked, changing the subject from the one that had dominated proceedings for the whole of the night, taking some light relief that we were talking about something *other* than the fact we had three players admitted to hospital. One who - now stable - had, for a few hours, been fighting for his life. It would've been nice for us to have been able to change the subject to something *other* than the problem the two of us had landed ourselves with not too long into the trip but what can you do, eh?

'Something like around a thousand euros between us, and another *two* needed, with three days left to get it'

It was - as far as I was concerned - an impossible amount of money for us to come up with in such a short space of time. It might've well as been fucking *fifty* thousand euros we'd had outstanding. Both amounts were as out of our reach as each other.

Aye, we'd *tried* to set about bringing the coin back in to be put towards the fines but had never came close and had it not been for the contribution of some funds from match fixing - well, *attempted* match fixing - gangsters then we'd have had barely a rupee between us put to the side to give to the Spanish authorities.

We'd eventually ended up sacking the stringing due to getting absolutely fucking nowhere with it and things becoming apparent that there had been a much higher chance of us getting lifted - when engaging in our craft - than there'd been of us strolling away with pockets full of cash.

Trust the pair of us to end up owing a fucking country a large amount of money like that, while we're stuck on an island where it had soon started to feel that *every* cunt knew about the old puggy stringing hustle.

You'd have thought the time that the security guard - at the hotel - shook us down, while telling Strings that what we were up to was by no means a new thing to the island. *That* should've been the signal to just fuck things off altogether, sending us away to call back home and ask our other halves to start looking out any of our possessions that might've made a bit of money and get them on Ebay, pronto. Twenty four hour auctions and that. Fast cash. Not like the pair of us had much of material value that cunts on eBay would've been fighting over themselves to buy. Times like that you wish you'd been into collecting stuff like trainers or designer clothes. The kind of possessions that could've been called upon in the most desperate of moments.

Aye, I'm sure my battered Superstars - that I used for walking the dog - would've had them all trying to outbid each other until the very final seconds of the auction, eh?

We still gave it another go - after the incident in the hotel with the crooked security guard - by trying a more old school amusement arcade that was situated down by the beach. The kind of place that could've boasted fun for ages eight to eighty. The perfect environment *for* a bit of stringing. Bairns running around all over the place making mischiefs of themselves. People of all nationalities - and language - constantly distracting those who were running the place. The *ideal* kind of joint for a couple of ghosts to sit there and do a bit of plundering.

Only, we weren't as invisible as Strings had first thought when assessing the place - as we walked in - and plumping for the first machine of the day. This, confirmed about half an hour into our shift when this kid came up to us. Wee Spanish boy, maybe ten years old at the most. Fair play, for a wee cunt like that, his English was decent.

The kid, stood there in a pair of dayglo orange swimming trunks and those jelly shoes that you see bairns wearing about the beach, tugged on my arm, as I stood there shielding Strings. Well, *thought* I'd been shielding, at least.

'Meester, meester,' he said in a cute wee Speedy Gonzales voice, getting my attention.

'You ok, wee man, aye?' I said as I looked down at him. Still holding onto my arm he turned and pointed at an old man who was sitting a few machines away, looking over at us.

'My abuelo, he no speak English, but I can, but he says that you are going to be taken away by the Guardia Civil'

My instinct was to say to him that the Guardia Civil only take away bad people who are doing bad things, put across like an adult to a bairn would do. Before doing so, though. I realised that *we* were doing what could've been described as 'bad things'

The old man - easily in his seventies with a face that looked like it had seen a long life and teeth which suggested that during this lengthy time on earth hadn't seen too much of a dentist. He flashed me a horrible looking smile, while making a stringing motion with his hands.

Is there *any* cunt in Magaluf that *isn't* on to us? I thought, with things now at the point where wee bairns were now casually pointing out to us what we were doing. Something that - generally - was done right under the noses of an unsuspecting public. It couldn't be any other way than that. If there *was* suspicion then you wouldn't be able to get away with fuck all.

Strings - by this point - had stopped playing. You tend to put your criming on hold when you hear words thrown around like *Guardia Civil*, mind.

The old boy shouting 'Pepe' and the wee boy running back across to him and stood there while the man - still looking across to the pair of us - spoke some more Spanish to the wee lad, who then came back across to relay the message to us in English.

'Abuelo says that if he can see what you're doing then the owners will'

The innocence of youth, eh? This wee boy looked so earnest in what he was saying to us. You got the impression that whatever it was that his grandad had told him to tell us he'd have happily ran back and forward and told us, playing interpreter.

'What's the fucking point, fuck's sake. This fucking island'

A frustrated Strings said, not really thinking of - or caring - about the wee boy being stood beside us as he booted the base of the puggy. His frustration getting the better of him. The wee Spaniard getting a bit spooked by this and me telling him it was cool and that my pal was just a bit loco, wiggling my finger round and round to the side of my head while crossing my eyes, making him laugh.

We left pretty much straight away, but not without one last piece of translation offered by the wee boy, after running back to his grandad one last time. From what he came back and told us, his grandad used to do what *we* did when he was younger, so it had been easy for him spy what we were doing.

There *was* - for a few moments at least - the temptation to put this down to him being a trained eye and that just because he was seeing what we were up to, didn't mean that anyone else could. Plus the puggy had been showing promising early signs of being a machine that was going to end up paying out big time for us.

Trying to see things from a more sensible perspective - which isn't easy when you're a desperate man - though, never in our life had we ever been caught in the act stringing, until Magaluf. And we'd been caught *twice* in a row. As far as signs for not pushing something. What more could you have possibly required?

'Mon, Benji,' a despondent Strings said, getting up to leave. Telling the wee man to thank his 'abuelo' for the advice while we both gave the old boy a thumbs up as we left. Him just waving us away as if it had been nothing. That was the watershed moment where - between each other - we'd been left with no choice but to admit that what had seemed like our only chance of scraping the money together to pay our fines, had worked out as barely worth our time and effort.

Which all brought us to the position of being on the eve of the final, and the team flying home the day after, and us sitting there with a third of the money - at best - that we needed to pay back before leaving the island. It had always been there - from the moment we'd left the Palma court house - but there had been an element of 'aye this is shit but we've got a decent amount of time to round up the money and a way to do so' about things. Only we hadn't done so, and now all the time that we'd had left had now almost expired.

Facts were now having to be faced.

Even though we'd never have been able to afford a proper English speaking representative for to deal with our court appearance. By then, I'd wished that we'd done so.

Because, we were now in a situation where we were due a foreign country an amount of money that we did not have, but would soon be looking to *leave* the country. What was going to happen, there? Were we going to get the KB once we tried to check in to fly back home? Were our names going to start flashing in red, the moment that we handed over our passports?

This was all stuff that we should have had established at the time but our heads were too rattled by everything to ask. The rate of words that judge had been shouting at us, there's every chance that specific part had been covered, and that junior lawyer boy just hadn't passed on. It had seemed that going by ratio of words spoken by the judge - to what was translated for us - had been a little low in terms of what *was* explained to us. The crux of it that I'd taken out of things had been that we had a month to pay the money, or we'd be going to jail.

Each country has their own rules, obviously, but I'd remembered watching one of those reality shows at an airport in Australia and - you know how para those cunts are about bringing almost *anything* into their country - some Chinese couple, there down under as tourists, were caught bringing food into the airport inside their suitcase and were dished out an on the spot fine with the timescale for paying back pretty much the same duration as what me and Strings had. Thinking about this, though. The chilling part was that I'd remembered that the customs officer - while issuing the fine - had also told them that they would not be able to leave the country, at the end of their holiday, *if* they had not paid the fine. Mental, like. All because they had some packets of beef and some radge looking mushrooms in their suitcase.

If the Spaniards operated the same kind of policy then, no question. Strings and me were utterly fucked. Stranded in a foreign country with fuck all money to survive and a wee stretch in a Spanish prison to come, for the non payment of the fine. *That* part, explained to us by the young guy in court. Definitely remembered that section as it had been the prime piece of motivation for us to be trying like fucking bears to bring in the money. It was almost like we weren't trying to raise the three thousand to pay the fine, it was more a case of to try and stay out of fucking jail.

'I remember reading somewhere that Palma Airport was one of the most busy airports in the world, which I had thought a bit radge in itself as I'd have always assumed somewhere like Los Angeles or Amsterdam or something, so you honestly think that they'll have things enough together for to know not to let us out of the country?'

Strings said, with a - more - hopeful tone to things rather than sitting and speaking with any kind of authority, or knowledge.

'Or put it another way, Benj. Look at those fucking Al Qaeda radgeys? You trying to tell me that a whole fucking mob of them could get themselves onto four planes and do with they did but that the Spanish authorities will have a S.W.A.T team on hand for when two clueless tourists who accidentally set fire to an island are trying to board a plane?'

Maybe he was right but the point was, he didn't *know* that he was, and was simply telling himself what he wanted to hear just so that there was some kind of positive spin to things, when there was absolutely *fuck all* positive to things, either in our own two person situation, or for the wider group.

By talking about terrorists, it had me thinking of the *last* time I'd flown from Palma and literally right beside the booth that you passed when you were boarding your plane, they had mugshots of ETA separatists who were wanted by the Spanish for bombings carried out in the country. So, aye. On that front, it seemed like the Spanish were a bit more clued up when it came to looking out for shady cunts in their airports than the Shermans obviously were. I felt no need to burst Strings' wee hope bubble that he'd found himself floating in, though.

And anyway, even if we *did* make it out of the country without any problems. The problems would soon catch up with us back home when the letters started coming through the door, and where we'd start to find that the - collective - three bags fine was now *ten*, or worse. In a perfect world you'd just have had to accept that you now couldn't go back to Spain because they'd have you on some list, but it wouldn't be as simple as that. No way were they going to just write the debt off, because we'd fucked off home. This was something that - however it was dealt with - wouldn't just 'go away.'

'Aye well, this isn't like we're bumping some Provie loan, Strings, mate. Even if we can get off this island, we're *still* going to have to pay what's due and I have the idea that the longer we take to pay it the *more* the debt's going to rise'

'The cunts are worse than Davey McKenna, eh?'

I didn't think it possible to even begin to compare the Spanish government and Davey McKenna, but Strings found a way.

'But, aye, Strings. To answer your question. We *are* proper fucked. Clearly, we're not going to be able to get close to coming up with the dough. I have a feeling that if we attempt to string one more place in Magaluf our luck's going to run out and we're ending up back in custody again. And now, as a result, we're going to be rocking up to the airport in a few days time with our erses flapping like fuck while we wait to see what happens when our name pops up on their monitors. We manage to get through, and on the plane, then we're *still* going to be left with thousands to pay the Spanish authorities, while at the same time in fucking McKenna's pocket, working off *that* debt. Forgive my negativity but I'm not seeing too much in the way of positives here, like'

We were already in a hole - back in Edinburgh - trying to combine enough time to do bits for McKenna while also working for ourselves to bring enough of a crust in for our families to live and eat each week. Where was this magical extra time, on top of all of that, going to come from where we could go into the wild and come up with the money to send back to Spain?

For the time being, at least, it was probably for the best that we introduced a wee bit of pragmatism to things. Because it was either that or just lose our fucking marbles thinking about it between then and when we would arrive at the airport.

Evidently, there were *other* things to be worrying about, than those that you couldn't do fuck all about, like our problem in paying back a fine.

Never mind the impact on the three boys lying in hospital beds - We'd been able to visit Wullie, who had been more pissed off at missing the final than he was about having had his leg broken, but Rossi, head bandaged to fuck, had been given some medication that had knocked him out so even though we'd been around him at his bed, he wouldn't have known it. Delaney had been the one who had been strictly off limits for us. For part of the night he'd been fighting for his life. They'd had to operate on him pretty soon after arrival and by the time we were leaving the hospital, was lying stable but without any visits permitted. The night had been a drain on us all who had came to the hospital, physically and mentally. We weren't supermen by any stretch and were not going to be able to avoid sleep for much longer.

Obviously, training had been cancelled. Jock - who had been stressing out of his tits from the moment I knocked on his hotel room door and woke him up - hadn't even needed to say to any of us. It had just been assumed, what with the whole team being awake for the whole night, whether they were there at the hospital or back at the hotel, anxiously waiting on any updates coming through.

Jock, in the end taking the decision to order us all back to the hotel for some kip, while he stayed. The hospital staff - who'd had the misfortune of having to deal with a mob of half pished and het up Muirhouse players throughout the night - looked happy at this prospect. Offering Jock the use of a visitors room that he could catch a few hours himself. Assuring him that if there was any news - regarding his players - that someone would wake him up.

'Aye, you lads get on your way back to the hotel and get some sleep, you bloody well look like you need it'

Jock said, clearly not aware of the horrific sight that was looking back at us. Poor cunt, I reckon he'd aged five years over the hours we'd been at the hospital, and Jock wasn't at the stage in life where he could just throw five years away, either.

As things stood, by the next morning, there in the hossie. Wullie was lying in bed with an injury that he could easily have picked up on a Sunday morning in the league, quite possibly as literally as likely from some cunt battering him with a baseball bat than being on the receiving end of a late challenge. Delaney, who had lost a shit load of blood and had the staff at the hospital working overtime to make sure the cunt didn't croak, was now lying classed as stable but definitely not what anyone could have classed as tip top, where Rossi? Well no cunt really knew yet when it came to him because he'd been out of it since he'd been admitted but had been hooked up to all kinds of machines that were monitoring him. Can't say I've ever had someone smack me off the nut with a hammer but surely it can't be a pleasant experience? Hitting your fucking finger when you're hammering a nail into a piece of wood is like pain you've never experienced, so fuck knows what it must be like to take one to the napper?

I'd shat myself at first, thinking that our star striker was literally in a coma but - from the monitoring that they'd been doing on him - the docs had said that from the brain patterns they'd been getting from their fancy machine that, while having received a serious blow to the head, should go on to make a full recovery. Jock was right, though. By that point of the morning, there was fuck all else we could really do, other than get in the staff's way, and I think they'd well had enough of that by then.

Ending the conversation, me and Strings, knowing that it wasn't as if we had any other choice, agreed to just go for a hit and hope - in terms of us leaving Spain via Palma Airport - but, in between, would concentrate on the wellbeing of our mates, alongside the not so small matter of a European cup final to be playing in the next day.

Although, after spending the longest of nights in a Spanish hospital anxiously waiting around corridors while praying none of our boys died, there was no guarantee that we were even going to *play* the final the next day.

Chapter 26

Strings

I don't think anyone - outside our own group of players and management - could have believed just how close - and after, quite literally, so much blood sweat and tears shed from us over those two weeks - we had come to saying 'fuck yer fitba' and just telling the suits - that were organising the Red Bear Beer Cup - that we were forfeiting our place in the final.

The night before the match? Fitba couldn't have been any further from our mind, as far as a priority. Which, obviously, was not a good sign, had we been a team who were intent on finishing the job that was ahead of us the next day. The match against the Russians had barely even been given a mention, and when it had it was the whispers between players over whether we were going to play the game or not.

It wasn't until the next morning - and a team meeting down in the lobby of the hotel - that we decided that we'd play. The main motivation for this was to play for Wullie, Delaney and Rossi, and that we'd win the trophy for them. Talk about having a cause to take yourselves into a game of fitba with though, eh?

Jock - who had pretty much lived at the hossie since the middle of the Saturday night, when the lads had been rushed in, - had appeared back at the hotel on the Tuesday morning, ready for the squad surfacing. The lot of us waking to a text from him, telling us to meet him downstairs.

By around half ten or so we were all sitting downstairs, having commandeered a large section of the seating area to see what the man had to say. Up until then he'd stayed there at the hossie while some of us would pop back and forward for a wee visit to see the boys.

'Right then, state of play? Delaney and Rossi are going to make full recoveries but the doctors reckon it might take a week, maybe two, before the both of them are released. Wullie, though, he's getting let out later on today'

We all looked around each other as the evident wave of relief washed over us. Things had started to look more promising - with the news that we'd occasionally receive via updates from the hospital - but you know how things can *also* take turns for the worse too? So, to get a wee bit more crystal clear information, and on the positive side, on the subject was just what we needed.

'I'll be honest with you, lads. With three of my boys lying in hospital injured, and with the seriousness of some of those injuries, I haven't even been able to *think* about the final. What kind of a manager puts *that* as their priority, when he's got players fighting for their bloody lives in a hospital?'

Me and Benji looked at each other, already knowing from Jock's tone where things were now heading.

'To be equally honest, Jock. We've been the exact *same* as you. Our heads have been completely fried by what happened. How you meant to concentrate on playing a game of fitba, with all of the other shite going on, eh?'

Terry said, breaking the silence from the squad and to be fair, while not some appointed spokesperson for the group by any stretch, in that moment he might've well have been, because what he'd said spoke for the group of us. Instead of it completely dominating the chatter amongst us - in terms of the build up to it taking place - the subject of the cup final had almost - unintentionally - become one of those topics that you just tip toe around tactfully, without ever having to actually *speak* about it.

'And *that's* why we are the bunch of magnificent bastards that we are, Tel'

Jock replied, pointing at him before extending his finger around the group.

'We're a bloody *team* and I'd have expected nothing else from a bunch of men with that mentality of looking out for one and other … BUT, while we still have the luxury of the cup final not kicking off until tea time, we need to talk about it. Now I'm not forcing anyone to play if they're not comfortable doing so but I've just come from a hospital where the three boys lying in beds up there have *all* told me to come back and tell you that they want you to not just play but *win* this bloody cup. If not for yourselves then for them. Delaney, who can hardly bloody catch a breath due to how messed up the insides of his stomach are right now near enough passed out in his attempts at telling me to say to the squad that if he found out that we didn't play the final because of him then when he's finally recovered he's going to bloody *stab* each and every one of you in the same way that *he's* been done in'

This bringing a wee bit of a laugh around the tables. It was such a Muirhouse Violet thing to do. Threaten to stab the rest of your team mates, if they don't go out and win a cup final!

'Now it's been a hard couple of days for us all, especially the three that were hospitalised, so I can appreciate that there may be a few heads maybe not finely tuned for tonight's match, and that's why I called this meeting as early as I did. To *allow* you to take a few hours out to prepare mentally. Like I said, though, anyone who thinks that they can't play in the game, they won't be judged by me'

'They absolutely positively fucking *will* be judged by him'

I joked quietly to Benji, while Jock was looking elsewhere.

If we were going to go on and play then we were already three players down for a kick off, and in *no* position - as a team - to handle any further absences.

'So what are you all saying then?'

Hunter asked, having allowed the group a wee bit of time to talk amongst themselves, following his wee speech.

'Well, put it this way, Jock, and I think I speak for the rest here and if not then speak up cuntos but if even just one of those players' life's were at risk this morning then there was not a fucking chance that we'd be sticking on a Violet shirt and running out onto that pitch to play the Farleys. How *could* we, with stuff at the back of our mind like that? If something similar had happened to a professional team, the cup final would've been postponed, so not really sure why we'd be just expected to carry on, business as usual. *But*, if things are looking a bit more rosy than they were, then I can't think of a better or more fitting gesture, towards Wullie, Delaney and Rossi, than to go out and kiss that fucking silver. Imagine the buzz we'll have taking the trophy into the hospital to visit Delaney and Rossi? I think we should just take it to a vote but already I'm standing up and saying that I'm IN'

Hunter nodded his head approvingly towards me and the leadership I'd attempted to inject. He'd have nodded it a lot fucking more had he known some of the shite that was in my head with regards to my own personal issues and how it was already at the front of my mind that the next night at the airport I was going to be stopped from coming home to Edinburgh. That alone could've - should've? - been enough to prevent someone from going into a cup final and giving it their all for ninety minutes.

'Fair enough, Strings. Can't argue with that, pal'

Jock Hunter replied with the air and confidence that - following my spiel - someone would've had, already knowing what the outcome was going to be. And he wasn't wrong, either. Not one single arm did not go up into the air when the time came, along with lots of expressions of defiance over what had been thrust upon the group in the recent days.

'These bastards think we'd come all the way here and give up? Obviously don't know the fucking Muirhouse Violet'

'Let's fucking do it. One more game, lads'

'We're going back to that fucking hossie with that trophy filled full of San Miguel for the boys'

'Fuck it, ninety minutes to win it for the lads, and make ourselves national legends in the process'

'Yasssss, we're Muirhouse Violet, we don't fucking give up, or give in, to no cunt'

Everyone had an opinion, all of the same vein.

Jock stood watching the fire inside us all build - that he'd appeared that morning and been the spark that had started it - with the first smile that he must've managed in days. He knew us well enough and what he was seeing that morning was the signs of a group of players that were going to be prepared to run through fucking walls for him.

I think, deep down and taking our players mentality into consideration, we all had *wanted* to play in the final but make no mistake, wouldn't have had a single issue in calling off, if we'd felt that it hadn't been appropriate. Something that we'd been of the opinion until that visit to the hotel from Jock. From a team mentality angle, though. We'd come all the way from Scotland to see how we would stand up against foreign opposition, and had wiped the floor with everyone that were put up against us. As far as I was concerned, the Estonia game didn't count. We'd won every game that we'd *tried* to win, a better way of phrasing things. And now we had just one match left to make us *champions*. I already knew - we all did - that there was not a single player in our squad that would not have been left extremely fucking moist at the thought of winning that trophy, but it had to be in the correct circumstances, and Jock had just brought them with him in that taxi down to the hotel from the hospital.

'Good lads, good lads'

Hunter looked around everyone, seeing the complete and utter *unity* that he had for his - now dismissed - squad, before moving onto plans for the match.

'Now, obviously I'm going to have to rejig the starting eleven, considering those three up at the hospital couldn't even currently manage a game of fitba on the PlayStation'

While not considering playing in the final - up to that point - it had already been clear that those Albanians had removed three vital cogs from the not so much will oiled and more well ale'd Muirhouse machine, and now they would have to be replaced, for a cup final no less. And it wasn't like we were - what you could describe as - wall to wall with talent, once you got past our first eleven. And with that, Jock didn't really have much deliberations of who he was going to have come into the starting eleven. Standing there, he confirmed which players would be coming in to start. Everyone else who had played in the semi final - despite looking like it had almost been one game too many for them due to the excessive playing of fitba as well as the equal amount of peaving over the ten days - all keeping their places in the team.

'Right, Milky, you're in for Delaney. You don't exactly need a crash course in what I expect and need from you, you've sat on the bench and watched Delaney, and before him, Bungalow enough times from the bench, so you know the requirements'

Jock clearly hadn't intended this to come across in the way that he had, but that's how I took it as. Another way of translating things would've been 'Right, I've got fuck all else to use and considering you've sat on the bench for fucking years without barely being used, you're clearly not my cup of tea but I've not got much choice right now so how's about you go out and play *like* the players that I've always picked ahead of you, because I rate them better than you.' Not exactly the most inspirational of talks but you wouldn't have known this by the look on Milky's coupon. Proper lottery winning smile at the news that - against all odds - he was going to get a start in a Muirhouse shirt, and in a fucking European final, as a Brucie bonus.

Milky, - named as such due to the National Health specs that he used to wear at school and, mixed with his blonde hair, made him look a bit like the wee boy from the Milky Bar adverts - to give Jock a wee bit of credit, was a complete fucking bomb scare of a central defender and literally there to make up the numbers. A player that milk would turn quicker than him. You knew you were fucked if he was going to be in defence and -

when he was - the policy was to always try and keep play in the *opponents* half of the pitch, simply so that Milky's deficiencies would not be exposed as much. You couldn't help but be nervous over the thought of playing in a cup final and have a liability like that in the team, but we had no other real option that morning.

'Stig, I'm bringing you in for Wullie. This isn't your first rodeo so I want to be seeing the Stig of old. The one who would've been in the starting eleven in the *first* place'

'I'll not let you down, gaffer, or the rest of yous'

The Stig said, looking around everyone. I can't think that his inclusion in the team would've been much of a surprise, considering it had been *his* full back slot that Wullie had came along and claimed as his own. All down to The Stig having to move to Norway for a year - through his work - but up until that point had been a permanent fixture in the side. Up until around six months before, he'd simply been known as Bayne - as in the the bakers - but after leading something like ten police cars on a high speed chase through Muirhouse, Pilton and then into Edinburgh city centre - after a jam sandwich had tried to stop him while he was driving while disqualified - it was a case of some nicknames writing themselves. Still, though. Radge cunt behind the wheel of an automobile but *fully* dependable when it came to a stand in for Wullie and - fuck all against Wullie here, mind - were it not for Jock's sense of loyalty, with Wullie playing that whole year with The Stig out of the country, I reckon lots of managers would've let The Stig back in the team because - and once again, not dissing the very much capable full back strengths of Wullie's - tactically *and* technically, he was the better full back out of the two of them.

The Stig - while someone who could gallop up the side of the pitch, overlapping and that - being a defender who could actually *defend*. Fucking *loved* it, actually. Aye, we'd not be going wrong with him slotting in for Wullie.

'Which leaves me to you then, Five O'

Everyone all turned around to see what his reaction was like. It wasn't going to be a day for passengers, we'd need *every* player to be up for it and at the very top of their game. And a lot of the time you just need to look at a player's coupon to know where they're placed, when it comes to pre match attitude. You can see those nerves written all over them in those moments.

But, nah. Five O's response to Jock was not one that would've left you questioning whether he was right in the head to play in a game of such magnitude.

The confidence - and almost arrogance - at the news that he was replacing the *one* player in our squad who was responsible for putting the ball in the net on a regular basis completely belied the reality that Five O was hardly as what you'd call a goal machine, on the times that he'd actually got a start, or the limited amount of substitutions that he'd normally get over a season. Handed the name after he'd turned up to the end of season player's award night in the absolute *worst* Hawaiian shirt you'd ever seen. He was a bit of a quiet boy off the pitch but a different animal *on* it. An absolute fucking mentalist with a fitba shirt on, to give an honest assessment of the boy. While he wasn't someone that you could have ever relied on replacing the goal threat that Rossi brought, he was definitely someone that was going to make it a long day for the Farley's defence.

The team meeting ended with Jock telling us to go away and prepare for later on, be that to do a wee bit of exercise in the hotel gym, or spend a few hours relaxing on a sun bed, recharging the batteries before this one final push.

I couldn't moan - considering the circumstances leading up to the match - but, confirming that we'd be playing in such a massive match, at the relatively late stage that we'd done, it had kind of removed that whole buzz that you get, before playing in a cup final. The build up that you and the team have when it's approaching. The whole feeling of positivity amidst the prospect of lifting that trophy. That one true moment where you get tangible validation that all of your hard work was for something. And now there wasn't really any time to soak up that feeling. It was a case of 'oh by the way, you're playing a cup final in a few hours.' It all reminded me of that morning I was driving up the road from Manchester with a van full of Ching in the back, while having the Kwik Save cup final hours ahead of me, and not knowing whether I'd even make the match at all.

Not quite the same thing - considering wars were being fought and that - but must've been something similar to the Danish players, in ninety two, who were all obliviously going about their life without a fucking *clue* that they were going to be playing in the European Championships. Imagine how buzzing those boys would've been for weeks ahead of that tournament beginning, instead of lying on a beach somewhere with playing fitba the last thing in their heads?

The hours flew by and - having taken them to just relax and try to get my head deep in what lay ahead for me and the rest of the team - it wasn't long before we were all getting on the two minibuses to take us up to the stadium for one last visit.

I wasn't sure if it was nerves or just some kind of steely determination from the squad but the short journey was more or less silent. The complete *opposite* of how you'd find the Violet players behaving. Pre, during *or* after a game.

Couldn't speak for Benji but my silence - as much as I wanted to focus on the fitba side of things - was more to do with the thoughts of how things were going to go at the airport the next night, when trying to leave. I was always good at that. Putting things to the back of my head - that were going to be a problem later on - until the very last moment and where it was now unavoidable to stop yourself from thinking about them. And I was now at that point, when it came to thinking about the whole skipping town without settling up your bill issue that was now very much incoming.

Best get those thoughts out the way now before the match begins, I told myself, while hardly doing anything to change my course of them as we pulled into the stadium car park.

Something that I was to find easier said than done. Me still carrying those thoughts onto the pitch for the start of the match, and during those first forty five minutes. And it showed. Although, with the rest of my team mates displaying attitude and commitment that screamed 'men on mission' my inadequacies had been easily glossed over.

Back in the dressing room - having done our warm up and now back in for our last moments before heading out for kick off - Jock rounded all the players up for his parting words to us all.

'Now, despite this being the most important match that any of you have ever played in, this should be the easiest team talk that I will ever have to give you. We all came out here, didn't know what to expect but that we travelled with the belief in *ourselves*. We maybe didn't know what the other teams that we'd play would be capable of, but that didn't matter, because we know *ourselves*. Since game one, they've cheated, they've punched, they've kicked, spat and conned referees. Whatever it's been to try and knock us out of our stride, they've tried it, because they bloody well could *see* who was the better team.

One team not even capable of taking their dinner given to them and arranging bloody *attacks* on the squad, because they weren't as good as us'

Jesus, if only Jock knew, when it came to the Albanians, and the *real* story behind that, I momentarily thought but while trying to keep up with his speech.

'All of this, it's because they know that we're here to win the trophy, and that on talent alone, they *can't* bloody stop us. They don't know *how* to cope with us and that trophy out there is only ours to lose'

With Jock's knowledge, Benji had arranged a nice wee touch for the team, providing them that last piece of inspiration and desire to win a game of fitba, before they left the dressing room that evening.

Pulling out his phone and making a quick call which - when he showed his phone screen to everyone - we soon discovered was a Face Time, showing an in bed Delaney and Rossi sat beside him, *both* in their Muirhouse strips. Jesus, man. Delaney looked as grey as that Man United top that Fergie said the players hadn't been able to see each other in. Rossi, still with a bandaged head looking well out of it on whatever drugs the doctors had been giving him. Fortunately his coma had only been a brief one.

The fucking noise from the team at that moment, seeing the boys - alive and kicking for one thing - in their tops, though? The other dressing room next door must've been wondering what the fuck was going on because the noise had to have sounded like a team celebrating at the *end* of the match, not before.

The two of them - both weak as piss - managed to put across some kind of message to us to go out and win the match. They couldn't have possibly understood all the different things being shouted back at them - from everyone - but for the impact that Jock and Benji had been looking for with this wee stunt, - if that's what you could call it - it did the trick.

The last thing we were to see before we left the dressing room, two of our mates - who we'd been well worried about, for very real reasons - sitting there in their tops? How could we have *not* went out onto that pitch like men possessed after that?

And it wasn't quite the *last* thing that we saw, before we left the dressing room. In what was classic timing. As the Face Time came to an end. Just as Montana was asking 'what about Wullie?' You heard ...

'Don't you worry about where the fuck Wullie is. Just get out there and give those fucking Russians hell, ya cunts'

Our Dundonian full back, coming into the dressing room, leg in a stookie while hobbling and looking like he was still trying to get used to having to use crutches to get around on.

The whole team, lifted further by the sight of him, fucking swamping the poor cunt until someone saw sense and shouted to give the boy some space.

By then, the knock on the door from the ref had come and it was the time for all the talk to end, and for the action to begin.

It felt a wee bit weird standing next to the Farleys in the tunnel, considering we'd stood next to the same players in the same tunnel just the week before.

'You cunts are like busses, eh?'

I said, to the Farley to the left of me as we stood there waiting on the signal to come down the tunnel. Maybe he didn't understand the English, the joke or had - like a lot of non Scots - taken offence at my usage of the word 'cunts' but I got nothing back from him. Negative or positive. Just a look which had felt like he'd stared right through me before turning and facing forward again.

Fuck you then, eh? I thought. Just trying to be a bit sociable, like.

The Farleys didn't know what hit them, that first ten minutes of the half. Proper shell shocked, like. Over the more recent days, we'd suffered a bit of adversity but, fuck me, if there's a group of men no strangers to adversity, it was us. The sight of Delaney and Rossi coupled with the last minute appearance of Wullie had sent us flying out the traps. Sometimes you can be that wee bit *too* hyped up, though, and it took me and Five O to pick up a booking each within the space of five minutes of each other for to be the signal for us to settle the fuck down. While it couldn't have ever been marked down as one of our team's strengths - and in fact we were fucking *infamous* for not having any - discipline was something that if we lacked in the game then we were going to have no chance. None of our usual shithousery that we usually relished in getting involved in. We couldn't afford to stray from the focus of our game plan.

They never laid a glove on us, the Farleys, in that first half. It was near on one way traffic which - fitness and tempo wise - is not an easy thing to keep up for forty five minutes. We'd already played these boys so *knew* how athletic they'd been in the first match, but they hadn't been able to live with the passion, power and desire from us. Out of anyone, I'd been the weak link out of the team. Unable to be professional enough to put my own 'stuff' to the side for ninety minutes and concentrate on the job in hand. I know that me and Benji had resolved to worry about leaving Spain until *after* the final, but the doing was harder than the saying part.

I hadn't made any mistakes that had cost us in any serious way and - because of this - had stood out, but I knew myself that I'd made them, and *why*.

Despite our near on total dominance, we'd only managed to convert one of the many chances that we'd created in that forty five minutes. While up the other end of the pitch all they'd managed had been wasteful long range efforts that hadn't troubled Sepp in the slightest. Ironically, our goal coming from Five O, Rossi's replacement. He celebrated exactly like someone who neither plays or ever scores, would've reacted. I think he combined at least three different celebrations in one as he wheeled away upon seeing his half volley - when the ball had deflected back into his path, following a shot from Montana that had been blocked by one of their defenders - hit the back of the net. First he was an aeroplane, next he had the front of his shirt up and over his face - until running right into Daz and tripping up - with him finishing by getting up off the ground and turning his back to the crowd while pointing his thumbs towards the name that wasn't actually printed on the back of his shirt.

That had come midway through the first half and - the way we'd been playing up to that point - the expectations were that we would go on and build on that lead. I remember looking at one of their midfielders coupon's and he'd looked visibly rocked by the intensity of our play. Like we'd done, they'd have been thinking about the team that they'd played earlier on in the competition. Even I'd been big enough to admit that while we'd won against the Farleys, on another day it could've just as easily been them. If they'd made the mistake of assuming that they were up against the same team, then they must've got the shock of their life when they found out that we were a completely different beast to that team in the group stages.

It *should've* been two. There was fuck all wrong with Montana's goal that the ref disallowed. The man in black making a motion that our striker had pushed their defender while winning the ball, before going forward and tucking. You didn't even have any of the Farleys complaining about it and *that's* when you know if it was a foul or not. They looked like they couldn't believe their luck when they saw the ref with his hand in the air. We were raging - as you'd imagine - and collected another couple of bookings during our protests which had now left us in the precarious position of having four players walking a tightrope going into the second half.

They say that decisions even themselves out? The fact that in our last meeting the Farleys having had a perfectly good goal chopped off wasn't lost on me.

With no further goals added, the ref eventually brought the first half to an end and - with the high tempo that we'd taken the game to the Farleys with - fuck me, weren't we happy to hear the whistle go.

None of us could've really complained, though. We'd went out and performed to the best of our abilities - some players, *surpassing* their talents - and were coming back in with a lead in our back pockets. The only regret? That it was only the one goal.

You know how fitba can be if you don't take your chances - while on top - and how this can maybe come back to haunt you at some stage but considering we didn't even know if we'd be *playing* in the match until that morning, *and* were missing three key first team players. Being one nil up at half time - in a first half that had it been the proverbial boxing match it wouldn't have even *seen* the forty fifth minute - wasn't exactly exactly shabby, either.

We walked off the pitch, ready to regroup, hydrate and see what words of wisdom Jock and Benji were going to have for us, safe in the knowledge that we were now only forty five minutes away from becoming Muirhouse Violet legends.

Chapter 27

Sepp

The atmosphere inside the dressing room - during the break - was electric. The intensity of our players, and the seriousness that they were all treating this particular moment in time, clear for all to see. We'd always been a tight knit unit that looked out for each other but even then, I don't think I'd ever witnessed such unity from everyone before. From the moment we decided to play the match, the morale boosting Face Time to the hospital to Delaney and Rossi - with Wullie's appearance the obligatory cherry on top - and right up to half time, *especially* half time. With how good the first half had gone, the eyes of the team were now starting to look on the prize.

And then there was me, sitting there silently. Watching everyone else, while feeling like a complete fraud.

Way worse than that. I felt like the world's worst cunt, the absolute fucking *worst*. I'm sat around a group of men who, - out on the pitch would fucking *die* for each other - full of hope and desire, were both patting each other on the back and offering encouragement on their game while - additionally - plotting what they now needed to all collectively do to go back out there for the second half to win the cup. On my side, though? I needed the *opposite* to happen. I didn't care how, I just needed my *own* team to lose the match.

Like I said, the absolute worst cunt. And absolutely *no one* would have needed to have told me that, had any of them known about the secret saboteur that was among them that early evening. Something I most definitely was not going to be informing them of. With some of the team mates I had? Aye, fuck *and* that.

'We've got our foot on these fucking Farley's throats, lads. No taking it off when we go back out there. COME ONNN'

Strings shouted out while clapping his hands, looking around at everyone. When he got to me, I could barely even look him square in the eye. How could I? Knowing that the first chance I got, I was going to be doing all I humanly could to let Zavorovo *back* into the match again.

'Strings is right, boys. We get the next goal and watch the bloody life get sucked out of those Russians. They're not coming back from going two down. Next goal's the big one, so make sure it's *us* that scores it'

Jock Hunter - seizing on Strings' words - rallied round everyone. I couldn't handle it. I just wanted to hear that knock on the door from the referee so that I could get back out there - away from the feel good environment of the dressing room - and be alone with my own thoughts, because the positivity inside that dressing room was killing me. I just wanted it to be all over, and when I say that, I wanted to skip the next forty eight hours and be back in my Muirhouse flat, feet up with a cup of tea while watching some shite on telly.

From a personal point of view, the first half couldn't have gone more wrong. Literally every one of our outfield players had played the full forty five minutes with such vigour that they could've easily had 'drug test me after the match' written on the front of their Violet tops. So much so that the Russians didn't even get fucking near me. Not even a single shot on target, like. As the first half had progressed I'd found myself looking across at the stand, hoping that Borovskiy had some men there watching. Because if there was one thing I was going to need - if the second half was to go the same way - it was an unbiased match report being given back to the old man that would absolve me of any blame, *if* Muirhouse won the match. I could hardly be blamed for not letting the Russians win if they couldn't even manage shots on target, for fuck's sake? Put it this way, I could've easily sat - during the first half - and had a wank watching a porno - as well as a cigarette afterwards - and there wouldn't have been the remotest chance of me letting one in. As a potential match fixer, I could only do so much and needed the other team to at least chip in a bit too. And if it all went tits up, I guess I was going to have to rely on how the game was relayed back to the big man, and then see how understanding a person he was.

That was all speculation at that point, but something that needed taken into consideration all the same.

It had felt like an hour we'd been stuck in that dressing room - not the fifteen minutes - before that knock on the door came and the wee Spaniard with the bandito style moustache popped his head around and tapped his watch. About time, ya cunt, I thought while taking no time to spring to my feet, just like the rest of the players. Eagerness written all over them.

I watched them all clap and gee each other up as we began filing out towards the tunnel. Their positivity and hope that they carried back out of the dressing room something that made me want to be physically sick. The fact that what I was doing was for my own survival, not really feeling much comfort to me. But still? The choice between being huckled - the day before flying home - by the Spanish police as part of some murder investigation, or taking a couple of bullets in the back of the head from one of Viktor Borovskiy's private army. The choice of either of those *or* going against my team mates and pals? Well, it wasn't exactly much of a choice, was it?

The boys were - if humanly possible - more fired up for the start of the second half than they'd been for the first, while looking like they hadn't even *played* a first half yet. Completely at odds with what was possibly going on inside their heads. I was hoping that biology would take over and they were going to run out of steam in the second half, so that I could at least be 'tested' and *given* a chance of being able to affect the outcome of the match.

Logically, though. There was no way that a professional, semi pro, junior, amateur or fucking *kids* team could keep up that kind of tempo for a full match, never mind a group of men who spend half their time in the boozer on a normal week.

As for the second half. Once both teams had taken to the pitch and the action back underway? Well it started more hopeful for Zavorovo - and by extension, me - with them taking the game to us right from kick off. Fuck knows what had been said - or taken - at half time in their dressing room but they came out with an attitude that showed that they were a team who knew that they needed to do much, much more than they'd shown in the first half.

The Violet were chasing shadows for the first ten minutes of the half. Inside this period I'd had an opportunity to give away a penalty, and did not pass it up. Gleefully accepted it if I'm being honest. I'd already thought about *how* I was going to be able to 'affect' the outcome of the match, without it looking fishy. A penalty was definitely something that would've fallen into that category. Keepers are fucking dafties at the best of times anyway so it's never out of the ordinary for one to give away a stupid penalty.

The first time one of their players even got a chance to be in possession of the ball inside our box close enough to me, I fucking cleaned the boy right out. Could've easily got my hand to the ball first but well, that was the whole point, wasn't it? It was the kind of incident that, while some of our players were disappointed about, did not draw any suspicious attention towards me.

I breathed a huge sigh of relief as the ref pointed to the spot. Walking back to my goal with my eyes closed while wishing their striker to put it away. Their big man - who I'd remembered being elbowed in the ribs from during the group game against them - stepping up and making a proper cunt of things by smashing it against the base of my left hand post. The Monk not requiring any kind of an invitation to get the ball away to fuck as soon, and as far away, as he could.

'Give me a fucking break here, eh? Help me out, lads for fuck's sake?' I thought to myself, while feigning delight that he'd missed the opportunity handed to him. The Stig and Milky first up to celebrate with me. Like I'd done anything to stop it?

This seemed to give us - and for that match, at least, it felt wrong to say *us* when I wasn't part of 'us' - a wake up call and we - we? - hit right back at them. Both Strings and Montana coming within a bawhair of making it two. Me standing up the other end of the pitch absolutely bricking it that I was going to see the ball hit the net, and the Muirhouse players wheeling away in celebration. Strings' shot, especially. Looked like it was past the keeper all the way until the very last second where he managed to get a hand to it, even if I'm not sure if he knew too much about it, how quickly the ball came at him.

As keepers do, I gave his save an applause from within my own goalmouth. An applause more sincere and appreciative than you'd have reserved for that whole 'keepers club' ethos.

It was from one of our attacks - broken up by the Zavorovo defence - that I presented the Russians with their next chance to get back into the match. This a little bit more suss than giving away a simple penalty, but still not exactly out of the ordinary. With us being so far up the pitch on the attack, I'd allowed myself to - very much consciously - take a wee wander out of my box. When Zavorovo stopped the attack, getting rid by knocking it over our midfield, it fell to one of their strikers to run on to.

I was still well outside my box by then and there was no question that he was going to reach the ball before I was ever going to make it back into my goal. Any cunt with a brain would've seen the chance that was there and just went for it. Instead, he took a couple of touches before switching the ball over to the other side of the pitch.

'Get back on your fucking line, Sepp,' I'd heard Daz screaming across at me as he'd sensed the danger.

Short of installing one of those massive fucking Las Vegas style casino neon lights with an arrow pointing towards the goal, there wasn't much more I could've done in that moment to try and engineer a goal for these useless bastards.

Once again, the lads were on Zavorovo's case. Five O - and thank fuck it was him instead of Montana - completely fluffing his lines and getting the ball stuck underneath his foot, when he should've been tucking it away, following being put in by Mr Benn with a pinpoint pass. Heart was in my mouth at that because we were getting near the sixty minute mark and - as far as my own prospects - this really wasn't funny anymore.

What I hadn't told Viktor Borovskiy inside the hotel room was that first of all, the Russians weren't actually a bad unit and it wouldn't have exactly been a major upset if they'd beaten us in the final. Secondly, we were a group of players who - through much more exercise than used to in such a relatively short space of time, the same going for alcohol - were almost on their fucking erses - by the semis - and that it had been a struggle to have enough energy to make it past the Albanians. And that one final game was possibly going to be a case of saturation point.

Taking those two factors into consideration. When I'd been left with the 'instructions' to make sure that Zavorovo won the final. There had been a part of me which had felt that this was possible *without* me having to play a major part in things, but yet my own individual part also being enough to get me off the hook.

The game wasn't working out like this, though. Muirhouse looked like they would fucking die before they'd lose the match, which was ironic given the high chances that I *might*, if they didn't.

With around half an hour left, finally, a bit of daylight came my way. The Russians bagging the equaliser. A weak attempt from Milky to clear his lines had only resulted in the ball landing at one of their midfielders, who slipped the ball into the box to a striker. Hitting it first time, it was a shot that I could've got to but, instead, elected to stand there flat footed and watch the ball pass me into the net while the relief of the Russians was evident, as shown in the celebrations they had for the equaliser.

Aye, wasn't fucking proud, like. Watching the disappointment on the faces of the players, almost an element of 'head down' which was always going to be a possibility to a team who had battered the opposition - with seemingly superhuman athleticism - but yet, with half an hour left, had just seen the other team draw level.

'Haw, Sepp? You know that you're allowed to fucking dive for the ball, eh?' An unimpressed Monk hissed at me while I retrieved the ball from out of the net and booted it back up the pitch.

'You want to tell Milky not to pass the ball out of defence to the other side and maybe I'll not have to dive in the first place, eh?'

I tried to take advantage of Milky's initial mistake by looking to shine the light on him, and away from me. Probably just looked like a fitba player looking for someone else to blame - to paper over their own inadequacies - but at least there was someone else that had played a part in their goal, just not moi.

'Fucking come on now, Muirhouse. This isn't over. Get the heads back up again. We've got a final to win here, like' Terry, shouted out to the players as they walked gingerly - and almost reluctantly - back up the pitch to take centre. Despite their wild celebrations, the Russians were now all back in their half of the pitch with body language that looked like it was screaming 'fucking come on then, let's get a move on.'

Having never been involved in a match fixing plot before - and never likely to be again - I wasn't sure what I should do next, as and when the ball came back down my end. Did I engineer a second goal straight away, or would that just look dodgy, even to the untrained eye? Then again, who was to say that the lads out there were going to take their equaliser as a sign to raise their game, and me hardly see Zavorovo back down my end of the pitch again? Talk about margins, like?

We tried to get back to basics. Keeping them away from the ball but not really doing much with the possession we had. The first time that the Russians mounted any kind of a meaningful attack, they scored their second. *Heavily* assisted by me.

Their wee number eight had robbed Coffee in the middle of the park and sprayed it out across to their winger, on the left.

Bringing it down the pitch unchallenged, - Daz having been caught up the park and out of position - the boy put a decent cross in where there were a collection of both Muirhouse and Zavorovo players waiting on it.

'KEEPER'S'

I shouted out to make my team mates aware that I had things covered. Unfortunately - for the other ten Violet players out on the pitch - my version of having things covered was not something that would track with how *they* would've imagined it. To be fair, I actually *did* come out all commanding and pluck the ball out of the air. It was the *dropping* of the ball, right in front of one of their players, that was the problem. Not believing his luck, he didn't muck about as he drove the ball home to make it two one to them. A despairing dive from me to give off the impression of a goalkeeper who has fucked up and is now desperately trying to redeem himself from his fumble.

I'm not even sure there's a word to describe the feeling of hearing a ball hit a net, the roar of the players you're up against, knowing that you're now a goal down in the latter stages of a cup final ... and for you to be *relieved* about it.

The Monk didn't say anything this time, he didn't fucking *need* to with the look that he flashed me after my 'mistake.' Terry, not so measured.

'All the fucking games you could choose to drop the ball right in front of the opposition and you choose today. You buy a watch out here from one of the looky looky men, aye, cause your timing's absolutely pish?'

Tel sarcastically said before turning his back and trying to rouse some of the players up, not even bothering to see what my response was to the comment. I had none anyway. I was literally selling my pals out and watching it all play out in real time.

One thing about Muirhouse Violet, though, - and on any other normal day you'd have had me firmly in this category - if you're going to beat them then they're going to do everything within their powers - legal *and* illegal - to make sure that *if* you're going to win, then you're going to have to fucking work for it. Lesser teams would've taken going behind in a cup final - after being in a winning position - and now going into the last fifteen minutes of the match as the signal that it's not going to be their day. Muirhouse Violet, however, are not what you could class as a *lesser team.*

Going right back at the Russians again I was a virtual spectator for pretty much the remainder of the match as wave after wave of attack went down both flanks as well as through the middle. Zavorovo just couldn't stop us, but neither could we grab the equaliser. Strings with another effort that looked in all the way until one of their defenders stuck his nut in front of the ball, sending it out for a corner. Montana hitting a post from a beautifully swung in free kick from Coffee. The same striker thinking he'd scored in a similar fashion only for their defender to scramble it off the line. There had been half hearted appeals that the ball had crossed the line before being hacked away but the ref and linesman weren't having any of it.

Despite us spurning chance after chance - and with the minutes ticking down - I just had that horrible sickening feeling that we were going to find the equaliser. We'd a habit of playing right until the end of matches, and quite a decent return when it came to scoring late goals to either snatch a draw or win the game outright. A one goal lead is always dodgy at the best of times too, for a fitba team and *definitely* for someone who knows the full time result is going to be the difference between a jail cell, coffin or safe passage back to Scotland.

I couldn't take the chance and, with around five minutes left, on what was their first attack since they'd gone a goal up, acted on this when - with all of our players committed to an attack we'd been on - our whole side was taken out with one simple slide pass from one of their midfielders, sending their striker with the long run up towards the box, and me waiting there on him.

I suppose, if you're any kind of a striker worth their salt, a scenario like that, the odds are meant to be in your favour. All the options open to what you can do in this scenario. Just a keeper to beat and with no defender near you to cause any concern.

As he got closer to the box I came running out and waiting on his arrival had deliberately positioned my legs wide open, knowing that anyone with a morsel of composure would've taken the chance presented to them.

As he fired the ball through them, I made a piss poor attempt at closing my legs, comfortable that it was too late for me to do anything about it but - once again - hoping the act of trying to prevent the goal would've at least looked the part.

'You could've driven a fucking arctic through those legs, for fuck's sake, ya Jim Leighton looking cunt?'

If Tel's looks could kill, it would've undone all of the work I'd put in to *avoid* being killed. You could tell he wasn't a happy man. Looking around, he wasn't the only one when it came to having a certain opinion on me. We'd left that dressing room for the second half having bossed the first half in such a way that had left the players feel that all they needed to do was maintain that same style and tempo and the cup was naturally going to be coming back to Edinburgh on the plane. Before the whistle had gone for the second half not one player could have predicted such a collapse. And it wasn't difficult for them to find the door to lay the blame for this at.

I felt like a complete piece of shit, but a *relieved* one at that.

That third goal - surely - being the one that would knock the stuffing out of the Violet who would - understandably - begin to accept that it was all going to end in tears. One goal? Aye, you've always got a chance, but not two. Not from a team who had ran an astonishing distance during the match but who had reached that one last brick wall that simply could not have been ran through. It had been a long tournament, a long - more for some than others - two weeks in general, and in those closing moments, it started to show.

Those last minutes played out in a weird kind of subdued way where the Russians had clearly decided to hang onto their nice wee cushion that they'd been gifted. Taking a midfielder and striker off and sending on defensive minded ones in place of them. On the other side, a Muirhouse Violet team who looked like they now had nothing left in the tank. Our chances - if we even had any by that stage? - further dented by the liability that was Five O making a frustrated - but with their player going absolutely nowhere, a stupid - 'strikers challenge' which landed him his second yellow.

I can't have said that I was too upset at this as it was both going to leave the match further out of our reach, plus also possibly add another person with a target on their back for when the game was over.

When the referee blew that final whistle, and put our players out of their misery, it had felt like when a vet puts a dog down. It was obvious that we weren't going to win the match and we just needed it to end. Well *I* certainly did, anyway. I'd wanted the game to come and go and me be left in any kind of position that was going to have me in the clear. And now I'd made it. Not that I was feeling celebratory over things being a case of *job done*, personally.

I crouched down, taking my gloves off, and looked out across the pitch. While the Russians were all going radge in celebration over in their half of the pitch, subs and management all running on to greet them, it was a different story for our players.

Some of them were mirroring me, crouched down and staring into space while others were flopped out on their fronts with head buried into the grass. The Monk and Terry both had what looked like actual tears in their eyes. This, a definite Muirhouse Violet first. Looking out at them all and just how devastated this loss had been to them - after all of the hard work put in across the two weeks, only to lose it at the death - and how hard it had hit them, knowing that it had been *me* who had caused it? I fucking *detested* myself. The heartbreak I could see etched on my team mates' faces and knowing that it all traced back from me just wanting my hole on a team night out? What a shitty, shitty thing to have on your conscience.

I'd never felt so low in my life. Things felt rock fucking bottom. Crouched there in the goalmouth looking out at everyone, I couldn't escape the feeling that I had never done anything so reprehensible in my entire life, and it had only been the week before where I'd ridden an old woman to death, to offer a little perspective.

We stayed out on the pitch long enough to receive our losers medals, applaud the Russians as they went to receive the trophy and then we were gone, leaving them all to get on with their celebrations.

I wasn't particularly looking forward to the dressing room - but was something that I needed to get over and done with and then hopefully begin to move on from the whole sorry episode - as whatever had been said to me out on the pitch - after my howlers - was surely going to be repeated inside the dressing room, only minus the filtered edition that I'd been subjected to in view of the match officials and all the spectators.

In all fairness, *whatever* any of the players had for me - verbally *or* physically - when we got back there, it was going to be fully deserved.

But that didn't have to mean that I was going to enjoy it, mind.

Chapter 28

Strings

I'd seen a few chaotic Muirhouse Violet dressing rooms in my time but doubt I'd seen anything like what had followed us getting back in there, after losing the final against the Farleys.

Half the losers medals handed to us - only moments before - were already lying in pieces on the floor, having been launched against the walls by several players upon getting back inside. Some cunts crying their eyes out, others screaming their heads off - to no one in particular - in frustration over the fact that we'd just thrown the game away and how it had been *our* cup to win. While for others, they chose anger. *All* of it sent in the direction of our poor goalkeeper.

Sepp, one of our normally more radge players, just sat there broken. On any other day, any of the shite that was being shouted at him would've been enough to provoke a response, which would one hundred percent have escalated into violence. That early evening though? He just sat there, didn't even lift his fucking head to acknowledge anyone shouting at him. Just taking it. Proper emotionless, like. Which I'd thought stuck out a wee bit because there's only so much grief you can take from cunts before you end up biting back.

You could see that he knew he'd let us down, though. I know I should've been one of the ones screaming and shouting at him as well but I kind of felt sorry for the boy. Not like he'd gone out there onto the pitch *intentionally* trying to make those mistakes, did he, eh?

'Just as long as when you're telling Delaney and Rossi that we lost the final, Jock, you tell them that it was that useless cunt over there responsible'

Terry said, looking and pointing angrily at Sepp the whole time. Looking for a reaction that wasn't coming. I could appreciate Terry's frustration. I had tears in my eyes by the time we entered injury time, and was coming to terms with the fact we were going to lose. Looking for a swedge from a team mate isn't the answer though. Especially when there's a shit load of holidaymakers you can take your frustration out on later, which Tel surely would go on to do.

'Woah woah woah, you're out of order there, Terry'

Jock said, not taking too kindly to what big Tel had said.

'We play as a team, win draw and lose as one too. How many times has that man, sat over there, saved our skin in games?'

I admired Jock standing up for one of his players over their mistakes, while the rest were feeling as raw - and unpredictable - as they were right then. He really was in the minority though, when it came to standing up for our keeper.

I really just think that it was an accumulation of things, and that he'd picked the wrong game at the wrong time to have a stinker. The lads were mentally and physically fucked. On their erses before the match but had managed to dig deep enough to pull out the kind of performance that I highly doubt we'd have managed had those Albanians not attacked our group in the brutal way they'd done. Had it not been for that 'cause' I genuinely don't think that we'd have played with such passion, because we really *were* fucked by the time that final came along.

Most of us couldn't wait to go home. The two weeks had broken us and we were nearly all out of money by then anyway. The feeling of - despite all of this - putting what we'd had into winning the game, and hadn't because of one man's errors. It was just a bit much to take.

A case of so near but yet so far, only, delivered with a punch to the gut that had simply hit differently to any other cup final defeat. It had been an adventure and a half. Full of the excitement - and at times, frustrations - of going toe to toe with teams from other countries and the buzz of finding out that we were *better* than them, enough to go all the way to the final.

For it all to end in the way it had? It was a feeling that I'd never felt as a player before. Aye, I'd experienced several boots to the balls before, but *nothing* like this. And for that reason I could understand why some of the players were coming for Sepp and just wouldn't drop it.

Eventually our goalie found his voice, although this only inflamed things further. Sepp pointing out about the mistakes made by Milky - for their first goal - as well as pointing out Five O being stupid enough to get himself sent off, while we were chasing the game, alongside mentioning the sitter that he'd missed while still *on* the pitch.

'Fuck you if you think you can blameshift your way out of this, ya cunt'

Milky didn't take too kindly to being apportioned some blame to the defeat. Quickly getting up from the bench and running over to confront Sepp before being stopped by a couple of fast thinking players, putting a stop to anything before it got a chance to even start.

Things didn't look like they were going to start to simmer down any time soon. The Monk and Terry starting to have another go at Sepp who, apart from bite back in the way he'd done, had just sat there facing the floor, continuing taking the torrent of abuse coming his way. Five O chipping in as well before Terry turning to our stand in striker and telling him to 'shut your fucking mouth, you're on thin ice yourself, ya cunt'

Thinking on my feet and trying to avert things escalating any further, feeling that a wee bit time out was required. I grabbed my cigarettes, lighter and Benji and walked over to Sepp and - grabbing an arm each - lifted him up - him feeling like a dead weight - from the bench to remove him from this whole dressing room situation. Give the lads a bit of time to get whatever they need out of their system and hopefully relations can then start to improve again somewhat, I thought of as something for the best.

The three of us took a walk back down the tunnel towards the pitch, now deserted of Russians - or fans in the stand - by this point. And stood near the corner flag to have a smoke. I crashed the L and Bs round the other two and lit up a much needed after match cigarette.

If you hadn't already known Sepp you'd have thought that he was a mute, so little had he spoken after the match. Generally you'd have at least expected him to apologise for his howlers or to raise whatever defence he might've felt he had with regards to them, but instead, you could barely get a word from him.

'Thought ten minutes away from the dressing room might've been a good idea before any cunt done something that they'd end up regretting, eh?'

I said to Sepp, as if this had needed explaining, which it didn't.

'Don't worry about it anyway, mate,' Benji added. We all have bad games from time to time, it'll be Terry's or The Monk's next time around, just you wait'

Benji's attempt at reassurance, counting for absolutely fucking zero going by Sepp's emotionless expression on his face. I thought I'd try a different tact by injecting a wee bit of humour, only to see it backfire on me.

'I'll tell you one thing though, Sepp. You're some cunt, like. You've played over two hundred matches for the Violet and you save your worst performance for the biggest match in our history!'

Looking back, it was maybe too soon for a comment like that, but that was how we operated as team mates and, well, mates in general. Take the pish out of someone during a bad situation and before you know it things are on their way to becoming better. It was tried and trusted amongst us, so why fuck with the classics?

'Look, boys. Cheers and all that, eh. I can see what you're both trying to do and I appreciate it, like, but right now, I need a wee bit time on my own, to process things, ken?'

Sepp said to us - in a non negotiable kind of way - before walking off and leaving us, heading off in the direction of the empty stand to take a seat in.

Chapter 29

Sepp

Sitting there in that deserted stand - still up at the stadium - I wish I'd been able to at least feel that the hard part was now over and done with, but that wouldn't be true. I'd done what I'd been given the choice of from Viktor Borovskiy. Either that or me being turned over to police *or* done away with. The old Russian prick taking delight in telling me that if it was going to be one of the latter options, he would decide on the flip of a one euro coin. So little he valued someone's life that he would decide on a coin flip. Nah, while it *had* been difficult to go out and play those ninety minutes as part of my 'team.'

The hard part was still to come, and fuck knows how long it would go on for before departing again. Because - from now on - I was going to have to carry on as normal and look my mates in the eye - aye, they were raging after the match but once they'd cooled down, all of that would've been fine - while *knowing* what I'd done to betray the lot of them.

Always being the type of person to look for the positives in something, the fact that I was now no longer fretting - as much - about killing the old Russian woman wasn't exactly much of a positive.

At that point, I couldn't speak for the rest of the squad - and it had hardly been a scene filled full of unity the last time I'd seen them together - but I was going to get absolutely fucking steaming. I *needed* alcohol, and lots of it. To kill the pain. It was the last night and while we didn't exactly have anything to celebrate, when had that ever stopped us?

I wasn't caring if I went out on my own, with the whole squad or something in between, I was going out. Because if I'd sat around in my hotel room that night just waiting on the next day rolling around so that I could go home, I'd probably have slit my fucking wrists.

Aye, what had happened during the final would still be there the next morning when I woke but at least, for one night, I wanted to put it out my mind, while already safe in the knowledge that it was going to be something that would dominate it for the foreseeable.

I was just sitting there, staring out onto the pitch, thinking of all the matches we'd played out on it since we'd arrived in Magaluf. All the varied teams we'd come up against and the different styles they played with, and the different versions of shithousery that some of them had stored in their lockers. It had been a mad couple of weeks all round but surely that was always on the cards the moment Jock Hunter announced to the team that we were going to be playing in Mallorca in some summer tournament? Fair enough, things like me killing a pensioner and Strings burning down an island was maybe taking things up a few levels than what we were used to, but it was what it was.

I was looking forward to going home, I think most were, though. You know when you just need your own bed and a bit of normality, like? I think by that point of the trip a lot of the team were at that exact stage. We weren't flying home until the next evening. Ending up in one of those situations where you get kicked out of your hotel room *before* it's time to get on the bus to the airport. So the choice was to sit and wallow in self pity until it was time to go home, or head out and spend every last euro you have on peave. Wanting fuck all other than to escape from my own head for a night, I chose alcohol.

I was just in the process of deciding to get up and head back to the dressing room and - *still* in my kit - brave showing my face again so that I could get showered and changed. Leave it any longer and you'll be having to get yourself back from the stadium under your own steam, I thought to myself as I stood up.

That's when I saw them walking up the stairs of the stand that were nearest to where I'd been sitting. Both stopping at the row of seats in front of me before walking along, in my direction. One of the two, I recognised. It was the same boy in the suit that had approached me in BCM that night and asked me if I would like to join 'Anya Borovskiy' for a glass of champagne.

Still rocking that whole Miami Vice detective casual suit look, sleeves rolled up, the lot. I'd always thought that - understandably - the Russians were a wee bit behind everyone else when it came to fashion and other things but, come on, eh? Miami Vice was the fucking *eighties*. This was two thousand and thirteen. Apart from the critique on his fashion sense - as I watched him swanning along the row, hand out bumping up and down against each seat as he walked towards me - I *did* have the question of why I was even looking at him *at all*.

'Hello, killer'

He said with a smirk, turning to look at the other boy, who looked a bit more of a serious character than Sonny Crockett there and by 'serious' I, of course, mean dangerous. Over the security details of both the Borovskiys that I'd seen, at different times. Miami Vice man had been the *only* cunt out of them all that I'd have fancied my chances with in a swedge. Well, him and his boss, obviously, because auld Viktor had to be over seventy. Probably not a good look, though. Giving an old aged pensioner the message *so* good that you literally kill her and then after that batter fuck out of her man?

The other boy, Russian, just smirked back at this.

Aye, funny as fuck, eh? Near on went out of my fucking nut over the thought of it all and then I find it leading to me having to throw the cup final.

I suppose, in worlds where cunts like that came from, though. Maybe you become desensitised to things like murders, or being *around* murderers? Even if I was more a manslaughter kind of guy, if we wanted to be pedantic. Would've just made me look like a fanny if I'd replied to his 'hello, killer' with a defensive *'hey, it was manslaughter, actually, ya cunt.'* I decided to ignore it completely. Not that I didn't go on the defensive though, mind?

I'd never expected to see any of them again. I'd been sure that a man with the reach of Borovskiy would've been able to find out the score of the cup final, if he hadn't been in attendance himself, of course. It would hardly have been a secret - by that point - that the Russians had won the Red Bear Beer cup, to take back with them to - fittingly - what would probably be the only country where anyone even *drank* that rancid piss of an alcoholic beverage. And if anyone had actually *watched* the match then they'd have seen that I had played a major role in *how* Zavorovo won the game. Fucking Les Mottram would've been able to see it, that obvious it was.

Seeing them coming towards me, though? I got *another* of those horrible dull feelings in my stomach - fuck know's how I never ended up with an ulcer, due to the sensations that fucking trip had put my stomach through - as I prepared to defend myself over whatever was coming my way. Fortunately, I'd managed to avoid going through life without having to find myself making deals with cunts that have private armies protecting them but from a lot of the films I'd watched in the past, there was always a lot of cunts double crossing *other* cunts. No honour with some of those types but then again, that's probably how they end up so rich in the first place, eh?

As far as the Russians were concerned, though. In my mind, at least, my conscience was clear. I'd done what was told and that the result quite literally stood for itself.

I don't think it had been intentional but the other boy - when he'd moved past his mate to be on the other side of him - managed to let me catch a glimpse of the gun inside the waistband of his suit. You know how gangsters pull the side of their jacket to the side to expose the gun they're packing, just to instil a bit of fear and respect from whoever they're facing? Aye, it wasn't like that, to be honest. Didn't fucking change the fact that he *had* one on him though, mind.

I'd been just sitting there not bothering anybody. Just having a smoke while pondering just what a massive wanker I was. It was them that had come looking for me. Out of all the possibilities, I thought that it would be safe to say that one of them was not going to be them coming to give me a wee pat on the back for my performance.

'Hey, boys. I done exactly what Mr Borovskiy asked me to do? Man of my word, eh? Not sure if you watched the game yourselves but if I was to tell you that at this very moment half of my team mates want to take me out into the sea and fucking drown me, then you'll have some kind of an idea, eh?'

I just launched into things. Billionaires pretty much by definition are bastards, so it really would not have been out the question for Borovskiy to have used me - cryptically, he'd said to win a bet on the tournament. Why the fuck would you put a bet on a competition full of players that are more professional at drinking than they are at playing fitba? - to make sure the Russians won the Red Bear Beer Cup. But then once that part was over with? No need for me anymore, and I would then find out that he'd planned to kill me all along?

If so then his men couldn't have planned it any better. Me sat, sticking out like a sore thumb in a stand that could've sat around a thousand people, but surrounded by empty seats. If that other boy had a silencer for his gun then they'd have been able to take care of things and stroll back to their car without anyone being any the wiser.

Maybe picking up on my fear, they just looked at each other and laughed some more.

'Mr Borovskiy sent us here to deliver a message to you'

Sonny Crockett said, leaving me doing a pretty good job of not shitting myself there in my Muirhouse shorts. Having a message 'delivered' to you on behalf of someone like a mob boss or some rich and powerful Russian businessmen - and you know how those cunts are all linked to that radge Putin boy, eh? - never has an appealing ring to it. And it definitely fucking didn't, that evening when I was having my own experience of such a situation.

Here it fucking comes, I couldn't help myself from thinking - while trying my best to magic up the faces of all the people in my life who were the most important to me, figuring I wasn't going to have much time to do so before everything went blank - as he reached into his jacket, smiling as he did.

Can't fucking believe these type of cunts take actual *enjoyment* out of stuff like this? The thought I got while I was trying to think of more happier ones. I couldn't help it, though. You're looking at the face of the boy who's about to end you, and he's just got a big fucking *smile* on his face. No right, that, like.

Heart beating out of its chest in a way that no amount of training over the past two weeks had come close to producing, he pulled his hand back out of the jacket and instead of a gun in his hand, he had an envelope. One that looked almost thick enough for the postie to have to leave you a 'sorry we missed you' card, if he'd had the job of putting it through your door.

He threw it at me, the envelope hitting me in the chest with a wee thud and then finding its resting position on my lap.

'What's this?'

I asked, even though it was pretty fucking obvious what it was, but why was it sitting on my lap?

'It is a token of goodwill from Mr Borovskiy'

He replied, nodding his head towards my lap, and the thick envelope sitting on it.

'A token of *goodwill*? From Mr Borovskiy? The same Mr Borovskiy whose wife ended up a wee bit dead after cutting about with me for the night? *That* Mr Borovskiy?'

No longer worried about being harmed by any of them, I thought I could have a wee black humour style laugh with them but while *still* trying to ask a valid question, because when you leave someone without their wife, you generally wouldn't be going looking for *any* fucking gestures of goodwill from the widower. That's just mental to think otherwise.

But, nah. I'm sitting there with a pile of money on my lap, courtesy of the old Russian gadgey.

'He instructed me to tell you that from what he has been told over the past few weeks, you play with a fearless team of warriors and how the boss, despite everything, appreciates how difficult it would have been to betray those team mates, and on the big occasion, like cup final. Going against warriors like Muirhouse is not so different than going against Russian oligarch. Because of this, he wanted you to receive a small gesture of goodwill before you leave Mallorca'

No denying it, it *was* a massive gesture, considering I thought I was going to be on the receiving end of a very different kind of sentiment. I appreciated the fact that the man had actually taken to time out to acknowledge that, aye, going against my team mates had been the hardest thing I'd ever done. Didn't need his appreciation but it was nice that he'd been able to see it that way all the same.

But I didn't want the money.

Instantly being in possession of it left me feeling grubby. At no point - during any of this match fixing caper - had I been driven by anything financially related. I only had a few percentage worth inside me that was going to be able to look at myself in the mirror, and that was only *because* money had not been a part of things.

Going into that cup final - as bad as things were for me, internally - I had just about managed to settle on the fact that I'd been left without a choice. Taking money from someone to then lose the match? Now *there* was a choice. I was doing it for something that money can't buy, your freedom. *Because* there had been no money involved, I had found it almost - not exactly noble by any stretch - acceptable, even if forced into it, like I'd been.

The thought of - after all that had taken place since that final whistle - me walking away with whatever amount of money that was inside the envelope made me sick.

'I'm not wanting it, pal'

I picked up the envelope, crouched forward in my seat and reached out to him to return it. Instead of taking it back from me, though. The boy in the eighties fashion stuck his hand up, not phased by the fact that someone was sitting there turning down free money. It wasn't free money in any case. Fucking *blood* money more like. If it was to ever come out - to the rest of the team - that I had purposely fucked things for us in the final but that they were to learn the reasons, there would be a gnat's chuff sized chance that I'd have found a bit of understanding to the situation. Had they found out that I had thrown the cup final and been *paid* for it. There really wasn't going to be any telling on just how far things could escalate and - I assure you - the instant sacking from being a Muirhouse Violet player would've been at the very bottom of my problems.

I didn't 'play' for the money and it wasn't my incentive. Had it been it would've propelled me even higher in the snake stakes. As hard as it might be to part with a wad of notes like that - which you now know to be officially yours - I wanted fuck all to do with the money.

'Go on, lad. Take it, eh?'

I kept my arm stretched out, with him having already taken his hand and batted my arm away a couple of times while shaking his head.

'Listen, friend. Mr Borovskiy tells me to bring money, I bring money, ok? Taking money back to Mr Borovskiy? If I take money *back* to boss, then he tells me that I haven't done my job, ok?'

I looked - hopefully - at the other boy who silently just shook his head at me, having still not spoken yet.

And that was them. Thought for one second that I was going to be assassinated by some cunt who had quantum leaped from another decade and, instead, he walks off - with his mute mate - having left me x amount of euros better off.

Not without - these unpredictable goons, what are they like, eh? - wishing me a safe flight back the following evening. Adding that maybe next summer holiday I should avoid Mallorca.

Something that I was in heavy agreement with him on.

Or put it this way, *if* I was ever to return to the island. It would be while a strict 'ride people your own age' rule was in force.

Through having to focus on that intense wee exchange with the Russians where I'd been expecting a bullet or two and, instead, was thrown a bung, I hadn't had the luxury of being able to look around the stand. *All* that existed - during that moment - were the two Russian men standing in front of me, blocking what had been, until their arrival, my entire view of the pitch. I hadn't appreciated that there might have been other people watching what was taking place.

The Russians had now disappeared from view completely while I sat there, back to my original thought of me having to get back to the dressing room before I was left behind. I didn't get far with those thoughts before they were broken by an angry voice from behind me, further up in the stand.

'Sold us all out, eh Sepp? You absolute fucking snake cunt'

I turned around to see an incensed Strings - followed by Benji - coming storming down the stairs. I'd played alongside the boy through thick and thin and had *never* seen him with a face like that on him as he literally skipped a stair with every step, such was his hurry to get down to the row I was in.

'Look, boys, I, I, I can explain'

I put my hands up - wisely without the actual money in any of them, like some mugger caught red handed with a purse in their hand - as they reached my row.

'What we've just sat and fucking watched, it kind of looks crystal fucking clear to me'

Strings said steaming towards me, along the row. Fucking hell, his eyes? *This* was what I 'felt' when I threw the game. I knew that Muirhouse Violet was a big thing to some of those men in the squad - ironically, me included - so for Strings to see and think what he was now angrily fuelled by, I *got it*.

'Honestly, Strings, mate. Just let me explain for a minute to the two of yous, eh?'

'Explain this, ya cunt'

Strings' last words before sending me falling back into the seats with a right hook to the jaw that was as surprising as it was potent.

Chapter 30

Strings

It's funny as fuck how the planet spins at times, eh? Near enough actually take the piss out of you at times, like? Because explain how you can find yourself booting fuck out of someone - your mate, as well - while not knowing that the *same* person you're assaulting is the *one* person in the world who is your saviour. Be nice if you knew that kind of stuff in advance though, eh?

Thing is, like. There's not a single person who'd have blamed me for reacting the way that I did. The only reason Benji didn't do what I'd done - with Sepp - was because he was *behind* me when coming down the stairs.

When you see your team mate - who has had a mare of a second half - sitting having a brief exchange with strange men, and them throwing him what looks like a fat envelope, before departing. You can draw your own conclusions from that, eh? Which I'd left no time in doing.

'IT'S NOT HOW IT FUCKING LOOOOOKS, STRINGS'

Sepp screamed out - for me to stop - while curled up into a ball as good as he could as I repeatedly kicked him. By this time, Benji trying to pull me back to get me to stop. That's when I'd known I'd went too far because - before we'd got down to where Sepp had been sitting - Benji himself was talking about ripping our keeper's head off. Wasn't like me to be so instantly violent about something, either, mind? More normally I'd be classed as someone who finds that words work better than actions. Not that I'm a sapp by any stretch and like anyone else in the team, knew that there was a time and a place for violence.

Caught in that moment, though? I don't think I'd ever felt so stabbed in the back, as right there. Complete and utter treachery from the boy, like. I'd never had Han cheat on me but could've imagined the feeling of finding out that your Mrs has been shagging someone else wouldn't have been too far away from seeing your mate accepting a bribe, having sold his friends down the fucking river at the same time, and on, arguably, the biggest day of their lives.

It had been me and Benji who had fucking *saved* him from getting a sore face - back in the dressing room - while, ironically, the cunt had been getting a pay off to play as shite as he'd done. Even more ironically, I was setting about him in a way that undone all of the good work I'd put in when it had come to *saving* him from a paggering off the lads, inside the dressing room. I couldn't have given a fuck about anything at that moment. The combination of hurt, fury and anger had proven a dangerous mix. Any other day, I'm never going to be able to deck a big hench cunt like Sepp. Not like how I'd managed there in that deserted fitba stand. One punch and he was on the ground, frantically trying to grab one of the seats to stop himself from falling but ending up grasping at thin air before hitting the concrete. And once he was down, I just flipped. Booting fuck out of his ribs and head while letting out all of my anger vocally as well as - obviously - physically.

Pretty lucky I'd changed from my Copa Mundials and into my flip flops, though. Who knows the damage I'd have maybe done to him had I still had the fitba boots on. Right then, in my mind. The more damage I could do to him, then all's the better. Actually, I remember the boot to the head I gave him and the thought that flashed into my mind over *wishing* I had something more sturdy on my feet to both protect myself from any injury while making the most out of any attempts at *doing* Sepp one.

What a fucking rat, though? All the problems that I had, yet I'd tried my hardest to shove them to the side and put Muirhouse Violet first, for ninety minutes, at least. I'm doing that while some cunt else in the team is looking out for themselves and for what? A wee bit of filthy lucre. No wonder I was raging although, to be fair, even if I hadn't been experiencing issues with the Spanish authorities I'd have *still* went fucking radge, after seeing what I'd just witnessed while stood at the back of the stand, having a smoke while Benji and me watched the exchange between Sepp and whoever the fuck those two boys had been. We were only still kicking around as we'd given Sepp the space he clearly needed but we thought he'd had enough and had went to fetch him and take him back to the dressing room with us, things having cooled down a *wee* bit back in the dressing room, from how hot it had been after the match.

'Come on, Strings. That's enough, mate. Let the boy speak, eh?'

Benji saying - and pulling at me - enough for to get me to halt.

After going a few vital seconds without feeling any more kicks come in at him, Sepp - sensing that the madness had passed - took himself out of the protective position that he'd tried to hold himself in and - while lying on the concrete in front of the seat - attempted to get himself up and into a seating position.

'You about done, mate? Aye?' He said, kind of joking while looking back up at me as he checked parts of his head for any possible blood. Fuck knows what he'd had to joke about, mind? Maybe - to him - the thought of me battering him was funny, because it would've been to a few as he was a bit of a hardy cunt, Sepp. Actually, while looking back down at him - feeling myself calming down a few levels but nowhere near to losing that sense of rage and injustice - it was only then that I'd realised that at no point had he attempted to fight back, which now that the red mist was slightly lifting, I was able to recognise as a good thing, for me.

'Fuck, me, Sepp? You think the last sixty seconds were bad? Wait until the *rest* of the fucking team finds out what you've done?'

Don't put me down as some bad grass or fuck all, either, but some things you *have* to tell other people. There were two camps here. The one that had done all they possibly could've done to win the Red Bear Beer cup for Muirhouse, and the other one? Different fucking agenda altogether. Give me one reason why the boys who had given it their absolute all - instead of choosing to be selfish bastards - should not have been told of *why* they didn't win the final? What had Sepp done - in clearly taking a bribe - to secure mines and Benji's loyalty over the rest?

'Well, if you'll let me explain, maybe it won't have to come to the rest of the team knowing, eh?'

Sepp said while grabbing hold of the top of one seat with one hand and stretching over to the seat in the row in front and managing to get himself up and into one.

'Hear the boy out, Strings, mate'

Benji passed the reeks around while we sat there, for the next ten minutes, engrossed in the tale that our 'goalkeeper' was sitting telling us. Speechless at some parts, shocked at others while at times - with how he had told the story - finding it hard not to laugh, as grim as he had painted events. It was one of those stories - excuses? - that when someone tells you, you already *know* that it has to be true because no cunt would've been able to make something like that up. And even if they *had?*

Would they actually attempt to *use it?*

Sepp sitting there telling us it *all.* What had happened the night he'd left the squad in that BCM club. Something that didn't square with how he'd described events the next morning when we'd all caught up with him when he'd got back from Palma. You could kind of understand *why* he'd told us a different version - which had just been a standard tale of champagne and sex on a yacht, which had left us all jealous as fuck at him - rather than deal with the chilling reality of how things had actually ended up.

'She was fucking ganting on it, as well. Telling me harder, harder, harder. Be careful for what you fucking wish for, eh?'

He said - in complete sincerity - while me and Benji looked at each other, trying to stop ourselves from laughing. Aye, I fucking bet 'Anya Borovskiy' would've thought it a right hoot, like. You know though how you can find yourself laughing at something you shouldn't though, eh? Doesn't make you a bad person or fuck all, eh? It's like how Homer Simpson said in an episode.

'It's funny because you don't know them'

He went on to explain how he'd had to go about the rest of the trip with the fear about either the cops finding him, or the woman's ex husband. Must've fried the poor cunt's brain, because for about the same amount of time, I'd been bogged down with the worry about paying back a debt I most likely was never going to pay. It kind of put everything in perspective.

'Think back to that match, against the Estonians? Absolute fucking bombscare that day, like. Head was all over the place as that was quite early on, following the night on the yacht'

I thought back to that game and, aye, he'd made some proper howlers in it. Thing was, though. We *all* did in that match since we were either still drunk or nursing hangovers.

'Me and Jock, from the bench, just thought that you were in as bad a state as the rest of the boys that day'

Benji chipped in but in doing so reminded me that Sepp had taken a bit of grief in the dressing room and it had been brought up that he hadn't that excuse - like the rest of the starting eleven that day - as Sepp hadn't even been *out* that night with us.

'So, anyway, the days kept passing and there was no tap on the shoulder from any one. Was just about getting to the point where I was thinking that I'd got away with it. By then, I just wanted to win the final and then get on the plane the next day and then myself back to Muirhouse - safe and sound - and try to forget all about it'

Good luck with that, I thought to myself. Having something like riding an old woman into her grave *has* to be something that's going to take a bit of coming back from?

'Almost fucking made it, as well. Fucking *days* away. When you two were up at the hospital, I had a visit to my hotel room. In comes these two carpet carrying looking cunts, with the old boy who was married to that Anya in tow. Basically told me that if I didn't throw the game today then I was either getting grassed on to the police, or he was going to take my punishment into his own hands. Sick bastard took out this euro coin, right, and told me that if Zavorovo didn't win, he'd flip it and decide what was going to happen to me but whichever side it fell on, I wasn't going to be leaving Magaluf tomorrow'

'Fucking know how you feel about having concerns about leaving this island though, like'

I half joked while looking at Benji, knowing he had those same worries.

'So, look. I did what I did, I feel like the absolute worst cunt in the world for betraying the lot of you, fuck getting past the whole woman dying on me stuff, that's small fry compared to how I feel about what I did out on that pitch, and I assure you. Riding an OAP to death is *not* fucking small fry. But, on my mum and dad's lives, I didn't have any choice in selling yous out'

You can't cheat your emotions and feelings, though. Even after *all* of what he'd told us, I was still incredibly pissed off with him. To me, Muirhouse Violet were probably the *least* likely team on the planet for one of their players to go against the rest of the side, and to do it on the kind of stage that he had? For all I knew, this was going to be our only chance at playing in the tournament. If one year later, a team's entry was down to how many 'sales' the beer had got over the year in that team's boozer, then we'd have had fucking no chance of being invited back. You can't cheat the disappointment you have in someone for when they stab you in the fucking heart, like Sepp had done. But, at least, I *understood*.

'Fucking, bit mad though, boys, eh?'

Sepp said, coming to the end of his outlandish story. It was a lot to unpack and - not sure about the Benji boy - but my head was a minefield of thoughts and counter thoughts. Wanted to still be going radge at the boy for causing the situation in the first place but - being no stranger to getting myself into holes that need climbed back out of - also understood what it's like to find yourself fighting for your life at times.

One thing that I thought I'd managed to piece together - with it being some rich Russian involved who had needed us to lose the match - was that this had to have been the same mystery man who had tried to bribe us back in the group stages? What a small world, eh? You try to bribe some Scottish amateur fitba players into losing a game of fitba and within forty eight hours one of those players who had taken your money - while they go on and win the match regardless - ends up riding your wife to death! Too fucking mad, like.

There was part that he *hadn't* mentioned, though. I didn't know if this was on purpose or simply because he'd rattled through so much to us in such a short space of time. He'd seemed all over the place at stages. Stressed out to talk about it but also *relieved* that he'd finally been given the chance to share this with someone. But he hadn't mentioned the actual thing that had been the catalyst for this scene between the three of us.

That we'd seen someone throw him something, envelope looking.

From the distance that we'd watched on from, it had been impossible to really see what had been given to him, but the assumption had been money.

'So what was that? That the boy threw at you before he left then?'

I asked, still keeping my pissed off tone, but sensing an angle. Something that might've seen the three of us all leave the stand better off than when we'd ended up there.

'What this?' Sepp said, immediately looking for it to then find that - with me firing into him in the way that I'd done - with all the commotion, he'd ended up with no idea where it even was. Eventually, he found it on the ground in the row to the front of us. It having fallen down in front when he'd been rolling around the ground.

'This?'

He held his arm up with an envelope in it that looked like it was almost at bursting point with notes.

'Aye, *that*. The reason that you ended up getting fucking chinned in the first place'

I replied, more than interested for the excuse that he was going to try and hit us with over the fact that - after everything he'd sat and told us, how he'd been *forced* into doing it - post game, he'd been paid.

'Look, mate. I know how it looks but I fucking *promise* you that money was not part of this. I'd been sitting trying to get my head around things, after leaving you two down by the corner flag, when the two of them just walked up to me, passed me a message from the old Russian, before chucking the envelope at me'

'Aye, we *saw* that. We were about to give you a shout when we saw the two of them approaching you. Held back to see what the score was but were ready to jump in and back you up if it was a case of cunts giving you grief. Who knows if those Albanians are even fully done with us yet, eh? Imagine what fucking fannies we felt when we found that we'd been stood there, having your back if required, watching you receive your payment for us losing the match'

I said, forcing him to expand on things.

'No, but that's the thing, Strings. I never *done* it for money, and never expected any either. If it had been a simple case of being offered money to throw the game I'd have either told the cunts to get tae fuck or taken the money and then went and had the game of my life anyway. There's a lot on me here, boys but taking a bribe to leave me financially better off isn't one of them'

Me and Benji looked at each other for a second. You don't have mates as close as you do Benj - and all the shit that you go through together - without having developed even the smallest bit of ESP between each other. It was the slightest of movements of my right eye, not even in the ballpark of a wink but slight enough for me to let Benji know that the game was afoot.

'Aye, he pure fucking had Muirhouse tapped, though. *That* was why he'd sent the money for me. Paraphrasing the cunt here, like, but he'd pretty much said that I'd gone against a team of players who would murder me if they were to find out what I'd done, and that the money was a wee goodwill gesture. As far as I'm concerned, when they left the hotel room yesterday morning, as long as we lost the match today, that would've been the end of things'

The three of us let a wee moment of silence pass while Benji got the Lamberts out.

'So, look, after all of that. My question is, are you going to go back into the dressing room and tell the rest of the boys?'

Sepp, breaking the silence before taking a nervously long draw on his cigarette.

There really were two ways of looking at this question. Aye, the boys deserved to know the truth. They'd panned their cunts in not just in the final but for the whole of the tournament, only for a bit of self sabotage from within their own ranks to bring it all crashing down. Had it been someone else being told the truth, like how Benji and me had been sat listening to, I'd have wanted to have known. Ignorance is bliss? Aye, not in every case.

But, maybe there was a different way, where the players would be *spared* the whole drama and never ending baggage that this information was going to bring. It would've been like me lobbing a hand grenade into the dressing room, walking back into it and telling everyone that we'd been cheated out of winning the final, by one of our own players.

That this second scenario also happened to be one where me and Benji would benefit out of? Purely coincidental, like.

I wasn't exactly comfortable about doing what I was about to go on and do, but had to keep remembering myself that this man had single handedly lost our team a shot at European glory, and that - at least for the next few minutes - he deserved to be *treated* as such. For that conversation sitting in that stand and that conversation only, Sepp was not my mate.

'Look, Sepp. As for telling the rest of the boys? I don't want to be *that* guy but me and Benji here are in a bit of a spot, financially, like. Don't even know if the fucking Spanish are going to let us leave the country tomorrow night. So, eh, I was thinking, when it comes to telling the rest of the team? Maybe you'd be able to *buy* our silence. The team never needs to know a thing about what happened to you over the past couple of weeks, gen up'

I decided to let Sepp know where things were.

'What's happened the past couple of weeks? I miss something, aye?' Benji said as a joke, but also to make the point.

Sepp, instead of reacting like he was in the middle of a blackmailing, which in a way, he kind of was, reacted to this without even barely thinking. Taking the envelope that was still in his hand and passing it to me.

'Take it, boys, and I hope that whatever the fuck's inside it helps cover your fine. I don't want it. Fucking blood money, that. Linked to an old woman who I managed to take sex and turn into manslaughter in one easy step, and me being coerced into what I did today, to all of you. I don't want a single fucking euro, dollar or pound of it, whatever it is'

Me and Benji not getting a chance to check the envelope until back at the hotel but - going by the size of it - surely to fuck there's going to be enough inside it to get me and Benji out of jail at the last moment, I thought hopefully to myself. Proper injury time winner from the boy Strings with how he finessed his way around his opponent to end up with not the ball in the net but a fistful of dollars shoved inside his shorts with shirt pulled out and hanging over the front, to cover the bulge.

It's funny, like. How all of that rage towards Sepp had kind of just floated away the very moment that he handed the money over, and I'd been left thinking that me and Benji might well have just pulled it off, typically when we weren't even looking to do so. Aye, it's all about replacing negative thoughts with positive ones. Things had started with me wanting to kill Sepp, *negative*, and ended with me feeling something I'd not had since I'd pinged that cigarette out on that island, a bit of hope, *positive*.

'So we square then?'

Sepp asked, having given up all he had to give. He'd told the truth and he'd handed over the money. What more could the guy have possibly offered after that?

'Well, look, Sepp. We'll leave you to deal with the fact that through your own stupid shit, you did what you done today, by going against us. But we all do stupid shit, mate. Look at *why* you've just handed *us* that envelope, and where the money's going towards. You're a good cunt, Sepp. Obviously if you could rewind you'd never have went near that old Russian hoor but what's done is done, eh? Consider things with a line drawn. You'd have to be off your fucking head to tell anyone else about this but know that no one will hear it from us'

I tried to ensure that he, eventually, *didn't* go on to tell anyone else because if it was to ever come out that me and Benji had known about it all along - and hadn't told anyone else, - *we'd* have been treated just as badly, as if we'd taken part in the match fixing ourselves.

'Nah, trust me. This stays between the three of us and the three of us only, boys. Think I'm wanting people knowing I shagged a pensioner to death? I'd never get a fucking ride again in my life back home. They'd be calling me the Black Widow or some shite like that'

He wasn't wrong, there. I'm not sure - if I wasn't married to Han - that I'd be too keen to have sex with a woman who had already been known to ride a man - who'd gone before you - to death. Just something about the possibility of losing your life during the whole sex part that I'd find a wee bit off putting, ken?

Me and Benji were in the process of telling Sepp that we were square when we heard the shout from Jock Hunter, from the touch line, up the other end of the pitch.

'COACHES ARE LEAVING IN FIVE MINUTES. IF YOU'RE NOT ON THEM BY THEN YOU'RE BLOODY WALKING BACK'

As the three of us walked back to the dressing room - left with no time other than to grab our stuff and jump on the bus - I honestly felt like kissing the pensioner shagging - and killing - match fixing big beautiful bastard.

Unless there was some nasty surprise waiting inside that envelope, like a stack of worthless roubles, Monopoly money or something to that effect, through him being nothing other than a complete fuck up, Sepp had saved the pair of us.

Chapter 31

Benji

It wasn't until we got back into the safety - and privacy - of the hotel room before Strings fished the envelope out of his bag. The game having ended hours ago but the boy still in his match kit, socks off and flip flops on. He was some sight. But then again, so was what was inside the envelope that Sepp had been bunged back at the stadium by the Russians.

From the moment it had been transferred from the waistband of Strings' shorts, and into his kitbag, I reckon had we been in possession of some superman laser vision - between us - we'd have burned a fucking hole right *through* the bag as we travelled back from the stadium. It's the hope that kills you, they say? *They* would not be far wrong, there.

I just wanted to know how much was inside the envelope, and if it was going to be enough to save my - and Strings' - Danish. Clearly, I wasn't the only one. Strings not even putting the bag down before opening it, with the hotel room door closing behind him.

Aye, it would still need to be counted but when he ripped open the envelope, and produced the euro notes from inside it, we couldn't help but grin at each other. Already sure that we were golden. Strings' worries about there being some sort of ironic booby prize sitting waiting on us, completely eased the moment we saw that the notes inside were twenty euro ones. Going by how many there were. There *had* to be three thousand euros worth in Strings' hand, maybe even more.

As it turned out, there was *lot* more than three k. We counted it twice, just to make sure, but it was the exact same amount both times.

'*TEN* thousand fucking euros, ya cunt'

Strings said as he threw all of the notes up into the air. The room covered in money while the two of us danced a jig all over top of it, high as kites. We'd just came back from a heartbreaking cup final loss. The kind of defeat that you already knew you might never get another chance at redeeming. Not one of those *well, there's always next year* type of deals. Nah, we'd returned from a cup final loss, and a crushing one at that.

But you wouldn't have guessed it from the look, sound and raucous behaviour of the two men inside that hotel room.

Shouting, cheering, laughing - in the kind of way that hadn't been possible since leaving the courthouse in Palma that day - and jumping around. Strings bouncing up and down on the bed like some five year old kid using it as a makeshift trampoline.

'Fucking hell, lad. That was a wee bit too close for comfort, eh?'

I pretended to wipe my brow with a wad of notes, scanning around the room and not even looking at what was littered all over as money. It was literally a symbol of our freedom.

'Aye, you're not wrong, Benji boy. Thank fuck for Sepp, eh? Poor cunt is probably broken right now but I have to say, I'm a big fan of the man. Huge, like'

It had been an absolutely mental turn of events that had led to him being the one to come to the rescue. Who'd have thought that one of your mates riding someone of an age - where he really should've known better - would've led to him being the one paying our fines for us?

'Tell you what, Benji boy. We might well be the first Scotsmen in history to come back from a holiday in Spain, with money *left*'

Strings laughed while looking at the three piles of money we'd counted out. First and most important of all, we separated the three thousand that we needed for the fines, which we could now go and pay the next day, before heading to the airport. Following that pile we then divided up what was left which gave us a tidy wee bonus of three and a half thousand euros each.

'Fucking pains me to say it though, having just got my hands on it a few minutes ago and that, but as many other things I'd like to do with it, I'm going to have to try and be an adult and hand every single cent over to McKenna, when we get back to Edinburgh. Eat a wee bit more into the debt, eh?'

Strings had a point, like. Fuck? If I was to hand over my share - and I'd have been off my nut *not* to - I'd have been officially debt free from the Edinburgh underworld's self appointed custodian, with some spare money left over.

'Very unlike you, Strings, taking the adult route, but wise, though. We never had the money in the first place. Paid a fine that, otherwise, we never had a fucking chance at squaring up so if the rest of it helps the two of us see a bit more daylight when it comes to Davey McKenna and looking out from within his pocket, then all the better for it'

I was happy enough to go along with him, when it came to the plans for the rest of the money. I'd have been chuffed with my lot if we'd counted it out and it had only been enough to pay off the fine.

'Still, that's not to say that we won't have a wee bit spare for one last night out in Magaluf, eh? Final chance to leave a lasting impression on the place, if we've not already, like'

I think, after the couple of weeks we'd had, never mind just that day, we owed it to ourselves to take the opportunity to have one last adventure - out on the town - before we headed back home the next day. Or put it another way. We were hardly going to sit in the hotel having a quiet night with a cup of Horlicks and a book, and the same went for the rest of the squad.

I'm not sure how wise this all was, but there was never a chance that the boys weren't going to go out that night and kick the arse out of things as far as they mentally and physically possibly could until they had either ran out of money, could no longer talk, or walk.

A drunk Muirhouse Violet - with the collective 'mood' that they were in, having lost the final - out on the piss in Magaluf, possibly a dangerous thing, to those that may have encountered them across the night. If we'd *won* the cup final you'd have almost feared for the town of Magaluf, but in a good way. As it turned out, - thanks to that magnificent bastard, Sepp - instead, Magaluf had to put up with the 'other' version of the Violet. The one who had *lost*.

Things started out not bad, mind. Keeping with tradition, we all popped our heads into The Arsed Rat to start the night off. We'd seen so much of the place over those two weeks that the owner - Ariel - knew us all by our first names and when we strolled in that night and he found out that we were heading back to Scotland. Without even thinking about it for a second, announced that he was making it a *free* bar for the next hour for all the Muirhouse players. What a gesture from the man, eh? In saying that, I couldn't even begin to imagine how much we'd collectively handed over to *him*, during those couple of weeks.

What a man, though but, also, what a maniac to offer the players and staff of Muirhouse Violet a free bar. Let's just say that we made every single fucking minute of those sixty - given to us - count.

Half of the squad could've easily just walked the few yards back across the road to our hotel and called it quits for the night by the time we were saying our farewells to Ariel, not that anyone did, obviously.

Apart from me and Strings, who were fucking buzzing. The rest of the team probably *shouldn't* have gone out, with the frame of minds that they were all in. Due to this, the whole night - once everyone had got to *that* drunk stage - had a bit of an atmosphere about it, like something was likely to kick off at any minute, and through the most tiniest of things. The majority of the squad - still hurting from the final - were just *itching* for someone to say the wrong thing to them, even a look might've been sufficient for your Tels and Monks of our group.

Miraculously - as far as I knew, anyway - we all managed the whole night without anything actually sparking, while some found themselves sparked out. There were many moments where potential trouble seemed just about ready to surface, only to be diffused at the very last moment.

Like The Monk, when he was playing pool. The boy was absolutely fucking burst by then and the only reason he should've ever had a pool cue in his hand would've been for to use as a weapon. But, nah. He'd insisted that he had the motor skills required to navigate himself through a game of American Pool, which he so very clearly *didn't* have.

Lining up his shot, - and going by the nick of the boy I'd have been astonished if he could even focus on the balls, never mind know if he was stripes or not - he somehow managed to send the tip of the cue - towards the table - at an angle that more rammed it into the baize than struck the white ball. In doing so, however, he's managed to send the white flying off the table right onto a nearby table, taking out four glasses in one go. If it had been something that he'd *meant* to do, it would've been impressive.

It was two couples that had been sitting at their table and with the sound of all the glass smashing and the drink going all over them and their table, one of the men who'd been sat there - who definitely had acted on impulse rather than survey his surroundings - shouted out in a Welsh accent

'Who the fuck did that?'

I'm not sure what he was seeking to gain out of this. Maybe try to show that he'll stick up for his other half, or that he thought that he was some kind of a hard cunt. I know this is maybe a bit hypocritical coming from someone part of Muirhouse Violet but sometimes you should have a wee look and see what you're dealing with, before you react like him.

Like the other three who had been sitting there until Ray fucking Reardon took to the table, the boy was now standing, wiping off the excess alcohol that was on his clothes. He turned towards the table to see who had just taken a bulldozer to their drinks.

'I fucking did'

The Monk, standing moodily eyeballing him, replied. Cue in his hand while refusing to look away from the boy. Wasn't just that, though. From the Welsh lad's point of view, he wouldn't have just been looking at a moody looking Monk. He was looking at almost a whole *team*, all standing there with the same look on their coupons, fixed on him.

The boy's wife - clearly having a bit more of an understanding of the situation than her man - having a quick look at us before grabbing his arm and pulling him towards her. She shouldn't have bothered. You could tell that he'd fucking shat it the moment he'd clocked how many boys were all looking at him. He'd have had to have been off his fucking nut - male pride or not - to have pursued things any further, which he chose not to. It wasn't going to end in a good way for him, had he opted to, indeed, crack on.

Due to the noise that the smashing of glass had made, it didn't take long before someone was out from behind the bar to clear up the mess. The boozer being absolutely rammed, meaning that these two couples - if they wanted to stay there and you couldn't have blamed them if they'd wanted to move onto somewhere else - had been left with no choice but to sit tight. When things had calmed down again - and The Monk's attention diverted towards something else - Strings, being Strings, went up to the four of them and apologised for his mate. Telling them that he got some bad news today and that it's never a good mix with alcohol, while throwing some euros on the table to pay for another round for them, since their last one had been taken off them.

'Maybe a good idea that you don't put them on the table until he's knocked off the table which, going by his last shot, probably isn't going to be long'

Even the bammed up Welsh boy laughed at this. That was Strings, though. Diffuse something as tense as that with one sentence and gesture.

As had been the case with every other night over the trip, we all ended up going back to the hotel at different times across the following morning. I didn't know *what* time me and Strings made it back but the sun had not long come up so must've been about five or six in the morning.

Was a fucking natch that neither of us would've - at the hotel - remembered to set some kind of alarm, with chucking out time being later that morning at eleven bells, either.

Didn't even know whether I was in Muirhouse or Maga-fucking-luf when that knock on the door came and I woke, still fully clothed, and answered to find the maid standing there in the hall, wanting in to clean the room. Clean the room? I hadn't even fucking *packed* yet. Should've done it the night before but well, you can't go looking back at the things you 'should've' done in life, eh?

'Eh, you're going to have to give me ten minutes, por favor'

I said sharply before closing the door on her again and rousing Strings, who had been woken by the maid before apparently going back to sleep straight away again. I was still drunk, hadn't given myself anywhere *near* enough hours sleep to have been able to wake up sober. Strings was worse. I had managed to throw half of my shite into my suitcase and the cunt was still lying on his bed snoozing.

'It's past eleven, squire. We're getting turfed out. Mon, get a fucking move on'

This, at least, managing to stir him. It was every man for himself. He could take care of his stuff, as long as I got everything shoved into that case and out of there, that's all I was worried about. When Strings started having a bash at gathering his own stuff, he found he could still barely walk. Not the state you need to be for fast thinking, never mind the required *actions* to go along with them.

When we eventually handed over the keys to the room, forty five minutes over the allocated time, the cunts on the desk at reception weren't too happy with us but, fuck it, eh? We were going home anyway so not like they could kick us out? They'd already *tried* that and found that we'd be kicked out under our *own* terms. They were still decent enough, from a customer service point of view, though. Letting us store our luggage in this spare room where they kept their customers' suitcases, kids push chairs and golf clubs and that.

With them dumped for the day - and after some helpful directions from the same reception staff that initially weren't happy with us - we headed out to find the local council office to pay our fine. We had a good few hours to play with - before the bus to the airport from the hotel - and, considering the states the pair of us were in, probably should've went somewhere for a breakfast and cup of tea, to get our heads together, but *also* had that whole 'siesta factor' to take into account.

'Just be our luck to *get* the money to pay our fine and then find out that the cunts we need to pay it to are all having a wee kip'

Strings slurred as we staggered along the road in the direction of The Britannia bar. From there we were to keep going straight until we saw a big yellow sign for a car rental firm, the council office a couple of yards before that.

'Bet you never thought you'd see the pair of us, eh?'

Strings said to the woman sat behind the desk who - having never seen us before in her fucking puff - looked at Strings then to me but when looking in my direction she seemed to be seeking a little help, in terms of who the fuck we were.

'But *wrong*, here we are, eh? Proved yous all wrong, like. Didn't we, Benji boy?'

'Can I help you?'

She - wisely - looked at me and asked. Already being one up on Strings - as in she wasn't drunk - she must've thought that she'd have got more sense out of me. Which she did, even if only just.

I managed to stammer something about us having a fine to pay but 'fuck knows where our paperwork is' while asking - hoping - that our passport would be enough for her to find anything in relation to the two inebriated fannies sat facing her.

A lot of the time, give these types any excuse to knock you back and they'll snatch it with both hands but I honestly think she just wanted rid of us - without any hassle - so was happy to go and look for our outstanding fee, us already telling her the amount she should be looking for.

'Ah, here it is'

She looked up from her screen with a smile while saying that she'd sort out the paperwork for us.

'Which form of payment would you like to pay?' She asked while battering away at her keyboard.

'Would *cash* be acceptable?'

Strings said in what had almost looked like he'd prepared to say it like that, when it came to the payment side. If this had been the case then I'm sure that it had all gone better in that pissed up reprobate's mind. Instead of dazzling the woman with the three thousand euros that he produced unexpectedly from his pocket, he dropped about half of it on the floor and was too busy picking it up to even see the look on her face when she confirmed that, aye, we could pay in cash.

After that, we were outside of there inside a couple of minutes. The council worker giving us the payment confirmation while advising us that it would take a few days to work its way into the system before our fines would officially be recognised as 'paid,' but that the paperwork she'd given us was as good as proof that we'd paid our dues.

Strings and me? Said adios to the woman and then walked out the front door to the office, Strings' right hand gripping my left as he thrust our arms up into the air while shouting

'Free the Muirhouse twoooooo'

He's some cunt, like. Love the boy to death, even if he is a complete fucking moron at times.

Officially, though. We now had the Spanish government off our cases, which had to go down as a plus and was - without question - one last thing to worry about.

The two *must do* things - pay our fine and be on the plane home to Edinburgh - that we'd started the day at the top of our list of things to do had now been reduced to one.

With the bus for the airport due around half four, we spent the rest of the morning - and afternoon - sitting things out at the hotel in that kind of way you can only do at the end of your holiday. Between the point where your hotel has kicked you out of your room but *before* the bus comes to take you to the airport for your flight back home. That kind of nether region where you're - technically - still on holiday, but no longer *feel* like you are.

Chapter 32

Strings

What a fucking fortnight though, eh? Aye, like there was ever going to be any other possible outcome, considering the rogues gallery of specimens who had boarded that flight out from Edinburgh, at the start of the whole adventure.

I wasn't feeling too clever - sat there on the bus to the airport - and the drink from the night before, which had taken a worryingly long amount of time to wear off the next day, was now gone and the hangover kicking in. Looking around the section of the travel company bus that held all the squad, I wasn't the only one. And that *definitely* included the grey faced Benji boy sat next to me.

Lifeless would have been the perfect way to describe the group, which couldn't have been more the polar opposite of that same group of men, chattering away with excitement - on that way *from* Palma airport - over the prospect of wall to wall fitba and peaving that lay ahead of them. Fittingly, it was that exact combination of playing association football and going on the batter with the squad which had left us all completely broken as human beings, mere shells of ourselves. I suppose it spoke volumes about how much we'd 'lived' while in Magaluf, though. And no one could deny that we had, good or bad.

Making our way - in that silent environment - I started to reflect on the trip. Looking out the bus window as we headed out of Magaluf and onto the motorway to Palma Airport while I replayed some of the moments from over the past couple of weeks.

The Red Bear Beer cup and how exciting it had been to take part in European competition. Being able to go up against teams from across the continent and find out just where we sat, when it came to a selection of pub teams from Belgium to Belarus and Russia to Republic of Ireland. As it was to turn out, we found that we ranked high amongst our contemporaries. Aye, so maybe it had all ended tragically in the way that it had but even so, I'll tell you one thing. I wouldn't have missed out on it for fucking three consecutive Balon d'Ors.

The epic sessions out on the peave that we'd embarked on and the tales that - would be coming back with us - would no doubt be retold, back home, in the years to come.

It had been impossible to think of both of those aspects to the trip without thinking of the whole sorry unfortunate episode - the day me and the ill looking man sat beside me - where the pedalo had been borrowed, which had resulted in an island being burnt to a crisp. Something that - as far as I was concerned - was best forgotten about although, in reality, there was no outcome that was not going to see every cunt in Muirhouse and Pilton know about it within twenty four hours of us being back in North Edinburgh. Still, alls well that ends well, as they say. Luckily Sepp had ended up with that old woman - leading to her death - which ended up, in a roundabout way, paying off our fine. Aye, pretty lucky, like. Probably not so much for the old Russian dear though, mind.

Aye, taking the rough with the smooth and putting everything in one neat wee package, though. I don't think anyone could've denied just what a fucking barry couple of weeks it had been. Well, maybe big Sepp would've had something else to say about that, I suppose. Even the poor cunts who were still lying in hospital beds - and wouldn't be following us back home for a week or two, Rossi getting out before Delaney - would've probably *still* admitted to having a top, top fortnight. Maybe they'd have knocked a couple of points off for being stabbed and hit with hammers which, if they had, you couldn't really have blamed them over.

I sat there thinking about some of the dark thoughts that the poor cunt was bringing back home with him, and how the boy must've been scarred by things and probably couldn't wait to get home, even if the memories would be travelling international waters along with him. I was trying to - while attempting to *stop* myself from doing so - picture what the scene must've been like when the still pished Sepp woke up on the yacht and realised that he'd been lying next to a dead woman. The last time he'd set eyes on her he'd been riding her silly. Can't even begin to fucking imagine what that must be like for someone after - what can only have been - a one night stand. Well he certainly wasn't getting a *second* fucking date, put it that way, eh?

With some messed up thoughts - of Sepp flapping inside the yacht - trying to decide what he's going to now do - while the dead body lay there on the bed - flying about my head, I found them disturbed by Montana.

Shattering the peace and quiet of the rear of the bus with a loud

'HOLY FUCK'

Everyone looked around at him. Even a percentage of the passengers on the bus who were fuck all to do with Muirhouse Violet but had pulled out the lucky ticket to get to ride to the airport in the same bus as them.

He wasn't even looking at anyone. Instead, he was face down, scrolling on his phone. Eventually realising that everyone was staring at him, he looked back up from his phone before offering some kind of an explanation for his involuntary outburst.

'Davey McKenna's been shot dead in Edinburgh'

Ex-fucking-scuse me???

Were you even *from* Edinburgh if you didn't know who Davey McKenna was? This apparent from the reaction across the squad at this news. Me and Benji, though? Our reaction?

As soon as the words had left Montana's mouth, me and the Benji boy looked at each other - wide eyed - in the kind of way where you're sat there - on your hands - in the Wheatfield Lower at Tynecastle while watching the cabbage and ribs score a last minute winner in the derby. Every single ounce of you sitting there trying to suppress your natural instinct of going completely fucking radge while expressing your extreme joy.

'Aye, according to Twitter, there's already rumours that it was down to some deal with a South American cartel that McKenna's finances fell through on. You know what those cunts are like over there, like, eh? They don't take any shit and aren't big fans of being fucked about in any capacity'

I wasn't really caring *how* the man had died, not at that point there on the bus. What *was* important, though, was that he was dead. With the predicament that me and Benji had been in with him, it hadn't been exactly something that we'd broadcasted to anyone. Fuck, even Han didn't know the full extent of how much I was in debt with him for. Sometimes its better for your other halves health that you *don't* tell them how many thousands their husband - and by extension, the *family* - is into with Edinburgh's most dangerous person to be owing money to.

With our issues that we both had with the man being on a need to know basis, neither of us could even say a single word about what we'd just heard, in relation to what it now *meant* for the pair of us.

We would need to wait a while before getting a chance to talk privately so I had no idea what was going through Benji's head while Montana sat and read out what was on the BBC Scotland news site. But his eyes alone told the story of an extremely happy man, probably just like what he was staring back at.

I wanted to run up and down the bus screaming and shouting. Stopping to kiss, hug and high five random cunts I'd never seen in my life. Apart from the fact that I didn't want anyone to know about my own personal situ with McKenna, it would've also looked extremely poor form to react in this fashion on hearing of a death of a fellow human being. This wasn't a Thatcher moment, even if it *was* a man who wouldn't have hesitated to put someone else in the ground if he felt they deserved it, and a death that certain individuals - in both law enforcement and criminal underworld - *would've* been joyfully reacting to.

Being a stranger to it most of the time, I couldn't help but think of just how much luck I'd had over the previous twenty four hours. Not only had I - through no effort of my own - managed to get out of jail - almost literally - via Sepp paying for my fine, but had come out three and a half thousand euros *up*. And now I was receiving news of the assassination of the man who'd - for years - had a hold over me, like he was some puppet master. *Luck?* That level of good fortune was simply fairytale stuff for me. Again, like Anya Borovskiy, not so much luck involved for Davey McKenna, though, mind.

It was well ironic, like, but I'd felt reborn, while hearing about someone's life being taken from them. Probably should've felt a bit ghoulish to be like that but nah, I was comfortable with my inner self. Thinking of an Edinburgh sans McKenna, I was overcome with a feeling that I hadn't experienced in a good few years. A sense of freedom. *Everything* changed, the moment Montana broke the news to everyone. I'd be heading back to Edinburgh with 'my life' waiting on me again. The one where I'd be working exclusively for myself, and no longer a prisoner to *that* phone of McKenna's going off - and on some occasions - morning noon and night.

Now I could *finally* get back to working to bring in money for me and the family, and no one else.

The only real issue that I had - as our bus pulled up outside departures with some of the passengers already up on their feet anxiously waiting to get off, in that way people behave anytime they get near a fucking airport setting - was that I'd maybe had *too good* of a twenty four hours.

Historically, anytime things were going good for me, there would always be something that came along and fucked things.

With my recalibrated life waiting back for me in Scotland, and one with all of those opportunities about to open again. It would probably be fucking peak me if our plane was to crash into the Pyrenees on the way back home.

But nah, self deprecating thoughts being put to the side, what an absolute result of a holiday it was. Aye, so maybe the Russians were heading back home with the cup on their plane, but I was flying home with something that *no* silverware could come close to touching.

A life.

It had been a difficult couple of years but Strings and Benji were *back*, and if you were the owner of any amusement arcades in Scotland, then it was time to watch your backs again, and your puggies.

Also by Johnny Proctor

The Zico trilogy

Ninety

A great portrait of a seminal time for youth culture in the U.K. A nostalgic must read for those who experienced it and an exciting and intriguing read for those that didn't' Dean Cavanagh - Award winning screenwriter.

Meet Zico. 16 years old in 1990 Scotland. Still at school and preparing himself for entering the big bad world while already finding himself on the wrong side of the tracks. A teenager who, despite his young years, is already no stranger to the bad in life. A member of the notorious Dundee Utility Crew who wreak havoc across the country every Saturday on match day.

Then along comes a girl, Acid House and Ecstasy gatecrashing into his life showing him that there other paths that can be chosen. When you're on a pre set course of self destruction however. Sometimes changing direction isn't so easy. Ninety is a tale of what can happen when a teenager grows up faster than they should ever have to while finding themselves pulled into a dangerous turn of events that threatens their very own existence.

Set against the backdrop of a pivotal and defining period of time for the British working class youth when terrace culture and Acid House collided. Infectiously changing lives and attitudes along the way.

Ninety Six

Ninety Six - The second instalment of the Zico trilogy.

Six years on and following events from 'Ninety' ... When Stevie "Zico" Duncan bags a residency at one of Ibiza's most legendary clubs, marking the rising star that he is becoming in the House Music scene. Life could not appear more perfect. Zico and perfect, however, have rarely ever went together.

Set during the summer of Euro 96. Three months on an island of sun, sea and sand as well as the Ibiza nightlife and everything that comes with it. What could possibly go wrong? It's coming home but will Zico?

Noughty

Bringing a close to the most crucial and important decade of all.

Noughty - The third book from Johnny Proctor. Following the events of the infamous summer of Ninety Six in Ibiza. Three years on the effects are still being felt inside the world of Stevie 'Zico' Duncan and those closest to him. Now having relocated to Amsterdam it's all change for the soccer casual turned house deejay however, as Zico soon begins to find. The more that things change the more they seem to stay the same. Noughty signals the end of the 90's trilogy of books which celebrated the decade that changed the face, and attitudes, of UK youth culture and beyond.

Muirhouse

Living in the 'Naughty North' of Edinburgh, for some, can be difficult. For the Carson family, however? Life's never dull.

You'll give them that.

'Muirhouse' by Johnny Proctor is a story of the fortunes of Joe 'Strings' Carson.

Midfield general for infamous amateur football team 'Muirhouse Violet' on a Sunday and petty criminal every other day of the week. Above all, though. Strings is a family man and, like any self respecting husband and father, will do whatever it takes to protect his household.

A commitment and loyalty that he's about to find being put to the ultimate test.

El Corazon Valiente; The ballad of Peter Duncan

El Corazon Valiente ; The ballad of Peter Duncan. A Zico trilogy origins story.Picking up where Noughty left off. El Corazon Valiente offers a look at how life is for Peter Duncan following events in Amsterdam, 2000. Finally find out how Stevie Duncan's father - through his own charm, ruthlessness and sense of self preservation - went from small Scottish town chancer to a vital component of a well known Colombian cartel. And how it all came crashing down around him.

The Onion Ring

Rule number one in the drug game is to always pay your debts; but what happens when you can't?

Just how far would you go to find redemption? Something that best friends and business partners Drummond, Hammy and Hummel are faced with when their business experiences some "technical difficulties."

Leaving them to find out just how far they will go.

Keyboard Warrior

Be careful who you troll, it might be Norman Fulton on the receiving end of your words. And by then, it'll be too late.

Keyboard Warrior, follows Nora - Ninety & Noughty - ten years into his dramatic escape from prison and, seemingly, a reformed character, under his new alias, Matthijs de Groot.

But with people, like Nora.

Is someone ever really reformed?

Available through Paninaro Publishing, Apple Books, Kindle, Amazon, Waterstones and other book stores.

Printed in Great Britain
by Amazon

45961314R00239